The Tooth and the Nail

....

The Wife of the Red-Haired Man

....

BILL S. BALLINGER

Introduction by Nicholas Litchfield

Stark House Press • Eureka California

THE TOOTH AND THE NAIL /
THE WIFE OF THE RED-HAIRED MAN

Published by Stark House Press
1315 H Street
Eureka, CA 95501, USA
griffinskye3@sbcglobal.net
www.starkhousepress.com

ISBN: 978-1-951473-02-0

Book design by Mark Shepard, shepgraphics.com
Cover art by James Heimer, jamesheimer.com
Proofreading by Bill Kelly

First Stark House Press Edition: April 2020

Contents

Ballinger's Chill and Puzzle Parallel Plots
by Nicholas Litchfield

Prolific American novelist and screenwriter Bill S. (William Sanborn) Ballinger (1912-1980) authored almost thirty books, more than one hundred and fifty television scripts, eight screenplays, and twenty-five short stories. His mysteries, some of which have yet to be reprinted in his own country, have sold more than ten million copies in the U.S., and have been reprinted in thirty countries and translated into more than thirteen languages. Highly praised by book critics and legendary mystery writers like John D. MacDonald, Brett Halliday, and Lawrence Block, he is responsible for some of the best and most innovative mystery fiction of the 1950s.

Without question, his most famous work is the thrillingly unique *A Portrait in Smoke*, first published in August 1950. Earlier, the author achieved moderate success with a pair of conventional hardboiled detective novels. However, with *A Portrait in Smoke*, in which he employed an unusual but effective split-narration technique, alternating between two seemingly unrelated stories, he established his name as a major talent in the mystery field.

He found continued success in applying similar dual plot formats to subsequent stories, such as the Edgar nominated mystery *The Longest Second*, the suspenseful courtroom drama *Not I, Said the Vixen*, and the two tales contained in this Stark House volume. The first, *The Tooth and the Nail*, originally printed in *Cosmopolitan* magazine in condensed form in March 1955 and published as a novel by Harper a few months later, is considered by many critics one of the finest suspense novels of American writing in the twentieth century.

Set in New York City, Ballinger's residence at the time, the novel jumps back and forth in time between an intriguing murder trial and the events in a professional magician's life. Paying particular focus on the two persuasive lawyers—Charles Denman, chief council for the defense, and Franklin Cannon, the assistant district attorney—the author teases the reader with interesting details about the case while cunningly withholding key information and masking the identity of the defendant. The realistic and occasionally amusing courtroom drama is oddly coupled with a first-person narrative about a likable, small-time conjurer, Luis Montana, alias Lewis Mountain (Lew), who, convinced that his young bride was murdered, becomes obsessed with finding the culprit and avenging her death.

The disparate narratives, which don't feel like they quite belong together, might easily have spoiled Ballinger's ingenious mystery tale, making it seem confusing and disjointed. Remarkably, each of the two intersecting storylines are so entertaining and exceptionally well-written that the momentum of the plot isn't lost and the reader will relish the verbal sparring in the courtroom just as much as they will enjoy Lew Mountain's frank reminiscences of carny life, his budding romance with the troubled Tally Shaw, and his fanatical quest for revenge.

The book, which became an instant bestseller, reintroduced a gimmick (the Sealed Mystery) previously used by Harper from 1929 to 1934—a thin blue wrapper bound into the book, three-quarters of the way through, challenging the reader to either break the seal and read the conclusion of the story, or return the book and get their money back. The *St. Louis Globe-Democrat* Book Editor, Francis A. Klein, was one of those unable to keep from breaking the seal. "Few, we believe, will be able to resist this challenge; we couldn't, and were rewarded with a bang-up yarn, with an ingeniously-constructed plot and surprises at every turn," wrote Klein. "Even if you are a 'fan,' you've never read one quite like this before."

A syndicated reporter for the news agency United Press spoke of the book in the same glowing terms, describing it as "an ingenious and absorbing tale of mounting suspense, and few readers who have guessed the right answer will not want to find out exactly how the plot works out." Likewise, a reviewer in the *Hartford Courant* remarked: "This is a first-rate mystery-suspense novel of revenge. It's so good that the publishers have sealed the last 50 pages and invites the reader to get his money back if the seal is returned unbroken. It's like betting on a one-horse race. It's a dandy. Too bad there aren't more Bill Ballingers in the field."

The sheer volume of positive reviews for Ballinger's books, particularly this one, gives you an indication of just how much the author's fiction was appreciated during his lifetime. Notable mystery fiction critics Drexel Drake (aka Charles H. Huff) of the *Chicago Tribune* called *The Tooth and the Nail* "a cleverly original story," and Anthony Boucher of *The New York Times* declared Ballinger "a major virtuoso of mystery technique." Lenore Glen Offord of *the San Francisco Sunday Examiner & Chronicle* thought it a "masterly" novel with a really unusual plot and "sound" writing. She went on to describe Ballinger as a "two-headed" author, one who could be "hardboiled without being dirty," and who had "a remarkable technique of narration."

The Desert Sun also appreciated the author's innovative style of storytelling, declaring that the mystery was "guaranteed to keep the reader on his mental toes to the final dramatic detail." Ballinger's dual narrative method had helped achieve "an almost unbearable amount of suspense," and the final clever plot twist made "clairvoyance a necessity if the reader is to guess this one."

In 1971, Joe Green of *The Cincinnati Enquirer* confessed: "This reviewer has long been a devotee of Bill Ballinger and hesitates to offer critical words about a man who has written so many suspense classics." Little wonder, then, that more than a decade earlier, he had nothing negative to say of *The Tooth and the Nail*, considering it a worthwhile read with a "superior" plot to many suspense novels. His thoughts on the fictional murder trial echo my sentiments: "Its courtroom scenes are dramatic and handled with the same authenticity as seen in the Perry Mason stories."

For originality and unbridled suspense, it's a novel that cannot be bettered, as far as I'm concerned. All the same, Ballinger managed, in the ensuing years, to advance this nifty tales-in-tandem structure, producing yet more masterful works that intrigue and startle and leave an indelible impression on readers.

His subsequent novel, *The Wife of the Red-Haired Man*, published serially under the title "My Husband is a Redhead" and released by Harper in March 1957, is a thrilling chase story about an escaped convict, Hugh Rohan, striving to elude capture by an astute detective who's determined to track him down. After escaping prison, Rohan returns to his wife, Mercedes, but discovers that she has divorced him and remarried, having presumed he was killed in the war. When her second husband, Albert, threatens to report Rohan to the police, the fear of returning to jail spurs the convict-at-large to execute the crooked, wealthy New York businessman and go on the run with Mercedes.

Assigned to the case is a NYC detective in the Nineteenth Precinct who, although he has very little to go on at first, manages to piece together the tiny trail of clues. As he traverses the country, from New York to Williamsburg to Kansas City to New Orleans and beyond, following in the footsteps of the man with hair "the blood red of a cockatoo, the splendored brilliance of a Mandarin cabinet," he begins to appreciate Rohan's motivations and patterns of behavior. While learning about the man's background, including his mistakes and disappointments, he discovers commonalities between them and gains empathy for his quarry.

His fixation brings to mind Danny, the collection agent in *A Portrait in Smoke*, whose fanatical search for the unscrupulous Krassy, a beautiful girl he knows only through photographs, leads him to believe: "She became just as real to me as if I was going to meet her for a date every night. I'd looked at her picture so many times, I could trace each feature with my eyes closed." In much the same way, the NYC detective's intense fascination with Rohan and yearning to find him echoes Danny's obsessive behavior. "My life, my thoughts, had become so entwined with those of the red-haired man that I could no longer think of him simply as a criminal to be hunted," he writes, perceiving him more like a "brother" than a criminal.

Told partly in the first person, from the point of view of the detective, and partly from an omniscient perspective, Ballinger intentionally focuses on plot over character, keeping character descriptions to a bare minimum. In spite of this, he still achieves a great deal of character development and makes the reader eager to discover the fate of the red-haired man and his former wife.

In terms of critical reception, the novel proved successful and memorable, with Anthony Boucher describing it in *The New York Times* as highly suspenseful, compulsive reading. Other newspapers, such as the *Daily Press*, regarded it as a "literate and conscientious" work. Although Drexel Drake offered tepid praise, Ham Park of *The Salt Lake Tribune* gave it his endorsement, and *The Fairfax Chief* lauded it as "a new high water mark in murder fiction—a real spine tingler."

Both of these exciting tales, milestone mysteries in their day, continue to be powerful and impactful works that, though seldom reprinted, are occasionally resurrected for film and radio. *The Tooth and the Nail* was the source for a 2017 South Korean movie, and *The Red-Haired Man* was adapted to radio by the author in 1973 as part of a thirteen-week *The Zero Hour* series hosted by *Twilight Zone* and *Night Gallery* star Rod Serling. Starring Patty Duke, her husband John Astin, and Howard Duff, it played across 150 stations in five half-hour daily episodes.

Although Ballinger went on to write plenty more critically and commercially successful manuscripts, this pair of inspired, unconventional chill and puzzle thrillers, centered on the hunter and the hunted, are among his most prized works. Few writers can match Ballinger's talent for inventiveness, relentless suspense, and delivering a startling reveal. And very few readers will be able to put this book down once they've started either story.

—December 2019
Rochester, NY

....

Nicholas Litchfield is the founding editor of the literary magazine *Lowestoft Chronicle*, author of the suspense novel *Swampjack Virus*, and editor of nine literary anthologies. He has worked in various countries as a journalist, librarian, and media researcher and resides in western New York. Formerly, a book reviewer for the *Lancashire Post* and syndicated to twenty-five newspapers across the UK, he now writes for *Publishers Weekly* and regularly contributes to Colorado State University's literary journal *Colorado Review*.

The Tooth and the Nail

BILL S. BALLINGER

Prologue

His name was Lew; his second name is unimportant, except for one instance, which I shall tell you about later; and he had been known as Lew Austrian, Lewison Clark, and Patrick Paris. Actually, however, he'd been born Luis Montana, which is Spanish, and later Americanized it to Lewis Mountain—which means the same. His name, in itself, was peculiar in a way, because his family have been Americans for many generations and by the time he was born were not Spanish at all. But the old names remained, and that's why he ended up with a name such as Luis Montana.

And, furthermore, he wasn't born in California, or Texas, or Arizona or New Mexico—or any of the border states where you'd expect to find the descendants of the Spaniards. He was born in Iowa which is approximately in the center of the United States and where you may expect to find anyone. He was born on a farm, a good one with rolling acres of rich soil; it had been his grandfather's farm, and after his grandfather died his father owned it.

When he was alive, he was a magician—a maker of miracles, a prestidigitator, an illusionist like Harry Houdini or Thurston. He had been a good magician, but because he died too soon he never became really famous like the others I've mentioned. However, he accomplished something that neither of these men ever attempted.

First, he avenged murder.

Secondly, he committed murder.

Thirdly, he was murdered in the attempt.

Chapter 1

The Judge of the Court of General Sessions, County of New York, smoothed down his black robe, deliberately arranged the papers before him and nodded to the assistant district attorney. The attorney arose from the prosecution's table and walked a few feet toward the jury box. In the somber austere room, with high ceilings, he was the center of attention and he paused confidently, for a moment, before he began the opening statement for the prosecution. As he turned slightly, his eyes swept the table where the defendant was seated beside the counsel for the defense, and the eyes of the jury followed his glance. In that exact instant, with the jurymen's eyes on the prisoner, he began speaking. He spoke fluently and well, in an easy conversational voice, pacing slowly and deliberately before the jury box which seated nine men and three women.

The assistant district attorney was named Franklin Cannon. A man of middle age, of middling stature and undeterminable colored hair, he was a deliberate and unemotional man attempting to fulfill the obligations of his office. He disliked histrionics and prepared his cases carefully—presenting his logic, facts, and evidence to a jury with an honesty and sincerity that often was severely damaging to his opponents. Cannon appreciated the importance of the opening of a trial; at such a time, the jury often formed lasting impressions of both the prosecution and defense to which it clung with bias throughout the entire trial.

Cannon, talking now, was conscious of the scrutiny of the jury's eyes. As he continued to talk in generalities, he felt the eyes probing his face, examining his clothes, observing his gestures; a dozen pairs of ears weighing the sound of his voice, sifting his words. With the minutes going by, he could sense the easing of tension among the jurymen, the visible disappearing of aloofness as each became accustomed to his appearance and the sound of his voice. It had been Cannon's experience that all new juries are uneasy at the opening of a trial, and he was content to spend the additional time and words to build this first rapport between them. One by one, they would come to think ... "He reminds me of Cousin Joe, the way he talks" or "he looks a little like Bob Elton out in the engineering department" or simply "Cannon talks like a pretty reasonable man."

Whichever it was the jury thought—the familiar comparison or the sudden acceptance of him as a person—whenever the decisions were made the barrier would suddenly go down and then the prosecution would get on with the business of sending a man to the chair.

Abruptly, Cannon stopped and walked slowly toward the jury box. Pausing, he seemed to be searching in his mind. Slowly, almost kindly, he said, "You must remember that the man accused here is not bound to prove his innocence ... it is the obligation of the state, my obligation ... too, to prove his guilt."

The chief counsel for the defense arose from his chair and stood beside the table. "Your honor," he said, "would you instruct the jury that what the counselor has just said is a matter of law. It has nothing to do with his own particular magnanimity."

Cannon turned and, in turning, seemed to bow to his opponent. "Certainly, it is a matter of law," he replied courteously.

The eyes of the jury were fixed on the defense attorney, partly hostile, partly surprised by the sudden intervention. Cannon, sensing the jury's sympathy for himself—which might quickly be dissipated when the defense made its presentation—turned now to the serious business before him.

"In many respects this is both an unusual case, and a very interesting one." Cannon's voice had assumed a grave note. "The defendant is accused of murder. The fact that he is so charged is the reason he is here, but it does not necessarily mean that he committed a murder. The State of New York will attempt to prove that he did kill a man known to him as Isham Reddick ... an employee working for him as a valet and chauffeur.

"We will attempt to prove the accused had a motive, and the opportunity." Cannon turned and walked to his table, pausing for a moment to pick up a sheaf of papers—through which he riffled. The silver-painted radiators, in the silent courtroom, released small puffs of steam. The rows of oak benches, the limply hanging flag, the green roller shades at the windows, the silent specters of other trials of other men, waited patiently.

Cannon was finished with his notes, and he replaced the papers and returned to a position a few feet from the jury box. "Undoubtedly each of you has heard the expression ... circumstantial evidence. And most probably you have heard it referred to in a rather derogatory way.... It's not uncommon to hear a criminal, after conviction, maintain complete innocence and insist that all the evidence was circumstantial."

The attorney smiled, and a number of the jurors returned it. "There are very few cases, particularly of murder, where the facts and evidence are not at least partly circumstantial. Possibly only in a case where there are eyewitnesses to the very act itself, where the witnesses can identify both the victim and the accused, do you find a case without some circumstantial evidence...."

The counsel for the defense interrupted. "Objection," he said. "This is a matter of argument, and is theoretical to the point that it can neither be proved nor disproved."

Cannon faced the judge. "If it please, your honor," he replied calmly, "I feel this matter of evidence ... particularly of circumstantial evidence ... is of the utmost importance to the jury ... and must be completely understood." Turning to the attorney for the defense, he smiled, "I'm sure the counselor is planning to refer to it himself."

"Gentlemen," said the judge, "on points of law concerning evidence I will instruct the jury!"

Cannon nodded politely and returned to address the jury. "It is the obligation of both myself ... and my associate," he turned and indicated Deputy Assistant Attorney Rickers, "to prove the *corpus delicti* in this case. In a homicide this term refers to the death of the person alleged to have been killed. Occasionally, newspaper feature writers," Cannon glanced with a quiet smile toward the press bench, "contribute to the myth that without a body, there is no conviction. This is not exactly the truth, although it makes excellent reading on a dull Sunday afternoon. What they mean to say, undoubtedly, is that without *evidence* of a body, there can be no conviction. But, ladies and gentlemen of the jury, that is something entirely different! In several notable cases, which I can quote, verdicts of guilty have been found without the actual physical presence of a *corpus delicti*, although the evidence of a *corpus delicti* was proved beyond a reasonable doubt.

"In most jurisdictions, only direct evidence will avail to prove the fact of death, although circumstantial evidence may, of course, be resorted to in order to show that the death was produced through a criminal agency. Now, with these points in mind let us return to the night of November twenty-second of last year."

The jury was listening intently. "It is the contention of the state," Cannon continued, "that on that date, sometime preceding midnight, the defendant killed a man named Isham Reddick. Reddick was employed in his household, an establishment located on East Eighty-ninth Street, here in the City of New York. Evidence will be introduced to show that Reddick had become a thorn-in-the-side of the defendant, that Isham Reddick was blackmailing him, and the defendant had on at least one occasion ... and probably on others ... paid Reddick a substantial sum of money. On the night of November twenty-second, there was a meeting between the defendant and Isham Reddick ending in violence...."

"Objection," stated the counsel for the defense. "That is a conclusion."

"What are you attempting to establish, Mr. Cannon?" asked the judge.

"I'm attempting to outline the position of the case for the state, and to indicate what we will later prove."

"Continue, Mr. Cannon," said the judge, "although I shall point out to the jury that at this time there is no evidence yet introduced to substantiate in any way what you are saying."

"Thank you," said the counsel for the defense. Returning to his seat beside the defendant, he continued to watch Cannon warily.

Cannon resumed, cautiously, the threading of his speech. He wanted no interruptions at this point. The afternoon shadows were filling the corners of the bleak, forlorn room and he glanced at the watch on his wrist. A little longer, and it would be time to adjourn until the following day. It would give the jury an entire evening to consider his remarks before the opposition took up its defense. "Sometime during the night of November twenty-second," Cannon continued, "and into the early morning hours of the twenty-third, the body of Isham Reddick was dismembered and destroyed in an attempt to remove all evidence of the crime! And, in the possibility of detection or discovery, to circumvent conviction and punishment for the crime! Fortunately for justice, however, all traces of the crime were not removed. All evidence of the body was not destroyed beyond recovery ... and other indisputable proofs of the crime were preserved by the early appearance of the authorities.

"This evidence will be presented to you. You will appraise it, weigh it, consider it. After you have heard the entire case, after you have seen the evidence with your own eyes, if you believe beyond any reasonable doubt that the accused is guilty ... it is then your duty, your obligation ... to return to this court your verdict attesting it." For a moment he stood silently, then added, "Thank you."

The judge glancing at the old-fashioned Western Union clock on the wall, gaveled his desk once, and adjourned the court until the next morning. The court stood respectfully while he walked to his chambers.

Chapter 2

It all began on the day I met Tally Shaw. Meeting her, with due apologies to the poets, was not the same as listening to a nightingale sing in a garden, or finding a spring of cool water after thirsting for days in a desert. But the fact that she was, that day, a complete stranger both to me and to New York, standing on Seventh Avenue arguing with a cab driver, put into motion all the events that were to happen later. And, if one believes in inevitability, then it was inevitable that I acted the way I did. A cab had stopped in front of the hotel where I was living and its passenger did not have enough money to pay her cab fare. The cabby was adamant about keeping her luggage, and the girl was pleading with him, desperately, to let her have one small bag.

The Delafield—a small, not quite shabby hotel—which receives most of its business from show people, does not have a doorman, or the girl might have borrowed the money from him. As I pushed past them to go into the lobby, I heard the girl say, "It's ridiculous! I only owe you a dollar!"

"I can't help that," replied the driver, "I'll hold the luggage and you can have it when you pay me the buck."

"I don't know how it happened ... I had the money, I don't know where it went...." She rummaged through her handbag urgently. "It might've fallen out when I had lunch. I remember I had it then. At the station just before I took the train ..."

I stood in the center of the doorway, holding open the door, listening to the argument. Urged on by my curiosity, I stepped back to the sidewalk letting the door close, still following the conversation. "Look, lady," the cabby protested indifferently, "maybe you did, maybe you didn't. I keep the suitcases till you pay me or ... I'll call a cop."

The girl was frightened. "No, don't do that! Keep one of them ... keep the hatbox. Is that all right with you? I'll just take the little handbag."

He shook his head. "Nope! I keep both of them!"

"But I must have at least one ... or I can't get in the hotel. They won't let me register without paying in advance...."

"I keep both of 'em." The cabby's voice was final.

I discovered I was standing by the girl's side and, to my surprise, I heard myself saying, "If the lady will permit me, I'll pay the bill." The cabby swung his small suspicious eyes at me, and the girl turned wonderingly. "How much does she owe you?" I asked him.

He replied, "A buck."

"Here it is ... and give the lady her luggage." He placed a large tan hatbox and a small leather satchel on the sidewalk. Circling around to the driver's seat, he slipped behind the wheel and drove away. The girl remained silent. "Well," I told her, "you now have your choice ... either say 'thank you,' or I'll take the luggage."

"It was nice of you," she gave me an embarrassed smile. "Thank you very much."

"Lost all your money, huh?" I asked.

"Yes." She regarded her purse, misery in her eyes.

"Any idea where you lost it?"

"It must've been at the station ... in Philadelphia." Her words began to tumble out. "I stopped in the station for a sandwich. Then I was on the train. I didn't look again until I reached the hotel. I didn't hire a porter ... or buy anything else...."

"Can you wire back for more?" She shook her head hopelessly. "Anyway," I said, "there's no sense standing out here on the curb. Come on, I'll buy you a cup of coffee while you decide what to do." The Delafield has a small luncheon counter, which is open twenty-four hours a day, and I headed for it. Picking up her luggage, I received a surprise. The hatbox was neither any heavier or lighter than you might expect, but the small leather satchel could not have weighed more if it had been filled with fire plugs. "Don't you find this a little heavy to carry around?" I asked politely.

She agreed, rather nervously. "Yes ... but it's good exercise," and then smiling, she shrugged it off.

We climbed on stools and she ordered a cup of tea. The counter was nearly vacant although it was invisibly festooned with the ghosts of generations of cream cheese and jelly sandwiches. "Just as a beginning," I asked the girl, "do you know anyone in town you can phone ... any friends or relatives?"

"No. I'm a complete stranger."

"Where'd you come from?"

"Philadelphia ..."

"The answer is easy," I told her. "I'll lend you five dollars and you can go back. Catch a train tonight … they leave practically all the time."

"I can't do it," her voice was very low.

"The five bucks? You can send it back sometime."

"I didn't mean that. I … just … can't go back to Philadelphia." Turning, she faced me, her eyes wide and set with determination.

"Why not?"

She didn't reply. Abruptly I realized I was wrong. What made her eyes so wide was not determination, but fear! I said, "All right, let's change the subject. Tell me about yourself; I'm not the Traveler's Aid Society, but I'll do until it comes along.…"

It was then she told me her name was Tally Shaw. She had no family; her last relative, an elderly uncle, had died the preceding week. She had taken what little money was left and come to New York. And here she was—no money, no friends, no job. As I listened, I watched her and realized it was an extremely pleasant pastime. While she talked, she held her eyes to the bottom of the tea cup—as if attempting to read the leaves. Occasionally she turned the cup slowly, around and around, in her fingers. There was an unconscious grace in the movement, her head arching on a slender neck, her profile lovely. She did not, however, possess what could be called a striking beauty although that was an asset in itself. Her charm depended on a shyness, a quietness—a blending of softness and repose.

High lights danced on her hair. The regularity of her delicate features was contradicted by her mouth—warm, and a shade too wide—and high prominent cheekbones which lightly brushed an enigmatic expression … a gentle touch of the Oriental … across her face.

"What had you planned to do here in New York, before you lost your money?" I asked.

"I really didn't have any plans," she shrugged. "I would have to find a job … of course."

"Have you ever had a job?"

"Well … sort of … before Uncle Will died."

"Can you do typing … take shorthand?"

"No … not without studying."

"Do you have any repressed desires? Can you sing … dance? Ever want to be an actress?"

She set the tea cup firmly on the counter and smiled. "I can't sing a note," she replied. "I like to dance … you know, just ordinary dancing to an orchestra. And I don't know a thing about acting. Do you?"

"No," I assured her, "I know very little about it either. Although through the force of economic necessity or the problems of seasonal employment, when I've had to … I've sung in the chorus of *The Student*

Prince, danced a mean waltz in *The Merry Widow*, done speaking parts up to, and including, five lines in summer stock." I lit a cigarette and added, "Tally, I've also sold tickets in a carnival, worked clown alley in the circus, and been a dealer in Nevada...."

"Oh," she regarded me gravely, looking a little puzzled, "you're an actor!"

"Only through necessity," I told her, "and not through choice. Through choice, if I have anything to say about it, I'm a magician."

"Can you do tricks?"

"Certainly. And someday you should catch me at them."

For the first time she really laughed. Momentarily, she seemed to have forgotten her problems. "I love magicians!" she exclaimed. "All my life I've loved to watch magicians and clowns."

"I agree with you," I said, "except personally I don't like clowns."

"You're just being jealous!" She looked at me carefully and then said marveling, as if just then she had seen me for the first time, "you said your name was Lew. What is your real name?"

"Lew Mountain. Lately, I've been working under the name of Patrick Paris ... or Professor Paris."

"Are you working in a show now?"

"I'm working in the floor show of a night club. Which brings up another subject. I don't have too much money. As a magician I know it's unkind to my profession to admit we can't make it materialize from the air. So with that thought in mind, I hurry on to what I can do. By waving my hand in the air, thus ..." I faked a pass and palmed the key of my hotel room, "I can make available to you ... tonight ... all the secrets, all the mysteries and joys, the romance and glamour of the ... Taj Mahal!" I held up the hotel key.

"What's that?" she asked.

"It's the key to a warm bath, a rather hard bed, four waterproof walls, and a doubtful ceiling and floor. It is the key to my room ... number 302, situated in the Hotel Delafield ... where we are now." She had been watching with a smile, but the smile disappeared. "Wait a minute!" I told her hurriedly. "Don't leap at the wrong idea. You must have a place to stay tonight ... perhaps for a few days. I rent my room by the month. You stay here, and I'll find a place to bunk for a couple of nights. Which reminds me! I know a fellow who has an apartment right near here. Why ... for years now ... he's been flooding me with weekend invitations."

The smile tentatively reappeared. "Oh," she said. Then brightening, "Will it be all right with the hotel?"

"Not entirely," I told her. "The management would far prefer that I pay the double rate ... and we live in sin. They're not moralists, you see, they're realists. But a little palm salve to the maid and the bell captain ... and you could stay forever." Rising from the stool, I picked up her luggage. "Come on," I said, "I'll get you moved in now." She arose and followed me to the back of the luncheonette where a door opened into the hotel. I placed her luggage on the floor, and poked my head into the lobby. Max, the bell captain, was leaning against the newsstand and reading the magazines. With the sure instinct of a man smelling a fast buck, he raised his head as soon as my eyes hit him. Immediately he put aside his reading and sauntered over to me. I stepped back within the lunchroom and he followed me.

"This is an old aunt of mine from Montreal," I told him, nodding to Tally. "She's here for the mud and the baths, you know. Because of the shortage of rooms in all the spas, she'll have to use mine for a few days."

"She's pretty well preserved," he observed, after eying her carefully.

"Yes, isn't she? It's the water that does it. Now, can you get her stuff up to 302 without the desk knowing it, and charging for a double?"

"I can get Yankee Stadium through the lobby without the desk knowing it," he assured me.

"Okay," I agreed, handing him a bill. "Here's your take for the luggage. I'll see you upstairs."

Max picked up the hatbox, and nearly dislocated his shoulder on the small leather satchel. "Jees, lady," he said, "what you got in here, a troop of midgets?"

Tally blushed and attempted to take the bag away from him. "I'll carry it," she said. "It's awfully heavy...."

Max squinted his eyes. "You don't look like a lady wrestler," he said shrugging off her hands. "I've carried plenty drunks that weighed more'n this." He seemed literally to vanish into the lobby.

Room 302 was located on the back of the building facing away from Seventh Avenue. It was a medium-sized room finished in plaid wallpaper, with all the wood trimming of the doors and windows painted white. The elderly furniture had been modernized to the extent of a coat of black enamel paint; this included the bed, dresser, straight-backed chair, and a small telephone stand. The handles and knobs had been removed from the furniture and replaced by small, round, circles of woods also painted black. The lamps, which harked back to the roaring twenties, retained their old bases, although supporting new shades of a particularly hideous elongated modern design. Only the prints on the walls remained unchanged. They would remain hotel pictures until the day the termites chewed them free from their frames.

Tally surveyed the montage calmly. "The nicest thing you can say about the room," I told her, "is that it's paid up to the end of the month." Surprisingly enough, she patted my hand.

"You don't know how lovely it looks to me," she replied.

"If that's the way you feel about it, I might as well show you the entire layout. Not that you'd get lost finding out for yourself, but this way you won't have to waste time walking. Here is the bath. It doesn't lead anywhere. This is the closet; but don't make the mistake of trying to get in it and turn around. I did that one night and missed a show." By the bed, I lifted the tufted chenille spread up from the floor and pulled out a wooden footlocker. "This," I explained, "is the kitchen. You are not supposed to cook in the rooms, but it's all right if the management can't get in the door while you're doing it." I unlocked the footlocker and handed her the key. "Keep it locked whenever you're not using the stuff. The maid knows … they always know … but tomorrow morning give her this dollar and she won't say anything."

From the locker I removed an electric hot plate, a nest of plastic picnic dishes, cups and a few pieces of silver together with several aluminum pans, a coffee pot, and a small, flat, iron griddle. "There!" I exclaimed, "All the conveniences of dining in! I keep coffee, sugar, and canned soup under lock and key; and the cream outside the window."

Tally nodded. "Utilitarian … to say the least. I don't imagine you often have large dinner parties."

"Just during the height of the season," I said modestly, "and then never more than … oh … well … myself."

She put the utensils back in the locker and shoved it under the bed. "I know I'm imposing on you terribly," she said soberly.

"Not at all," I replied, keeping it light, playing it flippantly. "I always expect people to drop in."

Rising to her feet, she smiled. Inexplicably, her face was dusted with a sweet and inscrutable expression. "I'll find something real soon."

"Take your time, kid," I told her. "Be choosy … start at the top if you can. Then you can always work down." Taking my hat, I stepped out into the hall. "I'll see you in the morning," I said, "around noon. And you can make me a cup of coffee."

"I'll be up before then," she said.

"Yes, but I won't," I told her. Walking down the street, deciding who was in town, and where I could find a place to sleep, I recited aloud:

> Meet me by moonlight alone,
>   And then I will tell you a tale.
> Must be told by the moonlight alone
>   In the grove at the end of the vale.

I felt very good.

Chapter 3

Charles Denman, chief counsel for the defense, was a dark sardonic
man with a lean alert face. Standing near a window in the courtroom,
his figure was silhouetted against the light and in the air behind him
dust motes stirred sluggishly. Denman had been addressing the jury all
morning, undermining the opening speech made by the district attorney on the day before. "Usually," he said, "this is the time when the defense states what it hopes to prove ... even while I again remind you that
neither the indictment of the defendant nor the prosecutor's statement
are proof ... but I believe that we will delay revealing our defense," his
voice dropped to a confidential level, "because, frankly, I don't believe the
prosecution has found soundness or merit in its case. At this time, theirs
is the burden of proof, and there let it remain.

"You are going to be asked to listen to quite a story ... in which someone ... has supposedly been killed. There is no corpse of the murdered
person, there is no motive, and there were no witnesses. From this skein
of gossamer fabrications you will be asked to decide ... beyond all reasonable doubt ... that murder has been committed. Except that this is
a learned court, and an innocent person's life is on trial here, I would
say that the entire story is so ... unbelievable, as to be unworthy of a half-
hour television play." An answering smile came from the jury box.
"However," Denman continued, "we will do what we can, as we go
along, to show you the inconsistencies, the doubtfulness of the charges.
I'm sure that you will need little help to notice the lack of proof supporting the charges which will be introduced."

Turning, he nodded in the direction of Cannon. "Yesterday, my respected colleague, Mr. Cannon, said ... and I quote him ..." Denman
walked deliberately to the table and selected a sheet of paper; carefully,
he put on a pair of heavy, tortoise-shell-rimmed glasses. Holding the
sheet before him, he read clearly, "You must remember that the man accused here is not bound to prove his innocence. It is the obligation of the
state to prove his guilt." Denman replaced the paper on the table and
removed his glasses. "Of course, Mr. Cannon also admitted many other
things, too." Denman swung around and returned casually to the jury
box. "I didn't read the entire statement, because I believe you will
agree it was rather wordy."

Denman's face was now extremely earnest. "I ask you to remember,
however, the seriousness of that statement. Saying it is one thing ... doing it, another. When evidence and exhibits are introduced into this case
... and undoubtedly they will be introduced very impressively ... ask

yourselves what it proves. Please say to yourself, 'What does this mean?' Is it evidence of fact? Does it actually *mean* anything when reviewed in the light of the entire case? Many persons who were innocent have been convicted by circumstantial evidence...."

Cannon was on his feet, interrupting. "Objection, your honor!"

"Objection sustained!" the court ruled. The judge instructed the jury, "You must overlook the last remark of the counsel for the defense."

Denman smiled to himself. Although the judge might advise the jurors to overlook the remark, some of them might remember it. Denman had been working hard, turning the opening sympathy of the jury away from the district attorney and attempting to win it for himself. He was beginning to tire with the advancing hours of the day. This case was one which he regarded uncertainly. As an attorney he believed it was his duty to defend the guilty as well as the innocent. To an extent circumscribed only by his own cynicism, he was dedicated to his profession. He fought for the rights of the defendants, protected their rights as defined by the law, and sometimes even financed the costs of their defense. He did this not out of friendship, and certainly not for financial gain, but for the satisfaction he derived in fighting for an equality before the law. Sometimes he felt more sympathy for the men he believed to be guilty. The client, in his present case, had maintained his innocence. Denman's clients seldom lied to him, and if he was convinced they were lying, he refused to represent them. But with this man, he could not be sure. Denman was not sure that he knew the entire story; what he did know of it fascinated him.

"There is very little more that I want to add now," he continued, "except to remind you that my client has pleaded 'not guilty.' That means he is *not* guilty ... until such a time as the charges are irrefutably proven. And, ladies and gentlemen, that time will never come! I ask of you, beg of you, to keep your sense of appraisement, maintain your feelings of skepticism, and keep your mind open until both sides have been heard." Denman stood before the jurors silently for a moment. Then nodded gently, turned, and retired to the defense table.

The judge recessed the court.

Denman's assistant, a young man with protruding blue eyes and a crew cut, helped him arrange his folders in a brief case. "I thought it went very well," he remarked to his superior. Denman glanced up to watch his client being escorted from the courtroom between two officers.

"Well enough, I suppose," he replied to the younger man. "No one can tell for sure ... until it's too late."

The reporters opened the little gate in the low wooden railing and approached Denman. "I suppose I can quote you as being optimistic, counselor?" one of them asked,

"What else?" asked Denman smiling.

Chapter 4

Of course on the morning after I met Tally, I returned to the Delafield around noon, and she opened the door. She was completely dressed ... in the same dress of the day before. Probably, it was the only dress she had. Or at least, it was the only one she had with her. Her hair was combed; she had her make-up on and she looked beautiful. The hotplate and coffee pot had already been set up, on top of the dresser, so we sat down and had breakfast—which included a sack of doughnuts I had brought along. I sat on the chair, balancing a cup, and tried to make conversation. "Have you been up long?"

"Oh, yes," she replied. "Hours ..."

"Well, I suppose it's fine if you can wake up in time. How'd you sleep?"

"Lovely! How did you?"

This was real sparkling dialog, but I liked it. Just sitting and talking to her, it was the tops. "Great," I told her. "I slept with a guy's dog all night. He has this mutt, which always sleeps on the extra bed; whenever anyone sleeps in it, the dog won't give it up. With some persuasion, however, the dog will share it. He shared it with me, but he insisted on the pillow."

She laughed, and in the morning it sounded as bright as the sunlight. "Did you work last night?"

"Sure. All three shows."

"Is it fun?"

"Not particularly," I told her. And then I realized it was just a pose ... it was fun. It wasn't difficult to remember when I thought it was the greatest thing in life. So I started telling her about it....

Our house, on the farm, had been a great, square, frame one. Across the front had been a porch narrow in depth but stretching the entire width. It had a series of plain, undistinguished wooden posts ... or pillars ... placed every eight feet which supported a railing. In the summers, my father and mother kept a couple of rocking chairs on it, and would sit there in the evenings after dark. Although the house was three stories high, it had a perfectly flat metal roof ... painted a faded red. Surmounting the roof was a glass-enclosed cupola ... about six feet square. On top of the cupola was a long elaborate lightning rod ... pointing up to the Iowa skies. The cupola could be entered only by a ladder which projected through an opening in the ceiling of a room on the third floor. No one ever entered it as it was usually occupied by mud hornets, yellow jackets, and pigeons. Why it was ever built, or even conceived—this misplaced captain's walk in the middle of the prairies, I'll never know.

The house had been built by some forgotten pioneer, long before the Civil War, and had been purchased many years later by my grandfather. Like most farm houses, it always needed another coat of paint.

In the front yard were great oak trees, standing in grass which seemed to spring from the ground a foot high, and never grew any higher. From the branch of one of the trees my father hung a rope with a worn-out automobile tire for a swing. But I don't remember ever using it; perhaps because I had no brothers or sisters to play with me, and it seems senseless to swing by one's self. Back, and away, from the house were all the farm buildings—the barn, the equipment sheds, corn crib, silo, and chicken house. Growing up with the animals, they had little attraction for me, and no novelty. Early enough, my first duties were gathering eggs and helping my mother feed the chickens; by slow degrees I graduated to the milk house, and then to milking ... and later to the fields.

It is easy to give the impression that I was worked too young ... and too hard. That isn't true. My life was the same as many farm boys and, I believe, it was better than most. Always we had a hired man to help with the chores, and my mother usually had a farm girl to help her in the house. Our farm was prosperous, and our way of life was good. But a farm, I think, is a lonely place unless it is truly part of your life. Unfortunately, although I lived on one, it was never part of mine. After dark, the land seems to expand, to push all things away, farther and farther, until the farm on which you live is an island. The rest of the world is far away; in the distance are the highways, but they do not lead to you. Across the miles a light gleams in the window of another house, but that light is part of a different island and has nothing to do with you. The tree frogs start hesitantly, always slowly, playing a chirping dissonance which gradually grows and swells in confidence and volume as if a conductor were leading; then lowering, it gently falls away following God-knows-what theme, until on cue it swells and crashes again. Sometimes the pigeons in the cupola mourn restlessly in the early translucent darkness, and the fireflies come out searching the night with their pin points of light for something which they never find. Unless it is death in the cold morning dew.

When I was nine, just shortly before my tenth birthday, I saw a magic set displayed in the mail order catalog which was delivered to us each spring and fall. For hours I read the description, read and reread it again until I could repeat it word for word. I wanted that set more than anything in the world. Until that moment, gripped in the fever of my new-found desire, I realize I had never really wanted anything before in my life!

My mother was helpless, before the intensity of my pleadings, to deny me the gift for my birthday, although I imagine the cost far exceeded what she had planned to spend. Together we sat down at the round kitchen table and filled out the order, and I addressed and stamped the envelope. That night I could hardly sleep for excitement, and in the morning I was waiting when the RFD mailman drove up in his Model T Ford. With the letter safely on its way, I drew a deep—and contented—breath.

There has never been a day like the day the magic set arrived. Never again will the sunshine be as bright, nor the sky as blue, nor the world as beautiful. It arrived in a large, flat, black box made of cardboard; on the cover was a Mephisthophelean magician with patent-leather black hair, and long curving sideburns. He was dressed in evening clothes and was pulling a placid rabbit out of a silk hat. Within the box was an instruction book, and the simple equipment necessary to make a quarter disappear in a glass of water, change a penny into a dime, and make silk handkerchiefs appear from eggs; there were large cardboard dice, glass wands, paper that changed colors ... the enchantment of all the world of make-believe and illusion. In my lap, in the black cardboard box, I held the secrets of the cabala, the mysteries of alchemy, the key to the Unholy Sabbath; a fellow of Paracelsus, a familiar of Cagliostro, a student of the Egyptians.

From that day on, I was never very far away from the set. As I grew older I spent my allowance, and then my youthful wages, on more complex equipment. I practiced in my room at every opportunity; in the barn and in the fields, I carried odd cards and silver coins to palm until my hands and fingers worked independently of my brain.

My first public appearance, as a magician, took place in the town of Fairfax—about seven miles from our farm. We drove each Sunday to the Unitarian Church, in Fairfax. On the occasion of a church dinner, I offered my services for the after dinner program. Somewhat cautiously the minister accepted. His acceptance was based partly on the fact that my father had been a member of the congregation for over twenty years, as well as the fact that there was little new talent to offer. The talents of the congregation had been seen on many occasions, by the same jaundiced audience. That evening I shared the bill with a fifteen-minute slide travelogue of the Falkland Islands—located off the southern end of South America and notable only for their dreariness; a piano concert by Mrs. Randy Fuller, a widow who gave music lessons; and a brother and sister duet by the Ostander kids.

I literally brought the house down ... or rather the church. I'll never forget the feeling as I stood in front of the small audience and listened to the applause of family friends, neighbors, and fellow church members. To me, it sounded thundering. Driving home that night, my father congratulated me and gave me ten dollars. I pocketed it ... for professional services.

The summer I finished high school I was seventeen. My parents had discussed sending me to the agricultural college at Ames that fall. I didn't seem to care about this one way or the other. I was neither pleased nor displeased. When fall came, if they wanted me to go, I'd go. That was the way it was. In July, though, a carnival played the Fourth at Oneida, our county seat town—about ten miles the other side of Fairfax.

My mother wasn't feeling well, that week, and so my parents were not planning to go. A family named Murray, on the next farm, was going to drive over to Oneida and they offered to let me ride along. In those days we had movies, although they were silent, and on the farm my father had erected a high antenna, and we had a huge, twelve-tube super-heterodyne radio. So movies and radio weren't novelties, but I had never seen a play in a theater or been to a circus or carnival. There were no towns with theaters where vaudeville or shows played within a hundred miles, and it was seldom that a carnival came within a reasonable driving distance.

The Murrays and I arrived at the carnival grounds after dark. Strings of orange, blue, green, and red lights swung in the velvet realm of night. Silhouetted against a great golden moon, a Ferris wheel churned slowly in its orbit, and a merry-go-round piped and trilled—the horses prancing and the lions racing. The smell of candy floss, of buttered popcorn, the frying hot dogs, the roasting peanuts, hot tamales and chili, the sawdust and hay trampled into the ground arose and hung, clinging in successive layers, in the quiet air of the prairie night. My senses were assaulted—by sight, by sound, by smell. In that first moment I was lost. I was drunk with an excitement, with an exhilaration which I had never known before.

Quickly I separated myself from the Murrays. Guided by knowledge which I could not identify, I walked straight to a small red trailer, parked to one side of the midway. A middle-aged man, with bushy sandy hair and heavily veined nose, was seated on the steps. He was coatless in the summer heat, his shirt open at a hairy throat and sleeves rolled high on his freckled arms. "Are you the owner?" I asked.

He turned his heavy eyes slowly to look at me, to acknowledge my presence. He grunted—it might be either an affirmation or a denial.

"I want a job," I told him earnestly. "I want to work for you. I'll do anything ..."

"I don't need anything done," he replied.

"I'm good with stock," I told him. My ears buzzed with sound and excitement.

"Go on home, son."

My hands had been thrust in my pockets, and now in my embarrassment I found a silver dollar in my hand, and I removed it from the trousers. Passing my hand before his eyes, I made the silver appear and disappear at will; it ran up my arm, stopped, rolled down to palm, and faded into the air. In the background I could hear the grind of the talkers pitching for the hanky-panks and string games, the fish pond, fortune wheel, and milk bottle games. The rides—dipper, scooter, and baby whip—crashed and clanked mechanically in the night. The jig show with its three-piece combo blasted loose-jointed music to mark the beginning of a new bally. And through it all, the fun house, the monkey drome, wild life and torture shows; the rattle of the shooting gallery, the penny pitch, the cork gallery, lead gallery, and scales—all the world was throbbing and contracting and calling as I manipulated my coin before the man with the red-veined nose. Abruptly he rose to his feet, standing on the top step of the trailer towering above me. "You ain't bad, kid," he said slowly. "You said you wanted to work?"

"Yes ... yes ... sir!" I stammered in my eagerness.

The man shouted a name into the noise and confusion of the night. "Hey, Hym!" Immediately a figure materialized beside the trailer; a heavily muscled man, with thick bullish neck, and terribly scarred ears. "Hym, take a look at the kid. He's good." He motioned me to resume my palming.

Hym watched me from mean speculative eyes. "Yeah," he agreed. "Nice clean yokel face. He could do all right selling." He turned to the man in the trailer. "You talked with him?" The man with the red nose shook his head. "Okay," said Hym, "I'll talk to him."

We walked silently to the chow-top—the cooking tent—and sat at a planked dirty table. Hym rested his arms on the boards, and regarded me cautiously. "You live near here?" he asked.

"No," I replied, lying ... not knowing why, except caution seemed to demand it. "I come from a town in Minnesota—about three hundred miles from here."

Hym grunted, pleased with the information. "Got any folks who might come after you?"

"No," I replied, resolutely shutting my parents from my mind.

He nodded, "Okay, kid. Here's the pitch. I'm putting you on as a ticket-seller. I start you at the girl-show 'cause the admission there is thirt' cents. That gives odd change outa dollar. Some mark hands you a buck, you give 'im a ticket and change for fort'-five cents. I got hustlers keeping the line movin' so's the mark don't geta chance to count change till too late." Reaching in his pocket, he withdrew a handful of sliver. "Like this, see. I'll show you. Make like I've already handed you your ticket—here, I shove it in your left mitt. Why the left mitt? Because the suckers, most of 'em, keep their change in their right pockets. I got a reason ... I'll show you later. Now you hold out your right mitt for your change. I count it for you.... Outa one dollar, sir, thirt' cents, thirt'-five, fort'-five, fifty, seventy-five ... and *oneee* dollar. T'anks, kindly."

I found myself nodding instinctively to his counting; in my hand was a heap of pennies, nickels, and dimes. "Okay," said Hym with a wicked grin, "count it yourself, kid." I did—there was fifty cents in it. There should have been seventy. Hym continued with his lecture, "So this mark is standing there with a handful of change, before he can count it, you say real loud: 'Move along, friend ... keep movin'! Please don't stand there blockin' all your neighbors. The show's just startin' and they wanta get in, too! Keep movin'!' Then one of my boys in the line give a shove, and the line moves along. The mark puts the change in his pocket, with his right hand. He don't have to change over from the left, so he can never be sure. And that's it. Got it?"

I found, suddenly, I was unable to say the words ... to agree. Miserably I looked at him, and his eyes were fixed on me in a hard, expectant stare. As if reading my mind, he shrugged and lurched awkwardly to his feet. From a distance, I heard my voice saying, in mingled shame and excitement, "Yes ... I've got it!"

"All right," said Hym. "You get your meals free in the chow-top, and you can find your own place to sleep in any of the sleeping-tops. You get paid ten bucks a week." He waited for my protest, and when it didn't come, his savage face relaxed. "Insida week, kid, you'll be stealing three times that much for me." He walked to the opening of the tent, pausing for a moment to add, "Never short change on a mark who gives you half a buck or less; on a big bill there ain't no limit to what you can grab. Don't let your fingers get too goddamned sticky and try to steal me blind." Shrugging his shoulders, he raised his palms in a little forgiving gesture, "Take a little ... give a little, okay. But don't forget, kid, I got mine coming, too." He walked out into the noise of the night.

Chapter 5

"The witness will please take the stand," the clerk announced. Cannon approached the witness chair and asked conversationally, "What is your name?"

"Daniel F. Mikleson."

"You are a member of the New York City police department?"

"Yes, sir. I'm a lieutenant, attached to the Homicide East squad."

"Do you remember what happened to you on the morning of November twenty-third of last year?"

"Yes, sir." Shifting his weight in the chair, assuming a more comfortable position, the lieutenant explained that he had been sent to examine the premises of a brownstone house located on East Eighty-ninth Street.

"Was it in answer to an anonymous phone call?"

"Yes, sir. On the telephone. A man called from the public phone booth on the Eastside subway station ... the stop at East Eight-sixth Street."

"Did you talk to him?" Cannon added, "And if you did, what did he say?"

"I talked to him. He said, 'There have been awful smells coming out of the chimney at that house. I think there's been a murder committed.'"

Cannon glanced thoughtfully at the accused, then turned his attention back to the witness. "And after the call, you proceeded to the premises. Did anyone accompany you?"

"Yes. Another detective named James Lowery."

"What happened when you arrived at the premises?"

"It's a large brownstone house, a private residence. There's a heavy plate glass door, in the front, which is protected by iron scroll work. We rang the bell and pounded on the door for some time...."

"How long?"

"Ten minutes. The bell was working because I could hear it ringing in the back of the house."

"What time was this?"

"When we first arrived, we parked the squad car in front of the house and I looked at my watch. It was 10:28 in the morning."

"Thank you. Now after ringing the bell, and pounding on the door for ten minutes, what did you do?"

"We couldn't be sure that the call wasn't the work of a crank, or just a neighbor being nasty. I had just about decided to check back to the desk, when the door was opened by a man."

"How was he dressed?"

"He was wearing underclothes, although he had a dressing robe around him."

"How did he look? Was she shaved? Did he have his hair combed?"

"No, sir. He was not shaved, and his hair was mussed."

"Do you see that same man here in the courtroom?"

"Yes, I do." The lieutenant looked steadily at the defendant. "He is seated over there."

"Please go over and place your hand on his arm." The officer walked stiffly to where the accused was seated, touched his arm briefly, and returned to the witness stand. "Now," resumed Cannon, "what did the defendant say when he opened the door?"

"He acted very astonished. He ..."

"Objection!" Denman's voice remarked.

The judge agreed. "Sustained," he ruled.

"All right," Cannon was unruffled, "after he opened the door, what happened next?"

"Nothing ... for a minute or two," replied Mikleson. "He was silent. I showed him my credentials and he asked what I wanted. I told him it had been reported there had been a murder on the premises, and it was my job to look around."

"What did he say, then?"

"Nothing. He was acting peculiarly and ..."

"Objection!" Denman's voice was curt.

"Sustained!" ruled the court.

"Was he shaking his head?" asked Cannon.

"Yes. He was moving it slowly from one side to the other. I had to repeat what I said before. Finally, he asked me if I had a warrant. I replied I didn't have one, but I could get it if he insisted. I told him I'd leave Detective Lowery to wait for me, and I'd come back with one."

"Then what did the defendant say?"

"He said to me: 'You might as well come in, now.'" Step by step, Cannon led the witness through a description of the house. Mikleson identified photographs of the defendant's bedroom, and the adjoining bath, as ones having been taken in his presence by the photographic detail. Cannon offered them into evidence and they were marked as exhibits.

"I'll return to the photographs later ... with the court's permission," explained Cannon, "but at this time I would like to continue with my present line of examination." There was no objection from Denman and the prosecuting attorney continued. "Tell me, when you reached the basement of the house what did you find?"

"There was a large furnace room, together with laundry and bathrooms." Mikleson added, "Also there were some other ..."

"Let's concentrate on the furnace room, please. Where is it located in regard to the front and back of the house?"

"It is at the back of the house."

"Are there any windows in it?"

"Yes, sir. Two. Both are rather small and located high up in the walls ... just about exactly at ground level."

"In other words, it is extremely difficult to see into it from the outside?" Cannon asked.

"Yes," replied Mikleson. "It is nearly impossible to see into it, from outdoors, unless you bend double to look in."

"Was there anything unusual in the furnace room?"

"The house requires a very large furnace ... it's a big place. That day was a warm one, but there was a real, blistering fire going...."

"One moment, please," Cannon interrupted. "With the court's permission, and opposing counsel's consent, I would like to introduce the official weather reports for the dates of November twenty-second and twenty-third of last year. I have secured them from the weather bureau's official records, and can introduce an expert witness if necessary."

"I'll waive the introduction," said Denman, indifferently.

"Proceed then, Mr. Cannon," directed the judge.

"During the warm spell last fall," said Cannon, "the official temperatures for November twenty-second were a low of 68 degrees, and a high of 74 degrees; on November twenty-third a low of 71 degrees, a high of 76 degrees." He held up a card and passed it to the jury. "All right, Mr. Mikleson, continue please."

The detective returned to his testimony. "The furnace was extremely hot ... so hot I couldn't put my hand on it."

"You attempted to place your hand on it?"

"Yes, sir. To test it. On the outside, the furnace was covered with thick insulation, but even through the insulation it was too hot to touch."

"Did that seem unusual to you?"

"Yes, it did. Because of the weather ... it was so warm that hardly any heat was needed at all. Also, it is very bad on a furnace to get it that hot; ruins them. Then I looked around the furnace room and saw that it had recently been scrubbed."

"How recently?"

"Very recently. Although the room was very hot, in one corner of the room there was still a small pool of moisture on the floor."

"Can you describe the floor?"

"It was a hard-surfaced floor composed of large, square, concrete blocks. Where the blocks fitted together, there were small cracks."

"What else did you notice about the room?"

"From the marks on the floor and the wall, there were indications a large wooden workbench, recently, had been in the furnace room."

"But it was no longer there?"

"No, sir. It was not."

"Just a moment," Denman interrupted. "I'm objecting to that. In the history of that house ... nearly seventy-five years old, there have probably been many benches in the furnace room. And they're no longer there! I'm sure the counselor is being ... ah ... overzealous in attempting to read an unsubstantiated interpretation into the workbench."

"It is entirely relevant, your honor," Cannon turned to the judge. "I can prove the bench had been in the furnace room, up until the night of the murder ... and the evidence is important."

"Continue," ruled the judge, "on the condition that all reference will be stricken if it's not proved later."

"With the overheated furnace, the water on the floor, and the missing bench, you decided to investigate further. What did you find?" Cannon asked Mikleson.

"In the furnace room?"

"Yes. Just the furnace room."

Mikleson moistened his lips with his tongue, turning slightly away from the direct view of the defense table. "Well," he said slowly, "on the floor, by the outside of the furnace there's a small area where the concrete is chipped away ... about like a small saucer. Part of this shallow hole runs under the outer shell of the furnace a few inches...."

"Is this a picture of the indentation ... or hole?" asked Cannon exhibiting a photograph.

"Yes," said Mikleson. Cannon offered the photograph into evidence and asked Mikleson to continue. "The cracked space," the officer resumed, "is a little distance away from the door of the furnace; to one side of it. The floor slopes slightly in that direction, too. In that small cavity in the floor, nearly hidden from sight, I found part of a human finger!"

Cannon exhibited a medical vial with a glass stopper. Within, floating in clear formaldehyde, was a section of finger approximately two joints in length. "Is this the finger you found?"

Deliberately, Mikleson identified it. "Yes, I cut a V-shaped notch in the fingernail. That's the nail!" It was offered into evidence.

"After you discovered the finger, Mr. Mikleson, what did you do?"

"I hurried upstairs to where Detective Lowery had been waiting with the defendant and called headquarters. I asked them to report my finding to the medical examiner's office ... and to send down the laboratory and photographic details."

"Thank you, Lieutenant. That will be all," said Cannon. Then turning to the counsel for the defense, he asked, "Do you wish to examine, Mr. Denman?"

"Yes," Denman said rising. He glanced at a sheet of paper, covered with notes, which he held in his hand, and leisurely approached Mikleson. "About this mysterious phone call you received ... it came to you direct?"

"No, it came to precinct and was transferred to me."

"You don't know who it was, but you are sure it was a man?"

"Yes, sir. I could tell it was a man."

"Was it a deep voice?"

"No. It was ... ordinary."

"It wasn't a bass or a deep baritone. It was in between a tenor and a baritone?"

"That's right."

"Isn't it true that some women have contralto voices?"

"Yes, so I've heard."

"Now, over a telephone a woman's voice ... a deep contralto voice ... can sound very similar to a man's tenor voice. Particularly, if a woman deliberately attempted to disguise her voice. Now I submit to you, Lieutenant, this point: You cannot say ... positively! ... that it was not a woman calling, who might be attempting to disguise her voice!"

"Well ... it's ..."

"Answer yes or no, please!"

"No-o-o, sir," replied Mikleson hesitantly. "I can't say positively it wasn't ... but I don't think ..."

"No opinions, please, Lieutenant! I just want facts. Let's get back to this mysterious phone call coming from an unknown person ... and you don't know whether it's a man of a woman, who's trying to stir up some trouble. What did this person say?"

"The person said: 'There have been awful smells coming out of the chimney at that house. I think there's been a murder committed.'" Mikleson under continued examination gave the address, approximate time of the call, and the efforts to trace the call back to the public phone booth.

"All right," Denman said finally. "Tell me, is it the usual procedure of the Homicide Squad to run around the city following leads reported by such unreliable methods?"

"Yes, sir!" Mikleson suddenly became emphatic. "Many times we receive information ... and tips ... from strange sources." His statement made a definite impression on the jury.

Denman attempted to turn the point aside. "I should imagine it must keep you busy chasing down leads furnished by cranks, crackpots, and mysterious strangers ... with personal feuds to settle. Then is it true, Lieutenant, that the Homicide Squad personally investigates all the trash and refuse burned in all the incinerators in this city?"

"It does if the incinerators got bodies in them!" Mikleson retorted grimly.

With a sigh, Denman returned to his examination of the witness.

Chapter 6

There was about Tally an inward assurance, a calm acceptance of life which, after my own years of wandering and instability, appealed to me deeply. For several weeks she tried unsuccessfully to find work. It would take her months, possibly much longer, to build the contacts by which she could make a living from modeling or to find a job as a receptionist; or any other of the better paying jobs that she might possibly do. There remained only the unskilled jobs, the ill-paid ones, the ones offering drabness and monotony.

At the club, the Martinique, where I was working, the first show went on at nine-thirty each night. Consequently, I arrived at the club before nine o'clock to get in my costume, check my props, and put on my make-up. But regularly each evening, I would meet Tally at the Delafield and we'd have dinner together in one of the inexpensive grab-joints along Eighth Avenue, and then wander over to Broadway. Sometimes we'd just walk along with the crowds, pausing to gander the lobby displays in the theaters and motion picture houses. At night the narrow grubby shops are dazzling in green, lavender, and rose neons; recordings blare over loud-speakers, from doorways of cut-rate record shops, blasting noise into the street; tiny turtles with hand-painted shells crawl aimlessly over each other in an endless attempt to escape from display windows; windows are crowded with plaster faces of a suffering Jesus whose melancholy eyes search one out in any corner of a room; litters of playing cards with naked, overdeveloped women on the backs. In some of the tiny shops busy merchants stitch personal initials on wild, absurd, top banana caps the width of manhole covers; in others one can buy natural-looking rubber dog turds available for practical jokers, at popular prices, brass replicas of the Statue of Liberty, equipped with thermometers, barometers, but not speedometers, rayon ties with one's birth date and individual sign of the zodiac, Spanish shawls, switch-blade knives, *moiré* photographs of women which can be manipulated to swing their hips and breasts back and forth, souvenir bracelets of New York City, wrist watches selling for $2.75 with a lifetime guarantee from the unknown (and unlocatable) manufacturer, shoddy Oriental rugs that would drive an Arab to tear up his Koran.

There are penny arcades with machines on which to practice torpedoing an enemy ship; machines to test the strength of one's grip; peep machines to watch a cloudy film of a strip-tease. There are stands selling orange juice, papaya juice, coconut milk, and mint-flavored grape juice; hamburger and hot dog stands. There are ballrooms where a roll of tickets permits a choice of dancing with strange, tired, and bored hostesses. There are spots to buy marijuana cigarettes, and other drugs.

The crowds push, shove, and parade—promenading to a beat and pulse which comes with the night and flees with the morning. It is a street of dreams, all right; and most of them bad!

In the evenings, after dinner, we walked hand in hand—talking, laughing, exploring. When it came time for me to leave for the club, I'd take Tally back to the hotel, leaving with a promise to see her in the morning. One night, while we were looking over the pictures in the lobby of a movie, I realized that Tally might have a chance to get on with the circus—the Big One—which had just opened its season in New York.

"I have an idea," I told her. "How'd you like a job with the circus? The pay for a show girl isn't bad—and you don't have to have any experience—just have to be beautiful. You get nearly nine months' work, room, and board. How about it? Tomorrow we'll go over to the Garden and catch the matinee ... and see about it."

"Were you ever with the circus, Lew?" she asked.

"Sure," I told her. "I was with it for two seasons. That was before the war. I was real young then ... and it seems a long time ago."

Tally tucked her hand over my arm. "The circus ... what's it like?" We started back toward the hotel, walking slowly through the crowds, sometimes stepping into the street, dodging through the human stream.

"Of course," I said, "when you say the 'Big One' ... you mean just one circus ... because there's only one Big One. It opens its season here, every year, in Madison Square Garden. It's a tough stand ... all cramped together. Later on when it moves out, it plays under the tops ... seventy-five thousand yards of canvas. It travels about fifteen thousand miles a year, and when it gets back to Florida in December it's really beat up. You know you've had it."

"Is it really as hard as all that?"

"Sure," I told her. And I remembered it ... the kid, the wise guy, the sharpie from the carney getting on with the Big One. After what I'd had in the carnival years, I thought I'd never had it so good. The Big One was luxury compared to what the carney had been. "But you learn to take it. In rain storms, cloudbursts, hurricanes—everything the weatherman can throw at you. Dust storms, sand storms, the old thermometer at 110 degrees doesn't mean anything. You play four hundred performances in a little over two hundred days, while you're standing, performing, and striking the show in eighty towns scattered over twenty-five states."

"But how can they do it?"

"Well, the Big One travels in its own train. The train has four sections. You sleep in it, and eat in it. With all the equipment and personnel ... and animals ... the show covers eighteen acres when it makes a stand and pitches its tents."

"If ... I ... should get the job, you wouldn't consider coming along with me?" she asked.

"No," I told her. "I'd like to ... it'd be fun. But I've spent too long now trying to build up my own act. If I ever went back, I'd have to return to clown alley, and behind that clown make-up, no one would ever hear of me again. There're perhaps fifteen hundred people working in the Big One, and of them all—none is so lost as a clown."

We were back to the hotel, now, and I had to hurry. "Tomorrow we'll go over to see it," I said. She looked at me and nodded, but not too happily, I thought.

The next day we stood in the great passageway, behind the arena, hugging the wall closely. Before us a great line was forming, broken here and there—leaving gaps—which filled, formed, and pressed together. Tally's eyes swept the confusing swirl of color before her—beautifully groomed horses with riders holding giant gilded candelabra; animated vegetables walking on red-hosed legs; the mighty bulls—the towering elephants carrying howdahs, the envy of Eastern potentates; tall, stately, lovely show girls dressed as calendar months, each surrounded by pages, courtiers, and grotesque little dwarfs; giraffes—tall, stumbling, and ungainly with tremendous satin bows on unbelievable necks; zebras hitched to clown wagons; tiered, pillared, rococo floats dusted in gold and silver, sprinkled with stars, draped with velvets and silks; space ships of plastic and chrome, spouting sparks and rocketing colored fire, crowded with interplanetary men; a phalanx of ancient Romans with plumed helmets, golden breastplates, and short broad swords; dancing girls in brief white buckskins and sombreros, with ivory six-shooters; tigers pacing restlessly in crimson and gold cages; monkeys dressed as tiny men; trained pigs, scrubbed pink and white as hospital nurses; acrobats in leopard skins and silken tights; Persian houris from the tales of Scheherazade, accompanied by Ifrits, jinni, and mamelukes; and they continued to form into line.

Mother Goose characters with gigantic, carnival heads—Bo-Peep and Little Jack Homer; Boy Blue with a tremendous horn, Old Mother Hubbard and the Knave of Hearts; chariots and broughams; coronation coaches and buckboards; Atlas carrying a huge globe on his shoulders; and clowns. Clowns.

Clowns in all sizes, costumes, and colors; laughing, crying, strutting, jumping; driving miniature cars; riding make-believe animals. Incredible, delightful clowns!

For a moment Tally closed her eyes to the confusion, and when she opened them a clown was standing by her side watching her. His head came to a point and perched on the top was a tiny hat, precisely creased with a gigantic pheasant feather in its band. Great, pendulous, red lips drooped in dejection, while the eyes—swooping upward in broad, painted, black lines—regarded her with perpetual and overwhelming surprise. "Go on, you dig me?" the clown's voice croaked.

She laughed without embarrassment. "I'm sorry. You surprised me, that's all."

"This is Hammy Nolan," I told her. "I've known him since we were in the alley together. Ham, this is a friend of mine ... Tally Shaw."

"Hi, kid," Ham acknowledged the introduction in his normal voice.

"How are things going?" I asked.

"So, so," the clown replied. "Same as usual ... too early in the season to tell, though. Nothing ever changes very much in this business."

"Ham, Tally here needs a job. Is Seaton still the program director for the show?"

"Yeah, still is."

"Do you think he needs any girls?"

Nolan shook his head slowly. A huge ruffled collar encircled his neck, and his ballooning costume magnified his size. "Now's not the time to ask him, Lew. The First-of-May'ers haven't cleared out yet."

Tally glanced at me, puzzled. I explained. "He means the people who join the circus in the south, and stay with it when it comes north. They leave around the first of May when the show takes to the road. They're called First-of-May'ers."

"Wait another three or four weeks," Nolan advised.

"I guess you're right," I agreed.

Ham regarded Tally. Behind the grease mask, it was impossible to tell what he was thinking. When he finally spoke, however, his words left no doubt. "A good-looking gal, Lew. Are you still doing that magic act?"

"Yes."

"She'd sure dress up your own act. Why don't you use her yourself?"

For years I had performed as a single, and the idea of giving the act more flash with a girl hadn't occurred to me. My bookings were getting better; I was working pretty steadily now; and my agent had been getting more money for the act. "That's an idea," I said. Turning to Tally, I asked, "How about it? Do you want to work with me?"

"I'd like to ... if you want me," she replied quietly.

That was the way I got a partner. After that day in the circus, I spent each afternoon ... all afternoon ... rehearsing Tally. I worked out special bits of business so she would have an opportunity to remain on stage. Basically my act was built around three major illusions—catching a goldfish in the air with a miniature fishing pole; pouring milk out of a pitcher and having it vanish in mid-air as I poured it; and a rope that crawled from a basket, and then stood on end like a cobra. Also, and this was very important, between each of the major illusions, I had a number of shorter tricks which I worked ... one after another ... very quickly.

By careful timing, and prearranged moves, to catch the audience's eyes for a split second, Tally permitted me to work free of the crowd's observation. Through this misdirection, my act was better, faster, and could be more complicated.

We arranged for a costume to be designed and made for her. It was a white, sequined leotard, as form fitting as a one-piece bathing suit; and with it she wore full-length black hose and black gloves. The first time I saw her in it, she took my breath away. She was stunning!

I added the traditional black evening cape to my own evening clothes—but this cape had a difference. It was made in such a manner that I could change the color of the lining from crimson to purple to yellow, by opening and closing it. But it was Tally who immediately put new color and new life into the routine.

After we were married, I moved back into the Delafield. I had been there only a few days, when belatedly I realized something was missing. It was the small leather grip, the very heavy one which Tally had owned. "Hey, doll," I said, "where's all the luggage?"

"What luggage?" At the moment she was digging out the coffee maker from under the bed.

"You know what luggage," I replied.

"Why ... my hatbox is in the closet, dear."

"Yes, but where's that little leather grip ... the one you had weighted down with uranium or something?"

"Oh, that." She replied casually, not looking up from the floor where she was kneeling. "I got rid of it."

"Why?"

"It wasn't worth keeping."

"What was in it?"

"Nothing. Just some old stuff."

I don't know why I thought it was important; perhaps it was because she only had two suitcases in the world ... and now she only had one. "Don't you have any other clothes stored away somewhere?" I asked.

"No." She arose from the floor, tossing the hair from her eyes, and dusting her hands. "You took me for better or worse. No, I have only the clothes that are here." Smiling, she leaned over to kiss me. "You knew I wasn't an heiress; do you want to divorce me?"

"I'll keep you," I told her, "and even occasionally buy you a bargain basement dress." She busied herself making coffee, and I didn't say any more about it. But I couldn't help wondering about that heavy case. Someday, I knew she would tell me about it; in the meantime, I couldn't stop speculating over a few things: why she had left home in such a hurry; why she had no strings anywhere; and why she hadn't brought more clothes?

I didn't pretend to know very much about women, but I still had enough sense to doubt that any woman ... if she had a choice ... ever leaves home with just the dress on her back, and a few pieces of lingerie.

Chapter 7

Cannon was involved in the examination of Harold Lafosky, a member of the laboratory squad, who was a witness for the prosecution. Lafosky testified that he had arrived on the premises together with officers Meyers and Cane. They had examined carefully the furnace room, first; and later the rest of the basement. Finally, they had completed the examination of the upper stories of the brownstone.

"Now," said Cannon, "I am going to show you several objects. I want you to identify them if you can. First, do you recognize this?" He opened a flat, cardboard box and extracted a small, charred, nearly flat piece of metal. The lump of lead was stained darkly by fire.

"Yes." Lafosky identified it, "I found that bullet underneath the furnace, within the ash receptacle."

Cannon handed him the bullet. "Please tell me how you can identify it without question."

Lafosky turned the bullet over in his fingers, and looked at it closely. "I scratched it with my initials, using a knife." He returned it to Cannon.

Cannon offered the bullet into evidence; the clerk accepted it and marked it as an exhibit. Cannon returned to his witness and extended another very small box, not more than two inches square. "Open it, please, and tell me what you see inside."

Lafosky opened the box. "I see a tooth, here."

"Have you seen it before?"

"Yes, sir." Lafosky continued, giving the location of the brownstone, the time, and the date he had found the tooth.

"Where, at what time and place, did you discover the tooth?" asked Cannon.

"The same place as the bullet ..."

"The same place as the bullet? Please be more specific, Mr. Lafosky."

"Underneath the firebox of the furnace, in the ash receptacle."

"Can you further identify it, without question, as being the same tooth you found?"

"Yes, sir. You'll notice the tooth is badly burned and stained by smoke. It was impossible to mark it with a pen or pencil. Consequently, I placed a small mark ... like a 'plus' sign ... on it, using red nail polish."

"Do you now see that same mark?"

"Yes, sir. I do."

"You are certain it is the same mark?"

"I am certain of it."

"I also submit this into evidence," remarked Cannon handing the box to the clerk, and then picking up a heavy, brown, Manila envelope. "Please observe this envelope closely. Have you ever seen it before?"

"Yes. I have my name, Harold Lafosky, written across the flap of the envelope, together with the date of November twenty-third of last year."

"What is inside the envelope?"

"A small amount of ashes."

"Where did you find these ashes?"

"Underneath the firebox of the furnace, in the ash receptacle."

"The same place where you found the tooth, and the bullet, is it not?" asked Cannon.

"Yes. The same."

"All right. Now about the ashes. Was there a large amount in the ash receptacle?"

"A fair amount, sir, although not a great deal. Enough to cover the floor of the ash receptacle. But the ash receptacle, itself, had been thoroughly cleaned out before."

"Cleaned out by you?"

"Cleaned out before the police got there."

"If it had been cleaned out before the police arrived, how do you account for the presence of the bullet and tooth?"

"Objection," Denman addressed the judge. "That answer will be simply a guess on the part of the witness."

Before the judge could rule, Cannon rephrased the question. "Let me ask you this: is it not possible that the tooth and the bullet had been in the body of the fire, in the coals of the furnace, and fell through the grate after the furnace had been cleaned?"

"Yes." Lafosky nodded.

"You then placed a sample of the ashes in this envelope, sealed it, and signed it with your name?"

"That is correct. I scooped up some of the ashes with the envelope, sealed it, and signed it."

"Thank you," said Cannon. He offered the envelope into evidence. Lafosky was excused, and Herman Meyers was called to the witness stand.

Meyers, in answer to Cannon's questions, identified himself as a member of the police department who had accompanied Lafosky and been present during the examination of the basement furnace room. "While Mr. Lafosky was examining the furnace, what were you doing, Mr. Meyers?"

"I was looking over the rest of the room." Meyers, a big man with beefy shoulders and an angry red face, seemed impatient with the questioning. "I was giving it a going over."

"Did you find anything?"

"Of course I found something." Meyers, as many police officers do, felt that time spent in a courtroom was time wasted.

"Objection!" Denman regarded Meyers with interest. A witness with a quick temper was always an undependable witness. "This witness is prejudicing his remarks."

"Please just answer my questions, Mr. Meyers," Cannon said smoothly. "That way we won't give Mr. Denman an opportunity to interrupt us." Meyers shot a belligerent glance at Denman and nodded. "Now tell me what you found when you examined the furnace room."

"I found a trash box."

"The trash box was full?"

"That is correct. It was filled with odds and ends of junk. All kinds."

Cannon carefully unwrapped a roll of oiled paper. The package was about twelve inches long, and when it was opened exposed a length of bone, badly charred and so smoked that it resembled a length of black stick. Attached to it was a paper tag. "Do you recognize this?" He handed the roll of paper, wrapped around the bone, to Meyers, who examined it reluctantly. The witness identified it, and Cannon asked, "Where did you find it?"

"In this trash box I was telling you about."

"The trash box in the furnace room?"

"That's the one."

"What is this you found?"

"It's a piece of bone."

"After you found it, what did you do?" Cannon asked.

"I tied this tag on it, and signed my name and the date." Offering the bone into evidence, Cannon continued. "Mr. Meyers, did you find anything else of interest?"

"Yes, sir."

Cannon handed him a small piece of two-by-four wood and a tatter of canvas—both badly burned. "Were these what you found?"

"Yes." Meyers identified both by his personal markings and the exhibits were handed over to the clerk. Meyers was then released from the stand, and Arthur Cane was sworn in. Cane testified that he, too, had been present with Lafosky and Meyers and had examined the rest of the basement, as well as some parts of the house.

"In examining the basement, what did you find?" asked Cannon.

"Well, sir," replied Cane, "there's a downstairs bathroom with a shower ..."

"Just a moment," interrupted Cannon, "before we discuss that, did you also examine the furnace room?"

"Yes, sir."

"What did you find?"

"I took some scrapings of dirt from between the cracks in the concrete floor. I put the scrapings into a glass vial, and on the vial I pasted a gummed sticker. I then wrote my name and date on the label."

"Is this the label? And is this the vial?"

"That is right."

"I notice the word 'furnace' marked on it also." Cannon held it so the witness could see it. "Did you write that?"

"Yes, I wrote 'furnace' on the label."

"Why?"

"The label is small, and I didn't have too much room to write on. I wrote the word 'furnace' to identify the scrapings in that vial as having been found in the furnace room."

"Very well. Now, referring back to the bathroom in the basement, which you mentioned, can you describe the room to me?"

"It's a small room, eight by ten feet in size. There's a toilet, a wash bowl, and a shower stall. The floor of the room and the floor of the shower were still very damp, with small pools of water."

"What did you do next?"

"I disconnected the trap in the drain below the wash basin, and from it collected some residue ... such as is usually found in such places. This residue I also put in a glass vial, pasted a label on it, and signed my name and the date. On this second label, however, I added the word 'bath-b.' This was to identify the vial as containing material found in the bathroom located in the basement of the house."

"Is this the vial?" Cane identified it, and Cannon submitted both vials into evidence. "Then," Cannon continued, "you examined other rooms in the basement. What did you find?"

"In the laundry room was a metal locker, or work box, which contained the usual household type of hand tools."

"Please describe them."

"There was a hammer, a hatchet, pliers, nippers, two saws, screw-drivers, a small soldering iron, and several packages of nails."

"Is this the hatchet you found?" Cannon handed the sizable, claw-type hatchet to Cane; the witness examined the initials which he had marked on the tool and identified it. "And now one final identification, Mr. Cane. This white envelope, containing a number of hairs, has your name and the date of November twenty-third marked on it. Can you identify this envelope, and state where you found the hairs?"

"The hairs are from a brush owned by Isham Reddick, a chauffeur living at that address. The brush was found in Reddick's room, located in the servants' quarters on the top floor. I removed the hairs from Reddick's brush, placed them in the envelope, sealed it, and marked it with my name and the date."

"Thank you. That will be all," concluded Cannon.

Denman arose for cross-examination, recalling Lafosky to the stand. Denman concentrated on Lafosky's damaging evidence of the tooth while ignoring his other testimony—for the moment. The tooth, which could be held for positive identification, was extremely dangerous evidence and Denman was anxious to minimize its importance. He referred to the notes he had taken. "All teeth look pretty much the same, don't they, Mr. Lafosky?"

"Not to a dentist, they don't."

"Are you a dentist, Mr. Lafosky?"

"No."

Denman regarded the witness as if he were examining a specimen. "Suppose you just constrain yourself to answering my questions. Mr. Lafosky, if I showed you ... say ... a hundred individual teeth, selected just one, and then asked you if it was the same one—many months later, you couldn't be positive, could you?"

"If I marked it, I could," Lafosky replied guardedly.

"Well, possibly. But did you write your name on this tooth you swear you found last year?"

"No. I—"

"No is correct, Mr. Lafosky. Did you write or scratch your initials on it?"

"How could I? It—"

"Yes or no, please. That's simple enough. Just reply yes or no."

"Yes or no," replied Lafosky grinning.

"Very amusing, Mr. Lafosky," remarked Denman, his lip curling derisively. "I see that in addition to not being a dentist, you also are not a comedian. You are rapidly proving a great number of things you are not. I grant you seem to have a certain parrot-like ability to repeat things. Perhaps you picked this ability up, in the same manner a parrot does— by coaching!"

"Your honor, I object!" said Cannon. "The counsel for the defense is demeaning the witness unnecessarily."

The judge replied calmly. "I feel the witness is not entirely blameless. However, Mr. Cannon, the court instructs Mr. Denman to continue his examination."

Denman, satisfied with the exchange, eyed Lafosky coldly. "As I understand it, you marked a tooth you found with nail polish? Is that correct?"

Lafosky squirmed uneasily. "Yes."

"Why did you select nail polish?"

"Well, it sticks to enamel."

"Interesting, very interesting. I suppose you have a particular shade you prefer to use?"

"No. Any shade will do."

"Do you carry a bottle around with you," asked Denman, "for the purpose of marking such teeth as you may find?"

Lafosky reddened. "No," he replied, "I found the bottle in the house ... in the maid's room."

"You found it in the house. What was the name and make of it?"

The witness glanced at Cannon, but received no help. "I don't remember," he replied slowly to Denman's question.

"What was the name of the color on the label?"

"I don't know ... just red I guess."

"No guessing now, Mr. Lafosky." Denman's voice was gently chiding. "Any of the ladies present today can tell you that no nail polish is just red. Each has a different name ... well, for instance ... Frosty Pinky or Sunset Memories ... Reddy Freddy ..." The spectators in the courtroom began to laugh. The judge quickly rapped the room back to order. "Tell me," Denman continued relentlessly, "why did you mark it with a 'plus' sign?"

"It was a simple, easy sign to make," Lafosky replied, walking into the trap.

"True ... true," murmured Denman. "There are only two signs more simple; one is a 'minus' sign which is only half as complicated as a plus sign; the other is a simple period. Now isn't it true, Mr. Lafosky, that you really don't know, but are only guessing, that this is the same tooth. You certainly can't recognize the tooth; you can't remember the kind of nail polish or its color; and all you did was make a mark which can be duplicated exactly by any boy or girl who ever finished first grade?"

"I'm positive it's the same tooth," replied Lafosky stubbornly.

Denman needled him gently. "I am reminded about the old saying, that only fools are positive, Mr. Lafosky."

"Your honor!" Cannon objected angrily.

"Strike the last remark of the attorney for the defense," the judge directed. He turned to the jury. "Forget what Mr. Denman has just said. In points of law it is necessary for witnesses to give as positive evidence as possible."

Denman bowed politely. "Your pardon," he said suavely, "I thought the witness was only attempting to prove something again."

"Objection!" Cannon shouted.

The judge nodded, and rapped for attention. "No more remarks, please, Mr. Denman." Behind his set face, he was unsmiling.

Denman dismissed Lafosky; he had done what he could to make the witness out a fool. Of the lasting effect on the jury, he couldn't be sure. Denman shrugged to himself, checked his notes, and then called Meyers back to the stand.

Chapter 8

Tally and I were doing three shows a night at the Martinique. This wasn't unusual; most clubs have that many shows, and some of the sucker traps do four and even as many as five. The early show starts sometime around nine-thirty; there's another shortly before midnight; and the last one is around one-thirty. It's rather an upside-down way of living, because by the time you get to bed it's nearly morning. You get up around noon, or early afternoon, and this gives you just the hours before dinner; in those few hours you try to do all the things that other people do during the course of their regular days.

What is important about living this way, though, is the perspective through which you look at things. The hours that count, the important hours are the ones of darkness, the hours of the night. Daylight means only the opportunity to get your laundry, or rehearse your act, or give your agent a call. At night when the lights are turned on, your life lights up with them. What I'm saying, perhaps, is that your life is like a night club, itself. If, for any reason, you've ever had occasion to stop at a night club during the day, you'll find it a dreary desolate spot. The rooms and halls are silent and deserted except for a few porters and cleaning women—and they are working, inevitably, under a bleak solitary work light. The chairs are piled on top of the bare tables, and the tables are pulled out from the walls so the cleaners can get behind them. The carpets look shabby, the pictures and mirrors seem in terrible taste, and the walls need painting. And over everything, penetrating each room, each piece of furniture and fixture, is the smell of flat souring beer. Out in the kitchen the steward is ordering groceries; and behind the bar, the liquor steward is checking, too. In the office, a bookkeeper makes entries from the day before. It looks like a restaurant which is going out of business.

But at night, it's different. The subdued lights glow warmly throughout the club; the orchestra plays, filling the rooms with music; the tables are draped with white linens; while the bartenders rattle cocktail shakers like ice-filled maracas. It's a different world.

After a while, this world becomes the real one.

Between shows there is very little to do. With not enough time to go very far, or do very much, the performers, as a rule, after taking off their costumes to keep them fresh, sit around back stage talking, or playing gin rummy. Some read magazines and newspapers, write letters, or make long telephone calls.

Tally and I shared a small dressing room. It was scarcely more than a large closet, with two straight back chairs, and a lighted make-up table. After the first show, we'd change into our street clothes and go for a walk; between the second and third shows, we'd wait in the dressing room.

And talk.

Each night, in one way or another, she told me a little about herself ... how her parents had been killed in an auto accident when she was a very small child, and she had gone to live with a great uncle and aunt. The aunt had died eight years later. "Then there was just Uncle Will and me," she explained. "Even then he was an elderly man, but somehow I never thought of him as such. He was big and solid, and nearly completely bald ... so bald, in fact, that it looked like his head had been shaved. He didn't talk much, and was uncomplaining; he was generous ... and impractical, too."

As she talked I tried to see her in relation to this man who had raised her, tried to imagine her as she was then. "Impractical?" I asked. "What did he do?"

"He was an engraver," she replied, "but he was really more than that. He was an artist. A real one. See ..." She unsnapped a small bracelet from her wrist, and opened a tiny locket attached to it. "This is me ... an engraving Uncle Will did of me on my fourteenth birthday." She handed the locket to me, and I tilted the flat golden surface against the light. Suddenly the face of a young girl was smiling into mine. The miniature details of the features, the feather-like tracery of the lines were exquisite. There was nothing to be said. Nodding, silently, I snapped it shut and handed it back to her. She continued, "He always wanted to be an engraver ... a great one, in the tradition of Dürer. As a young man, he went to Europe to study there. Engraving as an art was beginning to die out; when he returned to this country, he married and in order to earn a living ... he became a photoengraver."

"Is that what he did then ... the rest of his life?"

"Yes," her voice was tied by sympathy to the past. "He always had a job ... and made good money. He kept an engraving bench and tools at home, and once in a while he'd start a steel engraving or an etching at home. When he had finished it, he'd pound it up or destroy it. Or he'd give it to anyone who said he liked it...."

On another night, in the dressing room, Tally was brushing the long velvet gloves which belonged to her costume. She performed the simple job with a concentration that reminded me of a woman doing housework. There was an incongruity between the homey action and the sleek sophistication of her half-naked costume that touched me. I thought of her growing up in her uncle's household. "Tell me," I said, "more about the house where you lived ... the place where Uncle Will kept his engraver's bench."

Momentarily, she continued the brushing. The gloves achieving a satisfactory state of perfection, she hung them over a clothes hanger. Casually, she crossed the small dressing room, regarding me indifferently, then with a sudden laugh, she plumped herself down on my lap. Our double weight caused the aging chair to creak and groan, and it could be heard through the thin partition. In the next dressing room, a little dancer called, "Hey! You're not supposed to do that on company time!" Tally blushed, and hurriedly attempted to rise. Catching her around the waist, I held her quiet. "Don't bother to deny it, hon," I told her laughing. "Let them think what they like!" The dancer clapped loudly in return.

Tally slipped her arm around my shoulder. Lighting a cigarette, I passed it to her. "Go on," I said, "ignore the interruptions."

"Well," she replied, "we lived in Philadelphia on a little street ... but it could just as well have been the same street in Cincinnati or Chicago."

"Were you ever in Cincinnati or Chicago?" I asked grinning.

She shook her head, smiling back at me. "No. But our street looked like so many other streets in Philadelphia that I know there must be streets like it all over the country...."

"Sure, hon."

"It was one of those streets of row houses ... you know, they continue for a solid block on both sides of the street, and are exactly the same. But, while each block is exactly the same, no two blocks are alike. I mean," she sorted her words carefully, "the houses on our block were a little different than the row of houses in the next block ... and that was a little different from the next one ... and so on. Do you understand?"

"Yes," I replied, "I follow you."

"In our row all the houses were two stories, but not including the basement, naturally. The houses all used the same adjoining walls, and were built directly up to the sidewalk. There were six little cement steps up to the porch. I know the number of steps because I used to play on them. I'd bounce a ball up the steps, hopping on my left leg and counting; then I'd hop on my right leg, bouncing the ball down the steps again. All the little girls in our row did the same.

"Every house had a small wooden porch, painted white, and each porch had two wooden pillars. On the second floor, there was a green bay window. Ohhh, and here's something else! Everybody in our block was very proud that the windows *all* had marble sills. It wasn't really marble, but it was stone and looked a little like it. So we called it marble."

"Honey," I told her, "this may come as a terrible shock, but only in Philadelphia do you find row houses like that."

"Really?" she frowned, and leaning over the dressing table she snuffed out her cigarette.

"The bedrooms were built exactly over the dining room and living room … it wasn't very pretentious. A workingman's home …"

"With you in it, doll," I said, kissing the back of her neck, "it was a mansion."

"No," she replied gravely, "it was really a small house. In the winter, Uncle Will glassed in the downstairs porch. We used to store our galoshes and umbrellas there. When Auntie was alive, she always wanted to find another house … but we never did." She sighed, "It feels funny, talking about them this way."

One night, I was seated reading the paper in the dressing room, the chair tilted against the wall, my feet propped on the make-up table. There was a story in it concerning a con man who had been picked up for working the old sealed envelope switch. Briefly, it's this: the sharper hustles up a sucker, and gets the mark to put up some money … for one reason or another. The sharper gives him security to hold … usually government bonds, which he puts into an envelope and seals in front of the mark. Later when the sucker begins to wise up, he opens the envelope and discovers it's stuffed with newspaper. The con man had simply switched the envelopes and taken off with the loot. It's surprising, though, how the racket goes on forever.

I read the story aloud to Tally, and when I had finished, I chuckled. Surprisingly, she didn't join me. "No one ever pulled that on Uncle Will," she said, "but I guess it's the only one they missed."

"You mean the old man was a mark?" I asked.

"No, not that. He was always open to a hard luck story, and he was always an optimist; between the two, he was nearly always broke. All during the years he was working, he made a good salary but we never had any money. Oh, the rent was paid," she shook her head, "and the grocery bill, and we had enough to wear—but it was always just being able to make it. Uncle Will would lend money to anyone who asked him. And he was forever buying things … things that would make a fortune overnight … and never did! He bought land during the last bubble in the thirties and lost it; he speculated in funeral lots in cemeteries which were never developed; he put money in the stock of a rear-motor automobile and not even one car was ever made." She shook the memories away, wearily. "He invested in South American government securities at a big discount, and they were later canceled by a new government. Everything he did … went wrong."

Tears welled up suddenly in her eyes; mascara trickled down her face, streaking her make-up. "The poor old man," she said. "Uncle Will was ... he thought everybody was honest ... like himself. Even when he was old and sick ... and childish ... he still believed in miracles."

"Take it easy, kid," I told her. "You may not know it, but that mascara running looks like the marble face of Venus cracking up." I handed her my handkerchief, and she wiped her eyes. "There, that's better," I added. "Now, what was all that hollering about?"

She managed a smile. "I was being foolish. It wasn't anything. It's still so soon after Uncle Will's death ... I feel bad whenever I think about him." She stood before the dressing table, and began repairing her make-up. "It's funny," she said, "about the only two men in my life ..."

"Wait a minute," I said. "Is this going to be a confession? If it is, don't expect me to reciprocate with my boyish confidences unless my lawyer and agent are present."

"Don't be silly," she caught her hair in a velvet bow, and turned to face me. She smiled, "I'm sure you've been very trustworthy. Anyway, you interrupted me at exactly the wrong word. I was saying that the only two men in my life, who I have loved, are you and Uncle Will. And you are both so different. Uncle Will was ... a ..."

"A real blue-nosed Philadelphia square," I said.

"Don't be jealous, please!" Her eyes twinkled, and I grinned. "No," she continued, "he lived in a wonderful world all by himself. While you ... wise guy ... know all the answers, don't you?" Standing on her toes, she locked her arms around my neck, and kissed me on the mouth. Then holding her head to one side, she asked, "Well, don't you?"

"You're not just whistling up a breeze, kid," I agree solemnly. "Furthermore, I think the quality of lipstick has degenerated since I was a youth."

She refused to rise to my chaffing, and looked into my face, her eyes very near to mine. I realized, belatedly, she was serious. "I love you, darling," she said softly, "and I'm so glad you're in love with me." Gently, she loosened her arms, and taking a step back, looked at me. "But I'd hate to be the person you really hated, Lew."

"Wait a minute!" I said, trying to laugh it off. "Where'd this conversation come from? I don't hate anyone. I love the world. I'm a do-gooder! I beat a drum ..."

"Yes, dear." Tally turned, smiling sweetly and slipped into her coat. "I'm going out to get a candy bar. May I bring you one?" she asked, banteringly.

"No, bring me an oyster instead. One with a pearl in it."

And so, for a while, that was the way it was. It was a life held tightly within itself, in the night; a dressing room where we waited until the show went on, and the orchestra played our cue. The applause from the tables; the paychecks on Friday. Sometimes we walked the early morning streets back to the hotel, stopping for pre-dawn coffee and rolls with the truck drivers, milk men, and cops. It was Broadway when the night has gone and the lights have vanished, but day has not yet arrived. The sidewalks are bare and lonely; the hour is bleak and unlovely; but it's wonderful if you're walking along with the gal you love.

Then it's not bare or lonely at all.

Chapter 9

The man in the witness chair was Deputy Chief Medical Examiner Howard M. Eggleston. Dressed in a neat charcoal gray suit, with a lighter gray and maroon striped tie, he answered questions precisely and with authority. Cannon asked, "How long have you been in the medical examiner's office, Dr. Eggleston?"

"Seven years."

"In that period of time how many autopsies have you performed?"

"Each year?"

"Yes, each year."

"Well, between two hundred and two hundred and fifty ... the number is not the same each year."

"Yes, I understand that. But is it fair to say that in seven years you have performed between fourteen hundred and seventeen hundred and fifty autopsies?"

"That would be correct, sir."

"Dr. Eggleston, you would consider that figure a conservative estimate? If it were necessary, you could get the exact number as a matter of record from your files?"

"The number would fall between the two extremes of the figures you mentioned. It can be substantiated by the official records."

"Thank you Doctor. Now in those seven years, as a result of your duties, you have examined a great number of bodies ... literally running into the hundreds. You have examined both men and women, children too, of many ages and races?"

"That is correct. Under the law, an examination is required in all cases of homicide, accidental, unnatural, and suspicious deaths."

"You have made identification of bodies with members missing, such as head, arms, legs?"

"In some cases, yes."

"And in cases where bodies have been so badly decomposed as to make features and fingerprints unrecognizable?"

"Yes."

Denman arose. "This is very interesting," he addressed the judge, "but what is the counselor attempting to prove?"

Cannon, in turn, addressed the bench. "As the counselor for the defense knows very well, I am establishing the background of the witness for expert testimony."

Denman, who had no desire for the extreme efficiency of the medical-legal activities of the medical examiner's office to be too well established with the jury, snapped, "The defense will grant Dr. Eggleston to be an expert," and sat down.

Cannon returned to his witness. "Now, Dr. Eggleston, I have a number of exhibits. As I introduce them to the court, I will ask you to identify them. First, this hatchet identified by Mr. Cane; have you examined it in your laboratory?"

"I have."

"What did you find?"

"At the point of the V where the claws on the hatchet come together, there were traces of blood and broken sections of hair."

"Could you identify the blood as human blood?"

"Yes, sir. It was human blood known as type O."

"Was it possible to identify the hair?"

"The hair was identified as coming from a human head."

"Thank you. Now here is an envelope, also identified by Mr. Cane, which contains several hairs taken from the hair brush of Isham Reddick. Have you examined these hairs?"

"Yes, sir," replied Eggleston. "The hairs in the envelope are identical with the hairs found on the hatchet."

The jury, as a body, leaned forward, its eyes fastened on Eggleston. "You mean that without a question, without a doubt, the hairs from the hatchet and the hairs from the brush are identical?"

"That is right."

"Will you please show us how you reached that conclusion?" A projector and a small screen were set up, and cross sections of the hairs, greatly enlarged, were demonstrated to the court. Eggleston in a dry definite voice pointed out the duplication of cellular construction and points of identification. When he had concluded, Cannon resumed his examination. "Here is a piece of canvas, identified by Harold Lafosky. Have you examined it?"

"Yes, sir."

"What did you find?"

"The canvas had been burned by fire, and contained traces of paint, and stains of blood." Eggleston paused, then added, "It was human blood."

"Could you identify the type?"

"Yes. It was type O."

"Here is a vial with a label containing the name of Detective Cane, and bearing the word 'furnace'—identifying it as having come from the furnace room. What did you find in this vial?"

"Scrapings, such as are found in the cracks and on the floors in furnace rooms ... dirt, soot, coal dust, wood and fiber splinters, traces of oil and turpentine. Also, traces of human blood."

"Could you identify the blood by type?"

"I could. It was type O."

Picking up the second vial, Cannon offered it to Eggleston. This vial contained the sediment taken from the water trap beneath the wash basin in the basement. Cannon asked Eggleston what it, too, contained. "Dirt, fatty particles such as are used in soap bases, lye, both natural and synthetic bristles from brushes, and traces of human blood."

"You identified the blood by type, Doctor?"

"I did. It was type O."

"Again, Dr. Eggleston," continued Cannon, "I have an envelope ... a large, heavy Manila one. This envelope was identified by Mr. Lafosky. It contains a sampling of ashes gathered from the ash receptacle beneath the firebox of the furnace. You have examined the contents. Will you tell the court what your analysis showed?"

The deputy chief medical examiner withdrew a slip of paper from his pocket, referred to it briefly, and then recited a long list of chemical properties, in a flat unaccented voice. When he had finished, Cannon turned to the jury and said, "I'll ask the witness to reword his statement." He smiled briefly, "I couldn't understand a word he said." The jury nodded in grim agreement.

"Well," resumed Eggleston, "in addition to coal ash, wood ash, certain residues of vegetable origin ..."

"Such as what, Doctor?"

"Cotton, linen. There was also evidence of protein origin...."

Cannon interrupted him. Very slowly, pronouncing each word distinctly, he asked, "Does that mean the possibility of human flesh ... or rather, what might at one time have been human flesh?"

"That is correct."

There was a long moment of complete silence in the courtroom. Cannon stretched it to the breaking point, then coughing gently, broke the spell, and proceeded with his introduction of evidence. "Now, Doctor, another important point of identification." The prosecuting attorney unrolled the sheath of oiled paper. Within was the length of blackened charred bone, attached with a tag bearing the name of Detective Meyers. "Can you tell me if you have examined this," said Cannon, "and if you have, please tell me your findings."

"I have examined it," Eggleston stated. "It is a length of bone medically termed the *tibia*."

"In layman's language, Dr. Eggleston, that would be called the shin bone?"

"Yes."

"What more can you tell the court about it?"

"It is of human origin and belonged to an adult male."

"Could you determine the height of such a male?"

"Yes, within certain limits. The male was between five feet ten and six feet tall."

"How could you determine this, Doctor?"

Eggleston launched into a detailed discussion based on the measurements and proportions of the human body. Cannon put a question to the medical examiner. "Is it not possible that a deformity in the bone structure might affect other portions of the body?" Eggleston agreed that such a deformity was possible, but that where it existed, it could also be detected by additional research. "That possibility does not exist in this situation, then?" asked Cannon.

"No," replied Eggleston, "the bone was from a normally developed male."

"Thank you. And now, one final identification." Cannon presented the vial of formaldehyde containing the section of finger. Eggleston had examined it, and stated that it was a well-preserved section of a human finger, consisting of that portion between the middle joint and the tip of the finger. It was from the third finger of the right hand. "Can you tell the court how it had been severed from the hand?" asked Cannon.

"By a sharp instrument."

"Can you identify the instrument beyond being a sharp one?"

"No."

"Is it not true that a sharp instrument such as a hatchet might have done it?"

"It could have been done by a hatchet."

"Thank you, Doctor, that will be all." Cannon turned to Denman. "Your witness, Counselor."

"I will reserve the privilege to cross-examine the witness later," Denman replied without rising from his seat.

Cannon then called Officer Charles L. Risko to the stand. When Risko had taken his oath, Cannon asked him, "You are employed in the Bureau of Identification, of the Police Department, City of New York. Is that correct?"

"Yes, sir. That is correct."

"Your job is to keep a record of fingerprints taken by the police department, make comparisons, and identifications when possible?"

"Yes, sir."

"How long have you been doing such work?"

"For eleven years."

"You were given this section of finger?" Cannon held up the vial for Risko's identification.

"That's right. It was turned over to me by the Homicide Squad, and I proceeded to raise a print from it."

"It was a good clear print? One that could be examined with accuracy?"

"Yes, sir. It was. I secured a very satisfactory print."

"Then what did you do with it?"

"I processed the print for identification."

"What do you mean by that?"

"I sent it through the regular channels for identification," explained Risko. "First, through our own files here in New York."

"Was the print identified?"

"Yes, sir. Immediately. We had the prints of one Isham Reddick taken on his application for a license to drive a cab."

"Will you show us how this identification was made?"

A copy of the print made by Risko from the severed finger and a copy of the corresponding finger taken from the application were projected on the screen. Risko pointed out the identical characteristics of both prints, some thirty-four in number, which made a positive identification. He was then excused, again without cross-examination by Denman, and Cannon called Lincoln M. Means to the stand.

"You are employed in the Bureau of Licenses, Police Department, City of New York, Mr. Means?"

"I am."

"You have with you the original application made out by one Isham Reddick when he applied for a license to drive a cab?"

"Yes, sir."

"Will you please read the information regarding Isham Reddick's physical appearance that you have."

Reading from the original application form, Means recited aloud: "Sex ... male; age ... 36; eyes ... blue; hair ... dark brown; weight ... 175 pounds; height ... 5 feet 11 inches ..."

"Just a moment, Mr. Means. Will you please read again, his height as indicated on your record?"

"Yes, sir. Five feet eleven inches."

"That was written in Reddick's own hand?"

"It was written by the man who signed himself Isham Reddick."

At this point, Denman objected to the identification of the application as being in Reddick's handwriting. He was sustained in his objection, by the court. Means was excused from the stand, while Alvin G. Hartney, a handwriting expert, was put on the stand by the prosecution. A positive identification was made by the expert witness regarding the writing on the application based on other writing found in Reddick's room. Means was then returned to the stand.

"Once again, Mr. Means, in Reddick's own writing taken from the license application, please read what he wrote as his height."

"Five feet eleven inches," Means read.

"He did not write six feet, or six feet one?"

"No, sir."

"Nor did he write five feet nine?"

"No, sir."

"It was five feet eleven inches?"

"That is what he wrote."

"That will be all." Again, Denman waved the witness aside, reserving the right to cross-examine later. Obviously, he was waiting for Cannon to complete his web of identification. Beside Denman, the accused sat, head partly bowed, hands folded on the table.

The next witness taking the stand was Stanley Boss, a doctor of dentistry. He identified himself as practicing in the City of New York, and had been located in his present offices for nearly ten years. Cannon then began examining him concerning the tooth found and identified by Detective Lafosky. "Can you say if you have ever seen this tooth before?" he asked Boss.

"Yes, sir. I am very familiar with it."

"Will you please tell the court how you can identify it?"

The dentist, a small, slender man with an undistinguished face, adjusted his rimless glasses nervously. Clearing his voice, he began, "Well … last year, a patient called …"

Cannon interrupted smoothly. "Please give us an exact date, if you are able …"

"Yes. Yes I can. I looked it up in my files. It was the day, to a week, before the patient came in. He came in September nineteenth, so when he called it was September twelfth."

"Thank you, please continue."

"Well," Boss cleared his throat anew. "I received this call for an appointment. It was from a new patient … never heard of the man before. Said his name was Isham Reddick. I asked him how he happened to call me, and he said he'd looked me up in the classified book. I told him I was busy … filled with appointments for a week. He said he'd like to come the first opportunity, so I made an appointment for him on September nineteenth."

"He showed up for the appointment?"

"Yes. Right on time. My wife, Mrs. Boss, acts as my nurse. She took all the personal information concerning him. Including blood type in case of surgery. It was ..."

"Objection!" snapped Denman.

"Sustained," agreed the court.

"We'll call Mrs. Boss, later," said Cannon, "please continue, Dr. Boss."

"Mr. Reddick complained that his three back molars had been paining him. I took X-rays, but could find bad caries in none of his teeth. There seemed to be no reason for his distress. The patient, however, had a tooth missing from the front of his mouth and it greatly affected his appearance. We discussed the possibility of replacing it. He told me it would depend on how much it cost, and I made him a very reasonable ... actually a very low ... price to put in a removable bridge, and he accepted it."

"Doctor, will you please point to the identical tooth in your own mouth comparable to the position of the missing tooth in the mouth of Isham Reddick."

Boss parted his lips widely, in a grimace, and pointed to the first tooth in the front left side of his mouth. He held the pose for a moment, then withdrew his finger and closed his lips. "You then proceeded to make the tooth for Isham Reddick?"

"Yes, sir. I made it myself."

"You made it to exact measurements?"

"That is right, to very small and accurate measurements. I keep a complete record of all work done, measurements ... and degree of coloring."

"There are degrees of coloring? How many?"

"There are as many degrees in the coloring of teeth as there are degrees in the coloring of skin. False teeth, particularly when placed next to a patient's own teeth, must be very carefully shaded to match."

"So, Dr. Boss, when you saw this tooth which has been offered in evidence here, you could identify it as the same one you had made for Isham Reddick?"

"Yes, sir. It is the identical tooth."

"Will you please tell the court how you happened to identify the tooth. Did the police come to see you?"

"I read about it in the paper. What first struck my eye was that it was practically in the same neighborhood. Then when I read the name ... Isham Reddick ... I remembered he had been a patient of mine. The papers said a tooth had been recovered; I didn't know if it was the one I'd made or not. But I also had a complete chart of his teeth, as a matter of regular routine, and a set of X-rays. In the case of an identification, I might be of some service."

"That was very commendable of you, Doctor. So, you then notified the police that you would help?"

"Yes, sir. I felt it was my duty," Boss replied complacently.

Mrs. Boss next was called to the stand and testified that a blood-type record was made for reference in case of extractions and dental surgery."

"What type blood did Mr. Reddick have?"

"According to my record, it was type O."

"Did he tell you that himself?"

"No," the nurse replied. "He didn't know, or at least he didn't remember. I took a small sample and then sent it to the lab for typing. The laboratory returned the report on it, and I entered it on his card."

Chapter 10

To paraphrase a line of Porgy's, "happiness is a sometime thing." The feeling of happiness is difficult to recall—after any length of time—perhaps because it is transient ... intangible ... effervescent. Often it is misidentified as contentment—which, I believe, is a compromise between being happy and being miserable. Later, when one looks back into the months and years, it is impossible to recapture clearly the moments of complete happiness; but it is quite easy to remember long periods of time when contentment prevailed.

I know, however, that those months of our marriage in New York, when we were working at the Martinique, were happy ones. Our world consisted of two rooms—a hotel room with plaid wallpaper and a tiny bare dressing room. The two rooms were connected by a great long street which sometimes was lighted by neon, sometimes by the gray light of morning—just beginning to soften the black lines of night—as we returned from one room to another.

Tally recognized what we had at that time better than I. Perhaps that was why she didn't want to give it up, although actually there was no choice for us. Only a few days before we closed at the Martinique, I hurried back to the hotel with a new contract for five weeks at the Lark Club in Philadelphia. As I explained to Tally about it, she listened quietly. Seated on the bed, she nervously twisted the gold wedding ring on her hand, and all emotion was carefully screened from her face. When I had finished describing the contract, she said, "Lew, I ... wish you wouldn't take it." Her voice was so low as to be barely audible.

"Listen, honey," I said, "you've been away from Philadelphia nearly three months. That's long enough to start getting over your uncle. You ought to be able to go back now."

Shaking her head, slowly, she refused to meet my eyes. Then it came to me that beneath the impassive face she was struggling with other emotions ... ones which I couldn't identify. Swallowing several times, Tally said, "It ... isn't Uncle Will." She examined her hands, her head lowered. "Do I have to go with you?" she asked softly.

I lit a cigarette. "Sure, doll," I told her, keeping my conversation light. "The manager in the club at Philly said, 'I don't give a damn about that magician, but be sure the doll gets here.'"

But she couldn't smile. She replied, more to herself than to me, and her words were thoughts, wondered aloud. "Why did it have to be back there ... why couldn't it have been Chicago or Los Angeles, or someplace else?"

"In this business," I said, "you take the jobs as they come. In a way, we're lucky. We don't have to lay-over for a while."

Tally arose from the bed, wandering about the room—stopping by the dresser, repositioning her hair brush, going to the window, glancing out through the glass, returning to the chair, pausing; and all the time thinking, but what she was thinking—I didn't know. Finally she asked, "Couldn't you go, Lew, and leave me here?"

"Not very well," I told her. "They bought the act as it is—not as a single."

"I guess there's a reason for it happening this way," she said, her voice resigned.

The following week we closed in New York and began packing for Philadelphia. I had my old wardrobe trunk, and Tally head begun to accumulate a few things herself. The hatbox no longer could hold all her clothes. Proudly, she bought a set of matched luggage. Two of the cases were standard size, and a third was quite small, a small over-night case. When I returned to the Delafield after being out all day, making last-minute business calls, arranging for the trunk to go ahead, and finishing up all the other details, we checked out of the hotel. Max helped us into a cab. "See you around," he said. And so, Tally carrying her small case, we left for Philadelphia.

In Philadelphia many of the night clubs are concentrated along Locust Street ... and Thirteenth. Some of them are good, some of them bad. The Lark Club was small, new, and in the process of attempting to establish of policy of entertainment—struggling between smartness and sophistication, and dullness and vulgarity. When we arrived it was mixing the lot. On the bill, a comedian named Lemmie Hall performed with the subtlety of a sex offender out on bail, doing imitations with the aid of a hat, and introducing the rest of the acts. There was an attractive gal singer, with a good voice; a line of dancers called the Five Lovely Larks ... a nondescript collection of chorines with tight secretive faces, skinny legs, and rented costumes; and Tally and me.

The interior of the Lark Club was small, and the walls were hung with dark velours; the tables, chairs, and bar were made of modern light woods. Customers sat shoulder to shoulder, jammed into the room, and the dance floor was no larger than a waiter's tray. The performers worked from the floor, and the show was backed by seven musicians wearing red coats. The leader played a violin, and the guitarist played a guitar, but, unfortunately, both instruments were electric. Occasionally, the two musicians would accidentally mix their volume controls and the feedback over the mike resembled the disemboweling of banshees.

The Lark's main claim to fame was a larger-than-life marble statue standing in a prominent position near the center of the room. It was a sculpture of a nude man kissing a naked woman. The white marble was illuminated by small spot lights at the base, and against the black velours of the background, a viewer received the impression that Aphrodite and boy friend had been toying in a flour bin.

We had been playing the Lark Club for a week, when the phone call came. Tally and I were staying at the Hotel McAndrews, which is another show business hotel. It is located on one of the incredibly narrow side streets, near the night club district and is at least fifty years old. However, the McAndrews has been kept in good condition and is comfortable, although old fashioned. Except for the lobby, that is. This has been redecorated with fluorescent lighting, chrome furniture, imitation leather and tubular accessories, plus a coat of salmon pink paint on the ceiling. The lobby is L shaped with the registration desk and two elevators on the vertical side of the L; on the other side, a stairway leads to the floors above, and a doorway opens into the Highland Bar & Grill. Inside the bar, there are two doors each leading to a different street, as the Highland is located on the corner of the building.

Our room was on the top floor, on a corner, facing the front of the building. The corridors, in the McAndrews, are dimly lighted, and the walls are painted a dark chocolate brown to the height of a shoulder with a continuation of a slightly lighter brown to the ceilings. Ancient red carpeting covers the floors, and even during the brightest, daylight hours, the halls have a dark and archaic appearance. The rooms, however, are very comfortable.

In ours we had a large double bed, a television set which played one hour for each quarter deposited in the coin slot, several comfortable, faded, overstuffed chairs, and two large reading lamps. Connecting was an old-fashioned, linoleum-floored bathroom, with a high tub resting on metal, clawed feet. With two extremely large closets at our command, Tally set up our electric plate in one of them and we used it for a small kitchen.

When the day arrived ... the one with the phone call ... we were sleeping late. The phone rang, and I let it ring for several minutes hoping that

Tally would answer it. But when she made no effort to do so, I pulled myself together, sufficiently, to reach out an arm and take it off the receiver. Putting it to my ear, I said, "Yes ... what is it?"

A peculiar quality of silence on the other end aroused me to complete consciousness. Instantly I was awake, listening intently, although there was nothing to hear. "Hello! Hello!" I paused and jiggled the receiver. "Hello?"

After a long moment, over the line a voice said thinly, "I'll pay you twenty-five grand for 'em."

"Who is this?" I asked. "You'll pay twenty-five grand for what?"

"You know," replied the voice, and hung up.

Slowly I returned the phone to its cradle. Swinging my legs over the side of the bed, I reached for my cigarettes on the bedside table. Thinking it over, I decided someone was trying to kid me. Someone I knew ... possibly someone in the show was attempting to pull a gag. I shrugged the idea away, and now wide awake, began making some coffee. While the water was boiling, Tally awakened and sat up in bed. "Boy, are you a lousy maid," I told her. "Do you want a cup?"

"Oh, yes, please." Stretching her arms in the air, she shook her head, her hair fanning over her pillow as she leaned back. Taking the cup to her, I sat beside her on the bed. "Did I hear the phone ring?" she asked sipping the coffee.

"Those sure weren't the Bells of St. Mary's," I told her.

"Who was it?" she asked drowsily, not really caring.

"A voice. A mysterious voice ... and if I sound corny I can't help it."

"Stop fooling, darling," she replied. "Who was it, a wrong number?"

"I wouldn't be surprised if it was Lemmie Hall. Probably his idea of humor ..."

"What did he say?"

"Whoever it was said in a disguised voice, 'I'll pay you twenty-five grand for them.'"

"What!" Tally sat upright in bed, spilling her coffee. Leaping to my feet, I took the cup from her trembling hands. Her face was gray with fear, and she was unable to speak.

"Doll!" I placed the cup on the table, and gathered her hands into mine. "Tally! What is it? What's wrong ... tell me!"

She pulled her hands free, and throwing her arms around my neck buried her face against my chest. We sat like that for a long time, not saying anything ... just holding each other. Finally, she said, "Lew, I don't know ... I don't know what to do...."

"What is it, Tally? Tell me, and whatever it is, we'll figure out what to do." I lit a cigarette, and pressing her back against the pillows, placed it between her lips.

"I don't know where to start," she said slowly. "I don't even know exactly when it started ... there was this man. We called him Greenleaf."

"Who was he?"

"I don't know ... really, I don't."

"Did you ever meet him? What did he look like?"

"I never met him. I only talked to him a few times on the phone...."

She began trembling, and I patted her shoulder. "All right, doll," I said, "you talked to him on the phone. About what?"

"About the plates ... the counterfeit engravings Uncle Will was making ..."

"You did what?" I stared at her, not believing her words. Her mouth quivered, and I said more softly, "Look, perhaps you'd better tell me in your own words ... right from the beginning." Walking over to the dresser, I got her a clean handkerchief. She wiped her eyes, and attempted a smile.

"Once," she said, "I think I tried to tell you how Uncle Will was ... he believed everyone. All his life, he was generous and sweet ... and wonderful. And everyone took advantage of him, with crazy ideas and plans to make money. When he was an old man he didn't have anything left.

"The company he'd worked for all those years was sold and the new owners let him go because they thought he was too old. At first, he just couldn't believe it. He'd sit around the house all day and pretend to read the want ads, and write letters to different companies, but ... of course ... nothing happened. After a long time, he just had to believe it. When he finally did face it, it broke his heart and his spirit, too. He was just an old man, too old to work, too useless to be worth his pay."

Hugging her arms around her body, she sorted through the memories of the past. "His mind ... I don't mean he went crazy or anything like that. He simply refused to live in the world the way it was. Little by little, I could see him changing ... oh, unimportant things at first. He began to stop shaving ... skipping days, and then a week; he stopped wearing ties; his shoe laces would break, and he'd just tie them further down the shoe.

"He had always liked to eat, but he ate less and less—and refused meat and potatoes, and sometimes I'd find stacks of old, stale slices of bread hidden in his room. Like a kid ... you know how kids hoard food to have enough to run away from home? It reminded me of that; he was turning back into a child ... talking and thinking like a small boy."

"How'd you get along?" I asked.

"Well ... naturally ... I had to get a job. Uncle Will had a very small old-age pension, but it didn't begin to be enough. I worked extra as a cashier in a store downtown, and on Saturdays and Sundays I handled the cash register for Mr. Doremus. He owned the drugstore in our neighborhood, and we had traded with him all my life. Working like that, I was away from home a lot and that left Uncle Will alone ... which wasn't good, but it couldn't be helped. He was able to take care of himself; he wasn't helpless or anything like that. After a while, when I came home he'd be away. He'd walk downtown, and back, which was a long ways. On nice days he'd sit in Washington Square, in the little park, which is right in the middle of the printing and publishing district. He probably hoped to see some of his old friends." Nearly inaudibly, she added, "I thought it was good for him. It gave him something to do."

"Sure," I consoled her, "he liked to go back to the printing district, the same as an old railroad man hangs around a station."

"That's what I thought, too," Tally continued. "Then one day Uncle Will came home ... happy, walking on air. He was very secretive, all puffed up with importance like a kid. He let drop the fact he was going to get a job. Although he wouldn't tell me anything more about it, he hinted that it had something to do with the government. Very secret! I thought possibly he was making it up.

"For several weeks, he talked about a very important man he'd met. They would meet downtown and talk together in the square. And then one day, Uncle Will came home with a check; it was made out to cash and signed by a man named Greenleaf."

"How much was the check for?"

"For thirty-five dollars. At first, I didn't believe the check would be good. Uncle Will was very happy; he told me that Greenleaf was backing him and was going to lend him thirty-five dollars every week until he landed a big job. We needed the money so desperately that I decided to cash the check. Then I held the money ... without spending it ... in case the check was returned. But it wasn't returned; it was good. After that, each Friday Uncle Will gave me the check, and I endorsed it and had it cashed."

"Weren't you suspicious?"

"At first I was," she agreed, "but then ... oh, I don't know. For once someone was giving Uncle Will money instead of taking it, and we needed the money ... so badly. Uncle Will started working in his little shop down in the basement; he'd work down there all day long ... and sometimes at night. He kept the workshop padlocked, and never let me in. When I asked him what he was doing, he'd evade the subject and tell me not to worry ... he was going to take care of everything! Lew, I want you to know that ... well it sounds funny, but he was like a kid with a big secret. I didn't have the heart to hurt him ... so I left him alone. I knew he was still a wonderful engraver, and I believed ... honestly and truly ... that he was just making some gadget for Greenleaf."

"And all this time you never met Greenleaf?"

"No. Several times, he called on the phone to talk to Uncle Will, and I'd answer the phone if he was in the basement." Tally had regained complete control of herself now, talking slowly—sometimes hesitantly—and I poured her more coffee. She straightened against the pillows and held the cup firmly, occasionally sipping from it, while she went on. "One night Greenleaf called. Uncle Will picked up the phone and I could hear his part of the conversation. He'd finished whatever it was he'd been doing, and was now anxious to get his big, new job. I gathered Greenleaf told him it would take days; he wanted Uncle Will to come right downtown. Unpredictably Uncle Will became childishly stubborn ... and shouted he would take them, himself, to Washington. He began arguing and I was surprised to see him crying. Large tears rolled down his face, and he was shaking so badly that he couldn't remain standing. He sank down on a chair by the phone. Just before he hung up, I can remember he said, 'Nobody can have them, until I get my job!'

"Then he tottered to the kitchen and sat beside the table. He put his arms on it, holding his head, and he sat there, babbling and half crying. I was terribly worried that he might have a stroke or a heart attack. I tried to calm him, and after a while he told me what had happened."

Will Shaw had met Greenleaf one day in Washington Square. The meeting was quite by accident, but they had continued to meet after that and became acquaintances. The old man had told his newly found listener that once he had been a master engraver. Greenleaf, in turn, confided that he was a personal friend of the head of the Bureau of Printing and Engraving it Washington, D.C. Greenleaf promised to speak to his friend regarding a job for the old man. Will Shaw, in the dimming memories of his mind, recalled that the Bureau was always looking for expert engravers ... and once, in his youth, he had turned down an opportunity to work in it. Immediately, he took new hope.

Several weeks later, however, Greenleaf relayed the information from Washington that Will Shaw was too old; sympathetically, and confidentially, Greenleaf told the old man that his friend in Washington didn't believe that Shaw could do the work well enough. The spirits of Will Shaw plummeted to new depths of despair. Greenleaf eventually suggested a solution—one which the old man was in no condition to weigh or consider, but which he grasped eagerly. Will Shaw was to make a duplicate set of plates; he was to make them so expertly that they would be indistinguishable from the original engravings. Greenleaf would take the plates to Washington and show then to his friend. When the Bureau was unable to tell the duplicate plates from their own, the proof would be before its eyes, and the job would be given to the old man. Greenleaf had been careful in his discussion with Will Shaw not to mention the word "counterfeit," and now Shaw wishfully pushed the old knowledge from his head ... the regulations concerning the reproduction of government money ... and permitted himself to be persuaded by Greenleaf. Greenleaf because of his familiarity with the Bureau in Washington, Shaw vaguely believed, could safely waive rules and regulations.

In his enthusiasm to help Will Shaw, Greenleaf generously offered to advance money to the old man on which to live while he worked on the engravings. Kindly, Greenleaf cautioned the old engraver against the danger of hurrying the work—pointing out that all their plans would be ruined unless the plates were absolutely perfect. Will Shaw, to secure the job, must take all the time he needed to do the work; when finally he was hired on a good salary in Washington, he could repay the loan to Greenleaf.

"The old man must have been pretty far gone to fall for it," I said. "It was an obvious confidence setup from the very beginning. Will Shaw met Greenleaf ... accidentally ... like a chicken meets a chicken-hawk."

"Uncle Will was possessed with just one idea ... to get a job. Lew," her voice pleading, "you must remember that the old man wasn't ... right ... anymore...."

"All right," I agreed. "He was sick and senile. Then what happened?"

"When I finally understood, I made Uncle Will give me the key, and I went downstairs to his workshop. Inside, on his engraver's bench, were complete plates for five-, ten-, and twenty dollar bills. I knew the government would consider them counterfeit plates, and I was also sure that Greenleaf intended to use them himself. Something told me that I had to get them out of the house at once. It was still pretty early in the evening, so I put them in that little leather bag I had with a lock, and took them over to Doremus' drugstore. Everyone working there had a clothes locker, to keep coats and uniforms in, and I put my bag in my own locker, and turned the combination. I was worried sick, and I sat at the fountain and had a coke.

"I tried to decide what to do. Right here in Philadelphia there's a U.S. mint ... it's a big, brownish brick building and I've seen it many times. I made up my mind that in the morning, I'd take the plates there and give them to someone in authority. And then I decided that I wouldn't, because they might think Uncle Will was dangerous ... and send him to an institution. I thought about just mailing them to the mint, anonymously, but I was afraid to do that, too, because I've read about how the F.B.I. can trace things through the mail. I'd been there at Doremus' for over an hour, and the more I thought about it, the more confused I became. Finally, I decided that the next day, I'd just take the plates over to the Delaware River Bridge and throw them in the water.

"When I got home, the house was very quiet. Uncle Will wasn't around. I went into the kitchen where I'd left him, and then looked upstairs in his room. Back in the kitchen again, I noticed that the door leading downstairs to the basement wasn't tightly closed, and a light was on. Immediately I thought that Uncle Will had gone down to his workroom. Opening the door to call ... I saw him. He was lying at the foot of the stairs on the concrete floor."

"Dead?" I asked, but there was no question in my voice.

"Yes." She paused, then continued quietly. "I don't remember too much about the rest of that night. I called the doctor, and he notified the police. As far as the police were concerned, it was just a routine investigation of an accidental death."

"Wasn't it accidental?"

"At first I thought it was," she said. "I knew Uncle Will had been terribly upset. In that condition, he might have fallen or stumbled down the stairs ... even had a stroke ... and broken his neck."

"You didn't tell the cops about the plates ... or Greenleaf?"

"No. There was no trace of Uncle Will's plates and I thought it was better not to bring them up. The police were very nice and hardly talked to me at all. The doctor gave me a sedative, and one of the neighbor's girls stayed with me all night. By the next day, when the police returned to talk to me I'd had a chance to think it over. I definitely decided not to say anything about the plates or Greenleaf. I just told them about Uncle Will growing old and ill."

"What made you change your mind about his death not being an accident?" I asked.

"Well, after the police left the second time, I had a chance to look around the house. I was sure someone had been there and had searched it. Not obviously ... with things thrown around or drawers pulled out ... signs like that, because then the police would have noticed it. But when you've lived in a house a long time, it becomes a habit for things always to be in certain places ... the broom always stands in the right-hand corner of the closet, or the way you arrange laundry in your dresser. Little things like that had been changed. Nothing was missing, only it seemed to me that someone had been looking all through it. And the one time it could have happened was the night Uncle Will died, because I'd been there ever since."

"Didn't the cops search the house?" I asked.

"No, not like that," she replied. "They looked around the rooms ... but not in the same way."

"Okay," I said. "Then what?"

"It frightened me because I didn't know what it meant, and I didn't know what to do about it either. A girl I'd worked with at the drugstore agreed to stay with me until after Uncle Will was buried ... which was two days later. After the funeral, she stayed with me that night ... and then returned home. The following day, the phone rang—and it was Greenleaf."

"Could you identify Greenleaf's voice right now if you heard it?" I asked.

She thought a moment. "No, I'm not sure that I could ... although, as I remember, it sounded sort of affected."

"Affected? Was there something distinctive about it?"

She considered my question for a moment. "Not really ... I guess. He was an Easterner, I think."

"Did it sound like Philadelphia ... New York ... Boston?"

"No. More broad than those." She shrugged helplessly. "It was just ... different. Anyway, on the phone he said that he wanted the engravings, the ones Uncle Will had made. I told him that I didn't know what he was talking about and he laughed. That made me angry, and I said if I ever found them that I was going to turn them over to the government and tell how he had fooled Uncle Will into making them. He laughed again and told me to remember all the checks I'd signed. After that, everything was quiet for a moment, and I thought he had hung up. Suddenly he said, and he sounded cold and threatening, 'I'll pay you for the plates ... or perhaps you might prefer another accident in the family.'"

"And that was all?"

"Yes ... just about. But as he was hanging up he said something else that didn't make sense. It sounded like 'loon who ought to.'"

"Loon who ought to?" I repeated it. "Are you sure that's what he said?"

"Yes," she said, positive, "that's the way it sounded although it sort of ran together, and wasn't as clear as that. But he said 'loon who ought to' and then he hung up the phone."

I said, not too surely, "I suppose he might have turned his head away from the phone for a moment and you heard only part of the sentence ... about being a loon who ought to take advantage of his offer. Or something like that ..." In my own ears it sounded weak. Too weak and out of character for the man. "Anyway," I added, "it's not important now. What happened next?"

"I was really frightened," she said, "Uncle Will's death, then the house being searched, my lying to the police, and this threat of Greenleaf's about ... an ... accident. I wanted to get away, to run away from everything, so I packed my hatbox ... just as fast as I could ... and hurried from the house. At Doremus' I picked up the grip with the plates, from my locker, and took the first train to New York."

"The rest I know," I told her. "You met a tall wealthy man with talent and married him ... the dream goal of all red-blooded women!"

A smile warmed her strained face. "Exactly, darling!" she agreed. Bending forward she kissed me on the lips, the coffee cup rattling between us.

"Incidentally," I said casually, "you got rid of the plates in New York."

"Oh, no," she replied, "they're in that new little bag in the closet."

"Jesus Christ!" I leaped from the bed, slammed open the door of the closet and withdrew the small heavy bag. Opening it, I saw a magnificent set of deep-etched steel, counterfeit plates. Staring at the beautiful phonies, I could feel the cold sweat of fear break across my forehead.

Chapter 11

Denman had recalled Deputy Chief Medical Examiner Eggleston for cross-examination. The counsel for the defense concealed his worries well. Cannon had succeeded, Denman believed, in establishing the fact of a body in his case, identifying the body of the man who, when alive, had been known as Isham Reddick. Although there were still loose ends in the prosecution's case to be tied up to make the case more solid, Denman had few doubts that Cannon would make every effort to tie them. Now, however, the defense could see the course the prosecution would follow and it was necessary to counter the testimony which had impressed the jury.

"Dr. Eggleston," Denman began quietly, "You have identified blood discovered on a hatchet, a piece of canvas, and two vials of scrapings, as containing evidences of human blood; is that right?"

"Yes, sir."

"The counselor for the prosecution has established that you are an expert medical witness, and we certainly have no desire to question that."

"Thank you," Eggleston replied dryly.

"Now the traces of blood which you found, you have identified as a type known as O, is that correct?"

"That is correct. It was type O."

"As an expert medical witness, Dr. Eggleston, will you please tell the court how many known types of blood there are?"

"There are four types."

"Only four types?" Denman's voice expressed surprise. "You mean, Doctor, that in all the millions ... even billions ... of persons on this earth, they have only four types of blood among them?"

"Yes," replied Eggleston stiffly, "that's true."

"And everyone falls into one of the four types? Think of that!" Denman mused the point silently for a moment. "Well, now, Doctor, suppose you tell us what the four types are, if you will?"

Eggleston repeated clearly and distinctly, "There are four classifications of human blood. These are types O, A, B, and AB."

"What is the uncommon type, Doctor?"

"Type AB."

"And the most common?"

"Type O."

"Very interesting. Type O, what? The most common type ... there are literally hundreds of millions of people who have that type of blood? Is that correct?"

Eggleston cleared his throat. "Yes."

Denman turned and looked at the jury casually, then refaced his witness. "Among the twelve men and women in the jury box, the mathematical probability is that some of them have blood of O type?"

"Objection!" stated Cannon. "That calls for a conclusion."

Denman drawled, "Your honor, I don't think it calls for much of a conclusion that the jury has blood in its veins."

Cannon flushed. The judge, however, ruled in Cannon's favor. "Rephrase your question, please," the bench directed Denman.

The counselor for the defense shrugged and returned to the witness. "Dr. Eggleston," he said, "you definitely identified the type of blood found on the various objects as O. Can you, as a medical scientist, definitely identify that blood as having been the blood of Isham Reddick?"

"No, sir," the witness replied, glancing toward Cannon.

"Then all you have done is classified into generalities," Denman said depreciatingly.

"I identified it as belonging to the same type of blood as Isham Reddick's."

"But you can't prove it was Isham Reddick's blood?"

"No, sir."

Denman turned contemptuously away from the witness and faced the jury, although his words were still addressed to Eggleston. "In other words, you have proved nothing?"

"That is not true!" Eggleston replied firmly.

Denman faced around savagely. "Well then, Doctor, what did you prove?"

"That is was not impossible for the blood to have belonged to Isham Reddick." Eggleston regarded Denman steadily.

Immediately, Denman shifted his attack. "I hope you can be more specific about the mysterious ashes you analyzed, Doctor. For a moment I wish to refresh your memory concerning the testimony you gave Mr. Cannon." Denman reading from a sheet of paper, quoted:

A: There was evidence of protein origin.

Q: Does that mean the possibility of flesh ... what might at
one time have been human flesh?
A: That is correct.

Denman paused and regarded Eggleston. "Do you remember saying
that?" he asked.

"Yes, sir," replied Eggleston.

"Will you tell the court what you meant by the term 'protein origin'?"

"It means having a high protein content ... predominantly in protein."

"And what is protein, Doctor?"

"In biochemistry it means any of a class of naturally occurring complex combinations of amino acids ... ah, let's see ... containing carbon,
hydrogen, nitrogen, oxygen, and usually sulfur, which are essential con-
stituents of all living cells."

Denman pondered his next question carefully. Finally, he asked,
"Aren't proteins found in vegetable as well as animal substances?"

"Yes," replied Eggleston.

"Ah," Denman smiled, "then the ash containing a high protein content
could have come from vegetable substances?"

"No," replied Eggleston. "Chemically the dif ..."

"Please just answer my question!" Denman interrupted the witness,
and paused to weigh his situation. It was an extremely dangerous one.
Deciding to return to safer ground, he said, "Now just a minute ago, Doctor, you finished telling the court what was meant by protein, didn't
you?"

"Yes. I gave you a biochemistry definition."

Denman shook his head in reproof. "I asked you ..." he turned to face
the judge, "will the court please instruct the recording clerk to read back
the next question which I put at that time. Also, the answer of the witness." The bench so instructed, and the clerk read aloud:

Q: Aren't proteins found in vegetable as well as animal substances?
A: Yes.

"Now," continued Denman addressing Eggleston, "you heard what the
clerk has just read. I'll reword the question once more. Proteins are also
found in vegetable substances? Is that correct?"

"Yes," replied Eggleston. He was surprised to find himself so quickly
on the defensive.

"All right," said Denman with the air of a man who has just exposed
a fraud, "we'll leave the subject of vegetable protein." Walking slowly to
the exhibit table, he picked up the roll of oil skin, and turning, held it

up without unrolling it. "Dr. Eggleston," he said, "I'm not going to impose on the sensibilities of those present today by opening this exhibit again. You have already identified it once, so you know what I am talking about. You know what it is?"

"Yes. It's a bone called the tibia."

"A human bone?"

"Yes. A human bone."

"You are positive of that?"

"Yes, sir."

"It couldn't be the bone of one of the primates?"

"Yes, sir. It could!" Eggleston replied acidly. "Man is a primate."

Behind him, Denman could hear Cannon's soft laugh, but he gave no indication of his irritation. "Naturally, Doctor," he smiled blandly, "I'm sure we've all studied high-school biology. What I was going to ask before you anticipated my question ... incidentally," he turned to the judge, "will the court please instruct the witness to stop anticipating my questions?"

"Your honor," said Cannon rising, "I distinctly heard the counselor ask a question to which the witness made an intelligent reply. I feel that Mr. Denman is unfairly taking advantage of the witness." As he sat down, his eyes met Denman's and passed on happily. The court instructed the witness to content himself with answering only the question put to him.

"All right," said Denman, returning to the witness with dignity, "I will begin my question again. It couldn't be the bone of one of the primates other than man ... apes, monkeys, or lemurs? Naturally, I do not include marmosets because of their size."

"It couldn't be an ape, monkey, or lemur," Eggleston told him grimly.

"Without any question of a doubt it is human?"

"Yes, it is human."

"Now, Doctor, you testified that this so called leg bone ... the shin ... was from the leg of a normal, adult male. Which leg is it from?"

"From the left."

"You testified in some detail that the man was not less than five feet ten in height, and not more than six feet. Is that right?"

"That is correct, sir."

"When you examined the bone, what was its condition?"

"It was badly burned and charred."

"Was the entire length of bone you identified as the tibia present when you examined it?"

"I don't quite understand your question, sir."

"I'll put it this way. Was the bone entirely complete, was it present in its normal size and length except for being burned and charred?"

"No, sir."

"The fire then had consumed part of it ... made it shorter than it normally was?"

"Yes," Eggleston agreed, "the ends had been destroyed."

"Yet, from this damaged, incomplete bone you insist that the man could not have been less than five feet ten?"

"That is correct."

"You will take an oath that under no possible circumstances this man could have been five feet nine and three quarter inches?"

Eggleston twisted uneasily in his chair. No man, under the circumstances, could ethically have been positive of the quarter-inch variance. "I doubt it," he said.

"I'm not asking you to doubt anything," Denman replied, pressing his advantage. "I'm asking you this: Is it entirely beyond all medical possibility that the man could have been five feet nine and three quarter inches?"

"It's against all probability."

"I didn't say probability," Denman corrected him quickly. "I said possibility!"

"Well," agreed Eggleston reluctantly, "there's a possibility.... "

"Thank you!" Deliberately Denman began his attack on the other extreme of height, and after considerable maneuvering finally drew an admission from the medical examiner that the man might possibly have been slightly over six feet tall.

Standing beside Eggleston, although really addressing the jury with his remarks, Denman dismissed the witness. "Thank you, Dr. Eggleston. Actually this irregular piece of bone, which you have identified as not coming from an ape, monkey, or lemur, is in a badly burned condition, incomplete in material form, and you insist it came from man. It came from the left leg of a man who originally was not less than five feet ten and not more than six feet in height. This same unknown man, in the last few minutes, has shrunk in height, and at the same time gained in altitude. I'm sure if we had time, the Doctor and I could finally agree both on a midget and a circus giant."

Eggleston stood wearily, visibly relieved to leave the stand. At the last moment, Denman casually called him back, a trick the attorney had found effective with tired witnesses. Denman quickly drew forth the admission, from Eggleston, that the bullet found in the furnace had not contained evidence of blood. Skillfully, the defense attorney prevented the medical examiner from testifying that the extreme heat of the fire, which melted the bullet out of shape could also have destroyed blood and flesh segments which might have originally clung to it. Cannon tersely whispered to his assistant to make a note to recall Eggleston later and to solicit this information.

Lincoln Means followed Eggleston to the stand for cross-examination. Adding the minutes on the clock to himself, Denman decided that he might be able to finish two, possibly three more witnesses before the court adjourned for the day. When the jury was locked up for the night, his cross-examination would be the last testimony for the jurors to remember. Pressing the palms of his hands against the seams of his trousers, Denman began his questioning. After reidentifying Means as an employee of the Bureau of Licenses, he asked, "If I were applying for a license and told you that I was six feet tall, would you measure me?"

"No," replied Means.

"Why not?"

"Well ... we don't have a scale for that purpose. It isn't necessary; there's no reason to lie about your height."

"Would there be another reason?"

"You look like you're six feet tall. I'd believe you."

"If I'd said I was five feet two, though, you wouldn't believe me?" Denman asked.

"No, sir. That's obviously wrong."

"Now suppose I said I was one hundred and eighty-six pounds. Would you believe that?"

Means looked at him critically. "You're a big man, I'd say you probably weighed around one hundred and ninety-five pounds."

"Now for the moment, you believe I am six feet tall, and weigh one hundred and ninety-five pounds. Is that correct, Mr. Means?"

"Yes, sir."

"Six feet tall, one hundred and ninety-five pounds," Denman repeated the figures softly while he removed his billfold and took out his driver's license. Holding it up, he read, "Six feet one and a half inches, weight one hundred and seventy pounds." He faced the witness again, "We disagree by one and a half inches, and twenty-five pounds. That's quite a discrepancy."

The judge addressed the counsel. "How long ago was that license taken out, Mr. Denman?"

"A little over a year ago," Denman replied, "and I assure the court there has been no substantial change in my weight since then."

"Thank you," replied the judge. "You may proceed."

"Mr. Means," continued Denman, "what is your own weight?"

"About a hundred and sixty pounds."

"About ... you say? When did you last weigh yourself? On accurate scales ... say, in a doctor's office?"

Means thought back. "Couple, three years ago ... for an insurance examination."

"And your height?"

"Five seven and a half."

"With or without your shoes?"

"Without my shoes."

"And when was this?"

"At the same insurance examination."

"When I was examined for insurance," Denman said, "and when I was measured for height, my doctor didn't ask me to remove my shoes. He simply compensated half an inch for them."

"Well," replied Means uneasily, "maybe mine did too."

"Don't be concerned," Denman's voice was friendly, "I'm not attempting to trap you. I'm simply proving that the human memory is not infallible. Most persons only weigh themselves occasionally, and then on unreliable scales, or if they do have factual figures—it is possible that the figures have changed or are out of date. Right now, Mr. Means, you honestly don't know if you are five feet seven, seven and a half, or eight; also is it probable that you weigh one hundred fifty, fifty-five, sixty, or sixty-five pounds." Denman paused, then asked politely, "Is that correct?"

"Yes, I suppose so."

"Isn't it possible that many of the applicants for licenses have the same fallacious, out-of-date, or mistaken information that you have? They fill in the statistics with answers they believe to be true, but which could ... actually ... be quite inaccurate?"

"Well ... no ..."

"I don't mean obviously wrong, Mr. Means. But five or ten pounds off, an inch or two in height ... can you guarantee that every one of the thousands of forms you have are one hundred per cent correct?" Denman's voice had suddenly lost its friendliness.

"No," Means replied slowly, "sometimes somebody might make a mistake ..."

"Exactly!" Denman referred to his notes. "You read into the testimony regarding Isham Reddick: "Sex ... male; age ... 36; eyes ... blue; hair ... dark brown; weight ... 175 pounds; height ... 5 feet 11 inches." Denman glanced up from his reading and intently regarded the witness. "Now, Mr. Means, a few minutes ago you estimated my stature, but on the basis of your estimate ..."

Cannon was on his feet. "Objection! Objection!"

"Isn't it possible Reddick was over six feet tall and weighed two hundred pounds?" Denman concluded.

"You're honor," objected Cannon, "I move the statement be struck from the testimony, and the jury be instructed to disregard it!"

"On what basis, Counselor?" asked Denman smiling. "It is an opinion ... purely hypothetical ..."

"Sustained," agreed the court. The judge turned to the jury. "Please do not regard the last statement, made by Mr. Denman, as evidence in any way, and do not permit it to affect your decision."

Denman, however, was still smiling. He had built a smoke screen; how important it was, he couldn't tell.

Dr. Stanley Boss, the dentist, rather reluctantly returned to the stand. Denman stood beside the defense table, visibly sharpening up his weapons while the dentist was seated. Denman immediately launched his attack.

Chapter 12

Those engraved printing plates worried me! Plenty! I knew we had to get rid of them as quickly as possible. In a strange hotel, it isn't customary to call a bellboy, ask for a hammer, and then begin beating out an anvil chorus on pieces of heavy gauge metal ... in the hope of destroying them. Merely possessing the plates meant terrible trouble with the Treasury Department, in spite of their never having been printed from.

But even more dangerous, to my way of thinking, was the unknown and unseen Greenleaf. He had arranged with a great amount of time, and some expense, to con Will Shaw into making them. If Tally was correct, he had been in the house looking for the plates the night the old man died. Now it was impossible to return the engravings to the government without involving Tally—because of the money Greenleaf had advanced through the checks she had endorsed. And then there was the next point, too....

Suppose Greenleaf had been responsible for the old man's death? Wasn't it a probability that Greenleaf had struck him and knocked him downstairs when Will Shaw couldn't hand over the plates? Or possibly had struck Shaw first, and then with the old man unconscious had pitched him head first into the basement?

One thing was obvious, however; I must get rid of the plates immediately. And, furthermore, I had no intention of walking around the streets of Philadelphia, carrying them, while I found a place to hide them. Tally remained quietly in bed while I dressed. She looked worried. "Listen, doll," I said, kissing her quickly, "I'm going out for a while ... stick around until I get back." She nodded. I put the engravings back in the closet, and hurriedly left the room.

Out on the street, I cut over toward the city hall, looking for a place to hide the plates, and where they might remain undiscovered for a reasonable length of time. Preferably until we had finished at the Lark and returned to New York. The streets were filled with people all of whom seemed to be watching me suspiciously. Walking along Benjamin Franklin Parkway toward the Art Museum, I approached the monument of George Washington on a concrete island surrounded by traffic. Within the grounds of the Art Museum, however, I found another statue and the place for which I had been searching. There's a bronze casting of a man with a raised spear, astride a horse, and it's called the Lion Fighter. Growing directly behind it is a well-groomed hedge, heavy and thick, with a tangled mass of interwoven roots. By standing behind the statue, I could dig in the roots and conceal the plates without anyone observing me. The plates, buried deeply enough, might remain concealed for years—becoming corroded and ruined beyond any possible use.

I was anxious, now, to return to the hotel, pick up the plates, and to come back and bury them. Hurrying down the broad steps of the museum, I waved down a cab and rode back to the hotel.

At the McAndrews, a newsie opened the cab door, and I slipped him a quarter. He stepped back to the sidewalk, "A nice day, Mr. Mountain," he said.

"That it is," I agreed. He was a thin, skinny little guy with practically no shoulders at all, and the waddling gait of a penguin. Several times, when it had been raining, he had hustled cabs for Tally and me and consequently we were on nodding-tipping-speaking terms. For just a moment I stood beside him on the sunny sidewalk, and then it seemed a great flapping shadow covered the sun.

The newsie glanced up and, shouting loud senseless words, shoved me back into the street.

There was a tremendous report like the slamming of a door!

Death lay on the street beside me.

Stunned, the newsie and I stood there, stupefied, and in those few paralyzed moments the sidewalk swarmed with people, gathering from the streets and the buildings and the cars to form a tightening circle around the hideous heap. At my feet lay a slipper, a small, black, velvet bedroom slipper trimmed with gold.

It was Tally's slipper.

The tides lapping the beaches of all the oceans in the world stopped running and for a moment stood still. Then ebbing, they piled back one upon another, rushing faster and faster in a great black tidal wave dredging up the sickly bottoms of the seas, sucking the sun from the sky. Within the black heart of the wave a great roaring began, increasing louder and louder, and the wave grew higher and higher until nothing remained but the presence of a sound so great there is no other sound, a blackness so deep there is no sight. And yet, somewhere there were loud voices, and soft voices, and voices in between.

And one face kept appearing before mine. A face I had never seen before ... a large face, with dark close-set eyes and a heavy jaw. Finally, I could no longer hear all the voices—just the one voice. The voice that belonged to the heavy face.

The face belonged to a detective named Brockheim, and we were in my hotel room. Other men were in the room, too; some in plain clothes and some in uniform. It seemed as if everyone was there. Everyone, that is, except Tally.

"Come ... come," Brockheim repeated, "it's been a shock. Come, come, Mr. Mountain, you must answer a few questions. Come, come, man, pull yourself together." One of the cops had discovered a partly filled bottle of Scotch in my drawer and poured me a drink. I drank it, but I couldn't taste it. "Come ... come," said Brockheim.

Grasping the arms of the chair, I squeezed them. My fingers were lifeless—I was squeezing mush, whipped cream, the foam of beer. "Yes," I said finally, my voice coming from the void deep within me.

"That's better ... that's good," said Brockheim. "Tell me, Mr. Mountain, when did you see your wife last?"

"I don't know," I said.

"Come, come," Brockheim replied, "you were just returning to the hotel when your wife leaped from the window. You must have seen her sometime this morning."

"I don't know," I said.

"Well then, how long were you gone?"

Among all the watches, I saw the apparition of my wrist watch as I had looked at it in the grounds of the Art Museum. "Two hours," I said.

"Good!" Brockheim replied with satisfaction. "When you left Mrs. Mountain this morning, what was she doing?"

"She was in bed."

"Undressed and in bed?"

"Yes."

"After you left, she must have gotten up and dressed, because she was wearing her street clothes when she jumped. Why? Was she going out?"

"I don't think so," I said numbly as the memory of Tally lying against the pillows returned to me. "But she might have decided to get up anyway. I was gone quite a while."

"How was she feeling when you saw her this morning? Did you have a fight about something?"

"No. We didn't fight. We never fought...."

"Was she depressed about something? Anything?"

"I can't think," I said. "I'm all confused ... it's hard for me to understand what you say. Let me go in and wash my face." Without waiting for

Brockheim's permission I arose from the chair and stumbled into the bathroom. Pulling my tie loose, I unbuttoned my shirt collar; then turned on the cold water tap. Scooping up handfuls of water, I bathed my face and placed my icy hands at the base of my neck. When my head began to clear, the fog of unreality before my eyes slowly began to disappear. Drying my hands and face, I returned to the bedroom. "All right," I told Brockheim, "I feel better now."

"I asked you if your wife had planned to go out this morning?" Brockheim said.

"Yes ... I remember you asked that. You said she was dressed in street clothes. But she was still wearing bedroom slippers."

"That's right," agreed Brockheim. "Now tell me what she was worried about? A woman doesn't jump out of a window on the spur of the moment."

This was the moment of decision! This was the point of no return. It was now that I told the truth ... or never. Placing a cigarette in my mouth, I pretended to fumble through my pockets for a match. Before Brockheim could bring his lighter into play I walked over to the closet, opened it, and took a pack of matches from a jacket hanging there. My eyes touched the corner of the closet.

Tally's small bag containing the counterfeit plates was gone!

I returned to the chair and sat down. I knew that Tally had not jumped to her death—had not committed suicide. Not only was there no reason for her to do so, but it was impossible psychologically to reconcile the deed to her temperament. The final desperate act of suicide takes conditioning, over a long period of time, and Tally had given no indication of such thoughts.

The police, I knew, must also be considering the possibility that her fall was accidental. The two large windows at the end of the room were both wide enough and high enough to make it possible. Both windows had comparatively low sills, not more than twenty-four inches above the floor. The lower part of one window had been completely raised, sliding up to cover the entire top half of the frame, leaving a large wide opening. Suppose Tally had opened the window, leaned out—resting her hands on the sill—and her hands had slipped? As she lost her balance, was it possible that the momentum of the fall would pitch her out of the window? This would be impossible to prove or disprove as the outside cement sill would retain neither fingerprints nor palm marks.

One other fact remained; the big fact ... the most important fact of all! The plates were gone. They had been in the closet when I left. Could Tally have dressed and hidden them somewhere in the hotel? It was a possibility although I doubted it. She was waiting for me to return. Then, if she hadn't gotten rid of them, Greenleaf had been in the room and taken them.

From this, it might appear that I had thought about the situation in detail, while attempting to stall off Brockheim. That's not the way it happened. Actually, all the possibilities seemed to flash before me in an instant of lucidity. In another moment, I had made my decision. I knew beyond doubt that it was useless to explain about the missing plates, and to accuse Greenleaf ... whom I had never seen ... and couldn't possibly identify, and against whom I had no proof of any kind. To admit existence of the plates, worth millions in counterfeit money, was to point a damning finger of motive to myself. Logically, the police might believe that Tally had hidden the engravings to keep for herself, and I had killed her to regain possession of them.

Although I had an air-tight alibi ... with the newsie ... for the moment of her death, that did not rule out the possibility of an accomplice.

So in that second instant, as my eyes met Brockheim's, I said to him, "She'd been worried ... well, not really worried ... but distressed about her uncle's death. He died here in Philadelphia less than four months ago; he was my wife's only relative and naturally she felt very badly about it. Returning here to work depressed her, but not to the extent she'd take her own life."

Brockheim moved a stick of gum, peeled off the wrapper, and stuck it his mouth. Chewing it slowly, he explained, "Trying to give up smoking. Doesn't work very well." He eyed me contemplatively and asked, "How long you been married?" I told him. "Newlyweds, huh?" he observed.

"Yes," I replied.

"Did she have any insurance?"

"Not that I know of ... she might have had some before we were married. If she did, it couldn't be very much and she never mentioned it."

"You didn't take any out on her?"

"Not a penny."

"Sure about it?"

"Positive."

Brockheim shrugged. "I can find out." He relapsed to silence, and chewed his gum. After a few moments, he said, "The switchboard says you got a call this morning before you went out. Who was it?"

I looked at him. "Some joker in the show, I think. Whoever it was just called to wake us up. Pretended it was a wrong number ..."

"Oh?" Brockheim arose and ambled over to the window. "Seems there was another call later ... after you'd gone. A very short one. Soon as your room answered, the connection was broken. Same joker?"

"Could be," I agreed. "You always find them in this business ... in every show. They're not very funny."

"They never are." Standing by the open window, Brockheim stooped—

leaning out to peer down the fifteen stories to the street. Bending further, he rested his hands on the sill, his hands and wrists supporting the weight of his body. "Was your wife a fresh-air fiend?" he asked, his voice sounding distant through the window.

"Not especially," I replied. Brockheim pulled his body back through the opening and dusted the palms of his hands. "She wasn't against fresh air, either. If she had a headache, or wasn't feeling well, she might have opened the window to lean out."

"Did she have a headache?"

"I couldn't say. We slept late this morning. Perhaps she just wanted a breath of fresh air."

"Yeah," said Brockheim. Walking back across the room he faced me. "You think it possible she jumped?" he asked.

"No." I was positive.

"Then you think she fell?"

"Yes. It had to be that way."

"Well," he said slowly, "we'll leave you alone now. There're some more questions I've got to ask around the hotel ... and at that club where you're working. I'll talk to you later." He nodded to the men in the room, and they followed him through the door.

Instantly the room was deserted—a great square room, miles long and miles wide. Nowhere in the room was there a sound ... and nowhere was there movement ... except my fingers. After a while, I studied them and discovered they were doing a cull shuffle. In my hands, however, there were no cards.

I walked over to the dresser and picked up the bottle of Scotch.

Chapter 13

The dentist's eyes, behind his rimless glasses, watched Denman with wary interest. Nervously he ran his hand through his hair and cleared his voice. The defense attorney approached him indifferently, his hands shoved in the pockets of his trousers. "Doctor, you said a patient known to you as Isham Reddick called because he had three teeth hurting; is that right?"

"That is correct, sir," Boss replied.

"Furthermore, you examined those teeth carefully and took an X-ray ... but you could find nothing wrong with them?"

"I could find no reason for the teeth to be hurting him."

"After you told the patient this, what did he say?"

"He said they still hurt him."

"Following that first call, you continued to see him several times more. Did he ever say, again, that the teeth hurt?"

"I don't remember."

"But you remember everything else?"

Boss fidgeted uneasily. "When I saw him later, I was thinking about the new tooth...."

"But didn't it strike you as strange that your patient told you his teeth were hurting. You told him nothing was wrong, and very co-operatively he never mentioned his sore teeth again?"

"No," replied Boss. "Sometimes teeth hurt because they are temporarily sensitive to extremes of heat and cold ... then the condition passes ..."

"So after you decided nothing was wrong with Isham Reddick's teeth, you proceeded to make a false one for him. Tell me, Dr. Boss, who brought up the subject of the false tooth?"

"I'm sure Reddick did, sir."

"Why are you so sure of that?"

"Well, the loss of it greatly affected his appearance. He needed it badly. The amount of time and labor that went into making the new tooth greatly exceeded what Reddick could pay. It was more important to him to have the tooth than it was to me to make it."

"You have implied, Dr. Boss, that you did Isham Reddick a favor in making the tooth for him, and I consider it very generous of you, I'm sure." Denman paused, then asked, "Have you a very successful practice, Doctor?"

"Yes, I should say so."

"A large one?"

"All I can handle," Boss replied.

Denman turned his attack. "Yet busy as you are, you spent as much time ... as much effort ... as much skill in making this tooth for Isham Reddick, who couldn't pay for it, as you would for a wealthy patient?"

"I certainly did," Boss replied stiffly.

"Now, Dr. Boss, I don't deny that you made a tooth for Isham Reddick. I'm sure you did. But I'm not sure that you made by *hand* a tooth, specially colored, shaped, and shaded ... a tooth different than any other tooth in the world." Deliberately, Denman looked the witness up and down, "Well, did you, Doctor?"

"Yes sir, I did!" Boss' lips set determinedly.

"Consider it well," Denman cautioned. "Isn't it possible that you found a stock tooth suitable to use? There are stock teeth of individual sizes and shapes, aren't there?"

"Yes, there are."

"So you could have found one which matched Isham Reddick's well enough in color, ground it down to fit ... and have saved yourself a great deal of time and expense. Isn't that right?"

"No!" Boss denied it doggedly.

"Why not?"

"Because the patient is never satisfied with a poor job."

"But Reddick would have been better off, would he not? He would have a front tooth, one that looked reasonably well—which was something he didn't have before?" Denman was attempting to push Boss into admitting the use of a stock tooth. With such an admission, the dentist's identification of the tooth, as Reddick's, would be greatly weakened. However, Boss maintained tenaciously that the tooth he had made and fitted for Reddick was his own, and Denman was unable to shake his testimony.

Denman's examination of Mrs. Boss was cursory. She repeated her previous testimony that the laboratory report on Isham Reddick's blood had been type O. There was very little more that Denman could do with her. At the conclusion of his examination, the court adjourned for the day.

At ten o'clock the following morning Assistant District Attorney Cannon recalled Lieutenant Mikleson to the stand. "Now, Lieutenant, previously you have testified that on your first visit to the house on East Eighty-ninth Street, you examined the defendant's bedroom, the adjoining bath ... and that pictures were taken of those rooms." Mikleson confirmed this statement, and Cannon continued, "When you searched the bedroom, what did you find?"

"I found a revolver in the second drawer of the bureau."

"Is this the same revolver?" asked Cannon.

Mikleson identified it. "Yes," he replied, "a .32, with one shell fired."

"Did you find anything else?"

"Yes, sir, I did. I found a piece of note paper folded and placed under a number of items of clothing in the same dresser."

"Is this the note?" Cannon passed a small sheet of blue-lined paper, approximately three inches wide and five inches long, of a type commonly used in pocket memorandum books. A piece had been torn out completely along one side.

Mikleson examined the paper and nodded. "This is the one. I identify it by my initials on it."

Cannon turned, addressing his next remarks to the jury. "I'm going to read what is written on this paper." He held up the slip and read in a clear voice: "Reddick ... mt. 8500." Facing the judge, Cannon said, "Your honor, I offer this into evidence." Then turning back to Mikleson he continued, "Also in the possession of the defendant, you found a memorandum book. Can you identify this?" The prosecuting attorney handed a small leather-covered book to the officer who examined and identified it. "Thank you," said Cannon, dismissing the witness.

Next recalling the handwriting expert ... Alvin G. Hartney ... to the stand, Cannon showed him the memorandum book. "You have examined the writings and notes in this book and have compared them to samples of the writing of the defendant. Would you say they are written by the same hand?"

"Yes," said Hartney. "The writing in the memo book is identical with other specimens of handwriting of the defendant."

"Here," continued Cannon, "is a sheet of paper ... supposedly from that notebook. Have you examined the writing on it?" Cannon gave the blue-lined note to the witness.

"Yes," replied Hartney.

"Can you identify the writing?"

"Yes, sir. It is identical to both the writing in the notebook and the other handwriting specimens of the defendant."

"You would say, positively, they were written by the same person?"

"I would!" Hartney replied with assurance. Cannon excused him from the stand.

"Mary Deems," the clerk announced, and a middle-aged woman still retaining a trim and youthful figure made her way to the witness chair. Her round face was unmarked by lines, and she wore no make-up except lipstick. She identified herself as a house maid, in the house on East Eighty-ninth Street, having worked for the defendant. Dressed in a neat dark suit, she crossed her ankles, folded her hands in her lap, and continued with her testimony.

"You have said you were a house maid. Will you please tell us about your duties?" asked Cannon.

"Well, sir ... actually I kept the house picked up, answered the door and the downstairs phone, and in the mornings prepared a light continental breakfast...."

"Explain about the breakfast, if you will."

"I'm not a cook," she replied firmly, "but in the mornings, I'd make coffee, and warm up crisp rolls to be served with marmalade for breakfast." She nodded, thinking back. "When I was hired I said I wasn't a cook and I was told that there wouldn't be any cooking to be done. Breakfast, a real light one, was the only meal in the house. Sometimes ... there might be a little private entertaining, but then a caterer would just send something in."

"Did you live on the premises, Miss Deems?"

"Yes, sir. I had a room in the upstairs servants' quarters."

"Were there any servants other than yourself?"

"There was Isham Reddick. He lived in, too. He was employed as a combination houseman-chauffeur."

"Was that all the help to run a large house like that?"

Mary Deems shook her head. "That was all the help that lived in ... just Isham Reddick and me. There was a couple ... Mr. and Mrs. Lightbody ... who came in days to help. He was a super in another building down the street...."

"Just a moment. What do you mean by super?"

"Superintendent. He was superintendent, and janitor, of a small apartment building down the street. He came in every day to take out ashes, check the furnace, and fix anything around the house that needed fixing. Mrs. Lightbody, his wife, came in regularly to do the heavy cleaning and vacuuming."

"I see. Now, returning to Isham Reddick. You said, a few moments ago, that he was a houseman-chauffeur. I understood that he also acted in the capacity of a valet. Is that right?"

"Yes, sir, he did a little bit of everything." Mary Deems was not inclined to argue definitions.

"Now, Miss Deems, you have been in service ... for how many years?"

The woman hesitated, "Since I was a young girl ..."

Cannon was understanding. "I'm not going to ask for a definite reply. Is it fair to say around twenty years?"

"Yes ..."

"Good! Now in that time you've seen many servants when you've worked for other families. How would you compare Isham Reddick with other houseman-valet-chauffeurs?"

The woman considered the question and replied slowly. "Not very well, sir ..." her honest face was worried with the idea of speaking disrespectfully of the dead, "but he really didn't take an interest in his job. Of course," she added brightly, "maybe he didn't like the idea of doing so many things. Usually a valet is a valet ... and a chauffeur is a chauffeur."

"Did you get to know Isham Reddick very well?" Mary Deems blushed, and Cannon qualified his question. "I don't mean in any personal way, but did he talk to you very much?"

"No, sir. Not very much. Usually when he wasn't on duty, he'd remain up in his room. There was just the one time he ever acted very friendly. Once when we were alone, he asked me to go see a movie. Afterward we stopped and had something to eat."

"You remember that incident very well, Miss Deems. Is there any reason for it, other than it was the only time he ever took you out?"

"Yes, sir. There's another reason, too. There was a little restaurant near the movie up on Ninety-second Street. We stopped in there to get a bite to eat, as I said, I was reading the menu carefully because I didn't want to spend too much of Mr. Reddick's money. I decided I'd just have a sandwich and a cup of tea and he said, 'Go ahead and order anything you want. I've got plenty of dough.'"

"Isham Reddick said, 'Go ahead and order anything you want. I've got plenty of dough,'" Cannon repeated. "By that, Miss Deems, you understood that he had plenty of money, is that correct?"

"That's what I thought he meant, although there was the possibility he was just joking ... or bragging a little. Kidding him back, I said that I bet he didn't have an extra shirt to his name. He looked at me and said, 'What do you think of this?' He pulled a big thick roll of bills out of his pocket. He held them out in front of me for a minute, very proud like, and then put them back."

"Did Reddick tell you how much money there was in the roll?"

"No, sir. But when he held the bills up, I could see there were a lot of hundred-dollar ones among them."

"In your opinion, could there have been eighty-five hundred dollars in that ..." Cannon was interrupted by Denman springing to his feet.

"Objection," Denman stated.

The judge agreed. "Objection sustained."

"All right, Miss Deems," Cannon said, returning to his witness. "After Reddick had showed you a large roll of bills, many in the denomination of a hundred dollars, what did you say?"

"Naturally, I wondered where he had gotten all that money. I knew it wasn't from his salary...."

"Objection!" Denman shouted angrily.

"Sustained!" The court ruled.

"What did he say?" asked Cannon, addressing the maid.

"Well, first I laughed and said, 'Boy, you must have a private gold mine!' Then he laughed, too, and said, 'No, he didn't have a private gold mine. He was more like an undertaker—he knew where the bodies were buried.'"

"Let me get this straight now, Miss Deems," Cannon said deliberately, driving his point home. "Isham Reddick told you that he was like an undertaker—that he knew where the bodies were buried. Is that correct?"

"Yes, sir."

"And by that remark, you understood that Reddick was not talking about *real* bodies—but that he knew some important information?"

"That's right. That is what he meant."

"It hardly sounds to me like a man who could scarcely afford the cost of a tooth," observed Cannon. "Did it sound that way to you?"

"No, sir," the maid replied, "it didn't. It sounded like he had plenty of money."

"Was Isham Reddick wearing the tooth the night you went to dinner?"

"He couldn't have been," she said. "I remember there was a big wide gap in the front of his teeth—just like always."

Chapter 14

In the magician's land of make-believe and illusion what one doesn't see is always there ... only one doesn't see it until the conjurer is ready to show it. The silks are stuffed within the hollow egg, the flowers collapsed within the palm of his hand; the card concealed on the back of his fingers. But Death is the greatest necromancer of all; in a moment of inattention, he makes his sleight and palms a life, and one does not realize that the breathing figure is gone.

The illusion of life persists ... you listen for the voice in the next room; you await the footsteps coming up the stairs—the well-known, well-beloved ones; you anticipate the turn of a profile in a busy restaurant, the tinkle of a laugh in a bar, the lovely swiftly moving legs on a busy street. The illusion is there still; yesterday has not yet become today. Today must never become tomorrow, because tomorrow will be too late.

Hope lingers on, the last soft breeze in the trees before winter; the last strain of music before silence. It is there before despair wilts completely the last bouquet of make-believe flowers, and Death takes his curtain bow before the black velvet drapes.

The delicate, well-remembered lips brush your cheek in the night, but in the morning, there are only the twisted bedclothes beside you. In your own mind alone the voice remains; only behind your sleeping eyes does the face become reality. In the misery of the endless nights, the wretchedness of the matching days, hope vanishes. Then is the illusion completed! Because only then, is she gone forever....

I didn't lose Tally in the street before the McAndrews that afternoon, nor on Locust Street ... nor on any of the other little Philadelphia streets. She disappeared one night several months later in New York. I was lying on my back, on the sidewalk, in front of a bar on Eighth Avenue; I was lying there because I had been thrown out. I had been thrown out because I had been unable to pay for my drinks—and I couldn't pay for my drinks because I hadn't worked since Philadelphia. Thinking to myself without indignation what a cheap lousy joint to get bounced from, I lay there for a moment looking straight up into the sky. I could see no blue, no stars, no heavens. Only the murky haze ... half translucent, half opaque ... of blue neons and red neons, yellow fluorescents and green fluorescents; white Mazdas and amber General Electrics. They were all there in the murk above the street, mixed into a brown fog of quivering colors. Rolling over slowly on my stomach I pushed myself to my feet and staggered to the building—leaning against it for support. Wretchedly I spewed the cheap liquor back over the building in which I had drunk it.

That was the moment I decided to murder Greenleaf!

In the morning I went to see my agent. I had slept in my clothes for a week, my shirt was as filthy as an oiler's rag; I needed a shave, and I hadn't eaten in ... I don't know ... three or four days. I had to walk to his office as I didn't have the price of a subway ride, and I didn't think I would make it. Each block I was forced to sit down to rest. As I sat on the curbing, panting with exhaustion, passers-by walked around me in a careful antiseptic arc. Eventually I reached his office and I waited outside the door until he appeared.

"Sol," I said, "I want to talk to you." He nodded and opened the cubbyhole, helping me in. He is a little man with a round, compact potbelly. Seating me in a chair by his desk, he gave me a cigarette; the smoke gagged in my raw throat. "You've got to help me," I said.

"Sure, Lew," he replied sympathetically. "I heard about what happened in Philly, I'm sorry ..."

"I need some dough. I'm broke."

"Sure, sure. I understand." His eyes brushed past my filthy clothes to search my face. "You all right now, Lew?"

"Yes," I replied, "I'm all right now."

"You got a good act, Lew. It don't make sense to throw it away. Even ... as a single ... I can keep you going pretty good. You got to lay off drinking, though."

"Sol," I said urgently, his little office swiveling before my eyes while my stomach cramped and crawled, "don't lecture me. Just give me some dough ... let me get out of here!"

"How much you want, Lew?" He reached in his pocket and withdrew a thin, well-worn checkbook.

"I don't know ... whatever you'll trust me for. I need it bad, and it isn't for drinking."

"Sure, sure," Sol agreed heavily. He scribbled a check and handed it to me. "Two hundred enough?"

"Thanks," I said, folding the check and stuffing it in my pocket. Swaying to my feet, I held onto the desk. "Now I can get back in my hotel room."

"When are you coming back to work?" he asked.

"I don't know," I told him truthfully, "I've got something important to do first. But in case I don't come back, I'll see you get the dough."

"Forget it, Lew," Sol replied, "it's for old times' sake...."

A hot shower washes away many sins—at least the sins of dirt, grime, and grease. Back at the hotel, I showered, shaved, and slept the clock around. The following morning, in fresh clothes, I forced some breakfast into my protesting stomach. Although I was still lightheaded and couldn't concentrate for very long, I began planning to get Green-leaf. And each successive day, I continued to think about it, weighing the probabilities, considering the possibilities. Little by little, day after day, the idea began to go together. My most urgent problem, however, was money which I needed to complete my plans. And I needed it quickly. The money Sol had given me, after paying my hotel bill, left very little.

There was one fast way to get funds, and I decided to take it, although it was a dangerous and calculated risk. As soon as I felt better, and the shakes had left my hands, I looked up Max the bell captain. Tipping him, I said, "I've got a friend coming in from the sticks in a day or two. He likes a little action. Know where there's a game?"

"Craps?"

"No. Poker ..."

Max gave it to me straight. "Sure this guy's a friend of yours?"

"Absolutely," I replied.

"I know a game, but a stranger might get hurt. Particularly, if there's any fast dealing. The mug who runs it ain't no Union Leaguer."

I shrugged. "I can't guarantee this guy's morals," I replied. "But he's been around. I kind of figure it's up to him." I stared straight back at Max.

Max lit a cigarette. "What the hell," he said, "it's no skin off my ass. What's this guy's name?"

"Tom Murphy," I said. "His father's name was Tom Murphy, and his grandfather's ..."

"Yeah, I know," interrupted Max, "his name was Tom Murphy, too."

"I don't know how you guessed it, but you did."

"Okay. Tell Tom Murphy to ask for Jack at the cigar store. Tell him, I sent him." Max described a small tobacco shop, near Times Square. "Ask for Jack before nine-thirty any night. The game starts at ten ... it's a floater. Jack'll tell him where it's going to be."

The next night I contacted Jack. With the last fifty dollars in my pocket, I sat in a seven-handed game of dealer's choice, in the back room of a shoe store. It was a typical minor league, floating game. A consumptive and dangerous Greek named Steve operated it, taking a small percentage drag out of each pot. The other players were a used car dealer from the Bronx, a small restaurant owner, two out-of-town-ers attending a convention, a radio director, and a traveling salesman.

I played carefully and cautiously ... not being able to afford any losses, and I played it straight. When the game broke up about four in the morning, I was seventy dollars to the good. For my purpose, the amount was just about right. It wasn't too much ... large enough to cause comment ... and yet Steve noticed it.

During the next two weeks, I sat in Steve's game every night; we played in hotel rooms, garages, back rooms of restaurants, record shops, haberdasheries, barber shops, antique stores, and any other place where an owner was willing to pick up a fast twenty bucks for the use of his premises. The players came and went; new faces every night—except mine. The Greek, of course, didn't care who won as his take was a fixed percentage from each pot. However, to be careful, I deliberately lost small amounts on two occasions, and indirectly brought it to his attention. At the end of two weeks, I was about five hundred dollars to the good.

One night, when the game had broken up, I said to Steve, "How about grabbing some breakfast at the automat?" He agreed and we walked down Broadway to Times Square. At the table, I put it right to him. "I want to make some dough, fast! I'd like to sit in a big league game...."

Steve ate his Danish pastry without replying. When he had completely finished, he wiped his lips on a paper napkin. "You play a pretty good game. You make a little dough. What you want to lose it for?"

"I don't think I'll lose it," I said.

Steve shrugged. "Maybe not. But that's what they all think."

"All right," I said, "so I lose it. It's my dough. But if I win you get 10 per cent off the top."

The Greek's eyes swiveled around to meet mine. He stared for a minute, then dropped them indifferently. "You're pretty eager," he said obliquely.

I agreed. "There's a good thing I can get a piece of on the West Coast. It's not going to be open forever. I either get some dough, quick, or forget it." I kept my voice expressionless. "You've got contacts, you know where the big game is ... get me in it. I'll make it right."

"You said 10 per cent."

"That's it."

He looked over my shoulder, not seeing me. "Maybe I can do something," he said. Abruptly he returned his attention. "How much dough you got going in?"

"Half a yard," I said.

"Not enough."

Now came the gimmick. This was the important pitch. He was right; with only five hundred dollars going into a big game, I couldn't hold down a chair. "Okay, Steve," I said, "I need some front money. You lend me another five hundred, and I give you another 10 per cent."

"No dice. My five on the bottom, not playing." What he meant was that I'd bet my own five hundred dollars, and leave his on the table for show. If I lost my five, I'd cash in the chips for his money and return it.

"All right," I agreed reluctantly, "show and no play, but I'll only pay you 5 per cent on it."

Steve arose from the table, pushing back the metal chair. "I'll see what I can get going," he said.

Three nights later, the Greek gave me the nod for the big game. It was held in the suite of a midtown hotel, located on the plush East side belt. Steve was with me for a number of reasons: to get me in, to watch his money, and to collect his 15 per cent of any winnings. The drawing room of the suite was smartly and impersonally decorated with a false fireplace, huge antiqued mirrors, and weirdly designed modern lamps. A large oblong table had been arranged in the center of the room and covered with a piece of heavy green felt. Around the table were five players in addition to myself. Steve wasn't playing and he sat carefully to one side, away from the table where he could see no cards except mine. Half a dozen hard-faced men lounged around the room watching the game. The place quickly became blanketed with smoke notwithstanding the air-conditioning unit which was operating at top speed.

It was a strict game of five card draw with the deck and deal changing hands after each pot. Chips were twenty-five, fifty, and a hundred dollars. Who the other players were, I don't know; no one identified himself. But they were all experts.

As the hours crept by, I took it easy. By two o'clock we'd been playing over three hours—just long enough for everyone to be getting a little tired, a little slow with the eyes, a little slow with the reflexes. From the beginning of the game, I'd watched carefully and had detected no phony dealing. Unobtrusively, I checked the cards, at every opportunity, and could find no markings of any kind. The decks, six in all, were alternated regularly and in no particular order. The game looked to me like it was strictly on the square. There had been quite a bit of action with some big pots of three and four grand in them. Several of the original players had lost heavily and checked out; they had been replaced from the silent group of men watching the game.

I had been playing my cards pretty close to the vest and was a little to the good, and I continued to nurse along my chips, holding on, waiting for a break to come. In every game at some time, such a break occurs—either for good or for bad.

One of the original players was a heavily jowled man, with a broken nose, and black hair which he parted and combed in the middle. He'd won a few good pots during the game and had been betting his cards carefully, and dropping out often. As the night wore on, I kept getting a hunch about the fellow which I couldn't place. I continued to watch him; his hands were quick and sure; his heavy face impassive.

And then it came!

Heavy Jowls shuffled and offered the deck to be cut at his right. Casually picking it up with his left hand, his right hand covered the deck for a split second, and in that instant—with one hand—he completed the Ednase shift. It was done, literally, in the blink of an eye—and even then I couldn't have sworn he had done it. The Ednase is one of the fastest, smoothest gambling shifts in the world reversing the cut deck to its original position, and means just one thing. The dealer has stacked the deck.

This was what I had been waiting for. When I picked up my hand, I held three 8's and a pair of Queens. A full house. The betting opened and went around the table with four raises. Heavy Jowls had really set up his marks. Making my ante and raise, I sat there trying to figure out what Heavy Jowls held for himself. The other players called for their cards ... dealer's left asked for two, which indicated three of a kind; the next player stood pat, which might mean a full house, a straight, or a flush; the player to my right took one ... probably drawing to two pair. One thing was certain, in a stacked deck, the sequence is determined; it is important; break the sequence and you cause trouble. I discarded my three 8's and asked for three cards. The tiniest, almost invisible, twitch of surprise touched Heavy Jowls; he had planned for me to stand pat, too. The player to my left drew two.

Heavy Jowls, himself, checked his draw. At that point, I thought I had him pegged. He was holding four of a kind, and probably he would not bother to hold four extremely high cards ... it wouldn't be necessary to do so, in order to beat out a full house or a flush.

Picking up my new cards, I looked into a Queen, and a 6 and 9 of Spades. The Queen and 6 had obviously been intended for the player to my left, as I had not been expected to draw.

Heavy Jowls knew that I was holding three Queens, a 6 and 9 of Spades—which was a weaker hand than I held originally. We were using a blue Bicycle deck.

As a rule, the packs used in professional gambling games are Bicycle Brand playing cards printed with medium-colored red and blue back designs. These cards have become traditional ... probably because they are very difficult to mark successfully. I'd come to the game with a load, both a red and a blue pack concealed under my coat, the cards distributed according to suit and number over my body. This was simple; I'd been doing it in my act for years.

I stole the fourth Queen from my load, and palmed away the 6 of Spades while the original opener made his first bet. The second man bet and raised, while the original opener checked out; the man to my right dropped out; I met and raised; the player to my left dropped; and Heavy Jowls met and raised.

This left only Heavy Jowls, the man second to his left, and me in the game. Obviously Heavy Jowls held four of a kind; the man to his left held a flush, as I had been set up originally with a full house. We raised around again, and the flush had folded. Heavy Jowls and I stared at each other across the table. I now had seven hundred dollars of my own money in the pot. Squarely in the middle, that was me. Heavy Jowls raised two hundred and fifty; I met it and called. Behind me, I could hear Steve's angry breathing as I had taken the two hundred and fifty dollars of call money from his chips.

Heavy Jowls held four 5's.

I held four Queens!

Impassively, he pushed the pot to me. He knew ... and I knew, but he couldn't say anything. Picking up my hand, I palmed out the extra Queen, sleighted in the missing Spade, and mixed them into the rest of the discards. Heavy Jowls lit a cigarette. "Your face looks familiar," he said. "Are you a friend of Bill's?" His voice was offhand.

"Yeah," I said. "I know him well." That was the tipoff, of course—the round-the-world introduction of professional gamblers.

Heavy Jowls shrugged. "Haven't seen him lately," he said.

The game broke up about an hour later. I tried no more killings, playing the game straight, and stalling to protect my winnings. Walking out of the hotel, I was about three thousand five hundred dollars to the good. I peeled off seven hundred dollars ... making it 20 per cent for the Greek, and returned his five hundred show money. He grunted, and shoved it in his pocket. "I didn't like for you to use my show money," he said.

"You unhappy now?" I asked.

"No, but it wasn't part of the agreement." He pulled his gray soft hat down firmly on his head and signaled a cab. For just a moment he hesitated before getting in the door. "It was a good night," he said softly, then climbing into the taxi, he added, "but card mechanics don't live long."

"I've had it," I said.

He rode off down the street.

In my pocket, including my winnings and my original stake, was a little more than three thousand dollars.

Enough dough to get Greenleaf.

Chapter 15

"Your name," asked Cannon, "is Gerald Lightbody. Is that correct?"

"Yes, sir." Lightbody identified himself as the superintendent of a small apartment building approximately half a block down the street from the house on East Eighty-ninth. He stated further under examination by

Cannon that he worked approximately two hours each day in the brownstone. Early in the morning, he would check and fire the furnace and at that same time set out the trash cans for collection. Then later in the morning, he would return and put the cans back in the basement. In the evenings, before retiring, once again he would check the furnace, remove the ashes, and fire it for the night.

"You've been in and out of the furnace room many times. Are you very familiar with it?" asked Cannon.

"Yes, sir," agreed Lightbody. "Know it as well as my own face."

"Before the night of November twenty-second, last year, and the next time you saw the furnace room—several days later—were there any things missing? Familiar objects which usually were in that room?"

"Yes. There was a heavy wooden bench, and a piece of canvas about eight feet square...."

"All right." Cannon thought a moment. "About the bench, what was it used for?"

"Sort of a workbench. Pound and nail things on it," replied Lightbody.

"Was it strong enough to support the weight of a man?"

"Yes, sir," testified Lightbody. "I've sat on it myself and smoked a cigarette."

"Was it long enough for you to lie down?"

"Just about. Never tried it, though."

"Now, about the canvas tarpaulin, what was it used for?" asked the prosecuting attorney.

"To put down on the floor, when there was a little painting to be done— so paint and turpentine didn't spill around and get all over things."

"And after November twenty-second, Mr. Lightbody," Cannon emphasized his words, "you never saw either the bench or the canvas again."

"That's right," Lightbody testified.

"Very clear," said Cannon. "Now those duties, which you told about, took only a few hours of your time. They did not in any way conflict with your other job at the apartment house?"

"No, sir." Lightbody was a small wiry man with heavy shoulders and large red hands. "Matter of fact, a lot of supers maybe hold a couple other little jobs like that...."

"Were you ever asked, or expected, to do other chores?"

"Well ... yes. Not very often, and they didn't amount to much. I usually kept the sidewalks and steps swept up. And once in a while, I'd fix something in the house ... plumbing, or an electrical outlet ... when it went wrong. Simple things like that."

"On these different occasions when you were around the house, did you ever see Isham Reddick?"

"Sure. I saw him a lot of times."

"Did you ever talk with him?"

"Yes. I talked with him quite a bit."

"Did Isham Reddick ever offer to help you with any of the chores you might be doing?"

"No, sir. Not exactly. He'd hang around and smoke a cigarette, and sometimes put out a hand to brace the ladder ... things along that line. But he didn't believe in getting his hands dirty, that man didn't! If you ask me, he thought he was too good for the job!"

"Did he ever tell you that, Mr. Lightbody?"

"He sure did. He put on a lot of airs ... well, like smoking Congress cigarettes. Special cigarettes they were, cost thirty-five cents a pack. And believe me, on his salary he couldn't afford 'em."

"Objection," Denman stated.

"Sustained. Strike out the last statement of the witness," directed the judge.

"Please continue, Mr. Lightbody," Cannon suggested.

"Well, this one time I came over to put in a little pane of glass which had been broken, and me and the missus was going out later. To see some of her relations across town, and I was dressed up. It was on a Sunday, and I hadn't a chance to get my pay check cashed, and I needed some money. I asked Reddick if he would loan me five bucks until Monday—when I'd get to the bank to get my check cashed. Reddick laughs and says sure, he'd lend me as much dough as I wanted. He pulled out a roll of bills and hands me a twenty! While he was doing this, he keeps laughing and I guess he didn't notice that an envelope fell out of his pocket. I picked this envelope up and hand it to him, noticing that a bunch of figures are written on it. Reddick takes the envelope, wads it up, and tosses it away on the steps to the entryway ... where I was working."

"Did Reddick say anything to you at that time?"

"Well, I thanked him for the loan and he told me to forget it ... real offhand like he was a big shot. It sort of raised my hair, and I said it was nice to know one rich man, anyhow."

"What did Isham Reddick reply to that?"

"He said he was rich, and soon he'd be richer."

"Let me get this straight, please, Mr. Lightbody. Isham Reddick said he was rich, and soon he'd be richer. Is that correct?"

"Yes, sir," agreed Lightbody.

"All right, please continue. What happened next?"

"Reddick went back into the house, and I finished up the job. As I was walking down the steps, I saw the wadded-up envelope laying on the stairs where Reddick had thrown it. It didn't look good there, so I picked it up. There wasn't any wastepaper container around, so I just stuffed it in my pocket and took it home to throw it away. When I got there, my missus wanted to leave right away—and I forgot all about it, until later." Lightbody paused for breath, then continued. "The next week the missus went through my pockets to send the suit to the cleaners. She found the envelope and showed it to me; she asked if I wanted to keep it, as she thought it belonged to me...."

"When your wife found the envelope, what did she say to you, Mr. Lightbody?"

"She said, 'Is this anything important'?"

"What did you reply?"

"I replied that I didn't know what it was. I asked to see it, then I looked at it and saw the list of figures, and remembered Reddick had thrown it away. So then I said, 'No, this isn't important. I'll get rid of it.' I tossed it on top of the desk where I keep my old bills and receipts and stuff, and intended to throw it away. But it just slipped my mind until the police started asking me questions."

"When the police came to talk to you, you suddenly remembered the envelope with the figures on it, and you gave it to the authorities, is that right, Mr. Lightbody?"

"Yes, sir. That's exactly what happened."

Cannon held up an envelope, badly wrinkled, and handed it to Lightbody. "Is this the same envelope you picked up, after Isham Reddick had thrown it away?"

Lightbody inspected it carefully, then nodded. "Yes, sir. This is the same one. The cops asked me to mark it ... right here." He pointed to his initials in a corner.

"Thank you, Mr. Lightbody," said Cannon. Turning toward the jury, he said, "I'm now going to read the figures on this envelope and offer it into evidence. On one side of the envelope is the name of Isham Reddick, his address, together with stamp and postmark. The name and address are typewritten, and there are no return name and address, on the envelope. On the reverse side are six amounts ... figures written in a pencil. These figures are listed one beneath the other, and the first figure is preceded by a dollar sign." Cannon held the envelope before him and read:

$$\begin{aligned}
&\$1{,}000.00\\
&1{,}800.00\\
&2{,}000.00\\
&4{,}000.00\\
&6{,}600.00\\
&\underline{8{,}500.00}
\end{aligned}$$

"Beneath the last figure of $8,500.00 a line is drawn, but no total is entered. If you should care to know the total, I believe the figures make $23,900.00. Also, by the side of the figures, are the words, written in pencil 'and more to come.'" Cannon handed the envelope to the jury for examination.

Turning back to Lightbody, Cannon said, "There's one other point regarding which I would like to ask you some questions. You heard Miss Deems testify that on the evening of November twenty-second, Isham Reddick told her that the defendant, here, had instructed him to inform the help that they could have the night off, as well as the following day. Did you have a similar discussion with Reddick?"

"Yes, sir. The phone rang ..."

"At what time, Mr. Lightbody ... and the date please?"

"It was the early evening and we were just sitting down to dinner— about six o'clock. It was the evening of November twenty-second. Isham Reddick called to tell me the boss said not to bother about the furnace as it was so warm, and to take the next day off as he was going out of town."

"So you didn't go back to tend the fire that night of November twenty-second, or the morning of the twenty-third ... as you normally would?"

"No, sir. Reddick said to tell my wife the same thing about cleaning. And I told her."

Cannon excused Lightbody from the stand, and Denman reserved the right to cross-examine the witness later. The prosecuting attorney then recalled Alvin Hartney, the handwriting expert, to the witness chair. "Mr. Hartney," Cannon addressed him, "you have examined this exhibit," Cannon handed him the envelope with the figures, "is that not correct?"

"Yes, sir," replied Hartney.

"You have also examined other identified specimens of Isham Reddick's handwriting ... a note which he wrote to a garage, a post card he once sent to Miss Deems, and other samples of his writing?"

"That is true. I have examined them carefully."

"Is the writing on the envelope written by the same hand which wrote the garage notation, Miss Deems' card, and the other identified specimens of Isham Reddick's handwriting?"

"The writing is the same."

"You can say without any doubt in your mind that Isham Reddick wrote the figures, and the other words, on the back of the envelope?"

"Yes, sir." Hartney was certain.

Cannon turned the witness over to Denman. The attorney for the defense took up his cross-examination. He carried his heavy horn-rimmed glasses in his hand, tapping them thoughtfully. "I've always understood, Mr. Hartney, that it's more difficult to identify figures than characters of the alphabet. Is that correct?"

"Well ... to some degree."

"Will you explain 'some degree'?"

"Figures are usually written more uniformly than letters of the alphabet."

"I see. Now ... in looking over the list of figures written on the back of this envelope, I find examples of the figures: 1, 2, 4, 5, 6, 8, and 0. The figures, or numerals, 3-7-9 are missing. On the post card which Isham Reddick wrote to Miss Deems there is the house address using the numerals 3 and 7 ... and of course the numerals for Eighty-ninth Street. The only figure then ... *in common* ... between the envelope and the post card is the figure 8! Do you mean to tell me, Mr. Hartney," Denman demanded scathingly, "that you can determine ... *without doubt* ... on the basis of just one numeral?"

"There were other reasons," replied Hartney.

"What reasons? Certainly no more numerals! On the note to the garage, Isham Reddick simply scribbled a reply on the back of the bill. I'll read you his reply, and point out that it was undated. He wrote: 'This bill was paid day before yesterday.'" Denman paused, then continued, "Well, I'm waiting for an answer to my question. What are the other reasons?"

"On the envelope he added the words 'and more to come.'"

Denman repeated the words "and more to come," satirically. "In his post card to Miss Deems, Reddick simply said: 'See you soon. Home tomorrow.'" He paused, and then asked deliberately, "On the basis of his signature, the words: 'this bill was paid day before yesterday,' 'see you soon, home tomorrow,' and, of course, the single numeral number 8, you can identify the handwriting?"

"Yes, sir," Hartney replied definitely. "The words may be different, but the letters are the same."

"I'm not talking about letters," Denman interrupted. "I'm talking about numerals. The only numerals you know definitely Reddick ever wrote are 3, 7, 8, and 9. So how can you possibly tell me that he wrote the rest?"

"Yes, it's possible," Hartney retorted angrily. "He wrote other numerals, too!"

Suddenly, Denman remembered. Quickly, he dismissed the witness. Hartney looked mutely at the judge, and began slowly to rise from his chair. The judge watched him carefully, then said, "It is the duty of this court to discover the truth. I wish to put a question to the witness. Mr. Hartney, you have just said that Isham Reddick wrote other figures. Will you please tell the court what other figures he wrote, and where you saw them?"

Hartney looked straight up toward the judge. "Yes, your honor," he said. "When Isham Reddick made out his chauffeur's application, he wrote his age, height, and weight ... and in these figures are included 1, 3, 5, 6, and 7. This gave me the numerals 1, 5, 6, and 8 in common between his identified handwriting and the figures on the envelope. These are more than sufficient."

"Thank you, Mr. Hartney," said the judge. Hartney left the stand. Denman ignored him, and asked permission to recall Gerald Lightbody. When Lightbody was seated, Denman considered him carefully. The attorney for the defense was uneasy. The evidence which in his opinion was at best highly circumstantial was, however, slowly tightening around his client. Evidence which should show, somewhere, a wide crack ... and into which he could drive a wedge ... seemed to become more solid as he attacked it. Denman hunched his lean figure forward, picking his way carefully, attempting to discredit Lightbody's testimony by establishing the witness's hostility.

"Mr. Lightbody, you testified in your own words that Isham Reddick 'didn't like to get his hands dirty.' Is that right?"

"That's right. He sure didn't!"

"In other words, Mr. Lightbody, because Isham Reddick wouldn't do the work you were paid to do, you thought of him as not wanting to get his hands dirty?"

"Well ..."

"Did Isham Reddick ever ask you to do his work?"

"No," replied the superintendent.

"But you still prefer to sneer at Reddick? Tell me," Denman's voice was casual, "do you like to bowl?"

"Yes," agreed Lightbody, guardedly, "I bowl a little."

"And you go to an occasional movie?"

"Yes."

"Perhaps a ball game ... now and then?"

"Once in a while ..."

"So," Denman summed up, "you bowl, you go to movies, you see an occasional ball game. You spend an optional fifty cents here, a dollar there. Perhaps a couple of dollars, but you like to do it. Is that right?"

Lightbody squirmed uneasily. "Well ... once in a while ..."

Denman's voice cut in quickly. "It's all right for you to enjoy your pleasures, but when Isham Reddick spent ten or twelve cents extra for a package of cigarettes, because he liked them, because he bought Congress cigarettes, you accuse him of putting on airs. What standards do you use to measure people, Mr. Lightbody?"

Lightbody cleared his throat and crossed his legs uneasily. "Well ..."

"Another question, if you please! It's Sunday, and you don't have any money. It's your own fault, because you have a check ... but you don't get it cashed. You ask Isham Reddick to lend you five dollars. Reddick is pleasant and generous. Instead of giving you five dollars, he gives you twenty dollars! You said it raised your hair ... and not only are you not grateful to your friend, but you try to read a sinister motive into the situation. Isn't that right?"

Lightbody, now red in the face and angry, shook his head. "No!" he shouted.

"What do you mean ... no? In one breath you say Isham Reddick is laughing, and in the next breath you infer that he isn't joking when he says he is going to be rich soon." Denman realized that he was on a treadmill. He had no interest in painting Reddick as a friendly sympathetic character ... other than to prove his client had no motive to kill him. At best, he was only leading Lightbody to give a wretched performance before the jury. Always, of course, there was the possibility the witness might lose his temper. Denman kept plugging at him, "So Reddick befriends you, helps you, lends you money—and in return you attempt to besmirch him in every way?"

"You didn't know him!" shouted Lightbody. "Sometimes you'd a thought he was head of the whole house. But not when the boss was around ... then he'd crawl and bow around just as pretty as you please. Even that night he called me. 'You don't need to make the fire tonight. Take tomorrow off, too,' he says. Why, you'd a thought it was a paid vacation he was giving me. It didn't mean anything at all! There hadn't been a fire in the house for a couple days anyway, because it was so warm!"

Denman, who had turned away, suddenly swung around and faced Lightbody. "Did I understand you to say, that there had been no fire in the house for several days? And there was none on the twenty-second of November?"

"That's what I said," Lightbody replied, sullenly.

"Isn't it odd that Reddick should call you, deliberately, to tell you not to bother with the fire ... when there was no fire?" Denman felt a rising surge of excitement. Perhaps he had finally found a thread; without knowing where it might lead, he would attempt to unwind it. "Did Reddick know there was no fire?"

"Sure, he knew it, but that was his way ... just trying to be a big shot." Suddenly Lightbody dashed Denman's hopes. "It was just Reddick's way of putting it. He didn't have no authority to say nothing, unless the boss told him to." Lightbody shifted his eyes toward the defendant, then quickly moved them away.

Chapter 16

Three thousand bucks ... well, it was enough to get started after Greenleaf. During the days and nights, while I was getting back on my feet, I had thought of nothing else. I'd lie on my bed in the hotel room and think about him—trying to draw his face into focus. I never could do it; I couldn't even pretend. Always I would see his figure—the body of a man with a blank face. It reminded me of the paper cut-out dolls which have figures completely clothed with hands and feet ... but no face. You slipped the clothes over another little body with a face, and then the doll was complete.

Only one person I knew of had known what Greenleaf looked like; that was old Will Shaw and he was dead. Only one person I had known might possibly have recognized his voice; Tally. And she was dead, too.

Lying on the bed, I'd watch the room grow dark. Far below, the lights of the city would climb up the side of the building and crawl over the sill, inching their way stealthily up the walls. I'd lie on my back and watch the shadows flitting and flickering on the ceiling while the rest of the room remained in darkness. My mind would pick at the identity of Greenleaf, pawing and worrying the few bits of information I had concerning him.

At first, I couldn't concentrate very long; my mind would wander away and all could think was "Greenleaf ... Greenleaf," over and over. But it didn't mean very much, because the word itself had no substance. I could just as well have been thinking "Atlantic ... Atlantic" or "Pacific ... Pacific." Suddenly, something would snap in my mind, and for a few minutes I could concentrate very hard and think very clearly. The ball of hate would roll around in my stomach until I could stand it no longer. I had quit drinking, so I'd go in the bath and draw a glass of water and sip it while I smoked a cigarette. In the dark the cigarette lost its taste and only the ember on its end would tell me it was alight. The glowing eye of it burning red to match my own hatred.

Over the days, and the weeks, certain things began to fall into place. Not all at once, but little by little. Obviously, of course, Greenleaf was not his correct name, but an alias. And an alias, unfortunately, which he had especially assumed in his relations with the old man. Greenleaf was a confidence man ... the select, the aristocracy of the criminal world. He was far more intelligent, more cunning, more shrewd than the average criminal. Greenleaf was a new and assumed name, and one that would have absolutely no criminal record.

Secondly, he was utterly ruthless ... a killer opportunist, rather than a premeditating murderer. Possibly the act of murder was distasteful to him; it might explain his selection of death by falling and accident ... rather than by a lethal weapon. On this point, of course, I could not be sure; it was merely conjecture.

Lastly, I felt that Greenleaf worked alone. Most confidence men prefer to do so, except where a confederate is needed to arrange and color a specific situation. There have been instances where a number of con men ... half a dozen to a dozen ... have all worked together to pull off a big setup; but this is the exception. With trusting, old Will Shaw, he needed no help.

Undoubtedly, though, somewhere Greenleaf had one other man ... a printer. He had to have a printer, and a good one, to print the false plates. This, however, was not unusual either. Every man in the confidence game has criminal printing connections somewhere; the con men need printers to make up phony letter heads, phony bill heads, fake stock certificates; worthless bond issues, and all the rest of the paper they hang. So, Greenleaf had a printer—someone to print up the beautiful authentic fives, tens, and twenties.

There was another point which was difficult to determine. Was Greenleaf passing the queer himself, or was he wholesaling it? A counterfeit wholesaler will buy up the queer money at ten cents on the dollar; resell it to passers for another markup; the passers, in turn, pass it as money and keep the difference. If Greenleaf was wholesaling it, I might never find him. If, however, he was passing it, himself, I might be able to catch him. After thinking about it for a long time, I finally decided Greenleaf was passing it personally. Although wholesaling is faster, and makes a buck easier, it is far more dangerous! Because tremendous sums of counterfeit dough will hit different cities at the same time, the chances of its detection increase as the queer money passes through more banks and is seen by more tellers. This in turn adds up to the phony bills being detected more quickly by the Treasury men. With beautiful plates, such as Greenleaf had, he might go on safely for years, passing the money himself. With care not to flood the market, he could live forever ... like a millionaire. Making only a split with his printer, Greenleaf would have no fear of other partners, wholesalers, and passers being picked up, possibly for another and entirely different crime, and squealing to the cops. It seemed logical to me that Greenleaf would pass the money himself.

After I had the money from the poker game, I went to see Dave Sherz. Dave operated an investigation and detective agency; before that, he had been captain of a squad of private guards protecting the wheel in a gambling house in Nevada. I'd worked there one season, a long time back, and knew Sherz from those days.

He remembered me and gave me a hearty handshake. "Sit down, Lew," he said. "How've things been going?"

"So, so, Dave," I looked around the office. "Where are the walnut-paneled walls, the oversexed secretary, and the dead bodies?"

Dave laughed. "You been watching too many movies," he said. He yawned, stretched his arms above his head, and leaned back in his chair—planting his feet on the desk. "This business is so quiet," he said, "I go to church baking sales just for the excitement."

"No murders?" I asked pretending surprise.

"Hell no. The cops would run us off, anyway. Nothing but suspicious husbands, more suspicious wives, and a few insurance investigations...."

"Well," I suggested slowly, "perhaps you'd be interested in trying to dig up something for me."

"I'm interested in digging up anything, including flowers," he replied.

"You kept up with the bunco boys?" I asked. Back in the Reno days, one of Sherz's jobs had been to watch for sharpers, con men, and known criminals to keep them out of the club.

"Some," he said. "After I blew Reno, I hired on in Las Vegas and I've been in business for myself the last few years. Anyone you interested in particularly?"

"Just one guy," I told him. "His name is Greenleaf which may be real, but I doubt it. I don't know what he looks like, where he came from, what's his background ... or anything else that's going to be very helpful."

"That ain't much," said Dave.

"The only other thing I have on him is that he was hanging around Philadelphia about a year ago. He was still in Philly up to a few months ago. He had a checking account in a bank there; what bank, I don't know. He signed checks which cleared using the name Greenleaf. I have no idea where he lived, or what his initials were."

"And that's all?"

"That's all."

"I can't place the name. Never heard of anybody in the bunco business named Greenleaf. I can check the police records for the name or alias."

"Okay," I agreed.

"Also I got a few respectable connections because of my insurance tie-ups. I might be able to find something on the checking account in Philadelphia, although I can't guarantee it. Would that be of any help?"

"Anything would help," I assured him.

"I'll get on it," Dave said. He took his feet off the desk, and shook a cigarette out of a pack. Lighting it, he asked, "Any reason for me to know why you're interested in Greenleaf?"

"No," I replied, "there's not the slightest reason."

He shrugged. "Soon as I have anything, I'll call you."

I took out several bills, placing them on his desk. "Whatever the balance is, let me know."

Dave grinned. "For old times' sake, Lew, that's enough. Unless I have to hire a couple dog sleds for Alaska."

There was another point which I had been thinking about; it might mean something—or nothing, but it wasn't anything on which Dave could help me. However, a professor at Columbia University could; his name was Thurman Simons and he was a professor of Romance languages. Professor Simons was fluent in Italian, Spanish, French, and Portuguese. In addition to these, he was pretty handy with German, Dutch, and a few other assorted tongues. I called the professor on the phone, making an appointment to meet him the following day after classes. To my surprise, Simons was a comparatively young man ... short, pudgy, and with brown colorless hair. He wore green sunglasses with pink plastic rims, and seemed absolutely incapable of sitting still. While we talked, he ran his finger around his collar, brushed his hair with the palms of his hands, nervously adjusted his sunglasses, shifted his position clockwise around the chair, smoked incessantly, and when there seemed nothing else to do, tapped the toe of his shoe on the floor.

Sitting down to talk to Simons, I made it clear that I wanted to pay for his services. He waved my offer aside, "If I can help you, I'll be delighted." Patting his hands together nervously, he added, "If you still insist, make a donation in my name to the Red Cross. But perhaps, after all, I can't help you."

"Well," I replied slowly, "it really isn't important ... except in an extremely personal way. You see, Professor," I ad libbed as sincerely as I could, looking him in the eye and being unable to find his gaze behind the green glasses, "my wife died a few months ago. Before she died, she was in ... well, a sort of delirium, and she kept repeating words which sounded like 'loon who ought to.' It meant absolutely nothing to any of us, and perhaps she was only making sounds ... entirely meaningless, but sounding like that. Naturally, a death makes a tremendous impression on a family, and all of us have often wondered if she was trying to tell us something."

"Very sad, Mr. Mountain," Simons said sympathetically, "you have my condolences. I don't know if I can help, but I shall try. Tell me, did your wife speak another language besides English?"

"No. Not that I know of ..."

"Hmmm." The professor flexed his fingers, putting them end to end forming a tent, then collapsed it. "Perhaps she had studied some language while going to school?"

I shook my head. "I honestly don't know, Professor. Perhaps in high school, although she never mentioned it." I paused and added, "The best explanation, after all, might be that she really was saying 'loon who ought to.'"

"Loon who ought to ... loon who ought to?" Professor Simons tilted his head, repeating the phrase with small interjections of sounds and cluckings of his own. Behind his glasses, I would have sworn that his unseen eyes had rolled up in his head. He cocked his head to one side and appeared to be listening to himself. After a very long time, he said, "What you have told me about the phrase 'loon who ought to' very conceivably has been distorted in pronunciation. Perhaps your deceased wife may have given it a wrong accent and possibly ... quite unknowingly ... you have distorted it more." He waved his hands slightly. "Several possibilities come to my mind, the most obvious one being French. The French have a phrase meaning literally 'the one or the other,' and idiomatically meaning 'either.'"

"What is the phrase?" I asked.

"*L'un ou l'autre*," replied Professor Simons. As he pronounced it, the phrase sounded like "lun-ooo-low-tra." "Does that help any?" Simons asked. Once again, in my mind I could hear Tally's voice telling me of her conversation with Greenleaf. He had called following Will Shaw's funeral, demanding the counterfeit plates. Tally frightened, and at the same time angry, denied having them and threatened to turn them over to the Treasury Department if she found them. Greenleaf laughed, reminding her of the checks she had signed. He had said, "I'll pay you for them, or you might prefer another accident in the family." Then possibly, he had added "*l'un ou l'autre*." The meaning of the phrase, as placed in his conversation, was logical: one or the other ... either ... take your pick. I turned to Simons, "I don't suppose we'll ever really know what she meant, Professor. But thanks for your help."

"I've done very little," Simons replied with a deprecatory shake of his head. "I'll think about it some more, and perhaps something else will come to mind. You might call me later in the week."

"Thanks," I replied. Shaking his hand, I said, "I'll drop a check to the Red Cross."

But I didn't call back the professor. After thinking over his suggestion concerning the phrase, I was convinced that he had hit the idiom right in the middle of the accent.

Several days passed before I heard from Dave Sherz. After he called me at the hotel, I dropped around to his office to see him. It didn't appear that he had moved from his chair since the last time I had seen him. Waving me to a seat, he pushed over a photostatic copy of a check. "This print is pretty grainy," he said. "We took it off of a microfilm negative, but it might be one from the guy you're looking for."

I examined it. The check had been written on the Philadelphia Mercantile Bank & Trust Company; it was made out to cash; was for the sum of thirty-five dollars; and had been signed by Derek A. Greenleaf. "We checked the banks pretty carefully," Sherz explained, "and settled on this bird. Other accounts under the name of Greenleaf, which we came across, didn't hold anything when we checked them. Some had been established for a good many years, others had permanent residences. This particular account—the one for Derek Greenleaf—ran for less than a year."

"When did he close it?" I asked.

"He never did, actually. The account was opened with a cash deposit for one thousand dollars. He checked against it regularly with four checks a month, each check for thirty-five dollars. Finally after about six months or so, he just stopped writing checks. One day, he cashed a check for the balance in the account. That was that."

"What address did he give?"

"A number on Spruce Street ..." Sherz checked a small book, and gave it to me. "You familiar with it?" he asked.

"Not that address," I told him, "but I know Spruce." It is a street of cheap rooming houses and light-housekeeping flats filled with a transient, restless population.

"Well," explained Sherz "we looked up this number on Spruce. It was a typical crummy boarding house. The landlady's never heard of anyone named Greenleaf."

"The bank had to send him a statement each month," I said. "What happened to them? Were they returned?"

Dave shrugged impatiently. "I thought of that," he said. "But I suppose in a joint like that boarding house where the landlady had so damned many roomers she can't remember them, all the mail is just tossed out unless there's a forwarding address."

"What did you find out from the police records?"

"Nothing that fits," replied Sherz frankly. "The alias Greenleaf is unknown. Derek as a first name has been used a couple of times, but the times and places are wrong. A real smooth operator named Eddie Jackson, alias Derek Moore, used it in San Francisco. He's still in the can, and has been for three years, in California. Another old timer, Fred Hoskins, once used the name Derek Tone, but ... hell, Hoskins is close to seventy-five years old and he's been going straight down in Birmingham, Alabama. Living with a married son ..."

Picking up my hat, I walked to the door. "It was a good pitch," I said. I felt depressed.

"Lew," Sherz said, "I'm sorry there wasn't more. I didn't want to run up a bill on you. Do you want me to keep after it?"

I shook my head. "This guy is pretty fancy," I said. "Maybe it's the end of the road. If I need some help, I'll let you know."

Back to the paper dolls again. Here and there—a glimpse, a fragment of a pattern, but no man, no person, no face. A man using the name Derek Greenleaf, a con man with a thousand-dollar account in a bank to swing a deal, a man who used French phrases, a man who would kill an old man and a young woman. Today, right now, a man with the means and opportunity to make millions of dollars.

But still no face!

Sometime during the night, while I was asleep, the idea came to me. Subconsciously I worked it out, because in the morning I awakened with the answer. Rolling out of bed, I dressed hurriedly and rushed to Penn Station. There I caught a train to Philadelphia. I had breakfast on the train, and kept going over the idea in my mind. Sherz had told me that Greenleaf used a Spruce Street address when he opened the account in the bank. Greenleaf knew, of course, that the bank took microfilm records of all checks as part of its own accounting system, but it was important to Greenleaf to recover the canceled checks. He needed them for his own protection … to use as a threat against either Will Shaw or Tally. So, when he gave his address as Spruce Street, he had some way of recovering the checks from there.

Dave Sherz had advanced the theory that the landlady probably threw out all the mail that wasn't claimed, or for which she had no forwarding address. This of course was possible, and if it was true made Greenleaf's job of recovering his mail quite simple. All he had to do was take it. Consequently, one had to assume that Greenleaf either lived in the rooming house—under another alias, or he lived close by in the neighborhood where he could pick up the mail without comment!

Arriving in Philadelphia at the Thirtieth Street Station, I telephoned the Mercantile Bank and got through to the personal checking department. I was informed that customer's statements were mailed the fourth of each month. Leaving the station, I took a cab to the address on Spruce Street. Approaching it, I had the driver continue to the corner where I got out. Walking back, I stopped in front of the number. It was a shabby four-story house refaced with imitation brick siding. A door, in need of paint, opened directly from the street into a cramped dark hallway. Overhead a weak light burned within a swirled brown and green glass globe. Against one wall, a heavy table stood beneath a chipped oval mirror. On the table were stacks of advertisements, newspapers, hand bills, and letters. The hallway branched into a Y … one dark corridor leading to the rear of the house, the other forming an extremely steep and narrow stairway to the upper floors. At that moment, footsteps approached from the rear of the corridor and a fat, red-faced woman dressed in a sleazy satin dress came puffing into the hall. She peered at me suspiciously, and in a strident voice asked if I was looking for someone. "Yes," I said politely, "I'd like to see the landlady."

"I'm her," she replied, "and I don't want to buy nothing, and I ain't got no vacant rooms. So in either case, good-by!"

"I'm sorry," I told her. "Your place was recommended to me by a friend of mine ... Derek Greenleaf ..."

"Who you think you're kidding?" she demanded belligerently. "And what you think you're putting over? A little while back, another guy was sneaking around here asking about him. I told him I'd never heard of no Greenleaf and I ain't, neither."

That had been Dave Sherz or one of his men. "Miss," I said, holding my temper in check against the old bag, "I really do need help. I wish you'd listen."

"I don't like cops poking their noses in my business," she replied. "I run a respectable house, and I got a right to my own privacy."

"Yes ... sure ... certainly." I agreed with her. "But I'm not a cop. This is strictly something personal between Greenleaf and me."

"I told you I don't know any Greenleaf!" She turned and started down the corridor.

"Wait!" I said, withdrawing my wallet and taking out two twenties; I held them up so she could see them. "I'll pay for your time, if you'll help me. You're a business woman," I added quickly, "and I imagine you've had deadbeat roomers run out on you without paying their bills."

"Not anymore I don't!" she snorted. "Now they got to pay in advance!" Perhaps I only imagined it, but the suspicion in her eyes dimmed a little.

"This guy Greenleaf owes me some money, and I need it," I said, throwing together a story. "I trusted him on credit ... and he beat me out."

"Your own fault!" she said.

"Not entirely," I explained. "It was really my partner's fault. He advanced the credit. My partner died last week, and I've been trying to find Greenleaf ever since."

"Nobody ever stayed here by that name," she replied. "What'd he look like?"

"I don't know. I never saw him."

"Jesus! How'd you expect me to help you?"

"Well ... think back carefully. For a period of six or seven months, each month about the fifth or sixth day a letter was addressed to this house. It was delivered in the name of Derek A. Greenleaf. Do you remember seeing it?"

"The same letter?" she asked.

"No. It was a different letter each month, but it always came about the same time. It would be in a large, heavy, brown envelope ... perhaps like the banks use."

"And it was made out to a guy named Greenleaf?" She squinted her little pig eyes in thought. "Any letters supposed to have come lately?" she asked.

"I don't think so," I told her. "There's always a possibility of course. But I think they finally stopped coming about five or six months ago."

"I've been running this place for nearly fifteen years," she said, "and mail keeps coming for people I can't even remember. I've gotten in the habit of just running through the mail looking for my own name. I leave the mail there on the table, and the roomers can sort through it themselves." She waddled over to the table, puffing from the exertion, and searched through the pile of letters on its top, looking also among the old ads and newspapers. "There ain't nothing here for any Greenleaf," she announced.

"I think that proves he got it," I told her. "Otherwise, it would still be around ... or you would remember seeing it. Particularly if all six or seven of the envelopes had accumulated." Pausing a moment, I said casually, "If he wasn't living here under an assumed name, then he must have come in to get it. Do you remember anyone who didn't live here— who stopped in pretty regularly? It would be a man, and he would have a good excuse if you talked to him. He probably always showed up during the first week of each month." There was always the possibility that Greenleaf had known one of the roomers who had passed on the mail to him. However, I didn't believe that Greenleaf would disclose his new name to anyone, if he could help it.

"I don't remember no one particularly," the landlady said. "The roomers, here, have friends of their own visiting. I see a lot of people. The only person I could think of wouldn't be the same man, because he was French...."

"What!" I offered her a cigarette which she refused. Lighting one myself, I said, "A Frenchman used to drop around occasionally? What did he want?"

Pursing her lips, she thought carefully. "Come to think of it, he did drop around pretty regular ... and usually sometime after the first of the month. I remember because he was always looking for a room ... asking me for a vacancy. My roomers usually move out on the last day of the month, or the first day ... if they're moving someplace else. This Frenchman would show up a few days too late every time. I recollect now, I told him to come around the last week of the month, but he never did. I never let him a room."

I thought it over. It made sense. Greenleaf evidently knew some French. A con man is always a good actor, and Greenleaf could fake an accent well enough, no doubt, to fool anyone as stupid as the landlady. He timed his visit to pick up the mail; and he was careful to inquire for a room—only when he was quite sure he couldn't get one. Undoubtedly, Greenleaf had no desire to be tied to the Spruce Street address in case anything went wrong with his plans. "What did this man look like?" I asked.

"He was a big man ... taller and thinner than you." The landlady struggled to recall the impressions erased by time. "To tell you the truth," she said, "I didn't pay much attention. Thinking back on it, I'd say he was in his fifties. One thing I do remember though, he had a big nose." She nodded her head for emphasis. "Yes, he had a thin face, with a big nose ... long, too, and gray hair. Dressed real nice."

I handed her the twenty-dollar bills. "Thanks," I said. "You've helped a lot. If you'd go down to the police station and look through some pictures to help identify this man, I'll pay you fifty more."

Her stubby fingers folded the bills into a tiny packet, and stuffed them into the front of her sweaty brassiere. Once again her eyes had become suspicious, and she shook her head angrily. "I won't have no truck with the cops," she replied. "I was just helping you out neighborly. But I don't want nothing to do with the cops!"

Walking down Spruce Street, I felt good. A thin face, a long nose, gray hair, fifty years, tall and lean ... all details added to the paper doll.

Someday, I'd cut the head right off that doll!

Chapter 17

Cannon, spinning the web of his case, was still concerned with the problem of motive. He was confident that he had impressed the jury concerning the *corpus delicti*; the evidence was, in part, circumstantial—but, in his opinion, indisputable. Sometime on the night of November twenty-second, or early in the morning of November twenty-third, a servant known as Isham Reddick had been murdered, his body dismembered and most of it destroyed through cremation in the furnace of the brownstone located on East Eighty-ninth Street. Not all evidence off the crime, however, had been consumed and there remained a severed finger with an identifiable print, a tooth, a handful of ashes, bloodstains on floor, canvas, and bench, a section of human leg bone; in addition to other miscellaneous evidence including the possible murder weapon—a gun and spent bullet, and the dismembering instrument—a bloody hatchet.

Cannon was convinced that he had established the fact of murder, and had identified the victim, as required by law. There remained, however, the motive. Why had the defendant killed Isham Reddick?

No murder is committed without motive unless the murderer is insane, and the defendant in this case, obviously, was not in such condition. There remained to be resolved then the reason behind the murder, and Cannon believed the motive was blackmail. The chauffeur-valet had been blackmailing his employer. Cannon had evidence indicating Reddick had collected nearly twenty-four thousand dollars ... possibly more. Murder has often been done for less! Seeing no letup to his financial bleeding, the defendant had killed his blackmailer.

Regarding this particular point, a key certainly in his case, Cannon had spent much time, much work to buttress his theory. He next introduced three witnesses. The first to take the stand was Miss Beatrice Hyman, a saleswoman employed in a jewelry store located on Fifth Avenue in New York City. "Miss Hyman," said Cannon, "among the effects and possessions in the room of Isham Reddick was found a receipt—a sales slip which you identified as having been made out by yourself."

"Yes, sir. It was a receipt for three hundred and fifty dollars for a wrist watch I sold him."

"When was this?"

"According to the records in the store, it was October seventeenth of last year."

"Now, Miss Hyman," continued Cannon, "I'm going to show you a photograph. Will you please identify it." He handed her a black and white, glossy print.

Beatrice Hyman, a slim, efficient woman, looked at the photograph carefully. "That is the same man to whom I sold the watch," she stated.

"Did he give you his name?"

"He told me his name was Isham Reddick. And I made out the sales record to that name."

"Now, you have testified that Isham Reddick purchased a wrist watch for three hundred and fifty dollars. Do you consider that an expensive watch?"

"Objection," said Denman rising to his feet. "That calls for an opinion." The court upheld him.

"Miss Hyman," Cannon continued undisturbed, "do you sell many three-hundred-and-fifty-dollar wrist watches?"

"Not many," replied the saleswoman.

"Do many of your customers spend a month-and-a-half salary to purchase a wrist watch?"

Denman objected again, but this time Cannon argued his point. Addressing the judge, he said, "I do not feel that this answer calls for an opinion. Miss Hyman has been selling watches, in this shop, for several years. As a saleswoman, it is part of her job to determine, within limits, what a prospective customer can afford, or will spend."

"But she does not know the financial background of each customer," Denman took exception.

The judge considered the arguments. Finally, he said, "Proceed, Mr. Cannon, but cautiously."

Cannon returned to the witness. "Many of your customers ... the persons who visit your store ... are wealthy, or at least well-to-do?"

"Yes, I believe so," Miss Hyman replied clearly.

"Do you have many customers of very little money?"

"No, sir,"

"Now, if a man earned two hundred and fifty dollars a month, and bought a three-hundred-and-fifty-dollar wrist watch from you, would you think he was purchasing an expensive watch?"

"Under those circumstances, yes."

"You have less expensive watches to sell, do you not, Miss Hyman?"

"We have some watches starting at seventy-seven dollars; those are our least expensive ones, although they are still excellent watches."

"Did you show any of the seventy-seven-dollar watches to Isham Reddick?"

"As I recall, sir, I did. I also showed him some at one hundred and fifty dollars, as well as two hundred and seventy-five dollars. But the one he wanted was priced at three hundred and fifty."

"He paid for it in cash?"

"It was in cash. And it must been in large bills."

"Why do you believe the payment was in large bills?"

"Well," Miss Hyman explained, "most of our customers have charge accounts. Some of them pay cash, occasionally, and when they do it is usually with bills of large denomination. If Mr. Reddick had paid three hundred and fifty dollars in small bills, it would have made a good-sized pile of money—and I would have remembered it."

"And you don't remember Isham Reddick giving you a large number of bills?"

"No, sir. I don't. It was an ordinary transaction for us." She paused, then added, "It was half a dozen bills at the most."

"One final question," said Cannon. "Do you sell many threehundred-and-fifty-dollar watches to chauffeurs?"

"I wouldn't say we do," replied Miss Hyman. Cannon excused the witness, but Denman kept her on the stand for cross-examination.

"Miss Hyman," he addressed her politely, "do you ask strange customers when they come into your store, what they do for a living?"

"Of course not!"

"If I walked into your store, and happened to be ... say, an engineer on a subway train, would you say to me, 'What do you do for a living?'"

"No, sir."

"Or possibly, Miss Hyman, you can tell at a glance what a man does for a living? If I walked into your store, you could take one glance at me and say, 'That man is a subway engineer'?"

"That isn't correct," replied Miss Hyman angrily.

"Then how did you know Isham Reddick was a chauffeur? Was he wearing a uniform?"

"No, sir. He wasn't wearing a uniform, and I didn't know what he did. I wasn't particularly interested, either."

"Then how did you find out he was a chauffeur?"

"Mr. Cannon told me, when he talked to me."

"So, until Mr. Cannon told you, you didn't know anything about Isham Reddick. As far as you know, you have sold watches, diamonds, and other expensive jewelry to chauffeurs—without knowing it!" He added, "If they weren't wearing uniforms. Is that correct?"

"I—I guess so," she replied.

Denman, having made his point, continued in another direction. "You mentioned, Miss Hyman, that the least expensive watch you have in your shop is seventy-seven dollars. Now, tell me what is your most expensive watch ... man's watch, that is?"

"I can't be entirely sure, but I'd say several thousand dollars."

"If I wanted, couldn't I buy something more expensive?"

"Yes ... on a special order."

"It would seem to me that a regular two-thousand-dollar watch should be good enough," Denman observed dryly. "But getting back to Isham Reddick, he bought a three-hundred-and-fifty-dollar watch—not a five-hundred-, or a thousand- or a fifteen-hundred-dollar one. If he wanted a good watch, and had saved money for one, if there any reason he shouldn't have bought the three-hundred-and-fifty-dollar one?"

"No, no reason, at all," agreed Miss Hyman. Denman thanked her, and she stepped down from the chair.

Mr. Dann, of Dann & Glend, Gentlemen's Tailors, impeccably dressed in a gray flannel suit, buttoned-down collar, and delicately knotted tie, somewhat fussily identified himself as senior partner in the exclusive shop which catered to many distinguished New Yorkers, as well as national figures. "Your shop is located on Madison Avenue?" asked Cannon.

"Yes," replied Dann, "we have been in the same location for over thirty years."

"Either you or Mr. Glend ... your partner ... personally take care of all your clientele."

"Naturally we have tailors who do the actual cutting, fitting, and finishing, but Mr. Glend and I wait on our customers. This is strictly a per-

sonal business, and we would not consider hiring paid sales people."
Dann glanced appraisingly at Cannon's suit, and what he saw, evidently,
did not entirely meet with his approval.

"You recall selling three suits of clothes to a man using the name
Isham Reddick?" Cannon handed Dann a photograph. "Is this the
same man?" Dann identified it, and Cannon continued, "Will you please
tell us, in your own words, what happened?"

Dann carefully crossed his flanneled legs. "The ... ah ... fellow came into
the shop, and I waited on him. He said he was interested in buying some
suits. I informed him that we made suits only to order. The suit he was
wearing was a ready-made suit of very ordinary material, and I did not
expect him to buy. On occasions, we have persons who wander into the
shop, evidently under the impression that ... well, we carry a stock of
clothes. This, of course, we have never done. Usually when we tell
them our prices, they leave very quickly."

"What are your prices, Mr. Dann?"

"Our suits begin at two hundred dollars. The prices vary depending
on the materials selected and other details of the suits."

"When you told Isham Reddick this, what did he say to you?"

"He replied that he would take three suits. That day, he selected cloth
for a charcoal gray, a medium gray, and a midnight blue flannel. Mr. Mat
measured him. I told the customer that inasmuch as he had not yet established an account with us, we must request him to pay for the cloth
and the cutting in advance ... the balance to be paid when the suits were
finished."

"Did Reddick object to that?"

"No, sir. He immediately paid us four hundred dollars."

"On that first trip, he paid you four hundred dollars? Did he pay you
in cash?"

"Yes, before he left the shop," replied Mr. Dann, "he gave me four one-
hundred-dollar bills."

"Do you remember the suit he was wearing when he came into the
shop?"

"I remember thinking only that it was mediocre, although now I cannot recall the details. Actually, I suppose, there were no details to remember—it was that kind of suit." Mr. Dann silently sniffed his disap-
proval.

"You say a 'mediocre' suit ... what would you say was a cheap suit?"

"Any mass-produced piece of clothing costing less than fifty dollars,"
Dann replied promptly.

"Did it surprise you that Isham Reddick bought your expensive
suits?"

"Yes," said Dann, "he certainly didn't look as if he could afford them!"

"Objection!" Denman arose to his feet, and the judge sustained him. "No conclusions or opinions, please, Mr. Dann," he corrected the tailor. Cannon, however, had finished his examination of the witness, and the attorney for the defense took over.

"Mr. Dann," Denman opened, "I wish you would look at the suit I'm wearing. Do you consider it a cheap suit?" Denman turned slowly in front of the witness, walking up and down.

"May I take a better look at it?" requested Dann.

"Certainly ..." Denman moved closer, standing before the witness. Dann examined the lapels quickly, and checked the buttons on the sleeves. "Well?" asked Denman, smiling.

"Your suit, sir," replied Mr. Dann with dignity, "was made by Meade & Thomas, tailors with a good reputation, and competitors of mine for twenty-five years." Shrugging, he added, "You paid at least two hundred and fifty dollars for it—and you could have done better."

A ripple of laughter lapped over the courtroom. Denman smiled and bowed to the witness. "Quite right, sir," he replied. "The next time I will come to see you." Mr. Dann nodded in agreement. "Now," continued Denman, "let's consider Isham Reddick's suits ... which at two hundred dollars ... must have been an excellent buy. Do you agree they were an extremely good buy, Mr. Dann?"

"Naturally," agreed Mr. Dann.

"You see nothing unusual in a man paying two hundred dollars for a suit?"

"I see it every day," the tailor pointed out.

"Even three suits at two hundred dollars is a good buy?"

"Excellent ... an excellent buy. The suits last longer, look better when you change them often. Every gentleman should have at least a minimum of fourteen suits."

"Yes, I quite agree," Denman interrupted the witness. "Now, as I understand it Isham Reddick paid you four hundred dollars on account. Did he ever pay you the balance?"

"No, sir," replied Dann. "He came in for all the fittings, and then we heard nothing more from him. After the suits had been completed for several weeks, we called the number Reddick had left with us. When we asked for him, a policeman took the call. Later, the authorities came to see me."

"And you still believe the suits were a good buy?"

"Absolutely!" Dann stated with finality. Denman then dismissed the tailor. The attorney for the defense felt a growing depression; regardless of Dann's ready agreement concerning the good sense of purchasing quality clothes, he knew that the jury was not in sympathy with a chauffeur paying two hundred dollars for a suit, and purchasing them in lots of three.

Anthony Gillick, an employee of the Monterey Travel Bureau, had a high reedy voice. He identified the picture of Reddick as the man who had called on him the afternoon of November twentieth, of the previous year, in his place of employment at the travel bureau. "What did Isham Reddick want?" asked Cannon.

"He wanted to make a reservation for a flight to Paris on November twenty-fourth."

"Could you make a reservation for him on such short notice?"

"It wasn't too difficult," Gillick piped. "That time of year there's little tourist traffic. Besides he asked for a luxury flight."

"What is the difference in the price of tickets?"

"Regular coach flights are approximately one hundred and fifty dollars less than luxury flights."

"When did Isham Reddick plan to return?"

Gillick shook his head. "I don't know. He purchased only a one-way ticket. I told him he could effect a saving by buying a round-trip ticket, as long as he used it within one year. He said that he didn't plan to return."

"You mean that he didn't plan to return within one year?"

"No," replied Gillick, his voice climbing. With an effort, he lowered it again. "Isham Reddick said that he didn't plan to ever return."

"He told you that?"

"Yes, sir. That is what he said."

"Incidentally, Mr. Gillick, what was the price of the ticket to Paris?"

"Five hundred and seventy-five dollars."

"Did Isham Reddick pay you for it?"

"Yes, sir. In cash."

"Did you ever see Isham Reddick again?"

"No, sir. Twenty-four hours before flight time we called his residence to reaffirm his reservation ... as is customary." Gillick paused and swallowed quickly, his Adam's apple bobbing. "It was ... well ... I was informed that Mr. Reddick was dead."

"Isham Reddick appears to have been a very busy man," Cannon mused aloud, elaborately watching the witness, "five hundred seventy-five dollars for a ticket ... four hundred dollars for suits ... three hundred and fifty dollars for a watch ... that's thirteen hundred and twenty-five dollars...."

Denman interrupted him. "Is this a soliloquy or an examination?"

Slightly exaggerating his motion, Cannon turned his attention to the attorney for the defense. "Oh, I'm sorry," he said, "your witness, Counselor."

Denman, heavily, began his examination of the new witness.

Chapter 18

Back in New York, I sorted out my facts. Shuffling them and reshuf-
fling them in my mind, I dealt them out for examination. Sometimes
they would fit, and sometimes they wouldn't. Patiently, I'd reshuffle
them and begin all over again. I discovered I could think better at night,
particularly while riding the subway. Very late, I'd board the last car in
the train, on the Seventh Avenue IRT. In the end car of the train, I'd
stand on the vestibule, at the rear, watching the black hollows of the tun-
nels rushing past on both sides. The lights flicked from red to amber to
green as we roared past, and the rails looked like long twining snakes
crawling back into their pits. There is no rocketing rhythm, no clicking
beat to a subway train, but in their place in a rushing sense of destination ... and my destination was Greenleaf.

Finally my facts were assembled, my conclusions reached. I knew that
Greenleaf was tall, slightly over six feet; he was slender; had a large, long
nose; gray hair; and he spoke some French. I did not believe, however,
that he was French; Tally had never mentioned her uncle remarking
about his accent ... and neither had she. Greenleaf had deliberately
played the role of a Frenchman for the landlady in Philadelphia. If
Greenleaf really had been French, I believed he would have done everything possible to conceal it.

Greenleaf's physical description typed him to play three roles, and undoubtedly he had played them all at some time or other. There is a certain physical type which the United States, England, and France have
in common. It is exemplified by a tall, lean, large-nosed man, and in
America fits the conception of a Western cowboy. But with a change of
accent, he becomes an English sportsman ... or a French army officer.
The British accent, particularly in the Eastern section of the United
States, many times becomes difficult to distinguish from, say, Boston ac-
cents.

The use of a French phrase by Greenleaf, in his conversation with
Tally, led me to believe that he had been playing the part of a well-educated Easterner (or an Englishman) when he had been conning Will
Shaw. It was possible, because of the story he gave the old man concerning his Washington connections, that he had represented himself
as being employed in some diplomatic capacity. Will Shaw, in his senile
condition, might never have noticed his English accent if indeed Greenleaf had posed as being English. I couldn't be sure, although I remembered that Tally had once mentioned that Greenleaf didn't speak
as a Philadelphian or New Yorker.

But Greenleaf, having secured the plates, I was strongly convinced would immediately adopt a new character ... one as removed as possible from what he had been using—English or Bostonian, and French. Thus of the roles he had left, roles in which he was physically in character, only one remained for him to play.

A Westerner.

Not a cowboy, naturally, but someone from, say, Texas ... Arizona ... New Mexico; that general area.

I would begin searching for a tall, lean, gray-haired Southwesterner ... but where? That was the problem; where would he go to pass the counterfeit money? Not to a small town, obviously, because a stranger with a great deal of money is always a person of speculation and curiosity. Furthermore, if there ever was a slip on a phony bill, it could be traced too easily in a small place.

I decided that if I were in Greenleaf's position and planned to start passing queer money, I'd do it in a large city—and a city in which there is a big tourist turnover. Automatically, that would be either New York, Chicago, or Los Angeles. This conclusion brought me face-to-face with another problem, and one that might decide whether I ever found Greenleaf. Was he planning to convert the queer into legitimate money, and in turn bank it; or was he planning to spend it, only as needed, for living purposes?

There was something about the shadowy Greenleaf ... from what I'd heard, though, and felt perhaps ... that made me believe the man desired a certain respectability. His propensity for using foreign phrases, his enacting the role of gentleman were not much, certainly, upon which to base such a conclusion; but my feeling regarding the kind of make-believe roles he liked was strong enough not to be ignored. For this reason, Greenleaf would want a bank account. And this in turn meant something else: he would not be foolish enough to deposit counterfeit bills in a bank. Instead, he would pass his phony bills and bank only the legitimate money which he had received in exchange. New York is one of the few cities in the country where a man can buy a package of cigarettes, paying for it with a twenty-dollar bill, and not draw comment on the transaction, when he receives his change. In Greenleaf's operation, he could pass twenties all day, and never enter the same store twice. One other factor helped me reach my final conclusion. Most con men are suckers, themselves, for liquor, dames, and bright lights. New York's night life was the largest, the most gaudy, and it would appeal to Greenleaf. Converting money during the day for a respectable bank account and spending the queer dough lavishly at night ... this, undoubtedly, was Greenleaf's dream of the best of all possible worlds.

In my reasoning, I had completed a circle. Right here in New York, right where I was, there Greenleaf was too!

Now, although I might not be able to recognize Greenleaf on sight, there was the possibility that he might recognize me. I didn't know if he had seen me in Philadelphia. He had seen Tally, and so far as I know, he might have looked me over while we were performing at the club ... or at the hotel.

As part of my act, I had grown a mustache ... a small, dark military model. It is strange that when a man grows a mustache, it does not alter his appearance as greatly as a man, who has always worn one, alters his when he shaves it off. The first thing I did, naturally, was to shave mine.

Once, while I had been working in the carney, there'd been a big clem in a hick Southern town and I had lost my front tooth from a flying tent stake. As soon as I could, I had the tooth replaced with a false one on a removable bridge. I now took out the false tooth, leaving a wide gap in the front of my teeth. My eyebrows and hair are dark ... an excellent combination for a stage magician, but easily remembered. However, I didn't want to dye my hair, because hair not only can be analyzed but it also requires a lot of work to keep it from looking phony and being detected.

I bleached my eyebrows to a lighter brown, which immediately changed the entire expression on my face. Most of my entire life I had worked with stage make-up as part of my job. One principle of make-up should always be remembered: keep it as simple as possible. A minimum is easier to maintain, day after day, and it's more difficult to detect. I kept it simple ... lighter eyebrows, a missing tooth, no mustache. To this, I added a pair of conventional horn-rimmed glasses, with ordinary lens. The plain glass, however, had been ground around the edges to reflect concentric circles of depth, and appeared to be extremely strong.

In the clem I mentioned ... the one where I had lost a tooth ... one of the truck drivers in the carney, a man named Isham Reddick, had been killed. I had ridden in the cab with Reddick over many long dusty jumps, and during the endless, dull, night hours he had often talked. That night of the fight, the Southern cops had fired into the dark, and Reddick had been shot. The next day, without fanfare or publicity, he had been buried in a plain wooden box; dumped in a small Baptist cemetery on the edge of town.

But I remembered the name of the town where Reddick had been born, because it had been strange enough to make an impression. It was Rocky, Colorado, and his parents had moved away when he was still a kid. Sitting down, I wrote a letter addressed to the city recorder at Rocky. Enclosing a five-dollar bill, I wrote that my name was Isham Reddick, and I wanted a copy of my birth certificate. Ten days later, I received a small printed card, an official form which affirmed the fact of my birth on page thirty-three, volume twenty-six, of the city records, etc. It was signed by the recorder in office and ... believe it or not ... he returned three dollars to me.

It was as simple as that. I became Isham Reddick.

The best place to pick up the trail of Greenleaf, I decided, was in the bistros around town ... the big-money, late-night spots. As I couldn't hang around the joints and ask questions without the possibility of alerting Greenleaf, I developed a good cover. Going to the City Bureau of Licenses, I applied for a license to drive a cab. It wasn't difficult, either; after filling out the application forms and passing the examinations, I was fingerprinted. Several days elapsed while the records were checked; I had no fingerprints on file, and evidently the original Isham Reddick had never had a record, either. The license was issued.

New York City has as many cab companies as it has pedestrians. I selected one of the largest ... the Eastern-Circle Taxi Company, reasoning that it probably had a big turnover in personnel, and applied for a job as a night driver. It was a twelve-hour stint, from six o'clock at night to six o'clock in the morning, pushing around a heap, painted orange with purple circles on the fenders. The cab rattled and banged and steered with the ease of a Coast Guard cutter in ice. But I was the lowest man on the totem pole ... the newest driver ... and I had to take it. Hacking is a tough business, and let no one maintain differently. I pushed the hack around Manhattan, the Bronx, and Brooklyn during the early part of the evening. I needed the fares so as not to cut into my small capital, and also to show that I had been working when I turned in my mileage reports, and fares, to the garage in the morning. After midnight, however, I skipped all the fares I could. Instead, I'd pull into one of the cab lines outside the night spots; standing around I'd shoot the breeze with the other hackies, picking up a little gossip here and there, watching the customers leaving the club. Watching for a tall, lean guy with a big nose and gray hair! One by one the cabs worked their way up the line into first place position to take the next customer. As a rule, when I had reached second place, I'd take off for another club, and repeat the procedure—starting from the end of the line.

Each morning, I was just under the wire from getting fired. The money I took in on hauls in the early part of the evening didn't justify the loafing I did after midnight. I don't know why the company didn't let me go, except drivers were still pretty scarce ... and possibly, I was the only sucker who would drive the oldest hack in the garage. Anyway, the night foreman kept me on, from night to night, but always with the threat of firing me the next day.

I saw plenty of prospects who might have been Greenleaf. Although they answered his description physically, they failed to hold up when I tried to check them. Either they were unknown at the club ... and I figured Greenleaf would be a pretty well-known customer when I did locate him ... or else they were too well and legitimately known. One night I thought I had found him ... "That guy looks like a big shot," I told the doorman. "Who is he?" The doorman glanced at a tall, distinguished-looking guy with gray hair, and a flashy babe on his arm, and said, "He's a rancher."

"What's his name?"

"Cready. All I got to say is 'good evening, Mr. Cready,' and it's good for a ten spot."

"I guess he must have a pile of it," I said, acting impressed.

"You ain't kidding," replied the doorman. "Spends dough like he hates it. He's a big man back home."

I watched Cready climb unsteadily into a cab, the girl crawling in after him, clinging to the rancher possessively. "You know where he's staying?" I asked casually. I really didn't care about an answer, because in a minute I was planning to take off and tail him.

"Sure," said the doorman, "he stays at the Van Dyke-Plaza ... he always stays there when he comes to New York." The doorman cocked an eye thoughtfully, "Must be four, five years now I've seen him coming to the club. When he's in town, he always stays at the Van Dyke-Plaza."

That was that. I shrugged, turning away to conceal my disappointment. It is fairly typical ... in one way or another ... of all the other prospects I turned up for Greenleaf. Naturally, when I found Greenleaf I knew he would be operating under another name.

Somehow, though, I began to enjoy pushing that old cab around the streets late at night. The hours ... staying up until morning ... were a return to the pattern of my old life. Tally now seemed more remote; the aching loss had gone. The hatred I felt for Greenleaf, however, I had lived with too long to be able to lose it. The desire for revenge burned as brightly as ever. The gospel of my execration, the litany of blood I had recited to myself too often. I had learned them too well to ever unlearn them again. I was like a man who, only partly believing in religion, ends up a raving fanatic!

Eventually, of course, I found Greenleaf. I found him just as I knew I would find him. The first time I saw him, he was slightly drunk standing beneath the canopy of the Copabonga Club, arguing with a blonde floosie who had come out of the joint with him. He gave her a gallant bow, and pulling out a roll of bills unwrapped several from the outside. Stuffing the bills in the woman's hand, he put her in a cab. Turning back to the doorman, he shoved him another bill. The doorman saluted, smiled, and said something before whistling up a second cab. I was about the fifth cab in line, and I was unable to pull out to follow. Waiting a few minutes, I climbed out of my hack and sauntered up to the doorman. "Who was that john?" I asked, lighting a cigarette.

The doorman, a seven-foot giant named Ozzie, grinned. "A Texas oil man," he said. "Carries his own oil well around with him." He unfolded his hand, and in the palm was a twenty-dollar bill.

The excitement began mounting within me. "Wish to hell I had him for a fare," I said enviously. "Does he come around often?"

"Oh ... maybe once a week," said Ozzie.

"A regular?"

"Yeah ... I guess so. Showed up here couple, three, four months ago. Something like that. Probably'll go back to Texas one of these days."

The time was right as far as Greenleaf was concerned. The masquerade was right ... Texas and oil. "What's his name?" I asked.

"Mistuh Ballard Humphries," said Ozzie imitating a drawl.

"Well, shut mah mouf," I replied climbing back in the cab. I hung around the club for several hours waiting for the cab which had hauled Humphries to return. It didn't, and I decided that the driver had picked up a return fare. Knowing the number of the cab, and the company, I returned to the Copabonga Club the following night and the cab was in the line-up again. Walking down the line, I leaned against the cab door. Pulling out my cigarettes I offered one to the driver who took it, and stuck it behind his ear for future smoking. "Hey, Mac," I said through the window, "how was that Texas millionaire you hauled last night?"

The hacky, a little man with cramped shoulders, shrugged.

"They're all the same," he said.

"Except some have money ..."

"Yeah." A slow grin crept cross his wrinkled features. "This guy gives me a ten spot for the haul and I keep the change...."

"How much was the haul?"

"Buck and a half over to the East Side."

"Uptown?"

"Yeah. Eighty-ninth Street. A brownstone ... middle of the block."

"I know the street," I said, lying. "Bet I know the house, too. It's got a brass railing leading up from the sidewalk."

The cabby thought a moment, then shook his head. "Naw ... no railing. This joint's got a big heavy glass door all covered with an iron grill."

"That doesn't mean anything, Mac," I said. "Lots of doors on that street look like that. I'll drive around tomorrow, and I'll bet you there's a brass railing going up the stairs."

He spat, disdainfully, through the window. "Naw. This house was the third house down from an apartment building. Same side of the street.

No railing ..."

"Okay," I agreed reluctantly, "maybe you're right." Walking back to my cab, I felt good, I felt positive, although I still had to nail it down. A little later, I got out again and strolled up to Ozzie. "Ozzie," I said to the doorman, "remember that Texas millionaire last night? What'd you say his name was?"

"Humphries. Why?"

"Well, I've been thinking. I'm getting plenty tired hacking, and I thought maybe this Mr. Humphries might want to hire a chauffeur. I'd like to hit him for a job."

"So, go ahead and do it. I ain't stopping you."

"How'm I going to? I just don't walk up to him when he comes staggering out and brace him for one. I got to be diplomatic. I figured if maybe I got a chance to haul him someplace, while we were driving along I might sort of start talking with him...."

A party of four came out of the club and Ozzie busily signaled up the first cab, opened the door, helped in each passenger, palmed his tip, and closed the door. I had lost his interest, and he grew impatient. "That's your problem, Mac," he said, "not mine."

"Okay, Mac," I shrugged. "I was going to make you a proposition. I'll give you twenty right now," I slipped two tens in his hand, "if you'll give me the chance to haul him the next time Humphries is here. If he gives me a job, I'll give you another twenty." Ozzie peered down at me from his altitude. "Incidentally," I asked, "do you ever get a nose bleed up there?"

He brushed my remark aside. "How do you plan to work it, Mac?" he asked.

"From now on, I won't get in the line-up," I explained. "I'll park down at the corner on the other side of the street. When he comes out, stall as long as you can before waving up the first cab. That'll give me time to get here, and pick him up on the cruise."

"The boys are going to be awful mad," Ozzie warned me.

"Tell the guy who loses the haul that I'll give him a ten. That ought to square it."

"Okay," said Ozzie grimly. He looked down again. "And don't forget my other twenty."

"If I get the job, it's yours," I assured him.

Humphries didn't show up again at the Copabonga all week. Each night I parked around the corner, across the street from the club, as if I'd been poured in the concrete. Every morning when I checked in, the night foreman raised hell, bawled me out, and finally one morning fired me. That night, however, he hired me back on again, and I returned to my vigil. At last, the following Tuesday night, Humphries showed up.

He came out of the club about two in the morning, and this time he was squiring a slender, willowy brunette who was young enough to be his daughter, but who looked experienced enough to be his mother. Ozzie went into his stalling routine, and I slung the old cab into gear and roared up to the front of the club with the back door practically open.

Ozzie helped them into the hack, and Humphries with a broad Texas accent gave me the address on East Eighty-ninth Street. As the cab pulled away, he and the brunette began playing around in the back seat. After a few minutes of driving, I cleared my voice loudly; during the moment of silence that followed, I said, "Pardon me, sir, but you appear to be a well-educated gentleman."

The remark caught Humphries by surprise, and in the mirror I could see him straighten in the seat. In a loud, flat drawl he said, "Huh? What was that again, son?"

I repeated it and added, "If you don't mind, sir, I'd like some information, and I think maybe you can help me."

"Well, shore," replied Humphries. "If I can help out a fellow human, I'm always right happy to...."

"It's like this," I said. "Earlier this evening, I was down by the United Nations Building. I picked up a gentleman and his wife ... they were French, I think ... and I hauled them up town. The gentleman spoke some English, not very much, and when he got out of the cab he gave me a bill and told me to keep the change. It was a pretty good tip. I thanked him, and then he said something in French. I asked ... what'd you say? He laughed and replied in English that he'd said 'don't mention it.'" Pushing the driver's cap to the back of my head, I continued, "Well, I been thinking about it, and I wish I could remember the way he said it in French. Would you, sir, happen to know any French?"

Humphries roared with laughter. "I'm going to tell you the truth," he drawled. "I'm right proud to say that I'm a graduate of Texas Christian University, in Texas."

"Yeah ... sure," I said. "I've heard of it. They have great football teams ... I've seen them in the newsreels. That's at Waco, isn't it?"

"Yore plumb right," Humphries agreed. "They got a great little ol' team. Well, as I was saying, I studied a mite of French at TCU and if I can remember correctly ..."

"Oh, Ballard," the girl giggled admiringly, "don't tell me that you speak French, too! Why, that's wonderful ..."

"Well ... yes, m'am, I do," said Humphries preening himself.

"And if I recall correctly what the driver heard his fare say this evening was *'il n'y a pas de quoi.'*" His delivery was abruptly weakened by a hiccough.

The girl attempted to repeat it after him phonetically, "eel knee ah paw duh qua." She clapped her hands. "I think that's cute," she said.

"Honey girl, I think yore plumb cute, yoreself," Humphries replied gallantly.

I was thinking other things. Here's a Texan who speaks French. And a Texan who was graduated from Texas Christian and who mixes it up with Baylor University. Texas Christian is at Fort Worth; Baylor University is in Waco. Drunk or not, no authentic Texan makes that mistake!

Chapter 19

The prosecution had closed its case the day before. Denman, counsel for the defense, had moved that the indictment be dismissed for failure to prove the defendant's guilt beyond a reasonable doubt. The jury had been excused during the argument between the two attorneys and, when the motion had been denied, the jury returned to the courtroom. "Will the court please instruct the jurors that the denial does not concern them, but is only the court's decision on a question of law?" Denman requested the judge.

The court so instructed the jury. "At this time, I also make my exception a matter of record," added Denman.

"Your exception is so recorded," agreed the judge. "Proceed please, Mr. Denman."

"If it please the court," said Denman, "I would like to begin the defense tomorrow morning. It is now drawing near to the end of the afternoon, and I move the court adjourns until tomorrow morning."

Cannon did not protest the motion, and the judge dismissed the court, and retired to his chambers. Denman walked beside his client to a small private cubicle with heavily barred windows, located directly behind the courtroom. A uniformed officer stood outside the door. The attorney seated himself at a solid oak table with a badly scarred surface. His client, lighting a cigarette, walked moodily to the window which overlooked an enclosed air shaft. Denman was tired, and for a moment he sat heavily in his chair, his chin resting on his chest. Finally, raising his head, he said softly, "Sit down, Humphries. Let's have a talk." The tall, gray-haired man with a deeply lined face turned away from the window and walked listlessly to the table. He, too, sat down. "Listen," said Denman, his voice quiet and unemotional, "tonight we make a decision ... and whether our decision is right or wrong will determine whether we save your life.

"Before we make that decision, I wish to do a little talking. Usually, I have my own ideas about the innocence or guilt of my clients. Whether a man is innocent or guilty is no personal concern of mine; it is my duty to see that he receives a fair trial, as defined by the country and state. I defend all prisoners to the best of my ability. The more I know about their cases, the better I can defend them." Denman paused for a moment, then said slowly, "But I'll be damned if I know what to think about you, Humphries!"

"I pleaded not guilty, didn't I?" Humphries replied.

"The man caught with his knife in his victim's throat can also make that same plea," said Denman. "My personal belief is that you are hiding something ... or someone." As Humphries began to object, Denman raised his hand, silencing him. "I've sat in this room many times before, Humphries. Look around it—how large is it? Ten by twelve feet? Two small windows with bars over them. Look at this scrubby table ... two chairs ... and a guard beyond that closed door. But this is elegant ... a magnificent suite compared to what is waiting up the river. Yes, I've sat here before. How many times? Fifty ... a hundred. I really don't remember, Humphries. Somehow over the years, all those faces began to look alike ... some of them already tinged with the gray of the walled-in years to come, or with death stamped, early, on their faces. I mention this deliberately to frighten you ... to put the fear of God in your heart. Don't you realize the position you are in?"

Denman hunched himself erect in his chair, pushing his legs out ... straight and stiff ... before him. "I've had men who came here, with an illicit fortune hidden away, who refused to talk. They gambled the chance that if they could beat the rap, they would walk out of here wealthy men. Some of them died in prison, caught by the years, before they could get back to their money. Others took their last walk ... shouting they would tell the truth, but then it was too late. A few have returned to find the money, and again be picked up by the police."

"I don't know what you're talking about," Humphries denied surlily.

"I don't either," came Denman's frank reply. "I'm not even guessing. But you haven't told me the truth ... you haven't told me the facts ... you haven't told me anything! Humphries, you and I have sat for over a week while Cannon has beat us bloody with facts and witnesses. And what do we have? No alibi! No witnesses—not even a character witness. Tell me again, but this time honestly ... was Reddick blackmailing you?"

"No!" Humphries brought his hand down hard against the table. "I've told you before! So help me God, he wasn't blackmailing me! He never asked me for a cent!"

"Suppose," Denman continued relentlessly, "he hadn't gotten around to it yet. Was there something that Reddick might have known ... that he might have used for blackmail?"

Humphries did not reply immediately, an infinite part of a second elapsed before he denied it. "No," he shook his head. "He had nothing to hold over me ..."

Denman ran his fingers, tiredly, through his hair. "Humphries," he pointed out, his voice laboredly calm, "look at the case Cannon has advanced. He maintains that you shot Isham Reddick in the furnace room with the revolver found in your drawer. After he was killed, you dismembered him ... using the bench and the large canvas tarpaulin, and the hatchet. The body was consumed in the large furnace, and most of the traces and ashes were disposed of by you. He has even found traces of the ashes in your car. In evidence, he has Reddick's finger, part of his leg, his tooth, and possibly his blood. After the murder, he advances the argument that you cleaned up and showered in the basement bath. Now why did all this take place? Cannon maintains that Reddick was blackmailing you ... he has evidence in your handwriting concerning a payment of at least eighty-five hundred dollars. Reddick was spending money like a sailor on shore leave. Where did he get it? Cannon says he got it from you. Witnesses have testified that Reddick, himself, implied he got it from you. Cannon has proved that you are not from Texas ... have no business, and no traceable income. Where do you get the money that you have? Is that something that Reddick knew? Is that what you were paying him to hide?" Denman shook his head in disbelief. "And you want me to believe you aren't hiding something!"

"Cannon couldn't prove I had a criminal record," Humphries said.

"No," agreed Denman, "he couldn't. But there are plenty of individuals who have done something they don't want known ... something which could land them in the prisons, if it ever came to light."

"I'm innocent," Humphries replied. "Reddick was a madman. Stark raving mad!"

"And you want the jury to believe he killed himself ... committed suicide, and then cremated himself in the basement?" Denman's voice was sarcastic.

"He could have gotten another body ..." Humphries' voice was disbelieving.

"Don't be ridiculous!" Denman snapped. "Believe me, it's impossible to steal a cadaver; it's easier to get into Fort Knox. No, the prosecution has some pretty damaging evidence ... but that isn't the question. What I want to know, Humphries, is why, WHY!!!"

Humphries turned away helplessly. "I don't know ..."

"Yes, you know, Humphries, but you aren't telling me. That's it, isn't it?" Humphries remained silent, although shaking his head. "All right," continued the attorney, "let's face up to the question we have to decide. Tomorrow, we start our defense. We have no evidence to establish an alibi for the night of November twenty-second and the morning of the twenty-third; we have no character witnesses; and we don't even have an alternate theory to advance concerning what did happen."

"I don't have to take the stand," said Humphries.

"Right," agreed Denman, "as a rule, with any kind of a defense, at all, it's better for the defendant not to testify. But damn it all, man, we've got to do something! With absolutely no defense, and if you don't take the stand, the jury is going to wonder why." Denman studied the brown painted wall opposite the table, his eyes tracing a feathery crack which ran ... a narrow dark line ... along one side of it. Heavily, he pulled himself to his feet, and walked around the table until he faced the wall. With one finger he traced the line of the crack, then plunging his hand into his pocket returned and seated himself.

"There're cracks all over the case," he said. "They're a mile wide in Cannon's evidence, but I can't plaster them up." Turning, he faced Humphries again. "Well, how about it? Will you gamble your life on the story you told me?"

"It's the truth," replied Humphries. "It's all the story I got."

"Are you willing to get on the stand and tell it? Afterward, Cannon is going to rip you apart."

"I'm willing, if you say so."

"Humphries, I don't want to say so. But, there's nothing else we can do. If just one of the jurors believes you ... or any part of the story ... there's a chance. Our only chance."

The guard opened the door, and let Denman out of the room.

Chapter 20

It took me about an hour to talk Greenleaf, or Humphries rather, into giving me a job. That first night, I drove him home, I played up to his vanity. Arriving before the house, I walked around to the rear door of the cab and helped him out—lifting his wallet off his hip as I did so. At noon, the following day, I was back at the house to return it. A maid let me in, and after a few minutes Humphries staggered into the living room, dressed in a silk dressing gown and looking miserable. He did not seem to recognize me.

"My name is Reddick, sir," I said. "I drove you home last night. Afterward, I found your wallet in the back seat of the cab. I'm returning it." I handed it to him, he received it blankly.

Finally, he opened it and fanned through the bills. There were nearly five hundred dollars in tens and twenties ... all new bills! I had counted them the night before.

"Why ... thanks," he said. He regarded the wallet vacuously.

"I hadn't missed it yet ... just getting up. Terrible, bad night last night ..."

"Yes, sir!" I agreed, looking around. It was a large room, with a high, lovely, old ceiling. The walls were hunter green, and a tremendous, ornately carved Italian marble fireplace dominated the room. Humphries walked over to an Empire chair, and sank into it. Picking out five bills ... all twenties ... he handed them to me. "This here's a reward for returning the poke," he drawled.

I shook my head. "Thanks, sir," I replied, "but that's too much. Twenty will be more than enough."

His bloodshot eyes looked at me with surprise. "Yore an honest man," he said.

"Yes, sir," I agreed, "I am. And you look like a sick one. Where's the kitchen, sir?" Humphries motioned toward the back of the house. Walking in the general direction he indicated, I found a large, white, little used kitchen with an electric refrigerator. Opening a can of tomato juice, I poured it out and spiked it with two spoons of Worcestershire, and added a dash of red pepper. When I returned to the living room, Humphries was seated where I had left him, his eyes closed. I shook him, and he took the glass and drank it. Sitting motionless for a moment, he swallowed abruptly and shook his head in a delayed reaction. He said, "Brother, I shore need that one ... what a hangover!" He attempted to lift himself from the chair, then sank back weakly. "I'm shore grateful," he said, "now I got to get dressed."

"I'll help you upstairs, sir," I told him. As he began to protest, I grasped his arm, pulling him to his feet. "I haven't anything else to do," I explained. Upstairs, while he stood stupidly under a shower, I selected a suit from his closet, laid out a shirt and underclothes. Later, helping him get into them, I said, "What you need, Mr. Humphries ... a wealthy gentleman like yourself ... is a good man to help out. If I may say so, frankly, I'm getting pretty fed up driving that hack. Tell me, sir, do you have a car?"

"No," he grunted, "too much trouble getting around this here city."

"Not if you have a chauffeur," I replied. "Someone to keep the car in good condition ... and to drive you whenever you want to go." I paused, then continued, "And to pick you up, too ... any place, any hour of the day or night. Why, it's the biggest convenience you can have, sir. You know, it's dangerous going around the city late at night ... carrying as much money as you do."

"Hogwash," said Humphries.

"Not at all, sir. Someone to see you get home safe at night, someone to help around the house during the day. Such a man would be invaluable, sir. And, if I may say so, I'm just the man—and I'm available, too!"

Humphries looked haggardly in my direction, "You hitched up ... married?"

"No, sir," I said brightly, although the bile was gagging in my throat, "I'm single."

"What about yore family, they live here?"

"No, sir. I've been working here a long time, but my home's in Rocky, Colorado."

"What's yore name again?" I told him: Isham Reddick. He frowned a moment, and I couldn't tell if he was displeased, or if it was just the hangover. After a while, he said, "I don't have many hired hands in this spread, Reddick. Just a maid, a cleaning woman, and a sort of handy man. Not too much of a layout, but maybe I could use another hand. How much you want to hire on?"

"Three hundred a month," I said.

"I'll give you two fifty, and yore room. I don't eat in 'cept for breakfast, but I guess you can rustle up enough to eat around here."

"Yes, sirrr!" I replied, quickly. "I'll take it."

That afternoon we went downtown to buy a car. I was anxious to see what he would do in the way of a splurge, but Humphries was cautious. Instead of buying a Cadillac, he settled for a smaller, medium-priced car ... a black sedan with white sidewall tires. I wasn't surprised as it confirmed my suspicions. A man as wealthy as Humphries was supposed to be would not have hesitated to pay a high price. But Humphries had to pay for the car with a check, a personal one. It would have been impossible for him to pay in ten- and twenty-dollar bills, so he was forced to check against that legitimate account he was building up in the bank ... and he didn't want to wipe it out. However, as far as I was concerned, he could have bought a rowboat and I'd have rowed him down Fifth Avenue.

That evening, I moved into the servants' quarters on the top floor of the house. With the door safely closed behind me, I was able to relax for the first time. I found myself trembling, both with hatred and triumph. I forced myself to remain quiet, although I wanted to pound the walls with my fists and shout curses down the stairs. After I regained control of my emotions, I thought about Humphries, analyzing what I had seen. His eyes, although heavily lidded, were not large and they set deep within his head; the nose, long as had been described to me, swelled slightly at the bridge lending almost a predatory air; and his lips were a combination of both cruelty and sensuality. The upper lip was thin, straight, and very narrow, the lower full and heavy. Yet, unmistakably, the man had an appearance of distinction.

My greatest problem was not to give myself away. In my role of ex-cab driver and presently of chauffeur Humphries had accepted my disguise—if you could call it that. He gave no indication of ever having seen me before, and made no mention to a familiarity of appearance. I was convinced that he was entirely unsuspecting—although I do not believe that Humphries was ever trusting of anyone in his life. Determined as I was to kill the man, I was afraid that Humphries might read it in my face. Consequently, I went to great lengths to be servile—scraping and doing everything but touching my forelock. And he liked it.

Late at night, with contempt and loathing in my breast, I'd sit in my room, smoking, and consider the best possible method with which to kill him. While I would have enjoyed strangling him with my hands, making it as painful and lingering as possible, I realized such a plan had a drawback. Although Humphries was twenty years older than I, he was also larger and possibly stronger. But I liked to consider it anyway—as well as guns, knives, blunt instruments, and all their variations.

However, I was also determined to escape the consequences after I had murdered him. It would be little satisfaction to offer myself as another sacrifice to Humphries after his death. No, I hoped to escape the law, and with this in mind I began planning a method by which to avoid the police after the killing. I determined to build Isham Reddick into a definite person, a concrete character; give Reddick a motive for killing Humphries; and then have Reddick disappear completely. While the police searched for Isham Reddick, the chauffeur with light eyebrows, smooth shaven, a front tooth missing, and wearing thick heavy glasses— I would simply, overnight, return to being Lew Mountain again.

It was, I believed, a good plan and I immediately put it into action. As I began to build up the background ... a piece here, a piece there ... I kept my eyes open for Humphries' other connection—the printer. Each day when Humphries went downtown, I'd drive him and usually he would get out somewhere in midtown Manhattan. I'd try to leave the car, and get back in time to follow him, but as a rule this was very difficult to do. On several occasions, however, I did manage to pick him up near the place where I had dropped him. As far as I could discover, after trailing him all day, he concentrated entirely on passing the ten- and twenty-dollar bills—buying innumerable, small, inexpensive little items which he often threw away after leaving the stores. And yet Humphries always had an inexhaustible supply of new bills. I had searched the house from top to bottom, attic to basement, to find the place where he concealed them. Searching an extremely large house is no easy task. It took me many hours as I could devote only a few minutes to it at any one time. Either the maid, a rather simple person, or the cleaning woman was always around and I had to be careful neither became suspicious.

The house on East Eighty-ninth Street had been rented, completely furnished, from a wealthy family living in Connecticut. Consequently, I didn't think that Humphries had access to the folderol of sliding panels, hidden rooms, and concealed passages. It was simply a large beautiful town house, and after my search I was convinced if Humphries had found a place to conceal the money, I'd have found it, too.

It took me some time, however, before I discovered how Humphries got his bills from the printer. Daily, while he was downtown, I'd go through his room and all his possessions. This aroused no comment from either Mary Deems or Mrs. Lightbody as I was doubling in the capacity of a semi-valet. I found no money in Humphries' clothes, or in his room, and I never came upon evidence of correspondence ... or any other clue. Except once.

By Humphries' bed, there was a telephone which had a direct outside line; this was in addition to another phone in the house which had a number of extensions. Although this bedroom phone had no extension, there was nothing mysterious about it, and there was no secret about its number, either. On the table, beside the phone, was a tablet of paper. One day, I discovered tracings on the pad. The top sheet of paper on which the words originally had been written, had been torn off leaving an indentation on the sheet beneath it. Holding the paper up to the light, I could catch a slight shadow on the indentations. I read the word "Magarian-2:00." I put the pad back in its original position and went down to the bus terminal.

At the telephone booths, in the bus depot, is a collection of all the individual telephone directories for the boroughs of New York, as well as some of the neighboring cities in New Jersey and Connecticut. There were a number of Magarians listed, but no Magarian Printing Company. Obviously, there wasn't much more I could do about Magarian right then, so I returned to the house. I considered going to Dave Sherz for help, but by this time I decided I was too involved. Murder is a lonesome task.

As a rule, around ten o'clock at night, I'd pick Humphries up at a café after he had finished dinner, and drive him ... with a girl ... to a night club. After dropping him off, he'd instruct me to return at an appointed time. Instead, I'd park around the corner, away from the club, and then return to a vantage point where I'd spend three or four hours waiting for him to stagger out of the joint again. Most of the time, the girl would be so drunk that I'd practically have to carry her over my shoulder. The women were all pretty much the same ... hard faced, sharply pretty, little chippies with predatory and acquisitive instincts well developed. It always surprised me that Humphries managed to meet so many, and eventually I decided that most of them were simply on lend-lease from call flats. Humphries often took the girl home with him, although sometimes he would slip her money in the car and then transfer her to a cab. On occasion, one of them would ride back to East Eighty-ninth with Humphries, and then I'd drive her home. Invariably, she would live in a cheap, walk-up flat, downtown.

When I did discover Humphries' method of getting money, it was a matter of an error on his part. I might never have found out, except Humphries went to a new club one night—one where there was no back entrance. He and a girl had been in the club several hours. I was waiting down at the corner, as usual, when I saw Humphries hurry out of the entrance by himself. Grabbing a cab, he took off in a direction opposite to the one I was parked. His cab swung around the corner and disappeared, and by the time I reached the intersection, it was out of sight. I returned to my original location and waited. In less than half an hour, Humphries re-entered the club.

I could figure it out from there. The recurring patterns of clubs, and drunken girls. Humphries would get his companion high, excuse himself from the table, make his contact with the printer, and return. The girl, in her drunken condition, wouldn't know if he had been gone three minutes or thirty and would always be able to give him an alibi for the evening.

After that, I watched the backs or side entrances of the different clubs, and invariably Humphries would show up. He'd take a cab, and I would follow him. Driving for only a few minutes, and stopping in front of a drugstore or a restaurant ... any place ... and with the cab waiting, Humphries would walk in—and in a moment be out again. Back in the cab. Back in the club! It was that simple, and he never went near the printing plant.

I decided that sometime during the day, Humphries would call the printer and tell him the club he was going to attend during the evening. They'd arrange to meet at a place near the club, and the printer would slip Humphries the money as he walked past. I never saw the actual transaction, or the printer either, because of the danger in following Humphries too closely, and being recognized. After watching Humphries perform the cab and pickup routine a number of times, for caution's sake I stopped following him entirely.

It was with a degree of sardonic pleasure that I realized Humphries wasn't getting any real enjoyment out of his life. He worked hard during the day passing the queer money to pay the cost of running the house, and the salaries connected with it. And always he was working under the pressure and tension of possible discovery. Every night, he was back at a bistro, getting a floosie drunk, setting up an alibi, and contacting the printer. He had no opportunity to make friends or relax—

except in drinking. Humphries was on a treadmill, running hard and fast in the same place just to keep even. Of course, he spent much money on clothes and personal jewelry, but after all where are the kicks—if only paid prostitutes and your valet can admire them?

Over the Fourth of July holiday, Humphries announced that he was going up to a lodge near Bear Mountain for a few days. I had to drive him up, and we edged our way in bumper-to-bumper traffic out of New York, cutting across the short slice of New Jersey, and then angling back into New York State again. During the drive, Humphries pulled a note-book from his pocket, scribbled on it, and handing me the piece of pa-per, drawled, "I'll call you to come fetch me ... when I'm ready to leave. If anything comes up around the house, you phone me. Hear?" He in-dicated the paper. "That there's the number for up here."

"What might come up, sir?"

Suddenly irritable, he climbed out of the car impatiently, and I followed him carrying his luggage. "How'd I know what might come up? But if anything does, call me."

"Yes, sir," I assured him. Back in the car, I examined the note. Humphries had scrawled on it: "Reddick ... Bear mt. 8500." Bear Moun-tain 8500 was the number of the lodge. He had written it across a small sheet of blue-lined paper—and I deliberately tore it across one edge. When I had finished, it read: "Reddick ... mt. 8500." I carefully placed the paper in my pocket.

Returning to the city, I stopped at Duval's ... a magicians' supply house on Eighth Avenue near Forty-fourth Street. Like all professional ma-gicians' shops, it is located on the second floor of a building ... to prevent non-professional trade from wandering in off the street. These places specialize in making up highly complicated productions and sell only a few great effects a year, although they also carry a stock of all the stan-dard stage props. A little guy named Harry Lohr has always operated Duval's as far back as most magicians can remember, and I have reg-ularly bought my mechanical stuff from him. In most of these shops, good regular customers are permitted to store their props ... when they're not using them, or are out on the road ... and the stores will keep them in good condition. When I had moved into Humphries' place, I had delivered my big theatrical trunk to Duval's, to hold for me. The store is open until late at night as many of its customers do not come in un-til evening. I slipped my glasses in my pocket, and kept my lip down over my missing tooth. When I walked in, Harry said, "How's the mechanic, Lew? You look different, kid."

"Just younger! I shaved off my lip-wig so I can practice catching that bullet in my teeth," I told him. This was a standard joke between the two of us. Some years back, an inventor had come up with a composition that disintegrated completely after passing through a quarter-inch pane of glass. A pellet made of the substance would pass through the glass, leaving a nice round hole, and then it disappeared without leaving any traces. A magician, with an authentic lead bullet concealed in his mouth, could create the illusion of catching the real bullet in his teeth, after a gun had fired it through the glass. It was a really great piece of business. The fellow who invented it sold the idea to Harry. Harry bought a supply of the stuff and showed it to me. I went for it. While I was rehearsing the act ... building it up as a topper ... I ran out of the material with which to make the composition, imitation bullets. Harry called the phone number, the inventor had left but the guy had moved away. We couldn't locate him, and we never saw him again ... and neither did anyone else. Because no one ever did the act. "Where do you have my trunk stored?" I asked.

"Third room back," Harry directed. "You can find your own way."

Passing through rooms filled with loaded shelves, built-in bins, costumes, masks, and a half century of collecting all the instruments of miracle-making, I arrived in a dark bare room, containing half a dozen large, metal-reinforced trunks. I had no difficulty recognizing mine. From it, I extracted a thick packet of stage money ... not the ordinary green and orange fake stuff which you see in novelty stores, but a reasonable facsimile of real money both as to size and color. Naturally, the stage money was covered with "goon" writing ... doubletalk words ... and fake portraits. It could never be passed as real money, but magicians substitute the bills when they pretend to tear up a genuine five-dollar bill before the audience's eyes. From a short distance, it is difficult to detect a difference between the two. My trunk was crammed with a hundred other props, and finally I managed to get it closed and locked again.

Back in my room at the top of the house, I wrapped genuine one-hundred dollar bills of my own money, and a number of legitimate fifties around the roll of stage money. I had a wad of dough that would have impressed even a bank!

The following night I took Mary Deems out to a movie and to dinner. She was a nice person who didn't go out very often and was very anxious to be pleasant. Carefully, she ordered the less expensive items on the menu; my plans, however, called for me to flash my roll of bills and play the lout. I did, and the sight of the money hit her, hard. That was what I wanted.

Humphries had been away three days when on the morning of the fourth, I read a small item on page nine of the morning paper. The story said a man identified as Adrian Magarian, proprietor of the Inland Printing Shop, had been found murdered in his office. From what I read, the printing shop was just a small place located near Canal Street, and the police regarded it as another hold-up killing. Magarian had been struck down and killed by a blow on his head, and his shop had been ransacked. Judging by the position and briefness of the story, it was evident that Magarian wasn't very important.

I decided that the police hadn't found Humphries' counterfeit plates, or the story would have been page one! I wondered if Humphries had killed him ... or had someone else killed and robbed Magarian. I was inclined to believe it was Humphries; it followed his pattern ... no guns, no knives. Anyway, I decided to see what kind of reaction I could raise from him, so I called Bear Mountain 8500 ... the number he had given me. When he got on the phone I said, "Sir, I don't know if this is important, but I thought I'd better call."

"Yes. What is it?" It seemed to me his drawl sounded a little forced.

"Well," I told him, "some man just called the house and asked for you. I said you were out of town. Then he wanted to know if I could put him in touch with someone named Magarian."

"Who?"

"Magarian."

There was a long pause. "Never heard of him," Humphries finally remarked. "Who was it called?"

"I don't know. He wouldn't leave his name."

"Is he going to call back?" Humphries attempted to sound indifferent.

"He didn't say."

After a moment, Humphries said slowly, suspiciously, "How come you called me?"

"You said to call if anything happened ..."

"Well? What has happened?"

"Nothing," I admitted brightly, "except this guy ... man called. I thought *maybe* it might be important."

"Well, 'tisn't," said Humphries, back in his old characteristic drawl again. "Incidentally," he added, casually, "I'm getting mighty tired of sticking around this here place. Ain't stepped a foot outside the door since I been here; guess maybe you better mosey up and get me ... this afternoon."

"Yes, sir," I replied. I didn't mention the item in the paper to Humphries ... then or later ... and he never said a word about it to me. However, I could never shake the conviction that Humphries had used his trip to Bear Mountain as an alibi, to slip back to New York to knock off Magarian. The facts were that Magarian was dead and, as I soon discovered, Humphries still had the plates.

That Humphries had known Magarian, and also knew that he was now dead, was proven by his acts of omission. For several weeks, until after the first of August, Humphries made no more sorties into the saloons and bistros. Then, abruptly, he began the old routine of sneaking out of the clubs at night, and I knew that he had found another printer.

In the meantime, I was still developing my own plans. As a motive for Isham Reddick to kill Humphries, I selected the motive of blackmail ... with a reverse twist. Usually, it is the blackmailer who is killed, and not the victim. I would reverse the plot; as the blackmailer I would kill my golden goose. The cops would figure that I had pushed my victim to the end of his endurance, and to prevent him from turning me in—I had killed him. Flashing my roll of bills around the house, at every opportunity, I dropped hints and insinuations regarding the source of my wealth. Deliberately, I went out of my way to lend the caretaker ... a prying ass of a man ... money. To make the story better, I doctored up an envelope, with a list of fantastic figures including the number 8500 ... and arranged for Lightbody to get it. I hoped it would give him something to remember ... and to talk about ... when the time came.

Although my three thousand dollars were dwindling fast, it was imperative that I make my story convincing. The cops had to believe that I had taken Humphries for a big bank roll, and had spent it like a profligate. Making certain to leave a wide and easily followed path, I brought a solid gold wrist watch, jewelry, suits, sport equipment, and about everything else I could conceive; I couldn't be positive that the police would dig up all the purchases, but I knew they would trace some of them.

At one point, I nearly made a serious error. It was imperative I have a complete set of teeth the day I walked out of Humphries' house after killing him. The cops would be looking for a man with a tooth missing. Somewhere I had misplaced my tooth with the removable bridge. I couldn't remember seeing it since I had moved to East Eighty-ninth Street, and I couldn't find it. Consequently, I had to have another made. I realized the dentist might remember making one, and possibly inform the police. This would change their broadcast description of me, but I decided that it would take him several days to notify the police, and that would be enough of a start for me.

I called a dentist named Boss and went to see him. Attempting to remain as inconspicuous as possible, I stayed within the role of Isham Reddick—poor, hard-working chauffeur. Knowing that I would have to give an address and telephone number to his office, I was afraid to use a fictitious name in case Boss should call me to cancel an appointment. If he should become suspicious of me, he might remember me that much more quickly. He made me another tooth.

There was still a decision to be made concerning the method by which to kill Humphries. I had been so busy painting in my protective coloring that I continually postponed reaching a conclusion. Deciding, finally, that the best plan would be to strike when we were out of town, I determined to strip the body of identification and conceal it where it might remain undetected for a few days. This would give me even more time in which to disappear. Humphries, however, remained in town.

Shortly after the first of November, I began suggesting he take another short vacation, hoping that I might arouse some restlessness within him. Indirectly, I recommended a trip to Virginia, but he refused to rise to the bait. With each day, he seemed to become more taciturn and moody. When I had first found him, Humphries had been loud, blustery, and partly drunk most of the time. Since his return from Bear Mountain, in July, he had begun a slow deterioration. Possibly the idea that someone knew about his connection with Magarian worried him; or perhaps the strain of passing the queer, day after day, was wearing him down. The veneer of the openhanded Texan was getting very thin; occasionally his drawl would slip; and he took less interest in his appearance.

There was a certain satisfaction in watching Humphries breakup, and because of this satisfaction, I continued to procrastinate. The idea that I should get him out of town, although a sound one, was based, subconsciously perhaps, on a premise to help postpone my final action. There were plenty of opportunities for me to walk into his bedroom at night, and simply put a bullet through his head.

But the decision was finally forced on me!

Humphries forced it himself. On the morning of November twentieth, he arose with his usual terrific hangover. The night before, at the club, he had been absent longer than usual, over an hour. When he returned, he had been carrying a very heavy package wrapped in brown paper, and securely tied. The girl he had with him had noticed his departure from the table, and they had argued about it in the car. Angrily, he had me stop and send her off in a cab.

Sitting on the side of his bed, eating aspirin, and sipping a pick-me-up, Humphries said, "Reddick, I've got some sad news. I've decided to close up this here house and haul stakes back to Texas."

"I'm sorry to hear that," I replied. Recalling the tightly wrapped package of the night before, I knew Humphries had secured the return of the plates. Possibly he felt that he had run his luck too long in New York, or perhaps he had printing troubles again. Either way, he was folding up.

"Yes," he said, "I'm going back. I'm planning to leave in a week. That's not much notice, but I'll pay yore wages for an extra week."

"What about Deems?" I asked.

"She'll stay on for the owner's family to keep the house open." For a moment, he whirled the liquor around in the glass, watching it intently, and not meeting my eyes. Finally, he said, "I'd ... shore ... appreciate it, if you didn't mention it until I'm ready to tell her myself...."

That was it. Humphries was planning to take a runout powder and skip out from under his lease. He was afraid that Mary Deems might notify the owners. Momentarily, I couldn't understand why he had told me, and then I realized it was because of the car. Humphries was a wretched driver, and he needed me to sell the auto. "Yes, sir," I agreed, "I won't say anything about it."

That afternoon, I went down to buy a ticket for France ... an airline ticket. I now planned to kill Humphries the night of November twenty-third. When the police discovered that Isham Reddick had bought a ticket for Paris, the news would confuse them for a day or two. Particularly, as I had not applied for a passport, the authorities would have no record, and they could not be sure ... without detailed checking ... that I hadn't slipped through under another name.

The next day, November twenty-first, I went through the motions of looking for someone to buy the car ... driving it around to several car dealers ... and repeating to Humphries the offers I had received. On the morning of November twenty-second, Humphries arose ... earlier than usual ... and sober for a change. He told me that he would be downtown all day, and wouldn't be home until late that night. I drove him down to Fifty-seventh Street and Fifth Avenue, where he got off in front of a bank. That evening, around dinner time, I pretended I had received a call from Humphries and told Mary Deems that she could have the night off, as well as the entire next day. She was very happy to go visit her mother who lived in St. Albans. I also notified the Lightbodys.

Mary Deems left the house around seven o'clock in the evening. At eight, I drove downtown and stopped for a sandwich; then I went over to Duval's. From my trunk I took a snub-nosed .32, a pistol which I had used while rehearsing the "catching-a-bullet-in-my-teeth" routine. On my way out, I asked Harry, "Do you have any bullets?"

"Blanks?" he asked.

"No, regular ones." I held up the revolver and forced a grin. "Remember this? I have another idea."

"Be careful, Lew. Don't forget that guy who got killed on the stage in London."

"Sure," I told him. "I just have an idea ... for a shot-in-a-pillow illusion. I need some shells."

"I think I got some here, someplace," replied Harry. He began rummaging through the shelves, and eventually came up with a partly filled box of .32's. "Will these do?" he asked.

Shoving one into the chamber, I said, "Sure, they'll do great. How much?"

"Take the box," Harry said. "Nobody else wants 'em."

"Thanks, but I don't need that many." I filled the remaining chambers, and returned the box to him.

It was a little after nine when I arrived back on Eighty-ninth Street. The premises were dark, with the exception of a light I had left burning in the entrance hall. I went upstairs, first to my room on the top floor where I removed my coat and hat, then I returned to the second floor. The great house, suddenly, seemed sinisterly silent. Expectantly, it waited in the night, drawing its shadows around itself, clothing itself in darkness. The well of the stairway, which spiraled through the heart of the mansion, was a black void which sighed and rustled uneasily. Around me the deserted halls, the empty rooms were filled with the specters of all the murderers since time began. Each of my steps seemed to shake the walls to their very foundations, threatening to bring down the masonry in rubble.

At the end of the dark corridor, I opened the door to Humphries' bedroom ... the master suite. It is located along one side of the house, a locked door opening from the corridor into a small service hall. Grouped around the hall are several closets, and a large bath. Adjoining the service hall is an elaborate dressing room which, in turn, leads to the master bedroom. This is an extremely large room with a heavy fireplace at one end.

Somewhere in this suite, Will Shaw's plates were hidden. Humphries had concealed them here; and I intended to find them. Retracing my steps to the service hall, I began searching the closets ... going through the boxes and built-in drawers, exploring clothing, shelves, and corners. Methodically, I examined the bathroom, looking under the top of the water reservoirs. In the dressing room, I explored closets, drawers, dressers, and commodes. Eventually, in the bedroom, concealed behind the logs stacked in the fireplace, I found them. Picking up the package, I walked to the bed and tore open the wrappings. There they were! The complete set of counterfeit plates ... now stained with ink, but as perfect as the day they were made, as faultless as the moment I had seen them, with Tally, in Philadelphia!

"You lousy, sneakin' son-of-a-bitch!"

Whirling, I faced Humphries. He stood in the door connecting the dressing room and bedroom, and his face was twisted with fury. Rapidly he strode toward me, the wrinkles in his forehead bunched together, pulling the flesh across the bridge of his nose into a long, deep V. In the dim light of the shaded room, his eyes were merely opaque shadows.

My hands, reacting more quickly than my mind, flashed up with the .32. "That's far enough," I said.

At the sound of my voice, he stopped. His arms hung loosely at his sides, and for a moment he peered at me—as if watching a stranger.

"Reddick," he said hoarsely, "what do you want?"

"Step back about three feet," I said, "and then raise your hands in that respectable, old-fashioned gesture of hands-up."

Complying with my command, he asked, "Who are you?"

"Well," I replied, "you've always called me Isham Reddick."

"That's not your name!"

"How about calling me Adrian Magarian? Perhaps I'm a reincarnation."

"God damn it! Stop playing cat and mouse. Who are you and what do you want?" He no longer even made a pretense of using his Texas accent.

"I'll tell you," I said, "suppose you call me Ath. That's spelled capital A-t-h."

"Ath? What kind of a name is that? Who do you think you're fooling?"

"No one," I said, "you least of all. My initials are D. E. My full and complete name, as far as you are concerned, is D. E. Ath."

Perspiration broke quickly across his brow. One second his forehead was dry, the next instant it was wet with a thousand little beads of sweat. "You're crazy!" he said, his voice croaking.

"Absolutely," I agreed. And at that moment I was crazy. My mouth was dry, so dry that it seemed necessary to form each word with my lips first—before attempting to pronounce it. In the back of my throat, I could taste the bitter bite of gall. Humphries quickly withdrew another step. "That's all right," I said benevolently as a Spanish priest lighting fagots at an auto-da-fé, "keep going. You and I are going to the basement. There, I shall kill you. I could do it here, but neighbors might hear the shots. In the meantime, turn around and keep moving." I motioned with the revolver, and turning with cramped, paralyzed movements he floundered from the room. I followed him. Stumbling down the stairs, he wavered through the hall and into the kitchen. "We're going to the basement," I explained, my voice so tight and rasping I could hardly speak, "because there are six shots in this revolver, and I'm going to put four of them into you. Slowly! The fifth I'll put in your head. The basement is nice and quiet ... practically soundproof. I know ... I've thought about it often."

Behind the kitchen, loomed the back hall—and the stairway to the basement descended from there. Slowly, in slow motion, Humphries opened the door; his eyes were blind, unseeing ... and distended with fear. "Switch on the lights," I ordered. His fingers clawed helplessly, scratching against the side of the door. Reaching past him, I switched them on myself.

Humphries began to descend.

I followed him.

Chapter 21

Humphries raised his right hand to the oath, "I swear to tell the truth, the whole truth ... so help me God!" As he seated himself in the witness chair, Denman approached him ... in the quiet of the courtroom ... and said, "I want you to tell the jury, and the court, in your own words exactly what happened between you and Isham Reddick the night of November twenty-second in your house on East Eighty-ninth Street." The attorney for the defense glanced at the jurors who were regarding both him and the defendant, impassively. "You will retell the circumstances exactly as you have told them to me, and I will not interrupt you—unless it is necessary to elaborate a point, or to ask a question. Now, Mr. Humphries, please begin."

Humphries sat quietly for a moment, staring into space and, seemingly, hearing only part of Denman's words. Finally, after the attorney had ceased to speak and stood waiting expectantly, Humphries wrenched his attention back to the present, and looking over the heads of the jury began in a toneless voice.

"I had been downtown all day," he said. "I went to the bank to withdraw some money, and during the afternoon, I bought some things for a vacation I had planned. After a rather late dinner, I decided to return home, and not wishing to wait until Reddick could pick me up with the car, I rode home in a taxi. When I arrived home, I noticed the house was dark, except for a light in the downstairs' hall, and a light in my bedroom. This seemed strange to me, as the house should have been well lighted—and my bedroom dark. I opened the door with my own key, and walked in. Mary Deems was not around, although there was always the possibility that she was in her own room...."

"You had not given her permission to leave for the night?" asked Denman.

"No, I had not!" replied Humphries. "I returned to the main hall and walked upstairs to the second floor, very quietly. The door from the corridor to the service hall of my bedroom was open and I entered it ... passing through the dressing room until I could look into the bedroom. There I saw Isham Reddick rifling through my belongings. He had taken some jewelry, and at the instant I saw him, he had removed a large sum of money from a wallet I had left on top of my dresser.

"At that moment, he saw me, too. Instantly, he drew a revolver and told me to raise my hands. I was unarmed ... entirely defenseless, and I did as he told me. I tried to reason with him, but he was a crazy man ... yelling and threatening me."

"What did he say to you, Mr. Humphries?"

"He talked very quickly ... almost babbling, and much he said didn't make any sense. Reddick kept referring to himself by the name of Ath ... and he said his initials were D. E. And put them together, he was D.E.Ath ... it was a nightmare! I told him he could have the jewelry and money ... to take them and leave."

"In all the months that Isham Reddick worked for you," Denman questioned, "had he ever given any indication that he was insane, or subject to spells of unreasoning fury? Anything like that?"

"No," replied Humphries, "he wasn't the usual type of man you find employed as a chauffeur, though. Often he seemed ... well, not quite disrespectful, but rather as if he was amused about something, or had a secret he was enjoying. However, he always did his work well enough. If I had thought for a moment that I had a ... a lunatic on my hands, I'd have let him go immediately."

"All right," said Denman, nodding, "please continue."

"I thought possibly, as I stood there with Reddick pointing the revolver, that I might be able to escape from the bedroom. I was not far away from the door, and I tried to ease away, but he saw me. Suddenly, he ordered me to turn around and march to the basement. As you know, it's a large house and it requires a few minutes to walk from the second floor to the downstairs back hall ... where the cellarway is located. It was quite dark, and on the way I tried to think of something to do, some way to escape; but Reddick was right behind me, with his gun, and he was raving every step of the way...."

"Again, Mr. Humphries, can you recall what he said to you?"

"Yes. He threatened me with a slow death ... he was going to torture me ... shoot me four or five times."

"It would be an understatement would it not, Mr. Humphries, to say you were in mortal fear of your life?"

"I have never been so frightened!" Humphries abruptly removed the pocket handkerchief from his coat, and wiped his forehead. Returning it to his pocket, he removed it again to dry the palms of his hands. "At the top of the basement stairs," he picked up his story again, "Reddick ordered me to turn on the lights. That is the last thing that I distinctly remember. I knew I was walking to my death ... to an execution ... and each step down was less clear, less real. It is a long stairway from the back hall to the basement floor, and somewhere along the way I completely lost contact with reality...."

"I wish you would explain that a little more," Denman interrupted. "You say that you lost contact with reality. Do you remember reaching the bottom step at all?"

"Yes," replied Humphries, slowly. "But only as an impression, not as an actual occurrence. Going down the stairs was like sinking into slumber ... a grayness closed in over everything. My body worked mechanically ... independently of my mind ... there was absolutely no contact between the two. Eventually, my body reached the cellar floor, the last step, and at that point my mind went completely blank. Everything sank into darkness."

"That is all you remember of that night?"

"Yes, sir. That is all."

"What is the next event which you remember?"

"It was possibly twelve, or fourteen, hours later. I became conscious of a sound ... a noise that kept repeating itself from far away. After what seemed a long time, I realized it was the bell ringing in the house. I aroused myself ..."

"Where were you then? When you regained consciousness?"

Humphries shook his head, unbelievingly, "I was lying on my bed ... upstairs in the master suite."

"Were you fully clothed?" asked Denman.

"No. I was wearing only my undershirt and shorts."

"Where was the suit you wore the night before?"

"It was hanging in the closet, I discovered later. There was a terrible aching ... throbbing in my head, and I wondered why someone—Mary Deems or Reddick—didn't answer the door."

"You mentioned Reddick. At that time, did you recall what had happened the previous night?"

"Not right then, sir, I simply got out of bed and put on a robe. Going downstairs, I opened the door ... and there were the police."

"When you saw the police, what did you say?"

"I couldn't understand for a while why they were there. Then I suddenly remembered Reddick from the night before ... how close he had come to killing me. Immediately, I thought he had run away and gotten into trouble. I thought the police were there because of him!"

"When they asked to come in, you let them in?"

"Certainly. I had nothing to hide."

From then, until noon, Denman painstakingly went over Humphries' story. He could only elaborate on the testimony as given; Humphries had nothing new to introduce. When he had finished, Denman studied the jury carefully as they filed out to lunch. Eleven of the faces were still impassive, but on one face ... just one ... Denman wondered if he didn't see a faint trace of credulity.

When court convened, again, in the afternoon, Cannon began his cross-examination. "Tell me, Mr. Humphries," he asked, "what happened to the jewelry and money Isham Reddick was supposed to be stealing when you caught him?"

Denman immediately interposed an objection, which was sustained.

"All right," Cannon continued, "you say Isham Reddick was stealing your jewelry, is that correct?"

"That is correct."

"Did you ever see the jewels again?"

"No. I didn't."

"The police found no trace of them. There were no traces in the house. Did you look for them?"

"I don't know ..."

"You don't know?" Cannon pretended surprise. "You knew Reddick had them, but you didn't look for them again?"

"I—I didn't think about ... he took it with him when he left."

"You had some other jewelry ... which he didn't steal?"

"Yes. There was some left ..."

"But you don't know what was taken? You only know what was left behind. Could it have been the same jewelry?"

"No, sir."

"And the money? You testified that you had left a large sum of money home in your wallet?"

"Yes. Yes, I had."

"And earlier in the day, you had been to the bank to get more money? Why did you need all that money?"

"Well ... I had planned a vacation ..."

Because of Humphries' evasive and indefinite answers concerning the jewelry and money, Cannon was convinced the witness was not telling the truth. The prosecuting attorney continued to pound away at him, wearing him down, dogging his answers. Finally, Cannon said, "Mr. Humphries, you state that when you reached the cellar floor, the bottom step of the stairs, you completely ... 'lost contact with reality.' By that you mean that you blacked out ... lost consciousness?"

"Yes, sir."

"And after you blacked out, you do not remember anything for over twelve hours?"

"That's right. I don't remember anything."

"You don't remember killing Isham Reddick?"

"No, sir. I didn't kill him."

"You don't remember anyone else killing him?"

"No, sir."

"You don't remember dismembering Isham Reddick's body and destroying it in the furnace?"

"I didn't dismember him ... and burn the body in the furnace."

"But you don't remember!" Cannon said.

"No, sir. I don't remember. But I didn't do it...."

"You don't remember anyone else dismembering Isham Reddick's body and cremating it in the furnace?"

"No. I don't!"

"You don't remember how the ashes got in the furnace, how the bloodstains got in the basement, how the fragments of the body were scattered around as if in a charnel house?"

"No, sir. I know nothing about it. I don't remember a thing. I only know that—I couldn't have done it."

"But you don't remember anyone else present in the basement that night, do you?"

"No."

"Absolutely no one?"

"No one. I don't remember anything until the next morning."

"In the morning you awakened in bed, refreshed from a night's sleep … after a miraculous escape from an insane killer … as you have described him?"

Humphries glanced helplessly at Cannon. He nervously tugged at his collar, and then with great effort clasped his hands, and forced them to remain quiet. The pressure of his hands, locked together, marked his knuckles with white.

"Was Isham Reddick blackmailing you … asking you for money?" Cannon pursued his questions relentlessly.

"No, sir …"

"You had no reason, then, to hate or fear Isham Reddick?"

"None … none at all."

"Did Isham Reddick have any reason to hate or fear you?"

"No, sir … except I caught him stealing."

"That was enough to make him want to kill you? Especially after you told him to take the money and jewelry—and leave?"

"Well …"

"Well … what?" asked Cannon.

"Isham Reddick was just crazy … that's all!"

"Was he crazy enough to kill himself, dismember himself, and then cremate himself? And afterward, clean up the mess?"

"No …"

"Then who killed Isham Reddick? Who dismembered him, and disposed of parts of his body?"

"I don't know," Humphries admitted, his voice hopeless, "except it wasn't me."

"This was a carefully planned, diabolically executed murder. Someone had to do it. To do it, someone had to be there. You were there, Isham Reddick was there. Was anyone else there?"

Wearily, Humphries retreated to his defense. "I don't know," he said.

"I can't remember ..."

As Cannon continued his ruthless questioning, Denman glanced cautiously at the one juror ... the one he had noticed at the noon adjournment. Their glances met—the attorney for the defense, and the juror. Before their eyes parted, Denman was uncertain that he had ever detected a look of sympathy there.

Chapter 22

The stairs yawned before us. The foot of the flight was washed in a reflection of light from the concrete floor, while the stairs, themselves, were wrapped in shadows. The descent was very steep, and a handrailing ran along the right side. I shifted the revolver to my left hand, my right grasped the rail as we descended. Just in front of me, Humphries' head was on a level with my chest, and his sweat ... the acrid smell of fear ... was heavy in the air. Its odor seemed to drive me into a deeper frenzy, and I thrust the revolver against the back of his neck. Slowly, legs moving in unison to the same macabre rhythm we marched down ... step by step.

As Humphries reached the basement floor, he moaned loudly and stooping suddenly—straightened, a glittering, swirling arc of light flashing by his side. Instinctively I ducked, and thrust out my right hand to steady myself against the post at the foot of the stairs.

An instant later, the hatchet buried itself into the wood, and Humphries slumped forward to the floor!

I stood woodenly holding my position in the tableau. I looked questioningly at the gun in my hand ... I couldn't remember shooting it. There was no smell of gunpowder in my nose, no echoing sound of a shot in my ears. And then I became conscious of warmth stealing over my right hand. Involuntarily, I moved my hand, holding it in front of my eyes. Part of a finger was missing from my right hand. Blood spouted from the severed flesh. The dismembered section was lying on the floor beside the post. Dazedly, I kicked at the motionless body of Humphries. He didn't move. There was no sensation, as yet, from my hand and I walked aimlessly around the furnace room, holding the pulse at my wrist, attempting to stop the flow of blood. The stream, however, seemed to clear my mind ... and I began thinking again clearly and rationally. The cobwebs of hate, the clinging entangling skeins of insane anger which had twisted my thoughts for so long, disintegrated—dissolving finally with the falling drops of blood which marked my steps and crimsoned the floor of the furnace room.

Returning to where Humphries was lying, I knelt on the floor beside him. He was unconscious still, but I could hear the irregular sound of his breathing in the quiet of the room. Breaking open the chamber of the revolver, I found the shells intact ... unfired.

With a sigh of relief, I realized I had not shot Humphries!

Humphries had collapsed from shock ... from sheer fright. In one fast, frenzied, unconscious effort he had grabbed up the hatchet from the floor ... a hatchet Lightbody used to split kindling ... and had swung at me in a desperate attempt at defense. Even as he swung, he had blacked out through shock and hysteria; sometimes condemned criminals do the same.

Almost immediately I realized something else: here was a man who had committed three murders, or had been responsible for them, and had escaped punishment. But there was still a way by which justice could be served.

By my watch, it was then almost 10:30; the night of the twenty-second of November. I lit a cigarette, and sat down on the bottom step to think the situation over. The greatest illusions, I knew, are compounded equally by the things you see ... and the things you don't see. Obviously, I could not leave my entire body, but possibly I could leave traces that seemed to prove I had left my entire body. The illusion must be of a murder committed ... and almost entirely erased!

Picking up the hatchet, I walked into the next room, a semi-laundry, where the tool chest was kept. I pasted several hairs from my head to the blood on the hatchet, and wiping the handle on the sleeve of my coat, tossed it in the box. Next to the laundry was a basement bathroom. Standing over the wash basin for a minute or two, I permitted a trickle of blood to run down the drain and into the trap. Turning away, I splattered more stains around the cracks and corners of the floor—and then I was forced to stop. Already I had lost too much blood. With a piece of twine, I bound the finger as tightly as I dared, to stop the flow, and bandaged the end with a strip from my handkerchief.

My greatest fear was that Humphries might regain consciousness. Under the basement stairs there was a small, securely constructed closet where logs for the fireplaces were stored. On the outside of the door was a heavy drop bolt. Lifting Humphries by his shoulders, I dragged him to the closet, and bolted him inside.

I returned to my room, upstairs, and found a pair of leather driving gloves. Slipping them on, I stuffed the empty finger with cotton; and put on a top coat. Taking the car, for the second time that night, I returned to my trunk at Duval's. Harry nodded to me, showing no surprise at my late return. From the big metal trunk, I removed Omar ... my skeleton. God knows who Omar had once been. I had bought him complete, with wired joints, from Harry Lohr ten years before when I needed a skeleton for a comedy gag in a disappearing-cabinet act. Harry originally had purchased Omar from some long since forgotten magician, or supply house. Omar, however, was a real skeleton … and not a composition one. Removing the shin bone … the one reaching from the knee to the ankle, I broke off the ends where it had been wired through small holes. While I was returning the rest of the skeleton to the trunk, I remembered, suddenly, to look in a small built-in drawer in the top where I kept a lot of tiny gadgets such as springs, card-feeders, and release gimmicks.

Pulling out the shallow drawer, I discovered my missing tooth. I had packed it in my trunk, through force of habit, the day I had moved to Eighty-ninth Street. Slipping it in my pocket, I placed Omar's shin bone flat against the small of my back, holding it in position with my belt. After I had again donned my topcoat, it was impossible to detect. My hand was beginning to ache terribly, now, and I was anxious to get away. But there were still other calls to make.

I drove around town, looking for all-night delicatessens, carefully avoiding uptown and midtown Manhattan. Eventually, I found four of them which were open, and from each I bought five pounds of beef. Then with twenty pounds of meat, Omar's leg, and my missing tooth, I returned to the house.

It was after midnight when I arrived. Immediately, I built a great roaring fire in the furnace, and knocking apart the workbench, fed it to the flames; a large canvas tarpaulin, used for painting, also went into the fire … after I had carefully removed a small section which contained bloodstains. The pain from my finger raced high up into my arm; the stub swollen and angrily discolored from the tourniquet forced me to stop for a while. A great weariness weighed on me, and it seemed impossible that I would be able to complete all the effects called for by the illusion. My head whirled dizzily. I forced myself to climb to the upper floors of the house where I searched through the medicine cabinets. In Mary Deems' room, I found a bottle with three codeine pills in it. I took all the pills at once—and they seemed to help relieve the pain, or at least numbing me to the point where I could carry on. I also made another discovery, an important one. In the same medicine cabinet I found a small bottle of ether, which Mary used for cleaning purposes to remove spots and stains. I took the bottle back to the furnace room.

I kept the furnace roaring and forced the draft and at four o'clock the fire had pretty well burned through the bed of coals. I removed the ashes, shoveling them into a tub. Loading the tub into the car, I drove across town, and in front of a large apartment building, I left it concealed among a large number of other tubs filled with trash and refuse. On the back floor of the car, however, the imprint of the tub and the dust of the ashes remained on the rug.

Dawn was not far away. I looked in on Humphries, in the closet, and decided I had better take him upstairs while I still had the strength. When I touched him, he stirred uneasily. It gave me a shock. Hastily, I poured ether on the remnant of my handkerchief, and held it to his nose and mouth—praying to myself that I didn't smother him. He quickly became quiet again, and I immediately removed the cloth. Without another quiver from him, I alternately hauled, hoisted, and dragged Humphries upstairs to his bedroom ... a long, difficult trip with the limp body of a man his size. Undressing him, I left him on his bed, and carefully hung his suit in the closet.

Back in the basement, I rebuilt the fire ... but not so large as before. When it was glowing hot, I fired the revolver into a chunk of the beef and threw all the meat into the fire. It began to glow, then caught fire and burned with a thick, dark, black smoke. Eventually, it burned to ashy cinders, and I broke the mass up with the end of the poker, then shook the furnace to sift the ashes ... both wood and meat ... together into the receptacle below, where I had previously placed the charred piece of canvas.

Omar's shin bone I laid carefully on top of the mass of coals. The broken ends first began to burn. I permitted the fire to gradually envelop it, until the entire bone was blackened, and partly consumed. Then very carefully, I removed it from the flames placing it in the trash box, along with a charred end of wood from the bench.

Time was growing short now; the hours were running out. Partly paralyzed with exhaustion, I took a long drink from Humphries' stock of liquor. My mind was so benumbed with fatigue, that the whisky was absolutely tasteless. Lurching back to my work, I attached a garden hose to an inside connection and sluiced down the floor in the furnace room, permitting the water to stand in puddles and dry by evaporation. In the downstairs bathroom, I did the same. When I had finished, the floors were clean, but the damning traces of blood could still be found in the cracks of the floor!

Now, there were signs of life, noises and activity on the streets outside, and I must make one final effort to hurry. As the last gesture, I placed the tooth that Boss had made on the coals, and when it had darkened I tossed it into the bottom of the furnace. The indisputable positive proof of my finger, I half concealed on the floor outside the furnace.

In Humphries' room, I buried the note ... the one reading "Reddick ... mt. 8500" ... in a drawer of his dresser, together with the fired revolver, after wiping it clean of prints. Then I undressed, and in his bathroom took a shower ... washing myself clean of dirt, ashes, and blood. When I had finished, I put on the same stained clothes again, as I did not want to leave them in the house.

Again, I climbed the stairs to my room on the top floor. Somewhat awkwardly, because I was forced to use my left hand, I darkened my eyebrows with a make-up pencil, and replaced my missing tooth; the glasses I put in my pocket to carry away. Carefully, I brushed my hair, making sure I left a few strands in my brush. Blood had soaked through the glove on my right hand, staining it; I put on a new pair, again filling out the missing finger. The stained pair, I stuffed in my overcoat pocket. Checking the room carefully, going through the drawers I removed all records except a few specimens of writing. Once more, I stopped in Humphries' room for a final look. He was still unconscious. Beside him on the bed where I had left them were the counterfeit plates. Wrapping the paper around them, I carried them away with me, to be destroyed later.

At the last moment, I stood within the main entryway on the ground floor, checking over everything in my mind: the hot furnace, the ashes, the bloodstains; the tooth, finger, and nail; the shin bone, the piece of bench, the square of bloody canvas; the hatchet with the blood and hairs; the hair in my brush; the blood in the drains; the ash-tub marks in the car; Humphries' note and gun in his drawer. I recalled the boasts I had deliberately made; the money shown to Lightbody and Mary Deems; the envelope with figures in my writing; the gold wrist watch; the expensive suits; the ticket to Paris. And, of course, the deserted house; Humphries unconscious for the night ... with no alibi; no witnesses. And the final cynical beauty of truth itself. Humphries himself could never dare tell all the truth. Even if he knew the entire truth, his lips were partly sealed ... or he would be exchanging one hangman for another; one executioner for his brother. Humphries' life had been built on lies; and he must continue to live it on that basis. His own truths would condemn him.

Yes, I was satisfied.

The illusion was complete!

Chapter 23

Two weeks before, the verdict had been returned by the jury. After nearly seventy-two hours of deliberation, and argument, the jurors had reached a decision. They had reported it to the court. "Guilty," the foreman announced in a firm voice.

And now the court was to pronounce the sentence.

Humphries stood before the judge, standing alone in front of the high paneled bench. No longer was there a crowd in the courtroom; no public, no spectators. Only the members of the judge's court, Mr. Cannon, attorney for the prosecution, and Mr. Denman, attorney for the defense.

The spot, standing before the sentencing judge, is a lonesome place. It is the loneliest place in the world.

The judge observed the prisoner before him, for a moment, then said in the age-old ritual, "Is there anything you wish to say before I pronounce your sentence?"

Humphries, raising his head, shrugged his shoulders hopelessly. He was wearing the same suit he had worn during the trial, but now it hung more loosely on him. His gray hair appeared whiter, and his long nose—projecting bleakly—looked like the bill on a ruffled bird. "No, your honor," he replied in a low voice.

"Very well," observed the judge. He lifted a paper from his desk and began reading the legal formalities as required by the State of New York. After a few minutes he put aside the paper and continued speaking, although he was no longer reading. "It is the opinion of this court that in many ways the case of the People of the State of New York versus Ballard T. Humphries has been a most unusual one. A jury of your peers has found you guilty of murder ... a murder most reprehensible and compounded by the inhuman disposing of your victim's body after the crime. That such a crime was committed and executed appeared to be proved beyond a reasonable doubt to the duly impaneled jurors. You have heard the verdict. It is: Guilty.

"And yet the law is not untempered with justice. It is the duty of this court to discover the truth, and to see that justice is delivered within its jurisdiction. It is my belief that not all the facts and circumstances of this case have been discovered, disclosed, and explored by either the prosecution or the defense. Perhaps, in truth, such facts many not exist after all ... regardless of this court's opinion, or if existing, will never be found and disclosed. But if they do exist, someday they may be brought to light. For that reason, this court has deliberated the sentence to be imposed. Hear it then:

"I hereby sentence you, the prisoner, Ballard Temple Humphries, to be delivered to the warden, or other duly authorized official, of the prison of the State of New York, located at Ossining, New York, during the week of May sixth, the next, and your person committed to him for all the remaining days of your natural life!"

The judge gathered his robe around him, arose from his chair, and retired from the courtroom. Denman reached the prisoner before the two armed guards had moved within hearing distance. The attorney placed his hand sympathetically on Humphries' arm. "You're lucky," Denman said. "You don't know how lucky you are!"

Humphries shook his head, blindly, and turned away. As he approached the guards, they took their places—placing him between them. The prisoner shuffled from the room.

Chapter 24

A magician with a finger missing is Merlin with a broken wand, a card mechanic with two thumbs. I traded my finger for the capture of a murderer, my future for a tube of grease paint in clown alley.

I have a copy of *Billboard*. It says the Big One is playing out West. The pennants are flying from the main top, the music is playing, the kids are laughing. Too long, now, I have been surrounded by the ghosts of the dead—Tally, whom I loved; Will Shaw, whom I never knew; and Magarian, whom I would have disliked.

And, of course, Isham Reddick. He died years ago, and then again just recently. And when he died the second time, Greenleaf died with him; not quickly, not suddenly ... but a little bit each day.

It's time to shake the ghosts ... the one I loved, as well as the ones I never knew. In the night, I hear the distant train whistles heading West.

I'm following them.

Chapter 25

In his cell, he walked to the window, standing beneath it, the few beams of light falling like dirty water over his hair. Humphries was unable to see out of the window, but he stood as close to it as he could.

He lit a cigarette, puffing it rapidly. Within his mind a question kept revolving. Day after day, night after night, it had spun there on an endless, never ceasing track. Who was it, he thought, who was it who was it who was it who was it who was it?

Angrily, impatiently, he threw the cigarette to the floor and turned his face to the high-up window. "The lousy son-of-a-bitch!" he said. "Who was it that jobbed me? Who was it, who was it?" Turning he fell on his bunk. He rolled over on his back, and in his mind the question started going around all over again. Who was it who was it who was it who was it who was it who was ...

THE END

The Wife of the Red-Haired Man

BILL S. BALLINGER

But the day of doom shall come,
And hills and harbours be rent;
A mist shall fall on the sun
From the dark clouds heavily sent;
The sea shall be dry.
And earth under mourning and ban;
Then loud shall he cry
For the wife of the red-haired man.

Last verse, "The Red Man's Wife."

Translation by Douglas Hyde
from the Irish original.

Author, unknown.

Chapter 1

The wind slashed through the night, driving the stinging drops of rain against his face. Rohan squatted on the floor of the heavy, open, stake-body truck as it roared through the darkness, concealed from the view of the men ahead of him in the cab. The floor of the truck vibrated with shock waves—tingling his feet, jarring the muscles of his face, twitching at the skin of his forehead.

The chill of the late fall night had long exceeded the protection of his soaking denim shirt and trousers, and the headlong rush of the wind made his cramped position nearly unbearable. For two days and nights he had been fleeing—hitching rides on trucks, thumbing lifts from motorists—on his way to New York from Canada. His fear of recapture had kept him away from the cities and towns; away, even, from the occasional highway restaurants and eating stands. He was weak and dizzy from his hunger, feverish from the cold and rain.

Hungrily, the truck consumed the miles in the night, and on State Highway 22 near Pawling, New York, it slowed and stopped at an intersection. Rohan staggered to his feet and made his way to the rear of the truck bed. As the truck slowly began to roll forward again, he climbed heavily over the tail gate and dropped to the highway, his feet pounding the cement as he raced forward to retain his balance. From the side of the road, he watched the red lights of the truck disappear down the highway; then he began plodding toward the town.

He had no watch, but he believed the time to be around eleven o'clock at night. As he neared the outskirts of Pawling, he moved deeper into the shadows of the road; he no longer could think clearly although he realized that he must be careful—for in any town he could expect danger. Also, he knew that he must find a place to rest and, equally important, find food or he could not go on. The wind raised in its intensity and whipped the rain until it seemed as if he once again was riding on the truck with the thick wall of the night smashing against his face.

Working his way slowly toward the heart of the town, he circled from shadow to shadow along the dark and silent streets. Ahead of him, he saw a house; it was unpretentious and over the door a porch light glowed. The light attracted his attention. For many minutes he stood beside a tree, blending to it closely until he became part of its trunk, staring at the light. His eyes crept away finally, tracing the fuzzy blurred circumference of its glow as it spilled beyond the steps into the night. The house next door to the light was silent and dark.

At first he stared at the darkened house without interest; his mind tired, his eyes failing to register objects before it. And then, vaguely, he recognized the outline of newspapers lying against the front door. Four of them scattered across the steps. It took him another half minute to realize the meaning, the importance of what he saw, but when he grasped it he pulled himself upright beside the tree and plunged into the darkness—warily avoiding the house with the light.

At the door of the darkened house, he cautiously gathered the papers and holding them close before his eyes read the datelines. They were morning and evening papers from New York City: the oldest two days old. Carefully, he replaced them in their original positions, and circled the house to the rear.

A small screened porch boxed in the kitchen door. The screen door was unlatched, and opening it he stepped silently across the boards of the porch. He tried the handle of the kitchen door, but the door was locked. Cupping his hands, and pressing them against the square pane of glass, he attempted to peer into the interior of the kitchen, but the inky blackness of the room defeated him. Momentarily, he stopped and listened intently for sounds from within, but he could hear nothing. Rohan stepped back and examined the door carefully. Beside the doorknob he discovered a bell button. He pressed his finger against it and could hear the whirring of metal as it rang in the house. He held his finger pressed for a long time, until there was no doubt in his mind that it was unheard and would remain unanswered. With a final movement of caution, he stepped from the porch and approached the garage. Opening the door, he slipped inside to discover that the garage was empty.

He returned to the porch, latched the screened porch door on the inside. Quickly he removed his shirt, and, wrapping it around his hand, drove his fist through the pane of glass in the kitchen door. The noise was very small, but the tinkling of the falling glass sounded loud in Rohan's frightened ears. Carefully, reaching inside the door, he unlatched it; then, withdrawing his hand, he opened the door and stepped into the kitchen.

At the refrigerator, he struck a match, shielding its flame with his hand, and opened the door. As the door opened, a light flashed on within the interior of the box and the man started in surprise. Then, smiling grimly, he dropped the match to the floor, and began rifling the interior of the small amount of food in it.

In the morning, he stirred with the first sign of light. Rolling from the bed, he stood shivering in the cold room, standing naked in the middle of the bedroom. His wet, sodden denims lay in a heap on the floor. He went to a closet, opened the door, and then closed it; on the opposite side was another closet, and when he looked in it he saw ties and several suits of men's clothing. Trying one suit on, he found it hung loosely on him. He gathered the waist of the trousers, pulling his belt tight, bunching the material so that it could be concealed by the coat. Quickly then, he found a shirt in the bureau, took off the coat, slipped into the shirt, and knotted a tie at the collar.

In the bathroom he could find no razor, but instead a pair of manicure scissors, and with them he attempted to trim the heavy stubble on his face. It took him a long time and it was not too successful. When he had finished, he powdered it down with talcum.

Daylight seeped through the house as he descended the stairs to the first floor. In the kitchen cabinets he discovered a can of soup and a box of crackers. Having heated the soup on the stove, he gulped it hungrily from a cup and ate the entire box of crackers. Then, methodically, he began to rummage through the house. The small house was plainly furnished, and its occupants were evidently persons of no wealth. Rohan took nothing from the drawers, passing by small, inexpensive possessions until he found a china bank on a whatnot shelf. Breaking it open, he discovered it partly filled with bills and silver. Sixteen dollars and forty cents. With a twisted, apologetic smile, he scooped the money into his pocket and slipped out the back door of the house.

He arrived in New York City shortly before noon, having ridden the train from Pawling. In Grand Central Station he went to a telephone booth and made a phone call to a small town in Connecticut. When the phone was answered he said, "Hello, may I speak to Mercedes, please?" A look of surprise crossed his face as he listened to the reply. Then it turned rapidly to consternation, to disappointment and, finally, anger.

Holding his voice steady, he said, "No, no, we didn't know that. My name is Grant ... Howard Grant, and I'm married to an old school chum of Mercedes. I promised Mary, my wife, to call and say hello after all this time, while I was in New York. Can you tell me her married name?" He listened intently, then nodded and thanked his informant politely.

Hanging up the phone, he stepped outside the telephone booth, and leafed through a Manhattan telephone directory. He memorized the number after the name of Albert Turner, 345 East Vanders Place. Returning to the phone again, he dialed it. "May I speak to Mrs. Turner?" he asked. He stood waiting, holding the receiver to his ear; after the passage of a few moments, a voice spoke into it. Rohan froze in his position, his body intent, his attention riveted to the voice speaking to him. Then slowly, very slowly, and without replying, he hung up the receiver.

At ten thirty that night, the doorbell buzzed in the apartment of Albert Turner. Mercedes Turner opened the door. For a moment she stared at the tall, gaunt man with a crest of blazing red hair. Her delicately constructed face went slack, her lips parted; her hand sought her throat, and she held it there as if to support her breath.

The red-haired man stood awkwardly in his pinned-up suit, and his voice broke. "Mercedes ..." he said, partly whispering, partly sighing.

Mercedes Turner backed slowly from the door, her eyes staring in disbelief. "Hugh," she gasped. "Hugh ... Hugh ..."

He stepped into the apartment, and suddenly the dammed-up emotion of the years broke his restraint. He swept her into his arms, burying his face in the soft curve of her neck and shoulder. "Darling!" his voice inaudible.

Behind Rohan, in the darkened hallway, a cynical voice asked, "The return of the native?"

The woman moved gently in the arms of the red-haired man, loosening them, stepping away. She turned her head, the profile sharp and hard as a cameo. "More than that, Albert," she said. "It's the return of the dead."

"Then ask him in," replied Turner, "and let's talk to the ghost." He walked to the end of the reception hall which led into the spacious living room. For only a moment, the woman hesitated, and then nodding to Rohan followed her husband. The red-haired man walked silently behind her.

When Rohan entered the room, Turner had seated himself behind a graceful desk. A small lamp with a metal figure of a Greek warrior as a base threw its light partly upward into Turner's face, accentuating the hollows beneath his cheekbones, sweeping the heavily lidded eyes into lines of Oriental cynicism. His arched nose seemed paper thin, predatory as a beak. He lounged gracefully in his chair, a portrait of decadent elegance. "Sit down, Ghost," he said, waving his hand toward a chair. Then turning to his wife, he said, "You might make the introductions, my dear."

"I can introduce myself," the red-haired man replied. "My name is Hugh Rohan."

Turner tilted his head, consideringly. "I'm sorry," he said, pausing just long enough to subtly taint his reply with insult, "but I'm quite sure I've never heard it before." Then, as if hurrying to cover an unintentional slip, he added, "But then, there are probably very many famous people with names I wouldn't recognize."

"I'm not famous," said Rohan.

The woman remained standing, half concealed by the shadows of the room, her arms crossed over her breasts. A stray ray of light tipped her hair, touching it with gold. "Hugh ... is ... an old friend of mine," she explained softly. "I thought ... he was killed in the war."

"Ah, yes," Turner's lips seemed hardly to move, "I think I remember now ... but the name escaped me for a moment." He nodded his head apologetically toward Rohan. "The sailor boy."

"Merchant marine," Rohan corrected.

"I'm sure that Mercedes must be ... ah ... delighted to see you again. For me, of course, it's not such a ... pleasure, but that's because I don't know you so well." Turner's lips smiled ironically. "There must be a reason," he added, "for this late night, unannounced call. Would I be prying," he lifted his eyes, the whites gleaming porcelain, to Mercedes, "if I inquired why?"

"No," said Rohan. His face was marked with lines, sallow in the dimness of the room. Only his hair seemed alive. It was the blood red of a cockatoo, the splendored brilliance of a Mandarin cabinet. "The last time I saw Mercedes, she was my wife!"

A stillness, a quietness descended over Turner like a cloak. The thin upper lip, the full lower lip merged into a taut, narrow line assuming the color of his skin, disappearing, except for the edge of a shadow, into his face. Finally, he expelled his breath; the sound of it unwinding slowly in the room. "Very interesting," he said softly. "Of course I didn't know that. You must excuse me," he added insinuatingly, "if our wife hasn't told me everything ... and I appear ignorant."

The woman stirred restlessly, hugging her arms more tightly. Her voice assumed a new dignity when she spoke. Her words became statements, not explanations. "I had planned to tell you, Albert, sometime. I knew it would be useless. You'd have been delighted to taunt me. I thought Hugh was dead, and I hoped to leave it that way."

Turner laughed, a soft scratching, irritating sound. "That's always the way, isn't it, dear? The best-laid plans, et cetera, and now you are a bigamist?"

"No," replied Mercedes, "I received an Enoch Arden decree before we were married."

Turner shifted his eyes to Rohan. "Well, old chap," he said lightly, "that clears that up. She isn't *our* wife after all. She's my wife." He shifted his shoulders, a shrug of synthetic sympathy. "But that is the fortune of love, wouldn't you say?"

"No," replied Rohan, his voice low in his chest. "If she still loves me, and will come with me ... she can divorce you and we will be married."

"What do you say, my dear?" Turner glanced inquiringly at Mercedes.

"You know how I feel about you," she replied steadily. "I hate you!"

"Ah, well," replied Turner indifferently, "and after all we've been to each other." His voice carried an intonation of amusement. "Do you still love this ... ah ... sailor boy?"

"I've always loved him," she replied simply, "and when I thought he had died ..." She glanced at Turner contemptuously. "Otherwise, I would never have married you!"

Turner did not appear to be listening to her. His eyes searched Rohan's face thoughtfully. The woman stepped from the shadows and approached the chair where the red-haired man was sitting. Gently, as if seeking assurance, she dropped her hand on his shoulder. "If Hugh wants me, I'll marry him."

"That's very touching," said Turner, "but you know how it is ... my ethics, my beliefs ..." his lips twitched with silent amusement, "I just can't see my way clear to give you a divorce. I've told you this before."

"Then I will live with him ... anyway."

"Of course," said Turner, "that would cause me a great deal of embarrassment ... my social standing, my business associates." He lifted his eyebrows, thin, narrow, which arched high into his forehead. In mock implorement his voice added softly, "Please don't do that. You see, every time you did, I should have to have you arrested for adultery. Not for divorce action, of course, but merely criminal prosecution. I'm afraid, my dear, that you wouldn't like all the time you'd spend in the Tombs." Abruptly, he leaned over the desk, his eyes still riveted on Rohan. "I think your boy friend here could tell you something about that!"

The woman's hand clutched Rohan's shoulder. "I don't know what you're talking about."

Turner's thin nose seemed to wrinkle in distaste. "An ex-con," he said to the man. "You have the stink of the prisons on you!"

"You're a liar!" Rohan shook gently free of Mercedes' hand and rose to his feet. His face was cold, expressionless as yellow marble.

"Possibly," agreed Turner affably. "But that suit fits oddly, your haircut would do no credit to a barber college, the shoes you are wearing are prison issue ... and believe me, I know." His eyes crawled calculating along Rohan's face. "And finally, unless you have TB, I'd say you haven't seen the sun in ten years!"

"You're crazy," said Rohan, but his breath was ragged and irregular. "This is the kind of haircut the crew give each other ... and as for these shoes ... they're government surplus stock ... I bought them in Europe!"

"Methinks, thou dost protest too much," replied Turner easily. "Also ... you have no alibi for that creamy, school-girl complexion?" Abruptly, his hand appeared from beneath the desk. In it he held a revolver. "Where have you come from? I believe it is my duty to inform the police of your presence. I know it will distress Mrs. Turner greatly ... but I honestly can't face my conscience ... as a public-spirited citizen unless I do."

Suddenly the woman's voice became imploring. "Albert ... don't."

"Don't be worried, my pet," replied Turner, lowering the lids of his eyes sympathetically. "If he isn't wanted by the police ... it will all be just one big, nasty mistake. And I'll be terribly sorry. I'll apologize to Mr. Rohan ... humbly." He nodded graciously to the red-haired man. "You'd accept my apology, wouldn't you, sir?"

"Don't make that call!" Rohan warned him.

"But, Mr. Rohan," Turner appeared bewildered, "you've told me you aren't a convict ... so if you're not wanted by the police, there's nothing to worry about, is there?" Turner's revolver was pointed straight at the stomach of the red-haired man.

Rohan took a step nearer to the desk, clearing the chair where he had been seated, and leaving the woman far to one side. "Stop!" Turner commanded.

Rohan stopped. "Turner," he said, "don't make that call!"

"Ahhhh," Turner smiled broadly, "something seems to have disturbed you. Well, let's get it over with." His eyes fixed on the visitor, he reached his left hand toward the phone. Carefully, he removed the receiver, and began dialing, but on the third number his finger slipped, and instinctively, his eyes flashed to the phone.

In that instant, Rohan moved, twisting to one side. The movement triggered the gun in Turner's hand, the blast of it vibrating in the room.

Rohan did not remove the gun from his pocket. When it replied, the noise was partly muffled by the cloth of his jacket. A small neat hole appeared directly over the heart of Albert Turner.

Chapter 2

East Vanders Place is a short street only two blocks long, located in the Fifties overlooking the East River in New York City. The street consists mostly of small town houses which have been converted into expensive apartments. If you live on East Vanders Place, or die on it, it takes a lot of money.

I'm a detective in the Nineteenth Precinct, and East Vanders Place is in our district. When the report was routed through our desk, I went out on it. At the scene of the murder, the street was blocked by two RMPs and I met the detective from Homicide Squad, Manhattan East. His name was Skors.

Now, I don't know whether you know it, but I think I should explain that not every detective working on a killing in New York City is a member of the Homicide Squad ... either Manhattan East or West. A detective from the precinct in which the murder takes place is also put on it. These two detectives work together from the beginning, although others may be added if it's necessary. In this case, Skors was from Homicide East, and I was from the Nineteenth Precinct which is located on East Sixty-seventh Street, between Park and Lexington. The only reason I point this out is later on I was appointed to follow through on the case because I was the precinct detective; this assignment came through as a matter of routine. But because of everything that happened later, it's important.

There are approximately 22,500 cops in New York who are white, black, brown, yellow, and red, and who are Protestants, Catholics, Jews, and Mohammedans. Some of them ride horses and motorcycles, fly airplanes and helicopters, pilot boats, drive trucks, ambulances, and cars; others speak French, Spanish, Italian, Chinese, German, Arabic—and nearly any other tongue under the sun. Among these men, it was my number which turned up as a matter of routine duty. The Police Department always operates along strict lines of procedure. That's important to remember, because once I was assigned to this case, unless I was incompetent—I couldn't be removed from it. To many cops, it wouldn't have made a lot of difference.

Chapter 3

At six thirty in the morning, the alarm clock awakened Mercedes Turner. Her eyes opened immediately, and for a moment she stared at the ceiling as the events of the preceding night rushed through her mind. The horror of it caught her up, and she trembled violently; tearing her eyes away from the spot at which they had been fixedly staring, she forced herself to leave the refuge of her bed. When she rose, she slowly gained control of herself, and with hands which shook only slightly turned the taps to run her bath.

While the tub was filling, she wrapped a dressing gown around her and walked hurriedly to the kitchen. At the door of the maid's room she listened intently for sounds from within; hearing none she cautiously opened the door to peer inside. Thelma Jordan had not yet returned. Giving a small smile of gratitude, the woman returned to the refrigerator and removed two oranges. As she sipped their juice, her composure returned more firmly. The night before she had met the problems proposed by Albert Turner's murder head on. The years of past training to face and make decisions had served her well. She had immediately realized that all decisions must be made by her; Rohan was no longer capable of making them.

As she reviewed the events, she decided that she had acted well. Until long after Rohan had left the apartment, and she had gone to bed, she had managed to seem calm. The red-haired man had not recognized the waves of panic which had swept over her, nor her shock of reaction to his killing Turner. Turner had shot first, but Rohan could never plead self-defense. As an escaped convict, he would be indicted on a felony murder.

Much as she had hated and detested Albert Turner, she was sorry that he was dead. She was sorry exactly to the extent that she hated all violence, and all death. Rohan she had loved ... had always loved ... and his act did not change that fact. It only presented the questions of what she could do to help him. Turner could no longer be helped, Hugh Rohan needed her now.

With a sigh, she placed the glass in the sink, and went back to her bath.

This morning, bath and dressing went very fast. After getting into her dress, she stepped to her closet and slipped into a light camel's-hair coat, took her mink from the hanger, and folded it to carry over her arm. Then she gathered up her purse and carefully checked the items in it ... safety deposit keys, bank book, and passports. For a moment she glanced over the living room ... inventorying it; attempting to remember what she must do; attempting to recall what she might have forgotten. She hurried to the kitchen and quickly wrote a note to the maid, leaving the paper on the stove where Thelma Jordan would find it.

Outside the service entrance, she walked to the front of the hall where she caught the passenger elevator to the ground floor. She glanced at her wrist, her tiny watch pointed to five minutes of eight.

It was a warm day in early fall and she felt conspicuous with her two coats. On First Avenue, she took a taxi to the Hamilton-Plaza Hotel, a hotel where she was not known, and checked the coats at the cloak room. She had breakfast in the coffee shop, and then returned to the lobby where she bought a paper. For a while she sat quietly, trying to read it ... a beautiful and well-bred woman completely at home in the luxury of the hotel. But her eyes saw nothing of the paper she was attempting to read, and her mind refused to register the news it printed. She carried the resignation of the shooting deep within her; and it weighed on her as if the tragedy had occurred months before instead of the preceding night. Accepting the fact that there was no escape from either the tragedy or its consequences, she held no hope of ultimate freedom. Rather, she clung only to the expectation of postponing the final consequences.

At nine thirty, she left the hotel and walked a few blocks, south on Fifth Avenue, to the New Amsterdam Trust Company. In the rear of the bank there was a small paneled elevator and she rode it to the basement. Her face composed, gravely serene, she stood before the heavy grilled door of the safe deposit section and as the electric lock buzzed, she pushed open the door and entered. She took out the key of her safety deposit box, and writing out its number and signing her name to a printed form, she handed the key and paper to an attendant. The man led the way through a massive round door and stopped before her number. Inserting a master key, he turned it once, then inserted her key in a second lock, and the small oblong door clicked open.

The attendant carrying her box led the way to a series of small rooms, each containing a desk, chair, calendar, pen, and light. At the door to one of the rooms, he stood aside and the woman entered; he placed the box on the desk, and asked, "Will that be all?"

She nodded. "Yes ... thanks." As he left the room, he closed the door and it locked behind him. Mercedes Turner opened the box and removed a roll of heavy red velvet, lined with white silk, and tied with a matching velvet cord. Unrolled, the silk disclosed a series of pockets, each with a small flap which closed with a metal snap. Deliberately, she opened the pockets, searching them carefully with her fingers, removing a piece of jewelry from each ... a jeweled lapel pin, cluster earrings, several bracelets of diamonds ... one with rubies, one with emeralds ... a string of beautifully matched Oriental pearls, a small diamond choker; and an old, heavy antique necklace, which had belonged to her grandmother.

She wrapped each piece in paper tissue, and then centered them in a large silk handkerchief, tying the four ends together to form a compact, little package which she dropped into her big purse. Replacing the velvet roll in the safety deposit box, she closed it and, rising, opened the door. The attendant returned the box to its compartment and handed her key back to her. She smiled her thanks, and rode the elevator to the main floor.

Without hesitation, she approached a long line of desks set in a neat row along one side of the bank. Behind the desks sat pleasant-faced, well-dressed men in conservative suits. On each desk, a small metal plaque announced the name of its occupant. She skirted the end of the desks, and approached a man seated in the second desk from the front. His name was Forrest, and his plaque identified him as first vice-president. Beside his desk was a comfortable leather chair, turned slightly from the window to protect its occupants from glare. As she approached his desk, Forrest arose. "Good morning, Mrs. Turner."

"Mr. Forrest," she replied pleasantly, "how nice to see you again."

"Mr. Turner was in the other day ... I understand you had a wonderful vacation."

"Oh, splendid. We hated to return as early as we did."

"That's the way it is," he smiled, "vacations always seem too short."

She nodded, and dropped into the chair beside him ... lovely, composed, and casual. She took her deposit book from her purse. Albert Turner had maintained a joint checking account, an account which accommodated both of their personal expenses, and the expense of maintaining the apartment. She didn't open the book, but merely held it in her hands, and asked, "Could you get the balance for my account as of today?"

"Certainly ..." Forrest lifted a phone on his desk and asked for the bookkeeping department. Speaking briefly, he requested the information and hung up. "They'll call back in just a moment," he told her.

She lit a cigarette. "I have a balance of my own ... but I want to be sure." She smiled easily at Forrest. "Albert is going to think me quite foolish ... but after all, I want it very badly and I've decided just to go ahead and do it."

"Do what?" he asked, making conversation while they waited.

"Why, buy the car," she replied idly. "A friend of mine has a beautiful Italian sports car which she bought last year. She paid eleven thousand for it and is willing to let me have it for a song." She smiled at him confidentially. "I love it ... it's absolutely gorgeous! So, I'm going to buy it."

"Yes?" he replied courteously. The phone rang discreetly and he picked it up. His hand moved smoothly as he wrote on a memo pad of heavy bonded paper: balance ... $4,339.28. Returning the phone to its cradle he said, "Your balance is $4,339.28."

"Oh, good!" she exclaimed. "I only need four thousand." She spread out her checkbook, selected a fountain pen from a set which stood on Forrest's desk, and leisurely made out the check.

Forrest asked, "Do you have any large checks outstanding that you know of, Mrs. Turner?"

"Nothing important." She added gaily, "Anyway, I'll have Albert make a deposit right away."

"Do you want us to certify this?" Forrest asked.

"No ... Marian wants it in cash. She doesn't want her husband to know she's selling her car yet."

Forrest nodded. It was not his concern. "How would you like it? Large bills ... or small?"

The woman considered it for a moment. "Give me a thousand in hundreds, a thousand in fifties ... and two thousand in twenties," she replied indifferently. Forrest motioned to a uniformed guard who approached his desk. The vice-president scratched his initials on the front of the check, in the upper left hand corner. Handing it to the guard, he explained what he wanted. The guard walked to the rear of the bank and entered a small gate behind the row of tellers' cages. He stopped and handed the check to a cashier. In several minutes he returned to Forrest's desk and handed him four packets of bills—each with a brown paper wrapper printed with the figures: $1,000.00.

The woman found herself thinking with surprise how small the packets were. She had never handled a large amount of cash before, having always written checks whenever she needed money. Somehow, she had expected the bills to be more impressive. Forrest placed the four packets in a Manila envelope and handed it to her. She accepted it, and put it in her purse.

"Be careful with that new car," he said, smiling at her.

"I'll drive it down here, someday," she replied airily, "and park it in front of your bank."

"If you do, watch out for the cop on the corner," he advised her, mock-seriously. "He loves to give out parking tickets."

She arose and stood for a moment by his desk. "That would make me some kind of a criminal, wouldn't it?" She smiled at the banker, her face lovely in the morning light.

Chapter 4

A maid named Thelma Jordan discovered the body of Albert Turner and called the cops. The first half-hour on East Vanders Place, however, neither Skors nor I touched anything ... just looked around until the man from the Medical Examiner's office, and the rest of the crew from the Bureau of Technical Services, arrived. Thelma Jordan was ready to blow wide open, so we left her alone until the doctor could calm her down a little. While we were waiting, Skors and I got a pretty good idea of the Turner apartment which occupied the entire second floor of a converted town house. There were four stories in the building with one apartment to each floor. The building had two elevators; a self-operating one in the front for tenants and guests, and a second one for a service elevator in the rear.

The Turner place had five rooms, a kitchen, and three baths. The living room wasn't exactly large, although it was good sized with a high, old-fashioned ceiling and an ornately carved marble fireplace. It was furnished in a combination of different styles ... modern pieces and antiques, light and dark, old and new ... all blended together. I had never seen anything quite like it before, and it looked good. Behind the living room was a small dining room with a crystal chandelier, and a delicately carved table and chairs.

I walked down a short hallway which led from the dining room to the rear of the apartment. Two bedrooms, each with a bath, opened into the hall; the hall, itself, ended in the kitchen. Behind the kitchen there was a maid's room with a bath, and a door from the kitchen opened into an outside hall next to the service elevator.

Thelma Jordan recovered her nerves enough for us to talk to her. The doctor had given her a mild sedative together with a good lecture which probably was as much help as the pills. Doctors can get away with it, cops can't. Skors and I began to talk to her, in the kitchen, while the M.E. was doing his stuff in the bedroom where the body had been found.

There was a pot of coffee on the stove which I warmed up, and poured cups for the three of us. Thelma Jordan didn't drink hers, but it gave her hands something to do and she kept turning it around with her fingers while we talked. Skors drank his, and so did I.

We sympathized with the maid for a while, admitting that finding a body was quite a shock and certainly something that didn't happen to a maid every day ... especially Thelma Jordan. Finally, Skors got around to asking, "What time did you find him?"

She seemed a little hazy about her answers, a little slow on the pickup. It might have been the sedatives, so we didn't press her ... just kept it calm and easy. Anyway, she finally said it was around noon when she found Albert Turner. So I asked her, "Did you hear the shot?"

"There wasn't any shot ... not at least while I was here today," she said.

"Did you hear any last night?"

"I wasn't here last night after I had finished up with the dinner."

"What time did you get back?"

"I didn't come back until this morning. Last night was my regular night off."

"Where did you stay?" Skors asked.

"With some friends of mine in the Bronx." She gave us the name of the couple and their address. According to the maid's story, they had gone to a neighborhood charity benefit and then she had stayed with them overnight. We would check it, naturally.

Skors nodded to me, and I took over the next question. "What time did you come to work this morning?"

"A little after eight. That left plenty of time for breakfast ... if anybody had wanted some."

"Where was Mrs. Turner when you arrived?"

"I don't know," she replied. "First, I went to my room and changed into my uniform. Then when I started working around the kitchen, I found this note on the stove." She reached in her apron pocket and removed a sheet of paper which she unfolded and handed to me. Skors and I read it together:

Thelma:
Don't bother with breakfast this morning. I'm going out early. Please don't disturb Mr. Turner unless he calls you, and don't bother him with phone calls.

                                                          MRS. TURNER

"What finally made you look in Mr. Turner's bedroom?" Skors asked.

The maid twisted nervously in her chair. Her elbow jarred the table and a little of her untouched coffee slopped over. She began daubing at it with a yellow rubber sponge. "Well, all morning I didn't hear a sound from his room. I thought he was asleep so I didn't disturb him. But around noon ... I got thinking maybe he'd like a cup of soup or something. I knocked at his door, and when there was no reply, I knocked harder. I knew he had to hear me, but even then he didn't call out, or anything. I thought he might be real sick and I got scared. I opened the door and he was in bed, the covers pulled up around his neck. I called from the doorway and when he didn't move, I walked over and I swear he looked just asleep ... nothing else. I ... I waited for a little bit, trying to decide what to do ... and I touched his head with my fingers...." She began to sob, hunching over the table.

"You could tell he was dead?" I asked.

"Yes ... his forehead was cold ... but cold and different feeling than anything I'd ever touched before."

"Have you any idea where Mrs. Turner is?" Skors asked.

Thelma Jordan shook her head. "No ..." she said. We left her at the kitchen table, sobbing, and went into the bedroom where the body was. The M.E. pointed to the bed where the body of Albert Turner was completely covered by the sheet. "Shot in the heart," he told us. The doctor's name was Branch.

"Just one shot?" I asked.

"That's all, I think. One would've been enough, but I'll check it at the posting."

Skors rubbed the palm of his hand under his jaw. "It doesn't look like he was shot in bed," he observed. "There's not enough blood."

Branch said, "A wound like that kills instantly. It's a small hole and bleeds very little. But you're right, anyway. He was shot somewhere else, probably here in the apartment. The Technical boys are trying to locate where ... now." The M.E. pulled down the sheet and Skors and I took a look. Turner was lying as if asleep, his eyes closed.

"Did you close his eyes?" I asked Branch.

"No. That's the way he was."

I looked at Skors. "The maid said he looked asleep when she first saw him. Whoever shot him must've closed them for him."

Skors agreed. We stood staring at the body, thoughtfully. The late Turner was dressed in a dark, charcoal gray suit. The doctor had opened the front of the shirt which had a red stain about the size of my hand. Other than that, Turner was completely dressed including his shoes. I judged him to have been around thirty-five; of medium size, probably five feet ten and weighing one hundred sixty pounds. It's hard, though, to estimate a man's build when he isn't standing. His hair was heavy, of coarse texture, and it was just beginning to turn gray at the temples. We'd seen enough. Branch re-covered the body with the sheet.

"How long has he been dead?" I asked.

"For at least twelve hours," replied Branch.

"That puts it around midnight last night," said Skors. Branch nodded.

"Before midnight?" I asked.

"Strong possibility. I can't tell much more than that until I get down to the laboratory. Incidentally, did he eat dinner at home last night?"

Skors replied, "I got the impression he had, from what the maid said. She told us she didn't leave the apartment until after she had finished up the dinner."

"Good." Branch began packing his instruments. "If she tells me what time he ate and what he had to eat, I can pretty definitely pinpoint the time he was shot." He walked to the adjoining bathroom. "Technical is all through in here, so I'll use it." He washed his hands. "I'll talk to the maid on my way out."

"When do we get your reports?" I asked.

"Soon as I can get them to you," replied Branch.

The Technical men were strung out all over the living room ... taking photographs, raising prints, examining the furniture and rugs. "I wish we knew where Mrs. Turner was," I remarked to Skors.

"So do I," he replied. We watched the Technical men for a few minutes, then returned to the kitchen. Branch had just finished talking to Thelma Jordan. He nodded and left through the service door. I asked the maid, "What do you think could have detained Mrs. Turner?"

"I don't know ... but sometimes she's downtown all day. She may be out shopping and will be back for dinner."

"Does she usually leave before eight o'clock in the morning?" asked Skors.

Thelma Jordan shook her head. "No," she replied, "most of the stores don't open until around nine thirty." Then her face brightened. "Maybe she had an appointment to have her hair done!"

"That's early, that's still pretty early," I said.

"Not if they're terribly busy," explained the maid. "If they can't do it any other time, sometimes they'll do it very early or very late."

"Do you know where she goes?" asked Skors.

"She keeps a list of all the places ... their phone numbers and things. They're in a little memorandum book in the drawer by her bed."

"We'll find it," I said. We started down the narrow hall and had to stop. Turner's body was being removed, carried in an oblong, covered, canvas box. The three of us backed into the kitchen again so it could get by. Thelma Jordan's eyes were wet and bulging and I was afraid she was going to start crying again. However, the box disappeared through the service door, and as soon as it was out of sight she regained control of herself. We went back down the hall and I turned into Turner's room. The maid stopped me.

"No," she explained, "that's Mr. Turner's. Mrs. Turner has this other one across the hall."

We turned around and entered the second bedroom. It was exactly the same size and shape as the one we'd found Turner in, but there all resemblance ended. The wife's room was decorated in white and ivory, gold, and a deep plum blue. There was no mistaking that it belonged to a woman. A poster bed, with tall white posts supporting gold acorns, was flanked on either side by small ornate tables with marble tops. On one of the tables there was an ivory phone. Thelma Jordan withdrew a tiny leather book from the drawer of the table, beneath the phone, and handed it to Skors. He began to leaf through it expectantly.

"Was Mrs. Turner's bed slept in last night?" I asked the maid.

"Yes," she told me. "It was all mussed up this morning ... and I made it up again."

Skors and I had a problem to face at this point. I looked at my watch. It was just a little after two thirty. The picture wasn't clear yet. There was a possibility that Turner might have been a suicide, although we hadn't found the gun yet and he had certainly been moved into the bed.

On the other hand, if he had been murdered, Mrs. Turner was a good prospect.

At this time there was nothing firm to go on. It's risky to throw your weight around ... wildly, too fast ... until you know where you're going. Or, at least, think you know.

Skors said to Thelma Jordan, glancing up from the memo book, "Was this Mrs. Turner's hairdresser?" He read aloud a name. The maid confirmed it, and Skors dialed a number. He asked for Mrs. Turner, and after a few questions, he hung up. "She hasn't been in today," he told me. "They didn't have any appointment with her, either." I nodded. Skors went back to looking through the book.

The men from the Technical Squad had been through the bedroom thoroughly, looking for the gun which had shot Turner. Across from the poster bed was a large, beautifully carved bureau with a heavy mirror in a gold frame hanging above it. Against the third wall was a small delicate dressing table. I went through them. The bureau contained lingerie, blouses, nightgowns, and stockings. The dressing table was filled with costume jewelry and beauty preparations. While I had been looking through the stuff, Skors had remained on the phone ... trying to locate Mrs. Turner without success. I motioned to Thelma Jordan who'd been sitting on the side of the bed, and she came over to me beside the dressing table. "Are you familiar with Mrs. Turner's things?" I asked. "Clothes ... and jewelry?"

"A little ..."

"Look in here and see if anything's missing."

In the dressing table there were two extremely wide but very shallow drawers. The maid glanced into both and said, "Her jewelry box isn't here."

Skors placed the phone back on the stand and listened to us. "What was in the jewelry box? Real jewelry, or imitation ... costume stuff?" I asked.

"Oh, the things in the box were real," she replied. "She didn't keep very much of it in the apartment, but what she kept was real."

"She had more? Where did she keep that?"

"In a safety deposit box in the bank."

"Was there much of it?"

"I think so...." she said.

I had a strange feeling as if someone had wrapped a hand completely around my stomach and squeezed it. I looked at Skors and could tell he was thinking the same thing. Abruptly the name Turner ... Albert Turner ... meant something. I said to Skors, "Albert Turner. I just thought ... this is going to be a hot one." He nodded and picked up the phone again. This time he called the captain.

I motioned Thelma Jordan to follow me to the closet, and I opened its door. The closet was large, extremely large, and lined with cedar. Dresses and coats were hanging in neat rows. Above the clothes were shelves with orderly stacks of matching hatboxes ... gray boxes with black tops and a black cord to carry each one. In one end of the closet was a stand which presented pair after pair of shoes. "Are all of Mrs. Turner's clothes here?" I asked.

The maid walked into the closet and looked around. She stood for a few moments before saying anything. "Maybe some of her things are at the cleaners," she said finally.

"What's missing ... whether it's at the cleaner or not?"

Pushing the clothes one way and the other, pulling out an empty hanger here and there, she said, "Well ... there's a black suit, and a heather tweed ... and a plain gray suit ..." Continuing to glance slowly around, she added, "And some dresses ... a beige woolen ... and a blue jersey." After a pause, she exclaimed, "If she took them she'd take shoes for them, too!" She began counting the pairs of shoes. "Mrs. Turner always keeps fifteen pairs of shoes ... the old ones she gets rid of." I counted the shoes; there were nine pairs remaining on the rack.

"So there are six pairs missing," I said. "What about the coats?"

This time the maid replied very quickly. "Her tan camel hair ... and the full-length mink."

I couldn't imagine anyone walking around the city carrying coats, dresses, and shoes in her arms. I asked, "Where did Mrs. Turner keep her suitcases?"

"There's a storage room in the basement, where the people in the building leave their luggage."

I said, "Let's go and have a look." The maid accompanied me, and we rode the service elevator to the basement. In the rear was the furnace room, but near the front by deep inset windows there were four, heavy, wooden partitions, with individual doors and padlocks. On each door was a painted numeral. We stopped before door number two. "Do you have a key?" I asked the maid. She shook her head. Removing the sap from my pocket, I balanced it in my hand and then struck the lock a sharp blow directly above the keyhole. The lock sprang open.

I went in and pulled the cord of an overhead light. There was an assortment of wardrobe trunks, steamer trunks, suitcases, and hatboxes of all kinds. Over everything was a light film of dust. On the floor, near the door, were two clean imprints where two suitcases had stood until very recently. I pointed to the spots and asked, "Do you know which ones they were?"

"No," the maid said, "I just can't recall what they looked like."

"Anyway," I told her, "the important thing is we know they're gone."

Upstairs I told Skors about it. "It looks like she scrammed all right," he said.

"She must have. If anyone kidnapped her, or forced her to go away, I doubt if she'd been able to pack up all that stuff."

Skors put a cigarette thoughtfully between his lips and lit it. "We better get out a pick up order," he said. "I just talked to Hortzman." Hortzman was captain of my precinct.

"What'd Hortzman say?"

"He's on his way over." We walked into the living room. The Technical men were clustered around a section of the rug near the desk. A chair had been pushed to one side, and one of the cops was on his knees clipping some nap and putting it in an envelope. Skors and I went over. "What'd you find?" Skors asked.

The Technical man doing the clipping said, "I think we found us a bloodstain."

I looked over his shoulder. It was difficult to see the stain at first, because it blended in very closely with the color and pattern of the rug. It wasn't a very large stain. "Was that chair standing over it?" I asked, pointing to a large white chair.

"Yeah," replied the Technical man. "We could have missed it pretty easy if we hadn't been going over it section by section."

Skors and I walked back out to the kitchen. Thelma Jordan was in her room. She was very quiet. "If Turner was shot in the living room, he couldn't have walked to the bedroom with a bullet in his heart," I said.

"No," agreed Skors, "he couldn't."

"And he couldn't have gotten rid of the gun."

"No."

"And Mrs. Turner is missing ... after writing a cover-up note, and taking her things and jewelry."

"It's all pretty clear," said Skors.

"I don't know ..." I said.

Skors raised his eyebrows. "What's bothering you?"

"Why would Mrs. Turner run ... before she even knew she was hurt?"

"Panic maybe."

"After staying here all night?" I shook my head.

"It doesn't feel right to you, huh?" asked Skors.

"No, it doesn't," I replied. Then Captain Hortzman walked in.

Chapter 5

The red-haired man stood beside the window of the third-floor walk-up apartment, and stared into the street below. It was in the Forties, on New York's west side, near Ninth Avenue, and the street was lined with parked cars and double-parked trucks. He searched the sidewalk with his eyes but did not find the figure for which he was looking. Why doesn't she come, he thought desperately, what's keeping her! Turning from the window, he dropped the grimy mesh curtain and jammed his cigarette into an ashtray already overflowing with paper match sticks and smoked stubs. Immediately, he lit another. In the center of the shabby room stood two expensive pieces of women's luggage.

Walking to a chair, he slumped into it; by his side, on the floor, were copies of the morning papers. Within several minutes he arose restlessly and switched on a radio in a plastic case, tuning in a station which carried classical music. Running a hand through his flaming hair, he listened to the music irritably. He swung away, pacing the room. Has something happened, he asked himself, has Turner been discovered? Another thought crowded into his mind—perhaps she has decided not to come after all! The music stopped, and the announcer's voice interrupted to identify the station and give the time. It was ten thirty.

Turner had been dead only about eleven hours. He thought about Turner for a moment ... thinking of him indifferently, and carelessly. He tried to recall the moment of the shooting, but the events already had begun to dissolve in unreality. In the echoing distances of memory he heard the pistol crack. The figure of the woman standing immobile in the shadows stirred slightly. Her voice sighed, "God help us! He's dead."

"I had to," he said, shaking his head, the blood red comb swaying from side to side. His mind raced with a legion of thoughts and he scrambled through them, sorting and discarding to find the answer. "He shot first ... he was going to turn me in."

As if reading his mind, the woman replied in his stead. "Now there is no answer...." She stepped from the shadows of the room and approached him. When she stood beside him, she was nearly as tall as he, with shining golden hair. Standing quietly, side by side, the light played upon them burning like the flame of a candle meeting and entwining ... one crimson, one gold.

"He was my husband," she said. "Now there is no hope ... no hope. Every hand in the world will be turned against us...."

"I was your husband first," replied the red-haired man. Turning, he put his arm around her waist. She remained very still, making no effort to draw away and his arm remained for only an instant, then it withdrew from her motionless body. Abruptly his voice became reckless, holding a note of blithe unconcern. "After a while, they'll forget."

"No. They won't forget," she contradicted.

He stepped a pace away, then turned back to her; closer this time, and their bodies touched. Sharply she drew in her breath, and he placed a hand beneath each of her elbows, holding them lightly as if balancing her between them and he looked into her eyes. His eyes were brown, of a brown nearly black, and they searched for hers. "We'll run away together?" he asked.

A bead of tear glistened on her lashes, and without its dancing reflection he would not have known that she was crying within the shadow of her eyes.

He moved his hands from her elbows, to the upper part of her arms and patted them gently ... nearly as a child pats his mother's arm for attention. "Please come with me ..." his voice trailed into nothingness.

She bowed her head, slowly, and he dropped his hands, stepping away. "Yes!" His voice sang. "I thought you'd see it that way."

Her hand gently motioned him to silence, and she stood staring past him, peering through the walls of the room into the world which would soon be drawing in upon them. "I have to come," she said softly, "for many reasons." She lifted her face thoughtfully and kissed him on the lips. "Yes," she reaffirmed, "we'll go together ... there's nothing to hold me here. We'll run as far and as long as we can. But first, we must have the means!"

The man's thoughts fled from the past, and he was back in his own room again. If she doesn't come, he thought, I'll go alone. Reaching in his pocket, he withdrew a small automatic, holding it as if for reassurance. At the sound of a light knock on the door, he quickly dropped the weapon back in his jacket and swung around. With a few long strides, he reached the door, unlocked it, and swung it open. Mercedes was standing there.

Quickly he gathered her in his arms, nearly smothering her in his wild delight. "Were you thinking I wouldn't come?" she asked smiling.

Kissing the side of her face, her neck, he said, "Yes ... I was worrying. I thought something had happened...."

She twisted slightly to disengage his arms. "Help me with these coats," she said. He immediately took the coat she was carrying. "That heavy coat worries me," she said, looking at the glossy mink. "It looks odd carrying it around ... we'll have to do something about it."

"Why don't I go down to the drugstore and buy one of those canvas bags ... you know ..."

"The ones with Vinylite straps," she said, nodding. "That might be all right ... be sure to get one that's large enough." He slipped out the door, and she could hear his shoes clattering down the stairs.

She stared around the apartment. She was looking at it for the first time. Rohan had rented it the day before, upon his arrival. It contained little, and was merely a shabby room with a studio lounge which converted into a bed. There was a small kitchen, and an even smaller bath.

Hearing his footsteps approaching, she swung her attention back to the door as he entered with a brown canvas, carryall bag. "Here it is," he said cheerfully. "I think it's large enough."

She folded her fur coat carefully, and packed it in the bag. When she had finished, she zipped the bag closed. "Are you ready?" he asked.

"Yes ... let's go." He picked up the luggage and headed toward the door. "Wait," she said, "don't you have a coat and hat?"

"No. Where are we going?" he asked.

"First," she replied, "to Penn Station, and while we're there we'll get you a hat. Then we'll catch one of the tube trains to Jersey...."

"And from there?"

"This is a wide, wide world," she said. She smiled, but in her heart was a heaviness which she knew would never go away.

Chapter 6

The pickup order went out for Mercedes Turner. We were in a hurry, but more important we wanted to keep her on the move. If we gave her a chance to hole up ... to stop and hide herself ... it might be months or even years before we found her. In New York City, a criminal can hide himself forever ... if he knows how to do it correctly.

I requisitioned a car to drive up to Connecticut to talk to the Turner woman's family. Her maiden name had been Clinton. Skors remained in New York to see what he could dig up in Turner's office. As an officer, I had no authority in Connecticut and I couldn't force the family to answer my questions ... theoretically. Actually, if there had been any real problem talking to Mr. Clinton, we could have arranged for cooperation with the Federal Government on some kind of an interstate charge. The village of Argyle, where the Clinton family lived, was a very small place and had no peace officers of its own; any police problems were handled through the town of Mountain Forge which had a force of three men, and which was about four miles distant from Argyle. I called Mountain Forge and talked to the chief of police, a man named Novak.

Surprisingly enough, in sections of New England you run into many Polish names all mixed up with the old time Yankees. In Mountain Forge the entire police force was of Polish descent—Chief Novak, and two others—Spodnick and Walsky. Novak, on the phone, sounded cautious because his job was an appointive one under the town selectmen, and up in that section the local people were suspicious of anyone from New York. The chief of police agreed, however, to drive me out to see the Clintons, but told me I couldn't get away with any rough stuff. I assured him that I had never gotten away with any rough stuff in my life. We made an appointment to meet in his office as soon as I could drive up. Novak said it was around a three-hour drive.

I reached Mountain Forge, up past Kent and Cornwall in Connecticut ... a town of possibly six thousand persons. It is built around a square. The police station was located across the street from the railroad station, and the street was called ... naturally ... Railroad Street. I went in, and Novak was waiting for me.

He acted rather disturbed when I first came in, and I showed him my credentials. He grunted, then gathered himself together in a feeble show of politeness. "Had your supper yet?" he asked. I told him I hadn't. "I hain't either," he said. "Let's go up to Boody's and git some. Mr. Clinton hain't expectin' us until a little later." We walked a block down the street to a restaurant which was also a combination tobacco store and newsstand, with New York and Connecticut papers stacked in front of it.

The chief led the way deliberately to the far end of the room and selected an isolated booth. Sitting down, he took off his battered gray hat and placed it on the seat beside him. Novak was a man in his late fifties, small and going to fat. He wore a pair of faded army dungarees, a light blue sport shirt buttoned at the collar, and a shapeless brown jacket from some long ago purchased suit. A kid, in his teens, sauntered up to the booth to take our orders. There was no menu. "Evenin', Chief," he greeted Novak.

Novak lifted a pair of faded blue eyes and nodded. "Why, hello, Elton," he said. "How's your father these days?"

"So-so," replied Elton indifferently.

"What you got on the menu tonight? Same?"

"The same."

"Guess I'll take that hot pot roast sandwich, some coffee and pie."

"What kinda pie?"

"Apple."

Elton looked at me. I said, "That goes for me, too." He disappeared into the kitchen.

"Nice boy," mused Novak. "I've known his dad for years ... bought the old Pease farm up past Beacon ... kid's dad, that is."

"Did you ever know Mercedes Clinton?" I asked him.

"Sure. I've known her ever since she was a little girl."

"What was she like?"

"Another nice kid. Real pretty and lively. Had blond hair and big blue eyes...."

"Did she ever get into any trouble around here?"

Novak shook his head. "Nope. 'Course Spodnick and me used a caution her once in a while for speedin' a mite too fast. Lyman Clinton, that's her father, gave her a little yellow car when she first started goin' away to school. Durin' vacations she'd drive it all over ... always kept the top down, rain or shine ... and drove real fast sometimes."

Elton appeared with tremendous plates of food. Placing them on the table, he returned immediately with coffee, pie, and one check. He left the check by my right hand.

"It sounds as if the Clintons were pretty well off," I said.

"They hain't as well off as they used to be, I guess," Novak replied, slowly, "but they hain't never had reason to worry where the next meal was comin' from."

"They're an old family in these parts?"

"Tolerably ... four-five generations. Think originally they was New Hampshire people. First Clinton around here had a little black powder factory durin' the Civil War. 'Nother Clinton, little later on, bought an interest in a bleachery down the river ... round New Milford someplace."

"The factory still operating?"

"Nope. Powder plant hasn't been goin' for maybe fifty years. Bleachery's still goin', though."

"Was Mercedes the only child?"

"Yep ... only one. Lyman Clinton was mighty proud of her. A little too proud, maybe."

"Why?"

Novak didn't reply immediately. He swirled three spoonfuls of sugar around his cup, then drank the coffee in one, long draught. "Maybe he figured nothin' was good enough for her," he said, finally. "Sort of thinkin' he knew what was best ... regardless of maybe what the girl wanted." He looked me straight in the eyes; his own, abruptly, no longer seemed faded. "You sure she shot her own husband?" he asked.

"No one can be positive right now, but everything seems to point to her." I paused, then asked for it straight. "Is there anything that makes you think she didn't?"

"Nope," he replied steadily. "I figure if Mercedes wanted to bad enough, she'd have the gumption to do it. She always had plenty of pride, and plenty of spirit. If she got real riled, she'd do it." He pulled a cheap cigar from his pocket and licked the end before biting it off. Lighting it, he blew a great cloud of smoke, delicately turning aside his face so it billowed into the aisle by the booth. "There's one thing, though," he added thoughtfully, "that don't line up with what I know about Mercedes Clinton."

"What's that?"

"Why she didn't walk in and hand you the gun. Mercedes has had a good bringin' up, and she's got a conscience. She knows right from wrong, all right. Maybe she got madder'n blazes and shot her husband. Maybe she even had a dern good reason for it. But if she shot him, she'd a knowed she shot him ... and she'd walk right in and take her medicine. It sorta puzzles me ... her lightin' out."

I paid the check and we walked back to the car, which I had parked by the station. "Might as well drive out in yours," Novak suggested. "Ain't no sense me wastin' town gas on what ain't our business."

Connecticut villages usually have two things in common—small populations and enormous, sprawling borders. The village lines enclose enough land to accommodate twenty or thirty times their number of citizens. Argyle was no different. Novak and I cut up the side of a mountain by a steep road, and halfway down the other side was a sign which read: VILLAGE OF ARGYLE. FOUNDED 1707. There was no indication of houses or people ... or anything else. About two miles farther down the road, the single lane widened into a straggle of houses, all of them old, the most recent being garishly Victorian among the more sedate New England styles. At an intersection, there were two churches, one Episcopalian and the other Congregational, a general country store, a volunteer fire department with the village meeting hall above it, a grange hall, and a small stone public school. Along the road beyond, one could see possibly twenty houses spaced at irregular intervals. Novak told me to turn left at the intersection, and we followed the new road for about a mile.

The Clinton place was a great, rambling, old, New England farmhouse which had been changed from its original square shape by the addition of two wings, one on each side of the dwelling. The house sat back from the road possibly five hundred yards and it was approached by a twisting, gravel drive. Huge old trees towered above the house dropping a great leafy umbrella over it. Behind the house, I could see an old red barn completely covered with vines, and a second, smaller farm building which had been converted into a garage. The house wore a shining coat of white paint, but the other buildings were in need of attention.

Having pulled the car to a stop in front of the door, Novak and I ascended the shallow steps, but before the chief could use the big, brass knocker the door opened. An elderly man, tall, thin, and slightly stooped stood outlined within the door. "Good evening, Novak," he said.

"Evenin', Mr. Clinton." Novak removed his hat and nodded his head toward me. "This here's the officer from New York I called you about," he explained.

Clinton stared at me, showing no emotion. "All right," he said, finally, "come in." We entered, and he closed the door. Stepping around us, he led the way down a large, wide hall, through an enormous living room and into a small study. The smaller room contained an old-fashioned, oak, roll-top desk. Half a dozen black leather chairs, worn shiny, stood around the room, and bookcases, extending from floor to ceiling, were piled with books. A goose-necked lamp arched on top of the desk, and Clinton switched on an overhead light as we sat down.

Clinton's face was long and thin, with deep creases running from cheeks to nose. His forehead was high, and his thinning hair made it even higher. The hair which remained was nearly snow white. He removed a pair of glasses from a case, and put them on. Turning to me, he said, "Chief Novak told me you wanted to talk to me about ... my daughter." He stopped and rubbed long slender fingers against his head. Although he had carefully suppressed the animosity in his voice, I was aware of it in his eyes.

"That's right, Mr. Clinton," I replied, "I appreciate your seeing me."

He dropped his hand. "Before we get started on anything, I want you to know that I have no idea where my daughter is ... and if I did, I doubt that I would tell you." I nodded. "Furthermore," he added, "I will never believe that Mercedes shot Albert Turner."

"Did she have any reason to shoot him?" I asked.

"None with which I'm familiar."

"Did anyone else have any reason?"

I thought that he hesitated for a moment, and possibly he did, attempting to recall. But he replied, "I know of no one."

"Would Mrs. Clinton have any information?"

"I'm quite sure she wouldn't. She's dead."

Novak explained hastily, "Mrs. Clinton's been gone now ... 'bout five years. Or better."

Clinton didn't reply. He sat silent and withdrawn.

"I didn't realize..." I apologized. "When was the last time you saw your daughter?"

"Several weeks ago. I was in New York for the day and saw her there."

"Has she been up to Argyle often ... to see you since her marriage?"

"Yes." He nodded slowly, and for a moment I thought he had finished his remark. Then suddenly, he added, "My daughter ... and I ... we were ... very close. I saw her as often as I could. She'd drive up regularly to see me, too, especially since her mother died." Novak nodded agreement. The old man looked absently through the dark window into the night. "I'd ... sometimes thought ... in my old age ..." his voice suddenly steeled, and he stopped.

"When did your daughter marry Albert Turner?"

"In 1950... about six months after her mother died."

"Would you happen to have one of her marriage pictures?" I asked.

"No. I have none."

I knew he was deliberately lying to me. "Well, then, Mr. Clinton, perhaps you have some others ... even more recent?"

"No. I've never believed in pictures." A picture of his wife stood on his desk. Beside the framed photograph of the older woman, there were scratches on the desk where another frame had stood. His eyes carefully avoided it.

Undoubtedly he had photographs of his daughter, if he was as crazy about her as Novak claimed. But I couldn't search the house to find them. By now, I realized that only his pride before Novak had prodded him into seeing me; he had no intention of telling me anything. I stood and Novak got to his feet too. Slowly Clinton joined us. "Thanks, Mr. Clinton," I said, "perhaps things will turn out better than we expect."

"Possibly ..." but there was no agreement in his voice. Coldly courteous he showed us out.

In the car driving back to Mountain Forge, I told Novak, "That was pretty much of nothing."

"Do you blame him?"

"No," I told him, "I don't blame him. Blood will always be thicker than anything else in the world. You should see the way it works in the slums ... in the city." Steering the car with one hand, I fished out a cigarette and lit it. "But I don't see why you aren't talking either."

He stared through the windshield. Finally he said, "I've talked."

"You've talked, but you haven't told me very much. There's a reason for the murder ... somewhere ... in the background. What is it?"

"I don't know," he replied. He became angry, a little too angry, too quickly to be genuine, I thought. He said, "After all these people 'round here are my friends. What happened in New York hain't no concern of mine!"

"Murder's everyone's business," I said, "particularly as you're a cop too."

He stared moodily ahead. "You fixed to talk to Lyman Clinton, and I cooperated with you. I've done my duty."

"What's the matter?" I asked. "Are you afraid of Clinton ... does he swing a big stick around these parts?"

"I hain't afraid of Lyman Clinton," replied Novak. "He used to be first selectman, but he hain't no more."

"But he's probably an old friend of the first selectman, now," I insisted, "and the other selectmen, too."

"You wanta be careful you hain't gettin' too big for your britches," Novak replied.

I had to fight down the anger that surged up within me. Carefully I held on to my voice, keeping it steady. "I'll see they fit," I said. "Also, if necessary ... I'll see what I can get done through Washington."

"Skip it," Novak said, "I wasn't meanin' to pop off." I accepted it as an apology. Novak lapsed into silence which he held until we reached the outskirts of Mountain Forge. Then he said, "Used to be a girl named Clara Coldwater who was sorta close to Mercedes. Lived in Argyle for a while."

"Where's she now?"

"Livin' in Mountain Forge. Married to Henry Battles. Henry works down in the foundry."

"Do you suppose I could talk to her?"

"You could try. Try on your own; I hain't gettin' into it."

Novak, I realized, was either afraid of Clinton's connections with the Town Council, or he was an old friend of the family. I couldn't tell which. Possibly it was a combination of both. He knew I could come back ... either with the help of the Connecticut State Police, or through the Federal Government ... and blast out what I wanted to know—if it was necessary. Now Novak was throwing me a sop. An old girl friend of Mercedes. She might not talk, either, but as long as Clara Coldwater had been offered, I had to talk to her. Novak's approach had been oblique, but I recognized it; it was his peace offering.

We drove past Clara Coldwater Battles' house, in Mountain Forge— a shapeless, characterless bungalow. Novak remained in the car, slouched down in the seat, while I walked up to the porch and knocked. Mrs. Battles wasn't expecting me, and she regarded me with both hesitation and doubt. Two little girls, both under five years, crowded behind her and peered out from around her skirts. It didn't seem possible that she could have heard news about the murder yet.

I introduced myself, showed her my credentials, and mentioned casually that Chief Novak was sitting in my car. This seemed to reassure her. Then I asked if she would give me some information about Mercedes Clinton Turner. Immediately, the doubt which had been in her face changed to open distrust. "Why?" she asked. "What do you want to know about Mercedes for?"

"She's disappeared," I explained; "perhaps something has happened to her."

"You mean she's just ... gone?"

"Something pretty much like that."

"Maybe she has amnesia ... can't remember anything!"

"Possibly," I agreed. "But we're talking to as many of her old friends as we can ... looking for information. I understand that you were a very good friend of hers, once."

A certain pride appeared in her eyes at the mention of her friendship, and her heavy unattractive face relaxed slightly. "I haven't seen Mercy since we were girls ... in our teens." Her eyes looked over my shoulder, seeing the old days. "I lived in Argyle then. After my folks moved over here, we just sort of drifted away from being close."

"Won't you please tell me about it anyway?" I asked.

She stood aside from the door, brushing the children out of the way. "Well ... you might come in for a few minutes," she agreed. The small living room was immaculately clean; although the furniture was of the cheapest quality, it gleamed with polish and wax. "Mr. Battles is down to the foundry, but he'll be home soon," she said. I nodded ... I didn't know if it was an explanation for bringing me into the house. She seated herself on the edge of the sofa; the two children crowded against her knees staring at me.

I do not believe that anyone would ever have called Mrs. Battles attractive. With heavy features, small eyes closely set together, thin pursed lips, and thin, fine hair which escaped loosely from any design to keep it brushed into place she had little of beauty about her. Her housedress was clean and starched, and the short sleeves disclosed the upper part off her arms were growing heavy, becoming flabby with a covering of fat. It seemed strange to me that she could ever have been a friend of Mercedes Clinton who, according to Novak, had been an exceptionally beautiful young girl. And then it came to me that Clara Coldwater had been a hanger on, one of those extremely plain, pitiful, unpopular girls who attach themselves to the train of the local beauty. They bow and scrape, run and fetch, working their way into the position of confidante, adviser, and confessor. Vicariously, they live on the popularity, the glamour, the excitement surrounding the beauty ... picking up the consoling crumbs of an occasional invitation because of their declared devotion and allegiance.

This, I guessed, was the bond between Clara and Mercedes, but I also guessed that the protestation of friendship, by Clara, did not make it so. Across all the years, Clara still envied, was still jealous of Mercedes Clinton.

I said, "You have a very charming home, here, Mrs. Battles. And very well-behaved children."

Her eyes ran over the house complacently, and returned to the silent children by her side. "Nothing fancy," she said, "and I have my own ideas about bringing up kids. Some people might not hold with 'em, but it suits Henry and me all right."

"There are certainly a lot of people who would envy you," I said. "Tell me, did Mercedes Clinton like children?"

"I don't know," she replied, "at least she never had none. She's been married to some rich New Yorker, long enough ... and I guess if she was anxious to have kids, she'd have had 'em." She moved her eyes to me, attempting to smother the curiosity in them. "Did you ever meet her husband?"

"Albert Turner?"

"Yes. That's his name. Did you?"

"I've seen him once or twice."

"What kind of a man is he?"

"Well," I said, "he was very quiet when I saw him."

"The quiet kind, huh? The kind that broods over things?"

"I really don't know," I told her. "Why? Did he have something to brood over regarding Mercedes?"

"He might've ..." Her dull eyes snapped for a moment. "Even up here, once in a while a person hears stories...."

"What kind of stories?"

"Nothing bad ... nothing like that. But before she married what's his name ... Turner, I guess she had a pretty high old time. Good job ... plenty of money, living alone in New York."

"What kind of a job did she have?"

"A very good job ... real important. She gave it up when she got married. Then, I heard, she wanted to go back to work, but nothing ever came of it, far as I know."

"In this job of hers ... what did she do?"

"She was ... an executive of some kind in a steel company. Got the first job during the war, and she worked her way up."

"What was the name of the company?"

"I don't know." She leaned over and removed a fist from the mouth of the smallest little girl. "You really feel that Mercy is in trouble? Real trouble?"

"Yes. I assure you she is."

"Enough trouble to make a person break her word?" She regarded me intently, her thin lips pursed tightly together.

"Under the circumstances," I told her seriously, "I honestly believe that if you know anything ... anything at all ... you should tell me."

"Mercy made me swear ... and I mean *really* swear with my hand on the Bible, that I'd never tell a soul. Even after her father found out about it and broke everything up ... she told me I still had to keep my promise."

"I'll assume the responsibility for anything you tell me."

She drew a deep breath, hesitating for the appearance of reluctance ... but anxious to discuss the falling queen. "I don't know," she began, "but I guess outside me and the Clintons no one else does know about it. But, Mercy was married before!"

"I didn't know that. Do you think that Albert Turner knew ... knows of it?"

"I wouldn't know," she shook her head. Then she continued, "After it was all over, I tried to get Mercedes to talk about it and tell me what happened. But she wouldn't say a word ... not one word."

"When was she first married?"

"Oh ... years ago ... just before the war in 1941. Mercy was just about sixteen...." The bars went down, the gates opened, and Clara's words poured out. That year Lyman Clinton entered Mercedes in Bently Collegiate Institute, an exclusive girls' school in Prester, located about twenty-five miles from Mountain Forge. Clinton gave his daughter a yellow roadster so she could drive home on weekends to see him and her mother. In January, the war had been declared in December, the latter part of January, Clara remembered, Mercedes drove home for a weekend and looked her up. The next week, Mercedes told her, she was planning to drive to Elkton, Maryland, the wartime Gretna Green, to be married. After swearing Clara to secrecy, Mercedes wanted her to come along as a witness. The two girls made elaborate plans, but Clara's fell through when her parents refused her permission to supposedly visit relatives in Massachusetts. So the next week, Clara was left behind.

"Whom did she marry?"

"I never met him," Clara replied, "but it was some boy she met in Prester."

"Was he going to school there?"

"I couldn't even tell you that ... not after all these years. I only remember that Mercedes told me he was very young and very poor, but they were extremely in love. They were going to get married and not tell anyone about it. She would keep on going to school where she could see him, and they'd be together."

"She actually did get married?" I asked.

"Yes. They got married. I wasn't there, but I know they did."

"What was the boy's name?"

"His last name was Rohan. I don't think I ever knew what his first name was ... Mercy always called him 'The Card.'"

"Card?" I was puzzled. "Why, The Card?"

"Because," Clara explained, "he had red hair ... hair as red as a red cardinal bird!"

Immediately after leaving the Battles' home, I drove the twenty-five miles to Prester, Connecticut. It was nearly ten o'clock when I arrived at the home of Dr. White—headmaster at Bently.

The Bently Collegiate Institute consisted of a large, red, brick building with Gothic turrets and sharply pointed doors and windows. The main building named Bently Hall was surrounded by a number of smaller structures ... most of them in brick, too, and all of them considerably newer than the old original hall. Paths running from the individual buildings all met at Bently Hall like spokes in a wheel. Heavy old trees dotted the campus. The headmaster was a Dr. White, and I learned immediately that Bently Collegiate Institute was a girls' school exclusively.

Dr. White, I also discovered, was going to be absolutely useless as a source of information. Punctiliously polite, he answered my questions monosyllabically whenever possible. Yes; he remembered Mercedes Clinton. No; he couldn't recall anything about her. Yes; she had been an average student. No; he had never had any problems with her. At my urging, he seemed to remember that she had permission to go home on weekends whenever she wanted. "You see," he explained coldly, "this was all so long ago, and we've had so many girls since then. Bently celebrated its one hundredth anniversary two years ago. We rather lose track of our girls when they graduate ... unless they do something outstanding."

"Mercedes Turner, if she shot her husband, is outstanding enough," I pointed out.

His face froze. "It's unfortunate," he said coldly, "but she's the first from Bently."

I arose and prepared to leave. Dr. White nodded politely without rising. Just as I reached the door, I turned and asked, "Do you remember a red-haired boy here in Prester named Rohan?"

"I've never heard of him."

I believed him and walked through the campus to the highway where I'd parked my car. Prester was a town of perhaps two thousand population, and it rambled over the countryside, the streets lined with trees. Bently Collegiate Institute was on one edge of town; on the other was a small furniture factory. I drove around and around the town, touring slowly, attempting to get an idea of what to do next.

It was here, I believed, that Mercedes Clinton had first met a red-haired boy named Rohan. I pulled into a gas station and while my tank was being filled, I went into the office and leafed through the tiny phone book which included Prester, and four very small surrounding villages. There was no Rohan listed in it. When I paid the attendant, I asked him if he was familiar with a family by that name. He wasn't. Further questioning brought out the information that the town constable's name was Fullbright and he also owned the local garage. Driving back to the main street, I found a small, white, frame building which housed a number of broken-down automobiles. Inside, Fullbright was working on a ledger.

"No," he told me, "I never heard of no one named Rohan around here. Used to be an Irish family named Bohan, which farmed up near Naquog for a while, but they give it up."

"Did any of them have red hair?"

He thought about it. "Nope," he said finally, "the old man was bald and his wife and daughter ..." he thought again, "seemed to me they had darkish hair."

"That's all the family there was?"

"Yep. Just the three of 'em."

That was that. "Do you ever have any trouble with the kids from Bently?" I asked.

"The girls hain't no particular problem," he said. "Hain't half the trouble they'd be if they was boys. Bently sorta keeps to itself pretty much," he said. "Girls don't come down into town often."

"What do they do? They must have some place to go?"

"There's a place called the Snack Bar ... about a mile goin' down the road this way, but only 'bout a quarter of a mile walkin' toward town from the campus. The girls can go there. Old fellow by the name of Beatty runs it ... him and his wife been runnin' it for years."

The Snack Bar was in an old converted frame house. The lower floor included a built-over porch with large glass windows running into one large room with a heavy linoleum floor; there was a juke box in the far corner, a soda fountain with stools, and a series of small booths. It was spotlessly clean, and on the walls were pennants carrying a yellow "B" on a navy blue field. Yellow and blue twisted paper streamers draped from the center of the ceiling to each corner of the room. A cheerful place filled with color and youth. As it was eleven o'clock at night, the room was deserted except for two young girls in a booth, studying. When I entered, they merely glanced up and returned to their books. An elderly man, short and with a round wrinkled face, wearing a white confectioner's apron, was working behind the fountain mixing a malted. He fussed over it carefully, and when he had finished it, he crowned the drink with a heavy layer of whipped cream. "I haven't seen one like that in years," I told him.

He beamed with pleasure. "Kids like 'em this way," he explained.

"Are you Mr. Beatty?" I asked.

"Yes. You lookin' for me?" He walked over to the booth and deposited the malted milk by the side of one of the girls.

When he returned to the fountain, I said. "In a way ... I'm wondering if you ever knew anyone around here named Rohan? This was fifteen or sixteen years ago ... perhaps before the war?"

"A red-haired boy?" he asked.

"Yes." I waited patiently, while he considered the question. He had already answered it to a degree by identifying the red hair, but there might be more to come.

"Seems I recall the name," he continued slowly. "Why're you interested in finding him?"

"I'm just trying to get in touch with him," I said casually. He regarded me closely, studying my face. I smiled, and it seemed to reassure him. He wiped the clean fountain with a soft, pink rubber sponge. "Well," he said, "I remember the boy ... but come to think of it now, he's a man ... hain't he?" I nodded. "Yes, indeed, he must be all grown up. My, how time flies!"

"It certainly does," I agreed.

"Well, I'll tell you ... Hugh was here for just about a year ... a school year, that is ... nine months more like it. Worked for the Mrs. and me." He turned from the fountain, and at the door to the kitchen called, "Mother ... come here." In a moment, he was joined by a tiny, birdlike woman whose white hair was drawn straight to the back of her little head in a bun. She wore gold-rimmed glasses. She greeted me pleasantly enough, although with a slight reservation. Her husband, nodding in my direction, said, "Mother always remembers things far better'n me."

She was in firm agreement. "Hugh came here in the fall of 1941 and worked until late spring of 1942. He was a good boy, and both the Mister and me didn't like to see 'im go."

"Why did he leave?" I asked.

"The war ..." said the old man. "I guess he got restless and left. Ever'one seemed to be leavin' in those days."

"He was such a handsome boy," said Mrs. Beatty. "It seemed a shame skin and hair like his should be wasted on a boy. A girl woulda given most anything to have had 'em."

"Did his family live around here?" I asked.

"Nope ... not as I recollect." The old man turned to his wife. "Do you remember where Hugh come from?"

She shook her white head. "No. Seems to me, though, it was from out West somewhere." She sifted her memory, gravely, and added, "As I remember, it don't seem to me he talked like a regular New Englander ... or New Yorker ... either."

"A course, Mother and me are sorta used to hearin' all these girls talkin' and we don't pay much attention. They come from all over, too."

"How did Hugh Rohan happen to go to work for you?"

"Came down to see about a job from Royal. He was plannin' to go to Annixter College there. I sort of leave a standin' invitation with the Registrar's Office, there, to send down a good boy ... one who's deservin' ... to help Mother and me out."

The old lady nodded her head vigorously. "It's comin' back now," she said firmly, "I knew it would if I just give it time. Hughie did too come from out West."

"I remember he never did like you to call him Hughie," her husband said.

"It seemed sorta natural to call him that, but I was the only one he wouldn't fuss at who did it. He came from some little town out West, but I recollect he didn't have enough credits to get into Annixter. He had to make up some studies and then take an examination to get in."

"Why would he come all that distance to get into Annixter?" I asked.

"Well," replied the old lady, proudly, as if it might have been her own son she was discussing, "the boy wanted to be a doctor and he wanted the best. Annixter is recognized to have one of the best pre-medical schools there is."

Mr. Beatty added, "A lot of the girls at Bently marry doctors who once went to Annixter."

Nodding, the old lady confirmed this. "But he hadn't counted on havin' to make up a lot of credits, and he didn't have any money to speak of. So he came here to tide over."

"He didn't have to do much work ... all day long he was free to study. Only after school was out up at Bently, and durin' the evenin', he handled the fountain and waited the booths when the girls came in."

"We give 'm his room ... a real nice little room upstairs, and all his meals ... and ten dollars a week," Mrs. Beatty said. "It was a great help to the boy and if the war hadn't come along, he'd a gotten into the college."

"What kind of boy was he?" I asked.

"A nice boy. Nice and polite to Mr. Beatty and me, and he done his work real steady. Hugh was always readin' and always workin' out plans of some kind of other."

"But he had a temper, too," added the old man, "and don't think he didn't. That red hair of his'n wasn't put on his head for nothin'. I recall once two boys ... town boys ... was botherin' a couple Bently girls out front here, and Hugh took off his apron and sailed right out that door." The old man chuckled, pleased with the memory. "He lit into 'em like a chicken hawk and was givin' 'em a real lickin' when I put a stop to it."

"While Rohan was here," I asked, "do you remember a little blonde girl named Mercedes Clinton? She drove a yellow roadster."

The two old people looked at each other. Mrs. Beatty shook her head. "No ... can't say that I do." As if apologizing to her husband, she explained, "Good gracious ... all the girls seem to be blonde nowadays ... and they all have cars."

A tall skinny youth, wearing a maroon sweater and three white letter stripes on his left arm, poked his head in the door from the kitchen. "I'm all through studying tonight," he called. "If it's okay, I think I'll go to bed." His bright eyes passed over me to light on Mrs. Beatty.

"Might as well, Johnny," replied the old lady.

"That's Johnny Windecker ... our new boy from Royal this year," said Mr. Beatty.

"A nice boy," added Mrs. Beatty, "real nice."

By the time I drove back to New York, it was nearly three o'clock in the morning. I'd had it for the day.

Chapter 7

They stood on the pavement in Jersey City, and even in the noon of the warm, fall day the street looked bleak and shabby. It was lined with used car lots, garages, auto parts stores, and tire vulcanizing shops which crawled and sprawled next to each other, shouting their wares with ugly blatant signs painted in fading colors. On one corner was a small diner, built to resemble a dining car, and its chrome trimmings were tarnished and half eaten away by the soot and fumes of the city.

"We'll buy a car here," Mercedes said, "so we won't have to travel by train or bus. There'll be less chance of someone remembering us."

Rohan stuffed his hands in his pockets and stared down the street. "I don't think it'll be much of a car," he replied.

"It will be good enough. We won't drive fast, because we can't risk being picked up for speeding."

"Do you have some money?" When she confirmed his question, he continued, "I'll see what I can find."

"No," she said, "I'll buy it. They'll remember you more easily than they will me. You go over to that diner and wait for me. Keep your hat on ... and don't take it off! I'll meet you there as soon as I can."

He agreed reluctantly and walked down the street, making his way to the shabby restaurant. The woman watched him depart; then she withdrew a piece of tissue from her purse and removed the lipstick from her lips ... wiping part of the makeup from her face. It took only a moment and her features were no longer vivid; in contrast, suddenly, she appeared quite plain. She began walking slowly, passing the different lots where cars were lined up in rows, the price of each painted in white on the windshield. She paused, finally, before a sign which announced, JERSEY JACK—THE DEMON TRADER. The sign was a faded red with dusty white letters, and it spanned the width of the driveway which led from the curb to the lot—raised on painted four-by-fours, bridging the drive like a triumphal arch. As she entered, a man wearing a houndstooth sport jacket with pockets sagging beneath the weight of trading books, financial rates, order blanks, circulars, pens and pencils approached her. He sidled up anxiously while attempting to maintain a thin air of casualness. "Nice day," he said, screwing his face into a wolfish welcome. "I'll bet you're looking for a car?" He gauged her appearance carefully, obviously undecided as to her financial potentialities, misdirected by the chicness of her clothes and the plain, unadorned face.

"I'm just looking," she replied deliberately.

"Go ahead," he replied with hollow enthusiasm, "we've got some beauts ... best buys in Jersey."

I must be careful, the woman thought, to do nothing that he might remember; I must let him believe that he sold me ... that I really didn't intend to buy a car. Clutching her purse, she looked slowly around the yard. To her right was a long gleaming Cadillac convertible, a year old ... and obviously the pride of the sales lot. She stared at it, forcing a gleam of covetousness into her eyes. Following her glance, the salesman said, "Lady, there she is ... there's a real buy! A real steal, and clean as a whistle, too!"

"How much is it?" When he told her, she shrugged and shook her head. "That's a great deal more than I could possibly spend," she replied.

"Not when you consider all the mileage left in that buggy," he replied quickly, "she's good for another hundred thousand miles!"

She made a pretense of turning to leave, "No," she said, "it's too much. I was just looking, anyway."

Anxiously, he stepped to her side, turning her away from the drive, speaking rapidly, "Well, we've got lots of others—while you're here you might as well take a look." With obvious reluctance, she permitted him to draw her to the center of the lot, walking through solid rows of used cars.

"Yes," she agreed cautiously, "I don't suppose it will do any harm to just get an idea." Half an hour later, she consented to purchase a Chevrolet; it was four years old and painted a nondescript gray—no different in style, age, or appearance from thousands of similar cars on the highways. It carried New Jersey license plates.

She insisted on an immediate transfer of title, giving the name of Mrs. Walter Brewer and an address in Trenton, New Jersey. The bill of sale and title she tucked in her purse. Driving the car away from the lot, she carefully circled the block to approach the diner from the opposite direction. She could see Rohan seated at a table by the window; he recognized her immediately and hurried to the curb to meet her. He slipped into the seat beside her, and she drove back to the station where they had checked their luggage.

That night they stayed in Delaware, in Rehoboth Beach, a seaside resort town deserted in the fall season. The big hotels were boarded up, and sand drifted lonesomely across the tourist walks. After dinner, they made the long drive back to Wilmington to pick up the New York papers, but the early mail editions carried no mention of Albert Turner. At a cosmetics counter, Mercedes bought a dye for Rohan's hair, and that evening back in their room at the tourist home, she applied it carefully, covering the flame of red with a disguise of dull brown. They left Rehoboth early in the morning: Rohan bringing around the car, while Mercedes settled their bill so his change of hair coloring would remain unseen.

Again they returned to Wilmington, and now the New York papers carried the news of the shooting of Albert Turner. As yet, there were no pictures of her, and no mention of the red-haired man. The stories speculated upon the disappearance of Mercedes Turner vaguely ... carefully indefinite ... and were based upon statements issued by the police. Direct charges had not, as yet, been made against her, and she was wanted, at that time, only for questioning.

They filled the Chevy with gas, and after breakfast drove steadily—passing through Baltimore, by-passing Washington, D.C., into Virginia. In Fredericksburg they applied for a marriage license, and using the names of Walter Brewer and Martha Choate, were married.

Chapter 8

In the morning, back in New York, some of the reports were in from the Medical Office and the Technical Squad. Albert Turner had been shot just once, with a .32 ... possibly an S. & W. The stains on the living-room rug were blood, and it matched the blood for Albert Turner ... basic blood group B, type MN, plus Rh1, Rh2. This is not too common a grouping. He had been shot between ten and twelve at night ... probably halfway.

Fingerprints found in the apartment were identified primarily as belonging to the deceased, his wife, and the maid. Other prints were not identifiable and were believed to belong to guests who, according to Thelma Jordan, had visited the apartment often. None of these prints had any criminal record.

A strand of short red hair had been found in the sweepings from the living room. The length and texture indicated that it had probably belonged to a man. The maid was unable to identify any visitor to the Turner apartment who had red hair.

Picking up the phone, I called Mountain Forge and when I got Mrs. Battles on the line, I identified myself. Her voice was extremely cold. "I've seen the papers," she said accusingly. "You never told me you suspected Mercedes!"

"We suspect everyone," I replied, "until we find the right person. Would you mind answering another question for me?"

"I don't know ... I don't want to get Mercedes in any more trouble."

"After Mr. Clinton found out Mercedes was married to Rohan, you said 'he broke everything up.' What did he do?"

"He had the marriage annulled."

"What happened to Rohan?"

"I don't know." She added ungraciously, "Mercedes never talked about him. Maybe he went into the war."

"Not at seventeen."

"He might've been eighteen." There was a short pause, then she said, "I can't say why, but I'm pretty sure he was in the war ... I sort of remember it that way."

"Have you ever heard any more about him? Was he killed?"

"I've never heard a word."

I thanked her and hung up. Skors walked in while I was writing my report. I gave him what I'd picked up. He brought me up to date on his findings. "The wife did it, all right," he said, "there's a general out on her."

"What'd you find at Turner's office?"

"Plenty. This guy Turner was quite an operator; you should see the collection of rackets he had. He had a holding company called Turner Enterprises, Inc."

"What'd he go in for?"

"Anything for a fast buck ... all strictly within the law, though. One of his companies is a personal loan operation—with duplicate notes paying ten per cent interest a month ... pay up, sucker, or get your face busted open sort of thing. Then Turner had a hack cab rental company, too, on a per-day basis for the down and out cabbies who'd been kicked out of every other hack company in town. Thirty-five bucks a day ... payable in advance; by working eighteen hours, the driver might get his rent back and clear a couple bucks."

"That all?" I asked. "Turner sounds like a sweet guy."

Skors glanced at me uneasily. "No," he said, "Turner had a lot of things going for him. He had an accident and burial insurance company which he operated through a front in Harlem. Ten cents for accident, two bits for burial ... both for thirty cents, per week. One of those deals where you had to get hurt or die exactly according to directions ... and even then you couldn't collect."

I could feel the anger hit me. "Yes," I replied, "I know ... I've seen 'em operate. Poor families pay their quarters all their life, and then end up in Potter's Field!"

"Well," said Skors, "that'll give you an idea. Funny thing, though, this guy Turner ran around with a collection of bums ... and nice people, too.

Belonged to some good clubs with hot shots in them. I guess he could look and act like a gentleman when he wanted."

"Did Turner leave any insurance?"

"Some ... not as much, maybe, as you'd expect. Twenty-five grand."

"That's hardly enough under the circumstances to make a good motive. Besides, if his wife was trying to collect it, she'd have stuck around."

"Yeah," agreed Skors, "but there's something else ... a little more interesting. Turner kept all his insurance papers in his office. It seems he had a policy on some jewelry his wife owned."

"How much?"

"It's insured for fifty thousand, and it's probably worth more than that."

"Did she take it with her?"

"Yeah. She went to the box yesterday morning ... just as soon as the bank opened. The D.A.'s office got a court order to open the box and take a look at it. When we opened it, all her jewelry was gone."

"We better get out that DD 60," I replied.

"An officer of the bank had to be there when it was opened ... a man named Forrest. He told us the same morning she stopped and cashed a check. Nearly cleaned out the account ... which was a joint one. He showed us the check ... it was for four grand."

"A nice round figure," I said.

"Sure," replied Skors, "and it'll buy a long ride ... for a long time."

I thought about it. If the jewelry was insured for fifty thousand dollars, Mercedes Turner couldn't pawn it for more than ten or twelve thousand at the most. "Did you get a description of the stuff?" I asked Skors.

"There was a pretty good description in the insurance policy." Skors patted his pockets. "I got it somewhere, and I'll take care of getting out the DD 60." This is a card which goes to the Lost Property Bureau covering goods lost, stolen, or found. All pawnbrokers and secondhand dealers are compelled by law, in New York, to list and report each purchase and sale.

I showed Skors a picture I had found. It was a photograph of Mercedes Turner in a shepherdess costume, carrying a long crook with a big satin bow. I had dug it up from the publicity department of the New York Children's League; it had been taken at the annual charity ball shortly after Mercedes Turner's marriage. It wasn't a very good picture because it had been taken with a flash and the light had washed out many of the details in her face. Her hair was piled up, beneath a wide hat, and she was smiling. Her teeth were white against the dark rim of her lips, and her eyelids were partly lowered against the sudden flash of light. She was a good-looking woman ... a very attractive one, but the photograph had managed to lose her individuality and she looked no different from hundreds of others.

"That's not going to be much help," Skors said. "Is it all we got?"

"That's it," I told him. "Turner didn't like publicity, which I can understand, either for himself or his wife." I put the picture back in my pocket.

"Oh yeah," said Skors, "here's something else." He withdrew a sheet of paper with a list of names and addresses. "Here's some of the names of friends of the Turners." He shoved the list across the desk and I copied down half a dozen names beginning at the bottom and working up. "I'll cover the last six," I told him. He nodded as I returned the list. "Incidentally," I asked, "did Turner ever have any kind of a record?"

Skors shook his head. "No," he said, "he was never arrested, but he sure as hell deserved to be."

I finished my report and then went out to talk to some of the names on the list I had copied from Skors. I wasn't very lucky; everyone seemed to be out. At five o'clock, though, I caught one coming home. Her name was Gresham, Mrs. William Hudnut Gresham. She lived on Beekman Place which is a little below East Vanders. She told me she could only spare a few minutes as she had to get dressed and meet her husband downtown for a cocktail party. "As a matter of fact," she announced, "I'm exhausted ... perfectly exhausted ... right now. I've been literally running around all day! I think I shall have a drink while we talk." She didn't offer me one, which I'd have refused anyway. But it put me in my place. Ringing for a maid, she asked for a martini and in a moment it appeared in a chilled glass. My tongue parched at the sight of it. Sipping it, she said, "My ... how perfectly thrilling! Mercedes and Albert! I've read all about poor Albert. Dreadful. Perfectly dreadful. And who'd have thought that Mercedes would have done it?"

"I don't know ... perhaps she didn't," I replied.

"Oh, she must have!" Mrs. Gresham's eyes flashed. "Why would she run away?"

"That's something we'd all like to know. Did she have any men friends whom you knew about?"

"Do you mean was Mercedes having an affair?" Mrs. Gresham savored the martini. "Well, frankly, I don't know ... I really don't. Not that I'd have blamed her."

"Why do you say that?"

"Albert. He was about as nasty an individual as I've ever seen ... even with all his money."

"Then why did she marry him?"

Mrs. Gresham seemed amused with my stupidity. "Oh, Albert could be fascinating to women ... until you got to know him too well. He had charming manners, he'd been around and was amusing. And then, of course, he simply had loads of money."

"Didn't Mercedes Turner know what he was like when she married him?"

She shrugged. "Who knows? Albert was probably different from any man she'd ever known. And then, of course, she might've become bored with her job."

"Where was she working?"

"A steel company ... Eastern Coastal something."

"I understand it was a very good position."

"Oh, yes. Very much the woman executive type of thing ... decisions and crises each day ... memos ... all very businesslike."

"Did Mrs. Turner have any difficulties ... any arguments or misunderstandings with her husband?"

"Doesn't everyone?" she asked. Then she said, very seriously, "Albert Turner was the kind ... of man ... who liked to hurt people ... to keep them in his grasp. And I don't think Mercedes would stand for that ... if she could help it."

"Was Albert Turner running around with other women?"

Mrs. Gresham laughed. "Albert? Of course!" Then added very hastily. "But you couldn't prove it by me. Nor from anyone else. Albert would conduct his affairs very slyly ... very secretly. He wouldn't have wanted to give Mercedes anything she could use against him legally ... particularly if she wanted to divorce him."

"You think she wanted to divorce him?"

"Certainly. For several years. But there was nothing she could do about it, unless he agreed. And knowing Albert, I doubt that he'd agree, unless he wanted to."

"Why do you believe Mrs. Turner wasn't interested in someone else?"

Mrs. Gresham finished her martini and said, "I'm going to have another!" She rang for the maid, handing her the glass without a word. In a moment she had another. Completely ignoring the maid, she said, "I don't want anyone to think I'm being catty ... because I am. I've always been very fond of Mercedes, but she's rather ... well, indifferent might be the word, as far as men are concerned. Perfectly self-contained. No real warmth." She took a sip of her new drink. "Perhaps that's what endeared her to all the girls. Felt perfectly safe about their husbands."

"Mrs. Turner was popular then?"

Mrs. Gresham's laugh tinkled as sharply as an iced drink. "Very ... millions of friends ... everybody simply loved her." She added, "I can't say as much for Albert Turner. They were invited everywhere ... but utterly because of her."

"She didn't love Albert Turner?"

"Don't be quaint!" said Mrs. Gresham.

"Did she ever mention a man named Rohan?"

Mrs. Gresham licked up the tiny seed onion with the tip of her tongue. "I always eat the onions first," she explained. "I can't stand to see them staring at me like a fish eye." She shook her head, "Rohan? No, she never mentioned him." Her face lit with sudden curiosity. "Why? Did she ... was she ... a man named Rohan?"

"It was just a name which came up," I said casually. She looked disappointed. "Did Mercedes Turner ever mention an out of the way place ... a hidden cabin ... anywhere?"

"Where she might hide?"

"She might be using it to live in now," I agreed, "but when she mentioned it to you ... it might have been just a place she had seen ... or liked."

"No." Mrs. Gresham looked at her watch and gasped. "Oh, dear! I'm late! Positively, I'm late right this second ... I must dash. You'll forgive me?" She was on her feet and heading toward the back of the apartment. "By-by."

"Good-by." I let myself out of the apartment and walked up to East Vanders Place. There was still a cop assigned to the Turner apartment and he let me in. In the kitchen, Thelma Jordan was cooking her dinner. I sat down at the table. "Would you care for some coffee?" she asked. I told her I would.

"Tell me, Thelma," I said, "do you think Mrs. Turner shot her husband?"

She poured my coffee and returned the pot to the stove. "She must have," she replied. "Who else could have done it?"

"Why do you think they were unhappy?"

"I don't know what you mean by unhappy. They were both pretty young yet ... and had a lot of money. They could do most anything they wanted." Her plain, tired face turned to me questioningly, "Why wouldn't they be happy?"

"I don't have the answer. That's why I'm asking you."

"With all their money, I'd be happy," the maid said simply.

"But Mrs. Turner wasn't happy?" I insisted.

"Maybe not ... real happy," she said defensively.

"Contented, then?"

"She never complained about it; just sort of did the things she and Mr. Turner was supposed to do."

"There wasn't a photograph to be found in this apartment ... anywhere," I said. "That's rather odd because most families have photographs of some kind."

"There used to be a big book of them," the maid told me, "but the pictures are gone. There's just the cover left." She thought a moment and then added, "Speaking of pictures … just happened to make me remember something. It happened right after I started to work here. There was some picture Mrs. Turner had. Mr. Turner found it and they started a fight."

"What was the photograph?"

"I never saw it. I only heard them arguing about it. It was a picture of a soldier Mrs. Turner had been keeping."

"What happened?"

"Not very much. Mr. Turner was angry and he tore it up … and threw it away."

"Who was the soldier?"

"Just a soldier as far as I could tell … someone Mrs. Turner had known during the war."

"Can you recall anything that was said … anything at all?"

"Nothing, except Mrs. Turner said something about letting the dead stay dead."

"Did you hear anything which might lead you to believe the soldier had red hair?"

"No … not a thing."

I finished the coffee and walked into the living room where the cop was sitting, reading a paper. He was supposed to keep a list of anyone who stopped at the apartment, and anyone who phoned. "Anything?" I asked him.

He put down the paper. "Usual stuff … household calls." He handed me a list. I glanced at it and could see there was nothing important. The building and neighborhood had been covered in the hope of finding someone who might have seen a stranger entering or leaving the building … alone, or with Mercedes Turner. No witness had been found.

I had never talked to the tenants living on the floor above. They had either been covered by Skors, or the other cops assigned to the case. I'd seen their reports. I decided I'd go upstairs to talk with them anyway. The family's name was Leighton. A maid opened the door and then called Mr. Leighton who was quite pleasant and invited me in. The apartment was laid out exactly as the Turners' beneath it. In the living room I met Mrs. Leighton. "I don't want to interfere with your dinner," I apologized.

"We've plenty of time," said Mr. Leighton, "we don't eat until eight."

"That's a terrible tragedy about the Turners," Mrs. Leighton said. "I suppose that's why you're here?"

"Yes. Did you know them?"

"Only to speak to. Sometimes we'd meet on the elevator … and mention the weather," she replied. I'd expected it. In New York, it's possible to live in an apartment, side by side with neighbors for twenty years, and never reach the point of even discussing the weather.

"That Mrs. Turner was sure a beautiful girl," Mr. Leighton remarked. Mrs. Leighton agreed and regarded her husband complacently. She was sure of him, I thought; they've been married too long for her to be jealous.

"You were home the night Mr. Turner was shot?" I asked. Both nodded. "He was killed around eleven fifteen. You didn't hear the revolver?"

"No," replied Mr. Leighton, "we didn't hear anything."

"Contrary to popular ideas," I explained, "a revolver sounds nothing like a car back-firing ... or a light bulb breaking, or for that matter ... like much of any other sound, except what it is—a revolver shot. It cracks, and is rather flat and with a closed space such as a room often has an individual type of vibration. If you had heard it ... and sound rises, which means the sound beneath in the Turner living room would rise to this one ... you couldn't mistake it."

Leighton pointed to an elaborate hi-fi phonograph, which was large enough to contain a 36-inch speaker. "We play that a great deal," he said, "and when we do, we turn it up loud to get as much tone quality as we can. When we bought it, we had this room soundproofed as well as we could ... without going into a lot of reconstruction and baffle boards and that sort of thing."

"Were you playing it at the time Albert Turner was shot?"

"We had been throughout the evening, but I don't remember if we had it on at eleven fifteen. Anyway, I don't think it makes too much difference ... we wouldn't have heard the shot. Listen!" He held up his hand and the room was quiet; from outside I could hear none of the usual city noises. "See?" he asked pleasantly. "This isn't a hundred per cent soundproof or perfect ... but unless we open the windows, it's pretty good."

I agreed. "I don't suppose the other detectives have missed asking you if you've seen any strangers around the building? Either on the day of the shooting ... or a few days before?"

"Strangers are strangers," replied Mrs. Leighton. "A person sees hundreds of strangers each day on the street. I see people every day on Vanders whom I've never seen before. How can I remember them?" Her husband agreed with her.

"Not unless they were acting suspiciously," I said.

"I've seen no one acting suspiciously."

"All right. Now just one more question. Have you ever seen a man ... recently, that is ... in this neighborhood with red hair? I mean real red hair ... extremely red?"

"Why, yes," replied Mrs. Leighton, "yes, I remember, I did see a red-haired man early ... the night of the murder ... oh, it was around six o'-

clock. I noticed his hair."

"What was he doing?" I asked.

"Just walking down East Vanders. That's all ... just walking, and looking around as if he were searching for a number."

Chapter 9

They stayed in an inn, outside the city limits of Williamsburg, Virginia. In their room, Rohan kissed her—their first kiss since they had left New York. The night before, in Rehoboth Beach, they had remained apart, each separated by thoughts—deep, secret, fearful. The future which lay ahead seemed too dreadful to contemplate. Behind them, the powers of retribution were stirring, collecting their forces, preparing to strike. But they had not yet struck, and the uncertainty had seemed unendurable.

However, with the discovery of Turner's body and the publication of the news in the papers, it seemed that the worst had happened. The waiting was over; it had been endurable, after all, leaving no marks on them. In Fredericksburg, their marriage had reunited them again, and with it irresolution disappeared. Now, and forever, they were bound together, by marriage—and by the death of Albert Turner. In neither of their minds had the marriage been other than a solemn one. Mercedes, however, had urged it for yet another reason ... a reason which she did not disclose to Rohan. She was a witness to the murder; as Rohan's wife, she could not be forced to testify against him.

With the address of East Vanders Place far away in miles, with the memory of the night far away in hours, they turned to each other again. Rohan kissed her. He held her close and ran his face through her hair. "I love you," he said, "I've always loved you."

"There were years when you didn't," Mercedes whispered, "too many lonesome years ..."

"Those were years I couldn't help," he told her. "They were years from my life when I wasn't alive. It wasn't until I found you again that I started to live."

She stirred, and against her breast she could feel his blood pumping in his chest. A feeling of tenderness and pity ran through her, and she touched his face gently with her fingers. "In a world of immorality," she murmured, wondering, "it's strange that we have been so moral. We've shared no illicit love affairs, we've had each other only in marriage. And," she added, catching her breath, "now in murder too."

He raised himself on his elbow, peering intently down into her face. "They'll never separate us again!"

"They will," she said. "Oh yes, they will." She shook her head hopelessly on the pillow.

"I'll kill myself first! They'll never take me!" But the man's voice was hollow.

"What we have already done, we can never justify. We can only pay for it, when the time comes." She kissed him, and he relaxed—lying beside her. Then his arms, again, slowly folded around her.

In the morning, they decided to remain near Williamsburg, a town in which it was unlikely that the police would suspect them of hiding. Williamsburg, although small, contained a college which, together with the town's historical sites and buildings, drew tourists and travelers the year around. Visitors were not conspicuous, nor were they regarded with suspicion by the local people, and the presence of strangers caused no comment.

The day was cooler and the air became a stimulant, slightly chilled and exhilarating beneath a sky clear and cloudless. They drove the short distance to the bay, where the water nibbled against the white sand with tiny blue tongues tipped with brilliants. The evergreen trees which covered so much of the area wore, unchangingly, their blue-green coats, while the maples assumed rare and unsophisticated splendors—outdoing one another in the reds and vermilions, yellows, oranges, and cocoa browns.

The short main street of the town, the shops built in traditional conformity to the early architecture of the settlement, the green, the Governor's Palace became as familiar to them as their own home towns. The anachronism of the town, its way of life, was soothing and wrapped the two in protective layers of isolation.

But the soporific effects of their life in Williamsburg were a cause of worry to the woman. She knew it could not continue forever. The town was still too close to New York to be entirely safe, and there was the daily danger of recognition from acquaintances passing through on their way from New York to Florida. The rest, however, had built a new confidence in them, and she told Rohan, "I think we should go on. It's safe now ... and we should be getting more money."

The man was surprised. "But we have plenty!"

"We are using up our supply of cash," she told him. "We should keep as much of our money as we can, and begin to sell our jewelry."

"I like it here, don't you?"

"Very much. And I hate to leave." She regarded him sympathetically. "Darling, don't you understand? It will always be this way. We can never stay any place very long. We'll find places ... good and bad places ... and we'll live in them all."

He nodded. "When do you want to start?"

"Tomorrow."

In Richmond, Virginia, Hugh Rohan remained in the auto while Mercedes Turner entered the store. It was the Dixie Jewelry Company in the downtown section just off Broad Street. A small permanent sign lettered on the window announced: WE BUY, SELL, AND TRADE OLD JEWELRY. As she walked through the door, a tall slender man wearing extremely heavy glasses peered up from an examination of a watch. A black jeweler's glass had been attached to the right lens of his glasses, and he swung it up and to one side as he arose. Approaching the counter where the woman was standing, he nodded politely and, speaking with a very slight Southern accent, asked if he could help her.

"Yes," she replied crisply. "I have a pair of earrings I've been thinking about selling. I saw a sign on your window." She opened her purse and removed the pair of cluster earrings wrapped in tissue paper, placing them on the counter. The jeweler picked them up with deft slender fingers and walked to the front of the store. Standing near the window, he again swung down his jeweler's glass and examined each closely. When he had completed his inspection, he returned to where the woman was standing and said, "These appear to be comparatively new ... usually we buy older, less valuable pieces."

"I've had them only a few years," she replied; "they were given to me as a gift."

"The larger stone in each is very good ... probably about a carat and three quarters ... the smaller ones in the clusters aren't so valuable."

"How much can you give me?"

He shrugged apologetically. "Five hundred dollars."

"Five hundred dollars!" She repeated the words incredulously. "Why ... why, the insurance company issued a policy on them for thirty-two hundred dollars!"

"I don't doubt it, Ma'am," he replied, his voice courteous. "That should be a fair valuation of their retail price."

"Then ... why can't you give me more?"

"Well, Ma'am," he explained, "the way the earrings are now ... they're a right smart expensive set. Chances are we might not sell them for years ... maybe never. We'd just have to keep them in stock. If we reset them as rings ... or put them in other pieces, we'd have all that cost to go through first. Even if we sold them to another wholesale buyer, we'd not get much more than five hundred for them. So, you see, we can't pay very much." He regarded her kindly, his eyes huge behind the heavy glasses. "I suggest you keep 'em, Ma'am; they're worth more to you than anybody else."

"But ... I need the money. I've just moved down South ... and it cost more than I expected." They discussed the situation and after some minutes, the jeweler politely agreed to pay her five hundred and seventy-five dollars.

Once again, he said apologetically, "I'm afraid, Ma'am, I'm going to have to ask you for some sort of identification. Law requires it."

Her mind turned rapidly, quickly estimating the possible risks involved. She wanted the cash, to add to her diminishing capital, available for any immediate emergency. The rest of the jewelry, too, she must sell as quickly as she could. They had not been traced to Williamsburg ... and certainly not to Richmond; and she decided there was little present risk involved although an inner voice of caution nagged her. Smiling, she removed the bill of sale for the car from her purse. "We lived in New Jersey before we moved," she explained. "Here's a bill for our car." After only a momentary hesitation, she produced their hotel bill from Williamsburg. "We're living permanently in Williamsburg now," she said, "at the Old Stone Inn." She made a studied pretense of looking through her purse for other papers, but the jeweler smilingly waved her efforts away.

"This will be sufficient, Mrs. Brewer," he said. "It's just a sort of formality, I reckon." He scribbled a few notes on his pad. "I don't have that much cash on hand," he added, "so I'll have to give you a check. The bank is right around the corner ... I'll call them and you can cash it right away."

"That will be perfectly satisfactory," she agreed. After she had cashed the check, she left the bank and returned to the car where Rohan was waiting. She sat down beside him, and he shifted the car into gear and began driving to the outskirts of the city. "Have any trouble?" he asked.

"None," she replied, although she didn't feel entirely satisfied. "I'm uneasy, now, about selling the earrings," she explained thoughtfully, "although I really can't see how they can be traced. Certainly ... any kind of report in Richmond wouldn't go to New York."

"Perhaps we should wait a while before trying to sell any more," Rohan replied.

"We can't wait," Mercedes argued. "We must keep our supply of cash large ... and to do that, we must get rid of the jewelry as soon as we can. All of it!"

"And then what?"

"We won't have enough to last forever. We'll find a place where we can make it go far ... where we can make it last for a long time."

"Mexico?"

"No. We'd be too conspicuous in Mexico. Sooner or later, we'd be picked up ... sure. We speak no Spanish ..." her shoulders moved eloquently, "we'd always be strangers wherever we went."

The man removed his hand from the steering wheel and patted her gently on the arm. "We'd always have each other," he said, his voice shy.

She looked at him, and in response he moved his eyes from the road to smile at her, and his face was strangely young. "That's all that's really important to you, isn't it?" she asked.

"Yes. Just as long as we're together." He returned his hand to the wheel, and his eyes swept back to the road. "It's all that has ever been important." But as he stared ahead at the highway slipping silently beneath the car, his face was no longer young. Instead, it was the face of a tired man; the lines around his mouth were not creases formed by laughter, but were the marks left by the years dropping bitterly on his cheeks. "Do you think everything will be all right?" he asked, suddenly. The strength had left him, and his voice was wondering and confused.

The woman's emotions were twisted by sympathy and love, but the helplessness, the weakness of the man appalled her. "Why do you ask? Aren't you sure?"

"I'm no longer sure of anything," he replied heavily. "I've no confidence left. Those years take it away from you. Regardless of what you hear ... or read ... they take it away, and it can never be replaced. A man may become sly and cunning, but he never becomes confident."

She turned in the seat, throwing her arm across the back, and the tips of her fingers caressed the back of his neck, nestling in the muddy brown hair. "It will be all right," she reassured him, her voice soothing, "we will make out, darling. Possibly for a long time ..." She struggled, momentarily, attempting to temper her love with the truth, but the lost face beside her swayed her decision. Briskly, she gave his neck a firm final pat, and removing her arm lit a cigarette, giving it to him. "But you never can tell," she said, "finally ..."

"I'll never go back!" His voice choked with fear. "I'll kill myself first!"

She said nothing for a long time. Her eyes remained thoughtfully on the highway, the long black line down the center pointing to nowhere.

Chapter 10

We got a good break early. When the pickup order went out, for Mercedes Turner, we had watched all depots, airports, railroad stations, and ships. In addition to this, we naturally kept a close watch on stolen cars, and all cars reported sold. The three states of New York, New Jersey, and Connecticut cooperate closely to provide fast action on car information, because of the heavy tri-state stolen car traffic which skips back and forth over the state lines.

A sale of a 1952, two-door sedan, painted gray, had been made by Jersey Jack Auto Sales Company, Jersey City, to a Mrs. Walter Brewer, 1769 Bixley Street, Trenton, New Jersey. The information also listed the serial number, engine number, and New Jersey license plates. The car had been sold by Holland Beale, a salesman for the company, and he had also made out the ownership papers, and filed for transfer of title for the customer. However, there was no such person listed, and no such address in Trenton. This made it a matter of false registration, and automatically the information was relayed to New York.

Taking my hat, and buttoning up my coat, I decided I'd cross over to Jersey for an unofficial chat with Holland Beale. The salesman's description loosely fitted Mercedes Turner, although he could not positively identify her shepherdess photograph. "This babe here in the picture was either a lot younger or a lot better looking than the woman who walked into the lot," he said. However, I felt that the odds were still good it was the Turner woman who had bought the car. A woman can alter her appearance a great deal more easily than a man. I sent out a teletype on it, and got back information from the Delaware State Bridge Authority that a car answering that description had crossed the bridge at the end of the Jersey Turnpike before entering Delaware. After that we lost it, but its direction indicated that it might be headed for Delaware, Maryland, or Virginia. In the meantime, I went on gathering all the information I could find about Hugh Rohan.

I decided to retrace my steps up to Connecticut again, and call on Annixter College, in Royal. It had been late when I had left Prester and returned to New York, two days before, and so I hadn't been able to stop at the college.

The office of the registrar was in charge of a Miss Hoffman whose granite face seemed about the same texture as the old granite building. She was, however, very cooperative. "I don't remember the student to whom you refer," she told me, speaking through her nose, "but undoubtedly we have some records concerning him. Will you please be seated." I sat down on a wooden bench which ran parallel to a long counter and lit a cigarette. Miss Hoffman shook her head firmly and pointed to a "no smoking" sign. I put out the cigarette feeling like a freshman. After a few minutes, she returned with several printed forms of paper.

Glancing at them, she said, "Hugh Rohan applied for entrance to Annixter in the summer of 1941. His credits were forwarded from high school at Germaine, Illinois." She ran her eyes over a second sheet, and continued. "His grades were excellent, and he was an honor student in high school. However, the Committee for Admissions found he was lacking a year's credits in Latin and chemistry." Miss Hoffman explained, "This happens often ... particularly in the cases of students coming here from very small schools. The college requires three years of Latin and chemistry for pre-medical school, and many of the smaller high schools only offer two years."

"What do the students do then?" I asked.

"Most of them come here to tutor ... some of the instructors hold special tutoring courses for them. The student is then permitted to take a special examination, and if he passes it, he is then admitted as having the required credits."

"Who would have tutored Hugh Rohan?"

Miss Hoffman didn't know. "Any of the Latin and chemistry instructors. But it was so long ago, it's doubtful if any of them are still here."

"Is there any way I could find out?"

Miss Hoffman gave me the names of two Latin and chemistry instructors who had been at Annixter since before the war. Between their classes I talked with them. Only one, an instructor in the Latin department named Biggott, had been tutoring at that time. He didn't remember Hugh Rohan. I got back in the car and returned to New York.

Skors told me, "That gun which shot Turner, the Technical boys goofed on. Now they don't think it was a Smith and Wesson after all."

"What do they think it was?"

"An Astra. It was a .32 all right, but they think it was an Astra, model 3000."

An Astra is a Spanish-made semi-automatic pistol; there aren't many in the United States. Usually, they are brought into this country after being purchased in South America, Europe, or Canada. "They can't be sure, though," I said. "That one slug isn't conclusive...."

Skors shrugged. "Not conclusive, but usually the Technical Bureau's right, and now they don't think it was a Smith and Wesson."

I thought about it. Mrs. Turner had traveled a lot; she had been to South America and Europe ... not once, but a number of times. She could have bought the Astra, and returned with it. On the other hand, a semi-automatic pistol isn't something that a woman buys, as a present or a souvenir, and brings back with her from a trip. I wondered where she had gotten it, and if it did belong to her.

The murder weapon—Astra or S. & W.—had disappeared; so had Mercedes Turner. I couldn't shake the facts around so they'd fit straight in my mind. Why had Mercedes Turner run away? If she had called the police and reported the shooting either as a suicide or an accident, it would have been nearly impossible to have proved otherwise. If she had shot Turner, and then stood her ground, we'd have been in a tough spot ... both for lack of motive, and undoubtedly the best lawyers money could hire. On the other hand, if she hadn't shot Turner, but Rohan had ... why would she run away with him? It couldn't help him—and could hurt her.

I asked Skors, "Did you ever find out anything more from the company where Mercedes Turner worked before her marriage?"

"Yeah," replied Skors, "there's a report going through on it now. However, here's what we dug up. She started working for the Eastern Coastal Steel Corporation in 1943 ... left school to take a war job. She worked in the office for the expedition department ... in those days they needed old iron and steel so bad that they had to work around the clock to find it. You know, they'd even buy old bathtubs! This Turner woman turned out to be real good on the job ... read newspapers coast to coast, and spotted all sorts of local news which might lead to scrap metal and stuff.

"She really kept her nose to the old desk ... didn't run around or take an interest in boy friends. The other guys in the department were gradually drafted out, or hooked on to better paying jobs, and so eventually she found herself assistant to the head of the department."

"She must have been pretty good," I said.

"She was," agreed Skors. "Her old boss said that he left most of the actual work in the department up to her. He offered her a whopping raise when she quit to get married. But she left, anyway."

The papers had managed to dig up a lot of stuff on Albert Turner and his activities, and were giving the murder a lot of play. Turner had had his hand in a lot of pies, including politics. Somewhere they had found pictures of him, but they still didn't have a photograph of Mercedes Turner. I knew where Turner was; but I didn't know where Mrs. Turner might be.

I picked up Thelma Jordan and we went to see an artist I knew in Greenwich Village. He was a good portrait artist, and I showed him the photograph of Mercedes Turner in her shepherdess dress. I told him what I wanted. Maurry turned to Thelma Jordan, "Does this photograph resemble Mrs. Turner the last time you saw her?"

"Not very much ... only sort of generally," the maid told him. "Except Mrs. Turner doesn't wear her hair under a hat like that ... and her face is shaped a little different."

"First, about the hair," replied the artist. Thelma Jordan explained how Mercedes Turner usually wore it, and the artist began sketching with a charcoal pencil. Occasionally he'd stop and erase with a piece of kneaded eraser. The maid watched him, and once in a while would say, "Yes ... that's right," or, "No ... not quite like that." After a few minutes, she exclaimed, "That's it! That's exactly the way she wore her hair!"

Maurry then began on the face which he had merely indicated with a sort of blank oval. "Mrs. Turner's face is thinner than it looks in the photograph," Thelma Jordan told him. They worked on it for a while, and when Maurry satisfied the maid, he began to sketch in the eyes. He had quite a bit of trouble with them. In the photograph they had been slitted down against the flash bulb, but the maid maintained they usually were quite wide open although they slanted upward, slightly, at the edge of the lids. Finally, she said, "Yes, that looks quite a bit like her eyes. But not exactly. I can't explain it ... they usually looked wide awake, but rather lazy at the same time ... if you know what I mean. Not that she was lazy ... but more as if she didn't care about things." Maurry decided to leave the eyes alone. The nose and mouth he finished very quickly.

"How's that?" I asked the maid. "Does that look like Mrs. Turner?"

"Oh, yes! I'd recognize her immediately," she agreed.

Maurry took a bottle of fixative and sprayed it over the charcoal drawing. "Be careful of it," he said, "it may smudge." I thanked him and offered to pay for it.

"Is this coming out of your own pocket?" he asked. I told him it was. "Skip it," he said, "you owe me a free homicide on the house." All of a cop's expenses are his own, unless he can get an authorization for them beforehand. We have our own artists, and I could never have gotten any money for an outside one. Maurry, however, is a better artist than the ones we have, and I had wanted the best picture I could get of Mrs. Turner.

I sent the sketch to the photographic department and had some photo copies made of it which I could carry and show around without smudging. I found myself staring, for a long time, at the face of Mercedes Turner. Why, I wondered, had I been spending so much time on Hugh Rohan? This was the woman accused of murdering her husband. Was Rohan just a product of my overeagerness, existing only in my imagination? Regarding him, I had nothing to go on; nothing definite. He might have been ten thousand miles away at the time of the shooting; or he might even have died in the fifteen years since his runaway kid marriage. All I had was the fact that people who knew Mercedes Turner couldn't understand why she had run away. Looking at her face, I couldn't understand it either.

Across my mind flickered two very tiny facts: a single red hair on the carpet, and a red-haired man walking down the street one day.

The phone rang and I was told to report to the office of the Chief of Detectives, in Centre Street. He leaned back in his chair and gave me all of his attention when I checked in. "You're the precinct detective on the Turner shooting?" he asked. I told him I was. "How're you coming along?" he asked.

"We're getting all the help we can use," I replied, "but we're still not doing very well."

"Why?"

"The woman has completely disappeared. We can't pick up a lead on her."

"Do you have any ideas?"

"Not very many. Everything I know is in my reports."

"You tell me," he said.

"Well ... I can't get used to the idea the woman did the shooting. Everything points to the fact she did, but I can't make myself buy it. Not yet, anyway."

"If she didn't kill her husband, who did?"

"I don't know." I admitted it frankly. You don't fool around with the Chief of Detectives. You lay what you have on the line, and you stand or fall with it.

He swung his chair around and looked out the window. A squad of gray pigeons with bottle green and brilliant blue necks swirled around the building and planed in ... landing on delicate pink feet just outside the sill. "What is it, just a hunch?" he asked.

"Yes," I said. "I have a hunch this goes back ... way back. I think the first pressure on that trigger started fifteen, or sixteen, years ago. But the gun just went off last week. And it was somehow triggered by a man."

"Any idea about the man?"

"An idea only. I may be completely wrong, but I'd like to find him, too."

"What's his name?"

"Rohan ... Hugh Rohan," I told him. "He has red hair, and was once married to Mercedes Turner."

The Chief of Detectives swung around again. "I'm putting you on special assignment," he said.

"You're taking me off the chart?"

"Yes. As of right now. I'll clear it with your captain." He opened a drawer and removed a cigar, and offered one to me. I took it. Not because I smoke them, but because I'd never received one from the brass before ... not even a captain. He lit his cigar and I lit mine. "From now on," he said, "you stay with the Turner case. If it takes five years you still stay with it."

"What about expenses?" I asked.

"Whatever you need. Send your request for funds direct to me. We have to get this one cleaned up," he said; "it's getting hot."

"Albany?" I asked.

"Yes. The capitol's getting into it." He placed the fingers of his hands together, tip to tip, and regarded them intently. The smoke of his cigar curled over his desk. "Turner contributed pretty heavily to campaign funds," he said, "and they're already thinking about election year."

"Is this personal or politics?" I asked.

"Both. The party is anxious about the newspapers. They're already hinting someone has been paid off to let the woman get away."

"That isn't so!"

"No," he agreed. "But it's good ammunition for the opposition. Turner shot by his wife ... the wife permitted to get away ... lay low ... in order to prevent a scandal." He collapsed his fingers and removed the cigar. "It could be pretty dirty. Anyway," he breathed deeply, his voice nearly a sigh, "the good word has come down. You get with it ... and stay with it." He picked up some papers and it was a sign he was through. As I reached the door, he added, "Anything you have to have, let me know." I nodded and closed the door.

That night I caught a plane to Chicago. I stayed there overnight, and in the morning I took a train to Dubuque, Iowa, which is located on the Mississippi at the junctions of the states of Iowa, Wisconsin, and Illinois. Dubuque was the nearest large town, on the main line of the railroad, to Germaine. In Dubuque, I rented a car to drive to Germaine which is located down the river, on the Illinois side, about forty miles. I reached it in the early afternoon.

Germaine, I discovered, was not actually on the Mississippi; it was several miles inland tucked away in a steep valley between the hills which run to the river. The main street of the town lay in the comparatively level bottom of the valley. Parallel streets ran along the steep sloping sides, and the vertical streets ascended at an improbable angle. The downtown section was composed of weathered, frame, two-story buildings, with an occasional one of three-story brick. Many of the ancient buildings had false fronts, and had remained as they were from the middle of the last century, growing more shabby each year. Along the residential streets arched over with huge old elm trees were large, quietly respectable houses which have died a little with each generation. Once it had been prosperous, like so many of the little towns near the Mississippi ... and Germaine had depended on lead mining for its fortune. The lead vein had played out in the 1870s, and the town had sunk back quietly into the countryside, turning to agricultural trade in its vicinity for survival. It had managed to keep going because as each new generation grew up, most of the younger people moved away, leaving fewer and fewer to live in Germaine until the ones who remained could make a living, such as it was, from the farm country.

The town hired one policeman who also doubled as chief of the volunteer fire department, and I found him seated outside the door of the engine house. He was reading a magazine and he tipped down his chair when I introduced myself.

"Come all the way from New York," he mused, "it must be important." He was a man of middle height and stocky build with a round good-humored face. I decided he was in his thirties and pretty close to the age of Rohan. I asked him and he said he was thirty-seven. Then smiling, he asked, "Ain't no law in New York against being thirty-seven, is there?"

"No," I laughed, offering him a cigarette, "there isn't. I'm trying to get some information concerning a man about your age. Possibly you might know him."

"Who?"

"Hugh Rohan. He's about thirty-three or -four, with red hair. He was graduated from Germaine High School in the spring of 1941."

He lit the cigarette and tossed away the match, stepping on it firmly to put out the flame. "No," he replied, "I don't know him. I didn't come here until after the war. Matter of fact, it was in '46, I got out of the army ... and I took this job in '47."

"How'd you ever end up here?" I asked. "You weren't born in Germaine."

"I was born up in Wisconsin. Mauston, way up. But after the war, I'd seen enough of the world to fill my belly for a lifetime." He grinned at me. "I like it here ... nice and peaceful."

"So's New York," I told him, "if you can find a dry well to crawl into."

He stood up and said, "Let's go into the fire house. I got a bottle in there. I've always wanted to brag I've been on a case with a New York dee-tective." His voice was friendly; he wasn't trying to be smart ... only kidding me a little. I followed him into the narrow frame garage. Within was an oversized Ford truck, painted red, and carrying hose and ladder. He removed a bottle concealed in a black rubber boot which, with its mate, stood on the running board of the truck. A steep stairway led upstairs. He motioned toward it. "I sleep up there," he explained. "Also use it for the police station since the old station was sold." He unscrewed the metal top of the bottle and poured a drink into a tin cup which he handed to me. Taking a long drink direct from the neck of the bottle for himself, he recapped it and concealed the bottle back in the boot.

"Who do you think might be able to help me?" I asked.

"I've been thinking about that," he replied. "Miss Parker is probably the lady for you to see. She's going on eighty and has been principal of the high school nearly fifty years."

I was surprised. "You mean she's still principal?"

He shook his head. "No ... she retired in '45 or so. But she's still alive and kicking, and smart as all get out, yet." He gave me the directions to find Miss Parker, grinning again, and as I left he said, "I'll be damned—a New York cop."

The old principal's house was on one of the vertical streets, perched precariously on a high brick foundation which slanted down from the side of the hill. The house was small, and squat, and painted a light brown. A narrow porch with thin turned posts ran around three sides of it. On each side of the cement steps, green flower boxes had been set

... the flowers now twisted and dead in the fall. A square plot of grass in the front yard had been carefully edged with clam shells, and the skeletons of brown bushes lined the front of the porch.

Miss Parker answered the door. Stepping out on the porch, she didn't invite me in. She was a tall, gaunt woman with big knobby hands, and large feet in solid, heavy, black shoes. Her old hair, gray and very thin, was carefully brushed flat against her head, and through it I could see the pink skin of her scalp. She wore glasses and peered at me near-sightedly, as her fingers buttoned a man's heavy sweater up the front. There was a chill in the air, and she glanced up and down the street ... looking and listening ... before she turned her attention to me. "This is the time of year I always remember best," she said, her voice remark-ably steady for her age. "The children are always so frisky, and they're still relaxed from the summer." She paused, then admonitory, "After Christmas, though, they're tired of winter... and they hate being cooped up. That's when a good teacher has to make learning ... interesting for them."

"You were a teacher a long time, Miss Parker," I said softly.

"All my life." She said it simply, with no regret in her old voice.

"Do you remember a boy named Hugh Rohan ... with red hair?"

"Of course I remember Hugh," she replied, "and it doesn't take his red hair to make me remember him. He was one of the best pupils I ever had." She turned away, looking down the deserted street. "He was set on being a doctor, I remember. How's Hugh doing?"

I didn't have the heart to tell her my suspicions. I merely said, "Hugh's fine."

"Yes. He's a fine boy."

"Does his family live here?"

"No." She thought back through the years, recalling the young, red-haired boy who had attended her small school. "He lived with an older brother ... I don't remember his name, but he was married and rented a farm ... out in the Garnetville direction. Seems to me that sometime during the war the older brother moved away. Gave up farming."

"But Hugh went to your school?"

"Yes ... all four years. He used to catch a ride in the mornings, on a milk truck, but after school he had to walk home. A long walk it was, too ... four or five miles. He was bound determined he was going to be a doc-tor."

"What kind of boy was he?"

Miss Parker said, "I loved him ... a teacher can't help loving the good ones. There aren't very many of them, you know. Just now and then ... over the years, you find one ... young ... and well, bright. They're alive and wondering, and everything you can show or teach them, they suck up like a desert taking water. And you think perhaps this one ... this is the one, who will make everything worthwhile; who'll be ..." Her old face suddenly seemed shy, "I rather hate to say it because it sounds stagy, but it's true. The word is 'great.' You think possibly this student may be great ... and if he is, it's the reason I was put here to be a teacher."

I didn't say anything. We stood there on the little porch, looking down the street over the tops of the old trees to the shabby town in the valley. Finally, I asked, "Do you think Hugh Rohan was happy? Did his brother treat him well?"

"I think he was lonely," Miss Parker replied without hesitation. "I never met his brother who must have been a great deal older. The brother, I think, had a hard time making a go of the farm; it was probably a real sacrifice for him to permit Hugh all the time he spent going to school." She paused and drew the sweater tightly around her thin shoulders. "A young boy can't love a brother—not the way he can a father, or a mother. I suspect Hugh's brother was as good to him as he could be, but the brother had his own problems."

I nodded. "What about school? Did he have many friends?"

Miss Parker shook her old head. "Not as I recall. He kept pretty much to himself—not unpopular, or anything like that. Just ... well, aloof a little, too busy for frivolous things, so to speak. He studied and read all the time he could, and then just as soon as school was out for the day, he had to start home. It'd take him an hour or two to walk there, and I suppose he had to help his brother with the chores—soon as he got back." She removed her glasses and wiped them on a neatly folded handkerchief which she took from her sweater pocket. "His last year he kept talking to me in my office ... about the different colleges, trying to decide which one he wanted to go to." She replaced the glasses and looked directly at me. "I told him about a little college near my old home in Massachusetts. My grandfather had gone there to be a doctor. Hugh had no money, he had to work his way if he went to college. I thought it might be easier for him in a small town, and a small college where everyone is a little more neighborly."

"That was Annixter?" I asked.

"Yes. He left that summer after he was graduated. And at first, he'd write me every once in a while ... just a few words about making up some credits. Finally, one of my letters was returned. He had gone and there was no forwarding address."

"You never heard from him again?"

"No." I thought her old face looked, suddenly, a little hurt, a little puzzled as the memories came back. She turned her wrinkled face and peered intently down the street. "It's time," she said, "for the children to be getting out of school."

On the trip back to New York, I couldn't rid myself of a crazy feeling which was growing within me about Rohan. It was nearly as if in some other life we'd been mixed up together. I could see the red-haired boy walking back from school—through the country, just as I'd walked back through the miles of concrete sidewalks, back from school to the tenements because I didn't have the money to ride the subway. A nickel. Rohan had loved Miss Parker, who had supported him and encouraged and helped him; I'd had Mrs. Johnson, who had pleaded with my old man to let me try for a scholarship at Columbia. Rohan didn't get to go to Annixter; I didn't go to Columbia ... not until years later. Rohan and I had lived in an intellectual desert together, and we'd both been thirsty ... thirsty for an education.

Chapter 11

All day the sky had been the color of gray worsted; occasionally the wind would tear narrow rifts through which peeped a watery sun. At evening, they pulled into a motel by the side of the highway, and Rohan registered them under the name of Mr. and Mrs. Walter Brewer. They drove the car down one side of the motor court to a small cottage built in the shape of a miniature colonial house with tiny pillars and doll-sized green shutters. Inside, there was a bed and dresser and two chintz-covered chairs, and an oval hooked rug on the floor. Off the single room was a cramped bath. The cottage had the impersonal air of a rented locker, and at the end of the late fall day offered little more than a surface comfort.

The man and woman washed their faces, and Rohan poured a drink in a thick water tumbler which he found in the bathroom. They tasted the whisky, drank it without pleasure, and then returning to their car drove down the highway, searching for a place to eat. Eventually they found a roadside tavern and they stopped. The food was poorly prepared and they ate it without enjoyment, although they spent as much time as possible over the meal to postpone their inevitable return to the cheerless cabin.

Speaking little, they drove back to the motel for the night. Rohan sprawled across the bed, watching Mercedes as she brushed her hair carefully. Finally, he said, "Mercy, are you sorry now you came?"

She paused, the brush suspended momentarily by the side of her face; then, carefully, she resumed the rhythmical stroking of her brush. "I'm not sorry," she replied, "I had to come. One can't be sorry for what had to be." Overhead, a hard, flat light burned in a tiny chandelier screwed close to the ceiling, casting dark shadows beneath her eyes.

"You could have stayed behind," he said.

"No. If I had I couldn't have helped Albert. But by coming, I could help you."

He arose from the bed and walked to the window, peering out into the night. He stood in an attitude of listening, and after a moment he began to button the jacket of his suit, folding the collar over the white of his shirt. Turning, he moved toward the door. "Where are you going?" she asked.

He paused. "Out ... I have a hunch." Abruptly, he asked, "Do you believe there's any such thing as extra-sensory perception?"

"I don't think so," she said, "and I don't think there's any proof of it, either."

"Perhaps the words aren't right, perhaps they don't say the correct things. But the meaning's there ... and it came to me from out there in the night." She watched him silently, alert to the tones in his voice. "I had a feeling a moment ago," he said slowly, grasping his words, "... a sudden peculiar ... odd ... feeling ... intuition. It was nearly as if a voice told me the chase had finally started."

"It started in New York," she replied.

He became impatient. "No. What I'm saying is they know about me being with you now. Up until today, they didn't know ... or at least they weren't sure. From now on, they won't be looking just for a woman, they'll be searching for a couple."

"There's no way for you to know that," she told him, calmly.

"It's come," he replied, not heeding her words, "it's the instinct of the ... hunted. The cons used to talk about it in Bordeaux, and I didn't believe it. But now I believe it." He looked at his hands.

She hesitated, trapped between laughing and crying. "The hunter ... and the hunted?"

"Yes. It's almost like telepathy—as if some mind is transmitting thoughts and I'm receiving them." He shook his head irritably, "Not all of them ... I'm ... oh, hell, now and then I can hear it ... just a little ... when I listen." He opened the door and stepped into the night. The woman completed her toilet, and was lying in bed when he returned again.

"What did you do?" she asked.

"I took the plates from a Michigan car, and hid them beneath the carpet in our Chevrolet. Tomorrow, after we leave here, I'll put them on, and we'll get rid of the New Jersey ones."

In the darkness of the room, they held each other closely. The woman could sense the attitude of strain, the restlessness of the man by her side. She lay rigidly awake, haunted by the memories of the night in New York. Resolutely, since she had run away, she had pressed them out of her mind, but this night they could no longer be denied although, subconsciously, the floodgates of memory refused to open completely....

"Hurry," said the red-haired man, "we must hurry."

"Yes," agreed the woman, "but everything in its own time." She walked slowly from the living room to the bedroom of Albert Turner. Returning, she carried a pair of white cloth gloves ... a man's formal gloves. She handed them to the waiting man. "Put these on," she said, "and don't take them off. Don't remove them under any circumstances while you are still in this apartment." He slipped them on, holding them out before him, smiling, but with no amusement, at the incongruity of their elegance and his rough jacket. "Now," said the woman, "find a piece of cloth and starting with the door where you came in, wipe each surface ... everything which you might have touched."

He followed her directions without question, his face passive and emotionless. With a dish towel he set to work erasing the marks of his presence. After a while, he began to whistle ... very softly ... a tuneless little sound between his teeth, as he worked.

The woman sat quietly in a chair. Then she looked at the tiny domed French clock on the mantel. The hands pointed to eleven twenty; forty minutes until midnight. "I must think," she said to herself, "think of everything to be done." Everything we think of now means an extra week, or an extra month ... or possibly even an extra year. She reached for a package of cigarettes, and, finding it empty, discarded it again. "You must be out of here by twelve o'clock," she said to the man; "the maid usually returns a little after then."

He stopped his polishing for a moment. "I suppose," he said mildly, "that we could always put the gun in his hand and you could say it was suicide?"

The vacant notes in his voice stunned her, until she realized that he had, as yet, refused to recognize its reality. "No," she said firmly, "it's too great a chance. Perhaps someone saw you come in ... or they might see you go out." She added gravely. "If only we could be sure ... but we have no way of knowing."

The man with the red hair said nothing.

"You may have been seen by someone ..." She shook her head decisively. "Somehow there would be a slip-up, the police would find out, and then it would be too late to try to escape."

"If they held you," the red-haired man said, "I would give myself up and confess."

"That would only make us both guilty," she replied. "This way we have time ... a little time at least."

"We'll be together," he said, "and we'll be happy again. Don't worry."

The woman didn't reply. She arose to her feet. "I must go to the basement to get some luggage," she explained. "While I'm gone, take ..." her voice stumbled, "please take ... Albert ... to his bedroom. Put him in his bed, and pull the covers up around him." She could see the red-haired man hesitate, and her voice snapped with new authority, finding again the old accustomed note of command she had learned in business. Her mind raced ahead to make decisions, working clearly and without hesitation. "You must do that by yourself! I can't help you!" She paused, turning her face away. I couldn't touch him, she thought, and fought against the weakness which suddenly surged within her.

The red-haired man put aside his cloth. Slowly he approached the body, and as he moved into the rays of the lamp, his hair flamed. His lips drew back from his teeth, in an involuntary grimace of distaste.

"I'm going for some suitcases," she said, "I'll be back in a few minutes." When she returned, he had resumed his task of wiping.

"He's in bed," he said, "and anyone would think he was asleep." She said nothing and went into her own bedroom. Quickly she sorted through her closet, selecting a few dresses, suits, and shoes. Lingerie she pulled hastily from her dresser, stuffing it without care into her luggage. Finally, from her dressing table she removed a small jewel case, burying it deeply in the pile of lingerie. Then she closed and locked both suitcases, returning with them to the living room. The clock on the mantel pointed to 11:55 P.M.

"You must leave," she said to the red-haired man; "go right now. But take my suitcases with you."

His veneer of impassiveness cracked. "You're staying ... here? In this apartment, tonight?" he asked in wonderment.

"Yes," she spoke rapidly. "It's necessary ... and unpleasant ... and revolting. But I must arrange for us to have a little more time in the morning. If the maid should call me to the phone ... or," her voice hesitated, "when Albert doesn't appear in the morning ..." She didn't finish the sentence. "Tonight, when you go," she explained firmly, "pack your things ... just the things you will need, what you can carry easily."

"My things," he said, "can be carried in my pockets."

"Do you have any money?"

"This!" He showed her a pitiful heap of dollar bills and silver. "It's like old times," he said wryly.

She ignored his comment. "Destroy everything in your room. Photographs ... especially photographs. Do you have one?"

"Hardly," he forced a smile, "and nothing else, either."

"Good! Now hurry ... don't take a cab. Walk up to Fifty-ninth Street and take a bus from there."

"When will I see you?" he asked.

"Tomorrow morning just as soon as I do everything that has to be done.

I'll see you then. Where are you staying?"

He told her. Then lifting her suitcases, he stood silently for a moment holding them awkwardly. "Kiss me," he said, his voice pleading, "kiss me good night."

She lifted her face briefly to his ... then hurried him to the door, but he refused to be moved by her haste. "I love you," he said, "I've loved you every minute of all the years." He kissed her again, hungrily, as if building a wall to prevent her escape.

"We'll need our kisses for later," she told him finally. "In a little while, they will be all we'll have." She lifted her hand, and ran it through his red hair, and her face softened.

Standing just within the door, he turned back to her. "Mercy," he said, and the use of this special name echoed hollowly through the years lost in her memory, "Mercy ... I ..." he tried to smile. She shook her head and closed the door.

After he had gone, she once again composed herself and brought her nerves under the domination of her will. She searched through the desk in the living room, finding her own passport and the one belonging to Albert Turner, the book for their joint checking account, and the key to her safe deposit box. She put them in her purse, and carried the purse to the bedroom. Remembering, she returned hastily to the desk and hunted through it without success. Then she walked to a bookcase, and her eyes searched each row carefully until she found a large, flat, leather-bound volume. She removed it from the row, looked briefly at the mounted photographs, wedding pictures, and snapshots taken on vacations. Then she returned the empty album to the bookcase, and carried the pictures to her bathroom. She burned each one carefully, and flushed away the ashes.

It was as if the completion of this task had drained away her last strength. She sank wearily to her bed and sat, head lowered while her hands rested emptily in her lap. After long minutes she stirred. Rising, half stumbling to her feet, she made her way hesitantly to the hall to stare at the door of Albert Turner. It was closed, but she strained her eyes fixedly as if she could see through and beyond the wood. Finally, exhausted, she returned to her own bed. From the table beside her, she removed a small bottle of sleeping pills. Shaking two into her hand, she recapped the bottle and put it away. On her dresser was an alarm clock with daintily painted face and gilded hands. She set it for six thirty. Once more she got to her feet, and stepping out of her shoes, and removing her dress in nearly one motion, fell back to the bed. The tablets she put in her mouth and swallowed, too weary to get a glass of water.

She fell asleep, but the lights burned brightly in her room.

Chapter 12

I wasn't sure just where the red-haired man entered the picture. There was only that single strand of hair to point to the possibility that he had entered it, and that one strand of hair could never be considered conclusive evidence in any trial court. However, something, a hunch, an instinct—call it what you like—told me that Rohan was in it. It kept telling me over and over again, and I couldn't get it out of my mind. When I got back to New York from Germaine, I queried our own fingerprint department and the FBI in Washington, but neither had anything on a Hugh Rohan.

It appeared that I was running up a blind alley; but the more impossible it appeared, the more convinced I was that I had overlooked something.

Naturally, I was hunting for Mercedes Turner, too. I put my latest descriptions on the police teletype ... which goes to all five boroughs of New York City, and covers thirteen states as well, and sent out the artist's sketch of the woman on telephoto. This activity reminded me what it was I had missed!

At the beginning of the Turner case ... as soon as I had become interested in Rohan ... I had systematically checked information and descriptions of anyone we had on record who had red hair. The few leads, from this source, had soon played out. Now I sat down and began reading through all the messages received at the precinct from the Correspondence Bureau in New York. These messages go to each precinct from the central Correspondence Bureau located on Centre Street in Manhattan. You'd be surprised at the tremendous amount of information which comes through each day ... literally thousands of messages each year. Each precinct detective is supposed to read it all, and remember it, too. This, however, is a physical impossibility.

Copies of the teletype messages are carefully filed in heavy, black, composition folders. I started going back through them from the day of the Turner shooting.

Dated four days before that time, I found it.

TO ALL SQUADS, PRECINCTS, AND DETECTIVES:
CROWN PROSECUTOR, OFFICE ATTORNEY GENERAL, MONTREAL, CANADA, ADVISES WATCH FOR AND APPREHEND THREE FUGITIVES WHO ESCAPED TODAY FROM BORDEAUX PRISON. THESE MEN MAY BE MAKING WAY TO UNITED STATES. DESCRIPTIONS AND FINGERPRINT CLASSIFICATIONS

FOLLOW THIS MESSAGE.
        (SIGNED), AUTHORITY CORRESPONDENCE BUREAU

Two of the descriptions were of no interest. The third was:

NAME: ALIAS JOHN CARGILL; REAL NAME UNKNOWN. MER-
CHANT SEAMAN USING FALSE IDENTITY PAPERS DURING
WARTIME. CONVICTED OF SMUGGLING INFORMATION USE-
FUL TO ENEMY IN WARTIME.
HEIGHT: FIVE FEET, ELEVEN INCHES.
WEIGHT: ONE HUNDRED SEVENTY-FIVE POUNDS.
AGE: THIRTY TO THIRTY-FIVE YEARS.
COMPLEXION: VERY FAIR.
HAIR: BRIGHT RED.
EYES: BROWN
IDENTIFYING MARKS: NONE. NO SCARS.
FINGERPRINT CLASSIFICATION: 20 M I U 101 10
                                        L I U 101
PHOTO: ACCOMPANIES.

Several points, of course, were immediately obvious. The fugitive's coloring was distinctive ... both his skin and hair matched what little I
knew about Rohan. The age was right, too. I remembered the story
Thelma Jordan had told me about the picture of the soldier over which
Turner and his wife had argued. I picked up the phone and called the
maid. She was no longer living at the Turner apartment, but had found
a new job. She had, however, informed us of her move, and left us the
new address and phone number. When she was on the line, I asked her
if she recalled telling me the story. She did. "You didn't ever actually see
the photograph?" I continued.
    "No. I didn't see it."
    "How do you know then it was a soldier?"
    "Well ... I just got the impression it was."
    "Did either Mr. or Mrs. Turner say he was a soldier?"
    She thought it over, and there was silence on the phone. Finally she
replied, "No ... I don't remember either of them saying he was a soldier,
but I still got the idea it was."
    "Could one of them have said something about a uniform?"
    "Yes," she agreed, "that's it!"
    "Look," I explained to her, "I don't want to put words in your mouth.
Don't agree with me if you're not sure."
    "I can't really be sure," she replied. "It was so long ago, and I've nearly
forgotten all the details. But in thinking back, I got the impression the

man in the photograph was very handsome ... and he was a soldier ... or at least he was wearing a uniform."

That was as good as I could get. It didn't rule out the possibility that the man in the photograph was Hugh Rohan in a merchant marine uniform. The merchant marine uniform might tie back to the fugitive Cargill. Cargill might be Rohan. But why would a boy like Rohan, just a kid at the time, be convicted of smuggling information during the war ... a real dirty piece of business?

Picking up the phone again, I called the United States Coast Guard office. During wartime, all merchant marine sailors and officers were fingerprinted by the Coast Guard. I gave them the fingerprint classification for Cargill, and also the name of Rohan. The Coast Guard told me they would call back as soon as they had made a search for the classification.

I put on my hat and went down to 240 Centre Street which is way downtown in Manhattan. There I checked in with the Correspondence Bureau and they pulled out a telephoto copy of John Cargill which had been wired from Montreal.

Even the flat police picture ... front and side view ... couldn't disguise the fact that the man was handsome, His features were regular and cleanly cut. The mouth was full and sensitive, but sensitive mouths can sometimes be misleading. On occasion, the lips may become thin and cruel, and this mouth held both strength and weakness. His eyes were well set apart, wide and filled, it seemed to me, with a wildness composed of wariness and fear. His was a face tainted by hysteria, but still a face of handsomeness, containing much of beauty.

I arranged to have additional copies made of the photo and returned to the Nineteenth. On my desk was a message to call the Coast Guard.

"We located the prints all right," the Coast Guard officer told me. "The prints match a merchant seaman named Hugh Rohan. Also we have a record of a John Cargill."

"Are they the same man?" I asked.

"No. John Cargill's prints do not match Hugh Rohan's."

"Do you have a physical description of Cargill?"

"Yes. Here it is ... do you want it?"

"Go ahead," I told him.

"John Cargill ... home Lexington, Kentucky. Height five seven; weight one fifty; age thirty-two ..."

"Hold it!" I requested. "You say Cargill's thirty-two ... as of what year?"

I could hear the rustle of papers as the officer examined his records. "Cargill was thirty-two ... as of 1943," he said.

"That would make him over forty-five, now," I said.

"Yes," agreed the Coast Guard officer, "but we presume he is now dead."

"Why?"

"He disappeared in Beirut, and we have no additional record of him."

"Did his ship go down?"

"No. He disappeared ashore. He was listed for deserting his ship when it sailed. He couldn't have gotten back into the United States without his papers, of course, and he's not been listed since."

"A lot of seamen were mugged, killed, and robbed in those days."

"Anything could have happened."

"What happened to Rohan? Any record of him?" I asked.

"He's listed as jumping his ship, too."

"In Lebanon?"

"No. In Canada." Again the rustle of papers. "Before the war, he had no record as a seaman. He probably deserted ship in Canada, returned to the United States ... and lay low until the war was over."

A thought struck me. "Did Cargill and Rohan both serve on the same ship? Did they sail together the last time you have a record on them?"

"They were both aboard the *Saragossa Keys* in '43. Cargill deserted in Beirut; Rohan in Montreal."

"How old was Rohan in 1943?"

"Nineteen," he replied.

"That's close enough," I said. I thanked him and hung up. Pushing a sheet of paper into the typewriter, I made out a query requesting more information on John Cargill and had it wired to the Chief Constable's Office in Montreal.

Skors came in and sat down, pushing his hat back from his head. "Well, pally," he asked, "what's new?" I gave him what I had dug up about Rohan from the old teletype alert and the Coast Guard. He rubbed his jaw thoughtfully for a moment. "Interesting," he agreed, "but I still don't see any direct tie-in with Rohan and the Turner killing. All we know for sure is Turner's wife has disappeared. It looks pretty sure that she did it ... and we can't even know if the guy was in the United States when it happened."

"Remember," I said, "they were married once when they were kids ... Rohan and the Clinton girl. Her old man annulled the marriage. But I think she still loved him; she kept a picture of him during the war ... and even after she had married Turner. Now we know Rohan escaped from prison in Canada and returned to New York."

"No!" Skors disagreed, "you can't be sure of that! There weren't any fingerprints of his there ... and we haven't found a witness to put him in the apartment."

"There was that red hair in her apartment."

"Sure, but that's not enough evidence. It's pretty fashionable for dames to have red hair. It might have been there for years, or somebody brought it in on his clothes."

"That's all the evidence we have now," I had to agree, "but we'll get more."

Skors lit a cigarette and stood up. He threw a carbon copy of a list of items on the desk. "The D.A.'s office sent this over," he said. "It's the stuff they found in Mercedes Turner's safe deposit box. Everything, except for the jewelry which was missing, has been turned over to the Clintons' attorney. I've looked it over ... and I can't find anything in it." He left.

After he had gone, I studied the list. There wasn't very much ... two life insurance policies on herself. One made out to her father for five thousand dollars; the other to her husband for eight thousand. There was the empty silk jewel case in which she had kept her jewels; the title to a hard-top sport coupe, a year old, which the Turners had kept at their small summer place near Easthampton; the title to the property itself which had been made jointly to Albert Turner and Mercedes Turner; fire and theft insurance policies both on the apartment and summer place; a perpetual title and deed to the Clinton family cemetery plot in Argyle; a number of old and miscellaneous letters and receipts, including an empty envelope with a return address on Chambers Street.

This was the list. It was complete as required by law and included everything in the box which had been opened in the presence of witnesses from the D.A.'s office, the bank, and representatives of the Turner and Clinton families.

Everything had been gone over and cleared as a matter of routine. Although I put the list in my desk and closed the drawer, I found myself going over it, checking it again and again in my mind. Just one little point kept bothering me; why would Mercedes Turner keep an empty envelope in her safe deposit box? It might have been an oversight, or carelessness; having removed the letter, she had simply tossed the envelope back in the box. But there was another alternative. Possibly, she had retained the envelope to keep the return address as a permanent record.

A permanent record of what?

I called the D.A.'s office and asked for Bob Banners, an assistant D.A. who had been present when the box had been opened. I knew Banners slightly, as I had worked on several cases which he had prosecuted in the past. When he got on the phone, I asked him what the name and return address had been on the envelope. "Sawyer and Bates," he told me, giving me the address. "They used to be a small firm of attorneys who did a little business in Wall Street occasionally."

"Did you check with them?"

"Yes. One of our investigators did. They're no longer in business as such. The senior partner, Sawyer, died several years ago. Bates, the junior partner, didn't think it was worth while keeping the old name going. He moved farther up town and went into business for himself."

"What did Bates say Mercedes Turner's business was with them?"

"Bates didn't say. He's been out of town on business and I don't think he's been checked since he's returned."

"We don't know what she wanted then?"

"Sure we do," replied Banner. "We know all about it. Her father told us. Mercedes Turner's mother died in 1950 and left her a little money. Not much … a few thousand in insurance. The Clinton girl wanted to reinvest it, and retained Sawyer and Bates to represent her."

"Oh." I thought it over and finally said, "Where is Bates located now?" Banners told me it was Madison Avenue near Forty-second Street. "Any objections if I drop in to see Bates?"

"Not at all."

The connection between Bates and Mercedes Clinton seemed logical enough and if the D.A.'s office was satisfied with it, I should accept it, too. However, here was just one more connection with the woman, and I felt that I shouldn't ignore it. An interview would quite probably end up in nothing, but I called Bates's office and made an appointment to see him the following day.

The office of D. Agnew Bates, Attorney at Law, was not very impressive. It was located in one of the smaller and older buildings which crowd each other along Madison Avenue near the Grand Central Station district. Bates was a middle-aged man, in conservative, dark, wrinkled clothes. A secretary sat in a tiny reception room, and Bates's office opened from it. His office, itself, had two windows which stared blankly across the street into other rows of windows, and the room had an air of hard-pressed respectability. Bates arose from his chair, and stood with his fingers pressed against the top of the desk when I walked in. He made no effort to shake hands. I introduced myself, showed my credentials, and he asked me to sit down. He was familiar with the Turner case but hadn't connected it, so he maintained, with his old client whom he had known as Mercedes Clinton. "Is it true you represented Mercedes Turner, then Mercedes Clinton, in 1950?" I asked.

"Certainly," he agreed, readily. "At that time we were Sawyer and Bates and we had offices on Chambers Street."

"Did you represent her in certain financial activities?"

"Yes."

"You have not heard from Mrs. Turner since she has been a fugitive?"

"No."

"You are not representing her now?"

"No."

Bates was answering my questions with no sign of reticence, but he was not volunteering any information either. If he did have any information to give me, I was going to have to get it the hard way. "Was there anything of a secret or confidential nature concerning the financial activities of your client at that time?"

I thought he appeared relieved at my question. "No," he replied, pursing his lips, "not that I recall. She had recently inherited a small sum of money and we merely helped her reinvest it in some solid building loans."

"That of course would be a matter of public record?"

"Yes."

"Mr. Bates, did you conduct any other business, or activity, for Mercedes Clinton which is also a matter of public record, but had nothing to do with financial investments?" Anything that is a matter of public record cannot be pleaded as confidential by an attorney nor can it be regarded as privileged testimony in a court. Bates knew this, naturally, and suddenly I wished that I had asked an attorney from the D.A.'s office to accompany me for the interview. I couldn't swap legalities with Bates. He was an attorney; I'm not.

Bates considered my question for a moment. "That is quite a question," he said. "Its scope is sweeping."

"Mr. Bates," I told him politely, "I can't hope to spar with you. All I can do is call the District Attorney's office and ask them to send up someone who can. In the end, the result will be the same as if you talk to me now. You know how much you can or can't say."

"I don't like to discuss my clients," he said.

"Mrs. Turner hasn't been your client in years. As an attorney you are also sworn to uphold the state of New York and its officers and representatives. As a private citizen you have a moral obligation to help me in an investigation of murder, if you can. That's all I ask."

"I'm not sure that my relations with Mrs. Turner ... Miss Clinton ... were in any way connected with your case."

"Anything connected with Mercedes Turner may be important. Now, please permit me to ask you a direct question. Are you familiar with the name Hugh Rohan?"

He didn't reply, but after a few moments arose from his desk and, stepping across the office, ran his eye down a series of metal filing cases. Finally, he stooped and pulled out a drawer. From it he removed a Manila folder and returned to his desk. Opening the folder he glanced over several legal-sized documents. He cleared his throat. "Yes," he said, "that is the name. I represented Mercedes Clinton Rohan in an Enoch Arden decree against Hugh Rohan in 1950."

"The decree was granted?"

"Yes."

"You wouldn't mind telling me about it?"

Again he leafed through the documents, scanning them quickly, refreshing his memory. "I'll tell you," he replied, "because it's a matter of record, and you could look it up. Mercedes Clinton married Hugh Rohan in 1943. At that time Rohan was serving in the merchant marine. They did not live together publicly, as man and wife, after the marriage, but kept it secret because of prejudice of the wife's father and mother. Rohan sailed for a port unknown, because of convoy restrictions, in the spring of the year. Mercedes Rohan never heard from him again."

"This marriage occurred in 1943?" I asked. "You're sure it was not 1942?"

"According to Mrs. Rohan's testimony, she married Hugh Rohan in 1943."

Mercedes had married the red-haired man twice. The first marriage was annulled; the second marriage was secret. "I take it she wanted the Enoch Arden action kept as quiet as possible?"

"Yes. She told me that her parents had never known of the marriage in 1943, and she was contemplating matrimony with someone else. She was convinced that Hugh Rohan was dead ... that he had been lost in the war."

"Naturally, you made some investigation regarding his disappearance?"

"Yes. It was a matter of record, his ship had been sunk although no official confirmation of his death was ever given. However, a great deal of additional proof wasn't necessary. Rohan had disappeared for seven years; during that time he had never been in touch with his wife in any way, and had made no contribution to her support."

"It might have been desertion," I said.

"Not in New York. A decree is simpler, particularly as the wife wanted a minimum of publicity. She was worried mostly about her parents discovering this marriage. When her mother died, she brought me a small sum of money to invest for her, and continued to use it as an excuse for correspondence between us. After her mother's death, she was more determined than ever that her father should know nothing about the whole affair." He closed the folder on his desk. "As a matter of fact," he continued, "she requested that I keep the copy of her decree for her, so no one might find it. It is here in this folder."

I thanked Bates and left his office. Walking down the street I had plenty to think about. The red-haired man. The red-haired man. Was it tragedy? Was it fate? What was it? What pulled them together ... inevitably, and without hope of escape?

Chapter 13

"Ah ... my love, my sweet, my own!" Rohan jammed his hands in his trousers pockets and turned excitedly around the room. He was gay, abandoned in his good humor, and he talked and walked with the exaggeration of a boy. Since the night in the motel, on the highway from Virginia, he had alternated between moods of hilarity and depression. His conviction that the police now knew of his presence at the time of the murder of Albert Turner had released his passions. It was as if he courted the discovery and was anxious for the course to be run. During the day, at least, he seemed content, although in the hours of darkness his fears and uncertainties returned. In the hours of light, he busied himself with wild and illogical plans for their escape. Mercedes listen to them, without comment, but knew that the course she had determined was the one which held their only chance of escape.

Rohan threw himself in the chair, twisting in the seat, and the pistol in his pocket bunched. Reaching behind, he pulled out the weapon, and held it in his hand, regarding it. "All that's left of Bordeaux," he said softly, and hefted the pistol in his hand.

"We must get rid of it," the woman told him, "it is a direct link ... evidence ..."

Rohan disagreed. "No," he said, "I'll keep it. It's become an old friend. And, besides, it's too difficult to get another."

"But if we're ever caught, and the pistol is found ..." She didn't finish the sentence.

Rohan laughed. "If they ever find it on me," he assured her, "it'll be too late to do anything about it."

Her eyes drifted away from him gently, but her thoughts remained. She doubted that he would ever turn the weapon on himself. Of all the events which had changed and twisted him, since they had first loved, she was not sure. She was remembering him as he'd been ... young, slender, and with hair the red of heraldic paint; shy and anxious, ill at ease in his new surroundings, fired by ambitions.

The day they had first met, his eyes had found her in a room of confident chattering girls. With uneasy dignity, he had taken their orders and waited on them, and something in her had been touched. She had spoken to him on that long-ago day with a gentleness and a new maturity, strange to her youth. To her surprise, she had returned to see him again and again, between classes, when the fountain had been nearly deserted—anxious to see him, to feel him near her.

She had invited him to the Thanksgiving dance, which Bently held each fall, and he had declined. At first, she had been angry with him until she realized that his refusal had been dictated both by shyness and pride, and she—possibly for the first time in her life, looking into her motive—discovered that her invitation had not been offered in equality but in charity. Contrite, she had given up the party entirely and, instead, they had taken her little yellow roadster for a drive in the night stopping in Massachusetts for malts and hamburgers—for which he had paid. They had talked in the hazy, blue-black of the New England night, with a great silvered lead moon molding the Berkshires into onyx creases and folds.

He had been lonely. And in the true pattern of the solitary ones in life, once he had dedicated his love to her, it had remained constant and unswerving. In it, she had found his strength and her weakness. His fits of sudden anger were followed quickly by gnawing remorse; his stubbornness followed by wavering indecision. He was caught by his own emotions, and chained by them, and he could not escape his helplessness and confusions except by shattering them in great, explosive furies.

His jealousy was all-consuming. It was blind, unreasonable, and illogical, and yet, strangely enough, the girl had found herself clinging to it. She had listened to his wild furious accusations and accepted them without anger, although they were unjust and untrue. Although she loved him with an intensity of emotion that was new to her, this did not surprise her because her age-old instincts as a woman were neither shocked nor outraged at his possessiveness, and in her heart she would not have changed any part of his actions.

And yet, in the complexity of his nature, he was shy and gentle, too, with a sensitivity and perception alien to most men. The touch of his hands could start her trembling, and the pressure of his lips fired her—consuming her reason and her resistance. Her sanity, her background, her morals, were no protection against his love, and she made no effort to protect herself, but surrendered to his needs. And as two children, surprised and awed at the powers they had unleashed, they clung together in fear and innocence.

In the times they were apart, she resumed control of her perspective, and she realized clearly her own power over him, and assumed her responsibility. Her ability to protect him, she knew, was as necessary as her ability to arouse him.

That had been so long ago. During the years of her marriage to Albert Turner, she had thought her love of Rohan had passed. She had sincerely believed that he was dead. But the night he had appeared from out of the dark, from a past of thirteen years, it had seemed he had never been away. In one moment, he had reclaimed and rechained her.

Now she looked at him, in the hotel room in Kansas City, and she realized that no longer was she sure of his every thought and every emotion. In the great expanse of years which had been stolen from them, Rohan had lost his confidence, his power of decision. In those same years, she had found what the red-haired man had lost. The balance of strength and weakness between them was no longer in equilibrium, she was now the strength. Rohan was the weakness. Looking at him, her mind detached, she thought to herself, if he had the strength, the courage ... then I would no longer worry.

"How long are we going to be here?" Rohan's voice broke in on her thoughts. "I'm getting scared ... we ought to keep moving."

"I think we'll he safe here for a little while."

"Let's get out of the country as soon as we can!"

"We will. But before we can go, there're so many things to do." She paused and lit a cigarette, dropping the match in an ashtray marked Arnhurst Hotel. "We had better try to sell some more jewelry here. Instead of trying to sell it to a pawnshop, I'm going to try something else. We'll get more money for it if I run a little ad in the newspaper and sell it directly—sell it myself."

Rohan was suddenly alert. "Won't that be dangerous?"

"I don't think so. Certainly not as dangerous as having to give some kind of identification to a regular jewelry buyer. I'll be careful, and then each time after I've sold something, we'll move to another hotel and use another name."

The man was only partly convinced. "Well, I don't know ..."

"Let's try it," said Mercedes, "and if we aren't successful the first week, we can stop. Kansas City should be large enough for us not to attract attention from the police, and we'll get a lot more for the things if we sell them privately."

"We could wait until we get to California."

"I think it'd be more dangerous in California than it is here. The police might be expecting us in California ... I don't know. Perhaps we shouldn't plan to go there."

Rohan shrugged indifferently. It seemed to the woman that his attention was becoming more easily diverted each day, sometimes losing interest quickly ... as a child might lose it. "All right," he agreed.

Mercedes changed the subject. "We must think about our passports," she said. "Somehow, we must get them fixed up."

"That won't be too easy."

"Do you know ... anyone?" she asked, her voice hesitant and embarrassed.

Rohan's attention returned. He regarded her steadily. "Do you mean ... do I know any cons? Have I any underworld connections?"

"Yes," she agreed very softly.

His voice was harsh with irritation. "That's what I thought you meant." Anger flushed the fair skin of his face.

The woman's voice was no longer embarrassed. It became matter-of-fact and measured. "Darling," she replied, "whether you like it or not, we must find help. Is there anyone ... anywhere ... who could help us? Be reasonable!"

Slowly the man's anger faded. "I just tried to serve my time and mind my own business. I never became friendly with anyone, because I didn't want to have any contacts hanging over me when I got out. No one knew who I was ... and I wanted it to stay that way."

"What about the men who escaped with you? Weren't they friends of yours?"

He shook his head. "No! They just happened, I hardly knew them. They had a plan worked out, and they needed me. I took their offer."

"Why?"

"Because I had given up hope. I'd been before the parole board three times ... and got turned down each time. I had a good record ... a perfect one ... but damnit, the English are tough about wartime sentences. They don't forget." He paused, and swallowed. "I couldn't stand it any longer, so I busted out with LeRoi and Rouse."

"Where are they now?"

"I don't know. We split up just as soon as we hit the streets of Montreal."

"What were their crimes?"

"What difference does it make?"

"None, I suppose," she agreed. "Please tell me, why were you sent to prison? Was it because of me?" She had known of his conviction, now, for some days, but none of the details concerning it. Rohan had steadily refused to discuss it, but she felt she could no longer disregard it. Now she must know.

"Yes," he said, reluctantly, "because of you ... or because of us."

Silently, she agreed to his statement. Then, "Had you thought about it for a long time?"

"Yes." He changed his mind. "No!" Then turning away, he added, "I don't know ... I really don't. One thing just led to another. Who cares now?"

"I do," she told him gently. "I'd like to know how it happened. I must know."

He arose from his chair and walked into the bathroom drawing a glass of water. When he returned, he remained standing ... leaning against the door. "When we sailed on the *Saragossa Keys*, in '43, we went in a convoy and we didn't know our destination ... where we were going. Aboard the ship was a seaman called Cargill; he was smart and had a good education and might easily have taken his officer's papers. He preferred to remain an AB, though. I got to know him pretty well, and after a while I found out why he was happy to remain an able-bodied seaman instead of pushing to be an officer."

"He was smuggling things?" she asked.

"Yes. Dope ... or anything else. He was quite a bit older ... a man in his middle thirties, and he'd been a sailor for a long time with connections in different ports all over. After the convoy had been at sea and opened its sailing instructions, the news finally filtered down to the crew that our destination was Beirut. Cargill asked me if I had any money and wanted to get in on a good thing. I had about six hundred dollars." His eyes suddenly fell, and he no longer looked at the woman,

"I remember," she said. "When we were married, I sold my old yellow car ... any car was worth a fortune in those days."

"Yes," he agreed, his mouth bitter with the memory, "you sold your car, and we used part of the money for me to live on so I could get around to see you while I was ashore. When I sailed, you insisted I keep what was left."

"It was worth it," she smiled, "wasn't it? That small amount of money bought such a lot of happiness."

Rohan remained silent for a moment before continuing. "Anyway, Cargill knew where he could buy rough diamonds—from Africa—in Beirut. He told me if I wanted to put in my six hundred, he would put up the difference and buy two thousand dollars' worth. Back in the States he could sell them to a wholesaler direct for ten."

"You'd have received three thousand dollars?"

"For my share, yes. At first I wanted no part of it, then the more I thought about it ... well, I thought of what the money could do for us. It meant we could ... after the war ... face your parents, and I could go back to study." His thoughts returned to the nights he and Cargill had discussed it, on the rolling decks of the old freighter. Ahead of them, and behind them, and on each side, stretched the silent ghostly outlines of the convoy, wallowing in the troughs of the sea, panting through the darkness. The world, then, had seemed so unreal, and his dreams had been the reality.

"Cargill pointed out," he continued, "that probably the stuff could be resold legitimately. During the war, diamonds were nearly impossible to buy—even cheap ones were rationed for industrial use. Anyway, he convinced me. I guess I really wanted to be convinced, anyway." He faced the silent woman, his eyes waiting for her judgment. She refused him her glance, and he continued, "Some of the convoys had been losing up to fifty per cent of their tonnage. On our trip to Lebanon we lost about thirty. Men were being killed all over the world on a few dollars a month army pay; others were making millions back home. Cargill said we'd take the money we made, and reinvest it again on the next trip ... and so on. When the war was over we'd have a fortune. We were risking our lives every lay, and we might as well risk a little more. He'd done it before, many times, and he'd never been caught. "Well," Rohan hunched his shoulders, defensively, "I finally put in with him."

"What happened to Cargill?" she asked. "Did he escape and leave you to be caught?"

"Yes!" He laughed loudly, and his laughter mocked himself. "Cargill escaped ... but not quite the way you think. He got knifed in Beirut. He'd been lying to me, of course, but I didn't know it. We'd gone ashore that night to buy the diamonds, and he'd left me to wait down by the docks."

In his mind, he saw again the mountains rising from the sea across the bay; the mountains split by gorges and tufted with thickets visible in the unreal brilliance of the moonlight. The great foothills were rounded and smoothed with the tops of orchards, and the tips of the bay curved into great horns. Behind him lay the white-walled, red-roofed village; pouring over the crest of the hills, the olive groves heavy with tents, the inns and hotels taken over by the staffs of the military. "In those days," he explained, "the town was full of English and French, Syrians, Persians, Jews, Lebanese, and Arabs. Hell! Everybody in the world seemed to be there. I waited for Cargill, and he was late getting back. I waited ... and waited, and finally he staggered up to me.

"He'd been stabbed ... badly, but not fatally. One arm and shoulder had been cut to ribbons ... and he'd gotten it in a couple of other places, too. We stood there, in the darkness, in a shadow cast by a shed ... near the docks. With his good hand, Cargill took a small package out of his pocket. He handed it to me, and told me to open it. It was wrapped in a piece of ordinary brown paper ... the paper was just sort of crumpled around it. Inside were two large, dull stones. Cargill explained they were rough, uncut diamonds. 'I'll give you the name of a fence in Montreal,' he told me. 'Take these to him and he'll pay you the dough. I'll meet you later in New York and we'll split.'

"'Aren't you returning with me?' I asked him.

"'No.' he told me, 'I'm all cut up and the security precautions here are plenty rough. They might get suspicious. I'll lay low until I'm patched up, and ship back later.'

"Then Cargill took a stub of pencil and scrawled a rough sort of triangle with a moon in its center, on the brown paper wrapping the diamonds. He told me to be sure to deliver the diamonds in the paper so the fence could recognize the marking he had made and know they came from Cargill. Just in case, Cargill continued, the fence was still suspicious, I'd better take his identity papers with me to show, too.

"'What'll you do for papers yourself?' I asked.

"Cargill laughed and said for me not to worry. He could get others."

The woman sighed, and the sound rustled loudly in the room.

"Cargill handed me the package and his papers, and whispered the name and address of the fence in Montreal. Then he just faded back into the darker shadow of the shed. I put the diamonds and the ID papers in my pocket. I didn't know what else to do, so I returned to my ship."

"Weren't the police or military suspicious when he didn't show up?"

"No. Cargill was listed as deserting ship when we sailed two days later. There may have been an investigation but I didn't know about it. In Montreal, I went to the address given to me by Cargill to get rid of the diamonds, and I was arrested. It was a drop for a spy ring, and the Canadian Military Intelligence were watching it."

"But the diamonds," said the woman, "surely they weren't military secrets."

Rohan laughed again, bitterly. "The diamonds were little better than lumps of coal. They were lowest grade yellow diamonds and weren't worth a hundred dollars apiece. But what was important was the brown paper they were wrapped in. When it was treated in the laboratory, it was covered with writing and carried plenty of shipping information. I never knew what it was, though. Cargill was interested in getting that paper to Montreal, that's why he went through the rigmarole of writing identifications on it."

The woman said nothing.

"Fortunately," Rohan added, "when I was picked up I'd been smart enough to hide my own identification papers beforehand, and was carrying Cargill's. I refused to talk about myself, and the *Saragossa Keys* had already sailed. But this time the old tub didn't get through. There was no way of proving who I was ... or what. The Canadian authorities knew I was carrying false papers because of the difference in the ages listed ... I was still just a kid. Nineteen. I guess that's why they didn't hang me." He smiled bitterly. "But they did throw the book at me. I clung to the name of John Cargill and claimed I was Australian. I was tried and sentenced under that name."

He walked to her, and sat on the edge of her chair, putting his arm around her and tilting up her face. "You understand, don't you?" he asked, hesitatingly. "I couldn't write to you ... or risk trying to send a message, because if I had they could have identified me. I didn't want that to happen; that's the main reason, too, I didn't try to cop a plea and explain what had really happened, because I'd still have been convicted of smuggling. When I returned to you, I wanted to be free ... no one knowing a thing about the time I'd served. I only wanted us to be able to start all over again ... entirely free."

"I understand," she said, her voice so quiet that he could hardly hear it, "... now. But if I could have understood then, there'd never have been Albert Turner."

Chapter 14

Montreal wired me details concerning Cargill-Rohan. They added nothing new to what we had already except for a little additional background material on the red-haired man. His record had been perfect, and he'd been working in the maintenance department of the prison as a trusty. Of the two men he had escaped with, Rouse had been recaptured in Western Canada; LeRoi was still at large.

Skors came in grinning. "Well, pally," he said, "you got another break. Have you seen the DD 60 on the Turner case yet?" I told him I hadn't. "The Missing Property Bureau called me a little while ago," he explained. "I think they called you too, but you weren't in. Call 'em back."

Looking on the top of my desk, I discovered a call-back message had been made out and pushed to one side. Skors said, "Efficiency ... efficiency ..." He walked out.

I got the MPB on the phone. "Yeah," a sergeant named Morgan told me, "I think we got something for you. The Empire Jewelry Company sent in a report on a wholesale batch of stuff they bought. Looks like they got the earrings from the Turner woman."

"Who's the Empire Jewelry Company?" I asked.

"It's a Manhattan outfit ... goes around the country buying up wholesale and pawn lots. Here in the city they act both as wholesalers and retailers."

"Where'd Empire buy the earrings?"

"From a small wholesale lot they bought in Richmond, Virginia."

If these were the Turner earrings, this was what I'd been waiting for. The DD 60 based on the insurance policy description had read:

Two matched, platinum mounted, cluster earrings.
Central stones (2) @ 1.75 carats; Modern cut; 6 prong mountings.
11 small surrounding stones @ 20 points each; European cut; 4 prong mountings.

This made possible several points of identification. First, a Modern cut diamond has a larger "table" surface than the European or Old Mine cut. A Modern cut is wider across the top, and less deep than the European cut stone. But in the case of the Turner earrings, using the European cut for the smaller surrounding stones meant more stones could be used in each circle. And with their greater corresponding depth, they permitted more secure mounting.

The large central diamond, a carat and three quarters in volume, was set in six prongs ... rather than the more common four prongs ... possibly because of the extreme width of the diamond's table and its relative shallowness.

The final point was the number of eleven stones which surrounded the central diamond in a circle. Normally, the numbers of stones run in an even denominator ... eight, ten, twelve.

By using the European cut, eleven stones could be mounted instead of the usual ten.

These three technical points differentiated the Turner earrings from the many hundreds of others very similar in appearance, workmanship, and value.

The Empire Jewelry Company released the earrings to us, and I attempted to get an identification from Thelma Jordan. She could only tell me, "They look like the ones Mrs. Turner wore." It was not enough, although I had expected it and had wired Richmond to investigate the original purchase of the earrings by the Dixie Jewelry Company, owned by two partners—Towne and Huston, who had bought them and resold to Empire. Because of the extreme urgency in time—the possibility that Mercedes Turner might still be in Richmond, although I doubted it—I called the Richmond Police Headquarters in the City Hall Annex, just as soon as I returned from speaking to Thelma Jordan about an identification.

A Richmond city detective, named Spears, had been assigned to talk to Towne; Spears was out when I called, but they located him and told him to report back in. He returned my call in about twenty minutes.

"Sure," he told me, "I talked to Towne. He sold the earrings to Empire. He bought 'em from a lady."

"Did he get any identification from her?"

"Why, sure. Her name was Mrs. Walter Brewer ... she was living in Williamsburg at the Old Stone Inn. Before that, she said her home was Trenton, New Jersey."

"Ahhh." I couldn't escape the sense of satisfaction I felt growing within me. "Did Towne keep a record of the Trenton address?"

"I got it right here ... 1769 Bixley Street, Trenton."

"Where'd that ID come from?"

"Off the bill of sale for a car she bought."

"Was there a man with her?"

"Not that I know of. Towne didn't mention anyone bein' with her."

"Look," I said, "is it okay with you if I call Towne and talk to him?"

"Yes, suh ... it's your money, you go right ahead and spend it."

When Towne came on the phone, he substantiated the information given to me by Spears. I asked him for a description of Mrs. Brewer and he said, "Well . . . she was a right nice-appearin' sort of lady. A blonde ..."

"Tonight," I told him, "I'm putting a copy of a drawing in the mail for you. See if you recognize the person in the drawing as the woman who was in your store. Please wire me your answer immediately." He agreed. "Then," I continued, "I want to ask you another question. Was Mrs. Brewer alone when she came in to sell the earrings?"

"Yes. She wasn't with anyone."

"You didn't notice a man ... possibly outside the store waiting for her?"

"I don't recollect any man."

"All right. Now, please, think hard ... can you remember what you talked about?"

"Why, nothin' ... except she wanted to sell the earrings."

"Did she say where she got them?"

"I think she said they were a gift."

"Did she say anything else?"

"No."

"Can you recall anything ... how she was dressed ... a casual word ... anything at all?"

"Nothin' special. She was just a nice friendly lady."

I tried again. Somewhere there had to be something. "Tell me, Mr. Towne," I asked, but not pressing, "was she anxious or uneasy? Did she appear frightened?"

"Not uneasy or frightened. Not at all. 'Course you might say she was a little anxious to sell the earrings. Probably needed the money...."

"What makes you say that?"

"I couldn't pay her very much for the earrings. You understand that. They're not the kind of jewelry we can sell very well ... too expensive for my customers. I told her that, but she was right disappointed with my price. I advised her, matter of fact, not to sell 'em. But she decided to, anyway."

I thought about it for a moment. "You say she was dissatisfied with the price? Was she *real* dissatisfied?"

Towne's voice immediately became stiff. "I paid a fair price ... all she'd ever get from a reputable jeweler or pawnbroker, unless he had an immediate turn-around sale for them."

"I know that, Mr. Towne," I reassured him. "I was only trying to decide ... if she has any more jewelry ... whether she would try to sell it the same way, again."

"I couldn't tell you." His voice was still a little stiff.

"You've been a big help," I told him.

His voice became more friendly. "Incidentally, Mrs. Brewer endorsed a check I gave her. Would that be of any use to you?"

"Certainly," I told him, "I might be able to get a comparison on the handwriting. Would you mind sending it to me?"

"Not at all," he assured me. I thanked him and we hung up.

Things were moving right along!

Chapter 15

They had reached Kansas City not through planning, but merely by heading west from Virginia. The plans regarding their eventual escape from the United States depended on many factors which the woman had been, as yet, unable to resolve fully. Prodded, however, by an urgency to put distance between themselves and their pursuers, as well as an uneasy restlessness in remaining in one place, Mercedes had instinctively buried them in the heart of the continent. Winter weather held Missouri in its bleak embrace, although the city attempted to cheer itself with holiday decorations, strings of lights, and vivid displays ranging from the Plaza to the downtown area.

Rohan, however, could not still his fears. His hope, becoming nearly an obsession, was to escape from the country. He was anxious to break and run; the woman, on the other hand, was determined that their plans be carefully executed. They discussed them often, and the red-haired man would end each period with, "I'd still like to be getting on."

"We've been lucky so far, and we've managed to sell some jewelry here. After we sell the coat, we'll go on."

The man nodded. "I'd better be looking for another set of plates. And I've been thinking ... as long as we're here, I'll get the car repainted."

"Blue," she said, "have it painted a plain, dark blue." She walked to the writing desk and sitting down, wrote on a sheet of the hotel paper:

For sale, by private party, $8,000 mink coat; only one year old. Will accept best offer. Phone Jefferson Hotel, room 1417.

She placed the advertisement in an envelope, leaving it unsealed, and handed it to the man. "Drop this off today at the newspaper," she told him. "Have them run it for Saturday and Sunday of this week."

Rohan dropped the envelope in his pocket. "We'll leave next week, then?"

"Yes."

"California? Mexico?"

"No," she replied firmly, "that's where they'll be expecting us."

Rohan lit a cigarette. "You know," he said, "there was a fellow in Bordeaux ... who came from New Orleans." Mercedes lifted her head in interest. "This fellow's name was Crosley ... Bert Crosley. He was just a small-time punk, but he kept bragging about a brother of his who was connected with the slot machine racket in New Orleans."

"Is he still in Bordeaux?"

"No. He was sprung several years ago. He may be back in again ... or someplace else," he shrugged.

"But you say his home was New Orleans?"

"Yes." Rohan nodded slightly, and exhaled his cigarette smoke before continuing. "Most of the cons in Bordeaux were Canadians. There were a few Americans, but not many. I've tried to recall them, but Crosley's the best I can do."

"At least he's a start, if he's still in New Orleans. We can hope he'll be able to put you in touch with someone to help us with the passports."

"He would for money," said Rohan.

"We have money," she told him with assurance.

Rohan made a turn of the room, hands jammed in his pockets. "What're you going to do this afternoon?" he asked.

"I don't know," her voice was softer. "Would you like to go see a movie?"

"I'm sick and tired of them," he replied.

"Well ... how about going to the museum again?"

He smashed out his cigarette on the window sill. "We've been there a dozen times already!"

"Not quite that often," she said, "but I'm sick of it, too."

"This hotel is getting me down."

"We've only been here a few days."

"They're all alike," he said petulantly.

"Yes," she agreed, "they're all alike. But that's what our life must be ... a hotel ... a rooming house ... a motel ... what difference does it make? They're all alike, and they will be our home for a while. Until ..." her voice trailed away.

"Until what?"

"Oh ... until we find a place to live."

"That's not what you were going to say. What you really meant was ... until they catch us."

She made no reply for a moment. Finally, she said, "And we can have very few friends ... acquaintances, perhaps ... but few friends. We don't have the time any longer, and we've lost our background to make friends. Friendships have to grow. We can't belong to clubs or groups because some day that might raise a question about us ... who we are, where we came from. There's just us now, darling, and there will be only us ... in the future."

"I don't care," he said, "I've never needed friends."

She disagreed gently. "That might have been true when you could come and go as you pleased. But now you're no longer free." She lowered her head. "You and I are still as imprisoned as if we were in Bordeaux."

He shook his head angrily. "No!" he said. "But I don't mind admitting I'm bored ... goddamned bored!"

"It will be better, perhaps, when we go to New Orleans."

"After that, what next?" he asked. "Where do we go then?"

"We must find a place," she said slowly, "out of this country where we can stay. Not to hide, but to remain."

"I don't understand you."

"If we try to hide, we'll be discovered quickly. Two Americans can't hide in France ... or Spain, or Italy. Why ... the French police, for instance, could pick us up within twenty-four hours if we were traced to France. We would be foreigners in France ... or any country where they don't speak English. And foreigners are always conspicuous."

"England?" he asked. "Are you thinking about England?"

"Possibly," she replied, "but I've heard of the British police. They're too efficient."

"How about Australia ... or Africa? One of the British possessions ... there're plenty of them."

"I've thought," she said, "and thought, and I just don't know. Not yet, at least. We must be so careful to find a place where we can stay and not be conspicuous; where the police are neither too efficient nor too curious."

He walked to the closet and put on his coat. Pausing, he looked at her for a moment, hesitating, then said awkwardly, "I need some money for the ad."

She arose, and with her key unlocked a suitcase; from it she removed a heavy flat envelope. "The ad won't cost very much. How much will you need for the car?"

"I don't know exactly. Anywhere from seventy-five to a hundred dollars, I suppose. They won't have to do a very good job ... just spray it."

She handed him a small roll of bills. "This should cover everything."

He shoved the money in his pocket and left the hotel. Dropping the advertisement off at the newspaper, and paying for it at the want ad desk, he began searching for an automobile paint shop. He didn't want a large efficient one which might keep too reliable records; finally, he found a small body and fender shop where he left the gray Chevrolet to be painted blue.

As he was returning to the hotel, he passed a giant drugstore. In a window was a small sign: HELP WANTED! FULL OR PART TIME! He stood before the frosted window, the wind blowing up Baltimore Avenue, biting into his back. Abruptly, he turned on his heel, and pushing his way through a heavy plate glass door, made his way into the store. He was directed to an office, on a mezzanine balcony, and a harassed man, wearing bifocal glasses, told him, "Sure, we need some extra help. Stockroom mostly. What's your name?"

"Tufts," Rohan told him, giving the employment manager an address he had seen near the City Hall, on Twelfth Street.

"We pay a dollar an hour for stocking the displays," he was told. "It's not much, but you also get a twenty per cent discount on anything you want to buy in the store."

"I'll take it," said Rohan.

"What's your social security number?" The personnel man pulled out a short mimeographed employment form. Rohan had never been under social security; he had never had a number issued to him. For an instant, his mind was blank and then he found himself pronouncing meaningless numbers: "4- 8-0-0-5-3-8-8 ..." He had no idea as to the number of figures in the serial. His voice trailed away.

The employment manager wrote the numbers on the form, and then lifted his eyes behind the bifocals ... a seemingly benevolent gesture, but his eyes were puzzled. "That's a strange number," he said. "Are you sure you remember it correctly?"

"What's wrong with it?"

"It's one numeral short."

Rohan leaned over the desk and pretended to read the numbers intently. "Oh," he said, "you're right. I left out an O."

"Where? At the end?"

"No," replied Rohan, having no idea as to where the number should go, but pointing deliberately to a point between the 5 and 3. "There!"

The numeral was added. "480-05-0388 ... is that it?"

"That's it," agreed Rohan.

The employment form completed, the personnel man conducted Rohan to the basement of the store. At first glance, the great concrete room was a shambles of cardboard cartons, packing cases, and stacks of merchandise. A metal stairway opened to an alley through which a wave of delivery men constantly flowed, and a sidewalk elevator ascended and descended with additional cases of merchandise. Cold winds blew through the opened doors, twirling through the room and whistling up the elevator shaft. But the men and women working in the room were perspiring, their faces, beneath the hanging metal-capped lights, were wet and glistening.

Rohan was turned over to a wiry, red-faced man ... the stockroom manager. His name was Dave, and he stood beside a long heavy table checking invoices. "Ever worked for this outfit before?" he asked Rohan.

"No," Rohan replied.

"You on full time?"

"No, just part time."

"Okay," said Dave. "When you report for work, punch in at that time clock over there, and bring the card to me. I'll okay the punch. When you leave, do the same thing. Then I make out a time voucher for you. When you give it to the cashier upstairs, she'll pay you what you got coming. This way you get your pay every time you work."

Rohan took his card and punched it. Dave signed his initials after the time which was recorded on the card. "Now," said Dave, "I'll start you off in the toy department." He pointed to a large, square, cardboard carton. "Take that carton upstairs. You'll notice it's marked T-3-2. That means Toys, counter 3, section 2. In that section, put as many of the toys as you need to fill up the display."

The carton was heavy. Rohan lifted it and climbed the stairs at the back of the store. Counter three, in the toy department, was divided into four sections filled with metal motor trucks, flexible rubber swords with great glass brilliants in the hilts, cap guns, and cheap plastic-covered footballs. Before section two, he placed the carton on the floor and opened it. It was filled with cap guns ... imitations of old-fashioned western Colts. As he began to pile them on the counter, he was conscious of his own gun rubbing in the pocket beneath his loose jacket.

Chapter 16

The skipper said he wanted to see me. I reported to his office in the Nineteenth Precinct. The captain looked tired and worn, and when I came in he motioned for me to sit down, "How's it going?" he asked.

"Regarding the Turner case, sir ... we've picked up their trail in Richmond. I received a positive identification of a sketch of the Turner woman from a jeweler who bought some earrings she sold there. We believe she's accompanied by an escaped convict named Rohan who crashed out of Bordeaux in Canada. They were known, last, to be driving a 1952 Chevrolet with New Jersey plates."

The captain moved some forms around his desk with the tips of his fingers, and shifted his body uneasily. He cleared his voice and said, "The news came down from Room 200...."

Room 200 is the office of the Commissioner of Police, in Headquarters Building. I didn't say anything.

"Well," continued the captain (his eyes evaded me), "I guess the Chief of Detectives was going to talk to you ..." Abruptly he raised his head, and this time he stared at me steadily, "But, damnit, I said you were my man ... and a good one, and I'd tell you."

I thought I knew what he was going to say; I waited for it.

"You realize, of course," he kept on, "there's a lot of inside interest in this case. That means the governor of the state, and the mayor of this city are interested. There's just one man who's boss of the commissioner ... and you know who it is."

"The mayor," I said.

"The mayor," he agreed. "The commissioner ... uh ... feels there should be more ... faster progress being made."

"You're telling me I'm being taken off?"

"No!" A phone rang, and he swung around in his chair and picked it up. He listened for a moment, then said, "I'll call back; I'm busy right now!" He turned to me. "I know what you've done ... as well as the Chief of Detectives. You're a precinct man from my station, and I'm with you. As my precinct man, you're the *first* man on this case ... and by God as long as you do your job, you stay *first* man. Nobody's going to take you off!"

"Thank you, sir," I said.

"The Chief of Detectives, however, is taking Skors off the Homicide East schedule and assigning him to this case, and the D.A.'s office squad is also assigning a man."

The District Attorney's office has a squad which cooperates with the D.A.'s various bureaus—including Rackets and Homicide. These men do a lot of leg work on incoming and outgoing extraditions and know their way through a lot of red tape. "Skors," I said, "is a good man. I like to work with him. Who's the man from the D.A.'s squad?"

"Overton," replied the captain, "he's just returning from light duty." This meant that Overton had been hurt, or shot, and had been laid up for a while. "You'll continue to remain off the schedule, as the Chief of Detectives told you, and you'll continue to operate as you have ... until further notice."

I arose and stood in front of his desk. "That's the only reason, sir? Extra men ... for extra help?"

The captain replied without looking at me. "If the Turner woman is as far away as Richmond, you'll need extra help."

I knew what he meant. He didn't have to draw me a picture.

It was Wednesday when I went down to Centre Street to the Bureau of Information. I had a theory, based on the information from Richmond, that Mercedes Turner might try to sell her jewelry some way other than to pawn shops. According to the Richmond jeweler, she had been disappointed in what she had received for her earrings. Most people are when they try to sell diamonds to a jeweler, or pawn them. Regardless of what the public is told, diamonds are not a good investment. Workmanship in mountings means nothing; only the amount of precious metal in them, usually very small, is of value. Stones can never be pawned for more than twenty per cent of their retail value, and when sold to professional buyers rarely bring that much.

I believed the Turner woman might attempt to sell her jewelry to private buyers. She had sufficient funds to hold her over while she sold them, and could afford to spend additional time in getting rid of them. Obviously, the best way to do it would be to advertise in newspapers. She might find a private buyer ... and possibly get as much as fifty or sixty per cent of what the stones were worth.

Mercedes Turner was a very intelligent woman and I didn't expect her efforts to be too noticeable. I doubted that she would use a name that might be remotely familiar ... such as Brewer which she had used in Richmond. Actually, it seemed to me, she would use no name at all, probably substituting a telephone or box number. Also, I expected her to select a medium-large city, one over a hundred and fifty or two hundred thousand population, as there are more people with money in the larger cities who are interested in buying jewelry.

I believed that she and Rohan were heading west from Virginia. That left a tremendous amount of territory to cover, and I couldn't anticipate her ultimate goal—Los Angeles, the West Coast, Mexico. However, it made sense that once she started west, from Virginia, she might hold a straight route to where she was going, or at least a generally straight route. Such a route west, with alternate adjustments, had enough large cities to fit her need such as Louisville, St. Louis, Kansas City, Oklahoma City, Dallas, Fort Worth ... possibly Phoenix, and of course the West Coast. On the other hand, if she swung south there might be Nashville, Memphis, Atlanta, Birmingham, New Orleans, and others.

Consequently, I arranged through the Bureau of Information to subscribe to a clipping service covering the above cities and some others—eighteen in all. Because of the distance and spreads it was impossible to secure the clippings immediately, and we were confronted with a three-day lag in time.

I was thinking about this as I climbed the stairs to Headquarters. The Centre Street building is old, gray stone with a copper dome patinated in green. The basement windows are covered with massive iron grills painted black, and the ground floor windows are protected with curving bars. As I reached the door, I ran into Luis Alvarez from the Thirty-second Squad. "*Cómo está, amigo?*" he said.

"*Muy bien. Gracias,*" I replied.

He paused in the doorway, buttoning his coat. "*Hace tiempo no to veía.*"

"Yo he estado por aquí." I told him.

Flicking away his cigarette, he said, "I understand you're at the Nineteenth now ..."

"Yes." I had known Alvarez when we were on the Twenty-eighth together; the Twenty-eighth and the Thirty-second are Spanish-Harlem squads. Later Alvarez had been transferred to the Thirty-second, and several months later I went to the Nineteenth. Alvarez spoke Spanish like a native; he had been born and raised in a Puerto Rican neighborhood, and his parents were Spanish. I had to learn my Spanish at the Police Academy; I really needed it on the Twenty-eighth; but at the Nineteenth I never used it. "What are you doing over here?" I asked.

Alvarez grinned broadly. "Seeing how the brass live," he said. He sauntered down the stairs, pulling his hat firm against the cutting wind. "Take it easy, *amigo*," he said.

At the Bureau of Information I picked up a heavy brown envelope filled with newspaper clippings. I returned with the clippings to my own desk, at the Nineteenth, and spread them out. Each clipping had been cut and pasted to a small pink slip which carried the name of the city, paper, and date it had appeared.

I went through them, scanning each one quickly. Most of them were useless, but several looked interesting. One, from St. Louis, offered a string of genuine pearls, and in Louisville another ad offered a diamond wristwatch. Both listed a telephone number to call. The telephone company gave me the names and addresses for the numbers, and checking them back in the telephone directories for the two cities, I found both names listed. Obviously, the Turner woman was not living under either the name Larkin in St. Louis, or the name MacAndrews in Louisville the year before when the directories were published. This eliminated both of the advertisements.

However, I rechecked all the clippings again. I'd been concentrating so hard on jewelry, I'd temporarily overlooked the fact that Mercedes Turner had taken a mink coat with her. This was the coat that Thelma Jordan had described to me early in the case as being nearly new and very valuable. The clipping, which offered a mink coat for sale, listed a room number in the Jefferson Hotel in Kansas City, Missouri.

Picking up the phone, I called the special service operator. I didn't want my call to the Jefferson Hotel announced as a long distance one from New York, thus warning the fugitives. While I was waiting, I began to feel a warm glow of excitement crawling over me. I dragged impatiently on my cigarette, and finally twisted it out on the top of my desk. The palms of my hands felt damp, and cradling the phone between my ear and shoulder, I shrugged my way out of my suit jacket. I can't explain why I was so positive that this was the trail. I've read where native

Bushmen trackers in Australia can run at top speed across beds of rocks following a trail which can't be seen, or even scented, by dogs. I've heard stories of black hunters in Africa who, following an invisible trail to the edge of a river, will strike downstream two or three miles, cross, and pick it up again at the exact spot on the opposite bank. Something "tells" them, I guess. Now, something was telling me.

A voice answered clearly on the end of the wire. "Jefferson Hotel," it announced.

"Room 1417," I said. I could hear a metallic buzzing, which was followed by a new voice as the room's occupant answered.

"Hello ... hello?"

"Are you the party offering a mink coat for sale?" I asked.

"No." The answer was abrupt.

"I'm sorry," I replied. "There was an ad in the paper last Sunday regarding a fur coat ..."

"I don't know anything about it," the voice snapped. "I just took this room last night." He hung up.

Getting the operator back on the line, I put the call through to the hotel switchboard again. When the hotel operator answered, I asked, "The couple who were in Room 1417 last Sunday evidently checked out, is that correct?"

"Just a moment," she said, "I'll give you the desk clerk."

I asked him the same question, and he said, "Yes. They checked out yesterday."

"Did they leave a forwarding address?"

"No."

That was that. I wired the Police Department, Kansas City, Missouri, and requested they gather all available information concerning the people in Room 1417 and let me have it as soon as possible.

The following morning, I had a reply:

MAN AND WOMAN REGISTERED MR. MRS. J. K. HARTMAN, DETROIT, MICH., MAN SIX FEET, 175 LBS.: BROWN HAIR, EYES: AGE 35. WOMAN TALL: BLONDE HAIR: BLUE EYES. NO IDENTIFYING MARKS, SCARS, MANNERISMS NOTICED. NUMEROUS CALLS AND VISITORS TO ROOM ON SUNDAY AND MONDAY LAST IN REPLY ADVERTISEMENT SELLING COAT. THAT IS ALL. END OR GA.

"End," I told them. I called Overton in the D.A.'s office; Skors and I went over to see him. When we got together, I explained the situation to Overton. Skors had seen the teletype. "We're at their heels, now," I said. "I think we should go to Kansas City."

"What makes you so sure it's the Turner woman?" Overton asked.

I told him, "Everything fits about it, the description, the coat, the place, everything. I've wired Detroit to check on J. K. Hartman, but I'll give you a month's pay right now they won't find anything."

"Do you think they're still in Kansas City?" asked Skors.

"They could be."

Overton shifted his stiff leg. "If they're not there, where do you think they'd head next? Mexico?"

"No. She's too smart for Mexico. I think ... oh, hell!" I shrugged. "I don't *know*. They could be going north, east, south, or west. Your guess is as good as mine. But, somewhere in Kansas City, we'll pick up their trail again."

"Kansas City cops didn't find out very much," said Overton.

"They found out something, but not enough."

"Sure," agreed Skors. "They found out about the Michigan address and the car."

"It helps," I said. "We know they're driving a Chevrolet. When they were in Virginia they were using the New Jersey plates which came with the car. In Kansas City, they gave a Detroit address. Why? Probably because Rohan stole a set of Michigan plates, and so now they register with a Michigan address."

"You can't depend on it," Skors said, thoughtfully. "If they're leaving Kansas City, they might pick up a Missouri set."

"Or Kansas," I added. "Kansas City, Missouri, is just across the river from Kansas City, Kansas. There're plenty of plates of both states cruising around. They could get either, but my hunch is they'd pick Kansas."

"Why?" asked Overton. Overton wasn't being obtuse or throwing his weight around. He didn't have the background on the case which Skors and I had, and was only trying to get the feel of the thing.

"Because it's less obvious," I told him. "Mercedes Turner is a cutie ... she's plenty smart, and she'll take the time to try to work out every angle. I'm not so sure about Rohan." Leaning forward, I lit a cigarette, attempting to put my thoughts together so I could explain them. "From the very beginning, I've felt his presence. I *knew* he was there ... before there was any proof ... before I even knew what he looked like, or what his name was. Hugh Rohan's our best bet!"

"What makes you say that?" asked Overton.

"Because he's a strange combination from what I've gathered. He's smart, too, although he doesn't use his intelligence all the time. He's emotional as hell, but he usually manages to keep himself under control ... even if he can't go on forever. A man like that is bound to break eventually. He's more of a drag on Mercedes Turner than he is an asset."

"Rohan has always been your baby," Skors told me. "You figured him from the first, although at the time I couldn't see it. As far as the Turner dame is concerned, I put in with you concerning her, too. She's cool ... and real smart."

"If Mercedes Turner were by herself, it'd be another story."

Overton said, "We have pretty wide open orders to do whatever has to be done. But if we go to Kansas City, we'll have to justify it."

"The Turner case is our problem. Sure, Kansas City will cooperate within reason, but they have their own problems, too. They can't keep on this, and we can't expect them to. I think we should go there and dig up everything we can—with their cooperation. If we're there, we can get more done."

"Yeah," agreed Overton, "maybe you're right."

Skors turned to the D.A.'s man and said, "You go with him, Overton, and handle the arrangements."

I shook my head, as I remembered the skipper's remark about the case getting pretty far from home. It was possible for the situation to get embarrassing. "You've been on this as long as I have," I told Skors. "You go instead of me."

Skors said, "I'm not going. You're going."

I kept my voice very calm. "It'd be better if you went. You're going to have to ask for a lot of cooperation from Missouri. You'd do better there than I would."

Overton watched us quietly, saying nothing. Skors turned to him, ignoring what I'd said. "He's sore ... thinks I'm stupid ... wants me to travel and get educated."

To me, Overton said, "I'll do every damned thing I can to cooperate, you know that." He shifted his hip tenderly where he had caught the .45.

"Okay," I agreed reluctantly. "Okay, then. I'll go."

Skors socked me one, with his hamlike fist, on the back. "That's my boy," he grinned.

Overton and I flew to Kansas City the next day. On the way down, he relaxed and said, "This is the life. Cold weather kinks up where I got it in the leg. Just think now we got summer and tropic winds." He was kidding, of course, but all cops like the chance to get away with expenses paid. When we arrived in Kansas City, it was as cold as New York.

On the way down on the plane, Overton and I had talked over our plans. In downtown Kansas City we split up, although perhaps it wasn't really necessary. I don't know. Overton went to the Jackson County Courthouse, on Twelfth Street, and checked in our papers with the D.A. From there, he headed to the Police Department also right there on

Twelfth, and picked up a Kansas City detective who had been detailed to work with us.

When we had separated, Overton told me he would check into the Moreland; I took my suitcase and went to another hotel which had been recommended to me. Then I headed over to the newspaper office and went through the back issues of the papers of the past week. Other clippings fell into a pattern. Each personal ad listed a different room, in a different hotel. One advertised an antique necklace, the second a diamond wristwatch, and the third merely said personal jewelry. I made a list of the hotels and started out.

I didn't show my credentials, or claim any official standing. Overton was covering the Jefferson Hotel with the Kansas City detective, so I left it alone and concentrated on the three hotels I had listed. My story was that I had once worked for some people in Detroit, and I had heard they had been in town. Were these the same people? The clerks remembered the couple, all right, because Mercedes had tipped them well to send anyone making inquiries concerning the ads to their room. However, at one hotel, the desk clerk had gone home ill, and the man replacing him refused to check the register. I made a mental note to have the Kansas City detective do a little pushing ... if it was important. The other two hotels remembered the couple, Barnes in one place, Lowell in the other, but in both instances, the couple had registered from Detroit, Michigan.

I was pretty sure, not only from the general, although indefinite, physical descriptions, that it was the same couple. Rohan, I realized, had dyed his hair brown. The time element at each hotel was exactly the same. The couple remained just long enough for their ad to appear. Too, the tie-up of Michigan because of the auto plates seemed pretty firm.

I figured that Mercedes Turner had unloaded a lot of stuff, and now had plenty of cash.

At the Moreland I met Overton. He had been to the Jefferson, but had found out nothing new concerning the Hartmans from Detroit. The Kansas City cops had started a search of the downtown garages looking for the gray Chevrolet with Michigan plates. However, a letter had arrived at the Jefferson addressed to Mrs. Hartman. There was a return Kansas City address on it, and the mail clerk at the hotel had not yet returned it. Overton and the Kansas City detective had driven out to interview the writer of the letter, but no one was home. They decided it could wait until after dinner.

Chapter 17

"Look," Dave said to Rohan, "better get that stuff up to counter four-teen, they're yellin' for it." Rohan nodded. "Just one more day! Tomorrow, and the next day's Christmas. Jesus! Will I be glad!" He was unconscious of his blasphemous humor, as he jabbed pink tissue copies of invoices on a long, spike spindle.

Rohan wearily lifted a large carton; it was heavy, filled with small bottles of a cheap perfume. A gray twill jacket, furnished to him by the company, clung damply around his shoulders. In the front, by the left lapel, the name of the drug chain, "Kurts," had been stitched in red. The unwieldy carton turned in his hands, its weight unevenly distributed over his forearms, making the muscles jerk and tremble. Twisting the carton up, he rested one end of it against his hip, grasping the box from both sides with his hands catching it beneath the bottom. Walking to the rear of the basement, Rohan began climbing the stairs to the sales room.

On the street level, the store was jammed with shoppers, lights, sounds, and smells. Red and green streamers hung in festoons along the walls, alternating with giant cutout faces of Santa Claus; over the front door, a great cardboard sleigh, painted white and drawn by golden reindeer, was poised for immediate flight. Imitation snow, applied with a fixative, glistened and gleamed on the front of the counters. A section devoted to the sale of cheap phonograph records poured a bedlam of Christmas melodies into the air, the whining of precocious children singers, the breaking gliding baritones of aging male crooners, the affected phrasing of popular chanteuses blended a cacophony of hymns, hits, and folk numbers. Emitting from the soda fountain, in front of which hungry shoppers stood three deep to slake their hunger and thirst, were odors of frying hamburgers, melting cheese, boiling coffee, and roasting nuts combining to produce a super-smell, indescribable, attractive, and repelling.

Rohan picked his way carefully through the crowded aisles, heading toward the cosmetic section located between the toy department and the linen display. He placed the box on the floor and began filling a section of the perfume counter with the bottles, arranging them in long neat rows. Perspiration clung to his hair, and sweat rolled down his face as, leaning over, he removed the perfume from the carton, never quite standing erect before the counter as he placed the bottles on it.

Suddenly his body stiffened, and he froze in his crouching position, head lowered as if listening. Then, abruptly, he lifted his eyes, his glance sweeping over the counters, lingering for an instant on one, then fleeing to the next. Completing a frenzied circle at the toy department, his searching eyes lowered to the floor again.

Keeping his head averted, and remaining in a semi-crouch, he scrambled quickly down the aisle mingling with the throngs of shoppers. Approaching the rear stairway which descended to the stock department, he darted down the metal stairs.

In the basement, he tore the twill jacket from his shoulders, crumpled it, and tossed it in a corner, as he broke into a run for the service door at the head of the ramp. In another instant, he was in the alley. The cold struck him with the impact of a physical blow, hitting him hard in the stomach, freezing his damp shirt to his shoulders, drying the moisture in his throat and mouth.

The woman was in the hotel room, reading, when he returned. His appearance startled her, the wildness in his eyes, the fear and desperation in his manner, the trembling of his arms, his face pinched and blue with cold. "Mercy," he cried, his voice raw with fear, "they're here … they're here!"

She arose quickly, putting aside her magazine. "What's wrong?" she asked quietly.

Rohan approached the bed and sat upon it. He struggled with his voice. "We've got to hurry … they're right here in Kansas City." Leaping to his feet, he went to the closet pulling out the suitcases. "Don't stall!" he shouted. "Start packing!" At the dresser, he grasped a handful of shirts and linens, throwing them on the bed.

"All right," she agreed, keeping her voice steady, free from panic. "But tell me what happened … please." She began removing her dresses from the hangers. "And what happened to your jacket and overcoat?"

Ignoring the last part of her question, he replied, "I … I was in a drugstore … stopped in to get some cigarettes. The store was filled with people shopping…." He stood erect, rigid, his hands holding a shirt, his mind reliving the scene. "Suddenly, it was as if … someone touched me. You know the feeling you get, when you're being stared at, but you don't know who's doing it?" He swung away, moving the suitcase, dumping his shirts in it. "There was a toy counter nearby. It had a lot of junk on it … footballs, toy guns, and stuff. Crowds were standing around it, looking through the things. One of them was a cop, I know it! Or a police informer!" He added, "A voice inside me whispered, 'be careful.'"

"What did he look like?"

He shook his head. "I don't know which one it was. There must have been at least a dozen men and that many women, too. But someone in that group had recognized me … was staring at me. As soon as I started to look up, whoever it was looked away again, so I couldn't tell." He turned to the woman imploringly, "Hurry! For God's sake … please hurry!"

Neatly folding her dresses, she packed them in the suitcase, while she asked, "Did he follow you?"

"Yes ... he started to, but I managed to shake him off. I ran downstairs as fast as I could and out the back door to the alley. I didn't stop to look, but I'm sure he was after me....I could sort of sense it. The crowds were so heavy ... and he didn't know the store."

"But you really never did get to see him?"

Facing the woman, he said, "Mercy ... for the love of God ... you don't think I'm making this up? I'm not crazy!"

"I believe you," she replied slowly. "I believe that those who live by their wits must have sharp ones." She closed her suitcase and snapped the lock. "Like all other animals who run for their lives, we develop protective instincts against our enemies." Her face softened as she looked at him. "What time is it now?"

"Nearly nine," he said. "If you're ready I'll go get the car." He swore softly. "It was that damned car that jammed us up in the first place ... if they had painted it in time ... as they promised."

"It wasn't your fault," she said. "Anyway ... we have enough time before the next edition comes out with the ad."

He caught his breath; fear surged within him anew. Hastily slipping on a suit jacket, he said, "I'll get the car now. It's in a parking lot down the street. I put Kansas plates on it." At the door, he patted his pistol for reassurance. "Meet me in front of the hotel. Have them bring down the bags, and you pay the bill at the desk."

When he left, she picked up the phone and called the desk, requesting that a bellman be sent up. While she waited, she wandered restlessly around the room.

He was frightened, she thought, terribly frightened. His terror had gripped him to the very point of helplessness. What would happen when they were finally cornered? When they could escape no longer, run no farther, what would happen to him? She shook her head to rid her mind of the picture, and her hair glistened in the light of the room, but the terrible problem remained. Rohan? What about him? She thought she knew: he would break and die slowly ... a little each minute of the days ... through the trip back with his captors, through the long trail, and be a partly dead man before he reached the death house.

In a false strength of his pride, she remembered, and in the weakness of his terror, he had maintained that he would not be taken alive. Standing in the impersonal limbo of the hotel room, she faced her reality ... recognizing the truth, realizing what she must do, how best she could still serve the man who was her husband, her lover, her own lost youth. When the end came, and the fragile hourglass of their time was shattered, she must give him her love, her courage to fight that he might yet escape. For herself, she knew, there was no escape; the hope of her escape had never existed ... and it would never exist.

The knock at the door aroused her, and her mind fled back from the future to the necessity of the present. She went down in the elevator to the lobby, face serene, manner composed. She paid the bill, and waited in front of the hotel, its white sign "Towbridge" flashing above her head. The bellman shivered beside her, his body trembling in the cold. It began to snow with heavy, thick, white flakes, not hard, but in gusts, the flakes melting as they hit the pavement, dissolving the streets into dark reflecting mirrors of the lights of the cars and buses. She remembered that it would be better if the bellman did not see the car, so she turned and put a dollar bill in his cold hand, smiled. "Don't wait," she told him, "my husband may not be here for a while."

"It's all right, lady," he said, "I don't mind."

"But you're going to catch cold out here without a coat. You don't want to be sick for Christmas."

He smiled, indecision on his face. "Well ..."

"Go back to the lobby," she urged. "My husband will throw the bags in the back seat."

"Okay!" He touched his fingers to his forehead in a brief salute. "Merry Christmas, lady." And he hurried into the warmth of the hotel.

In a few minutes, Rohan approached the hotel. He had parked the car around the corner, and he carried the suitcases away from the entrance. The Chevrolet was painted a dark blue, and it gleamed wetly beneath the melting snow. He stored their luggage and they climbed into the car.

As he sat behind the wheel, Rohan asked, "South, now?"

"Yes," replied the woman. "South."

"New Orleans, I guess?"

"Eventually ... but I'm not sure if we should head there direct. If the police have traced us here to Kansas City, they can't be sure which way we'll go."

"They'll expect New Orleans to be one of the possibilities," Rohan said.

She unlatched the glove compartment and removed a number of road maps. "Where's the map for Louisiana?" she asked.

Rohan looked up from his driving. "It should be in there."

"I can't find it."

"Well, we'll have to get another."

"I thought I'd like to check the towns. Oh!" she exclaimed, "I remember ... I looked at it last week ... and I must have left it at the hotel."

"We don't need it now, anyway," replied Rohan. "Do you have the map of Arkansas?"

"Yes." She spread it on her knees, peering at it closely beneath the dim lights of the dashboard. "But I think we should cut across to the east ... as much as possible, and get into Mississippi. If they're watching for us to go to New Orleans, they'll expect us to drive through Arkansas. We could go all the way south the length of the state of Mississippi ... and then cut back west to Louisiana and New Orleans."

They left the city behind them, and in the night the car was a warm, secure world of its own. The snow still fell, but away from the streets and buildings it seemed swifter, and rushed through the headlights of the car ... sweeping in to meet them. The woman curled up in the seat, tucking her feet beneath her. Finally, she said, "What would you have done if the detective, tonight, in the drugstore, had tried to arrest you?"

"I'd have shot him!"

"Good!" she said softly.

Her answer surprised the man. His face was startled, and it showed as he turned his head to look at her. "I thought you were against it," he said.

"I was," she replied, "... at first. I used to think that further killing was useless, senseless. But now I know I was wrong."

"Why do you say that?"

"Because now it's the only way for us to survive." In the darkness of the car, her voice reached him ... cool, logical, gently explanatory, soothing. "We can measure our time only in the day we have. Today. Anything, now, is justified to extend that day into tomorrow. The rest of the world, the people, the police ... everyone ... can simply wait for tomorrow to come. We can't."

"Believe me," he nodded, "they'll never take me alive!"

"If they take you," she replied, "they'll take me, too. One more life may mean another year ... another ten years for us. Let me see the gun, please." Her voice was as casual as if she were asking for a cigarette.

Rohan squirmed his body in the seat and twisting his right hand behind him, removed the pistol from his pocket. He handed it to her, a short, blunt, .32 automatic. "Be careful," he warned her.

"I know," she replied, "I've handled guns."

"Rifles and shotguns are something else."

"Hunting is hunting," she replied. She examined the pistol, checking the safety attachment, and removed the magazine. "How many shots does it hold?" she asked.

"Seven," he told her. "One in the chamber and six in the clip."

She returned the clip into position, locking it in. "I'll put it in my purse," she said, "and keep it while you drive. It must be uncomfortable in your pocket."

"Only when you sit on it," he replied, wryly.

"Well, I'm glad we have it." She leaned forward in the seat, peering intently into the night ahead. "Slow up," she said. The man removed his foot from the gas pedal, and the car coasted forward. On the shoulder of the road, pulled away from the concrete highway, an old maroon sedan sat without lights; its front left tire flat, half detached from the wheel. There were no signs of a driver, and the car was unoccupied. "Pull up behind it," the woman urged, tersely, "I don't think there's anyone around."

Rohan drove on the shoulder, his lights picking up the rear of the old car. "Look," she exclaimed, "it's from Nebraska!" Rohan climbed out of the Chevrolet and approached the deserted car cautiously. "There's no one in it," he said, "it's all locked up, though." Walking to the front of the car, he looked thoughtfully at the ruined tire. "The driver probably went for help."

"That means there's a town up ahead. Hurry and take off the Nebraska plates and put them on our car!" She let herself out of the door and began helping Rohan remove the Kansas plates from the Chevrolet. Quickly, they made the exchange. "Whoever owns this old car won't notice the plates have been changed until tomorrow," she said. Returning to their own car, Rohan threw it into gear and pulled back to the highway. Within a few minutes, they could see the glowing lights of a small town ahead. "How far are we from Kansas City?" she asked.

"About twenty miles."

"I'm worried," she told him, "I think we should do something."

"What's there to do?" he asked. "We just keep going."

Slowing down to pass through the main street of the town, they approached a large Greyhound bus which had pulled to the curb in front of a small cafe. An elderly woman was standing, bundled in a coat, waiting impatiently for the driver to remove her suitcase from the back luggage compartment. "Listen, darling!" Mercedes said, "let me off here ... in the middle of the block!" Rohan hesitated, looking at her bewildered. She explained hurriedly, "I'm catching that bus ... it's going south. Stop right here!"

"Wait a minute!" Rohan protested.

"There isn't time." She pressed a roll of bills into his hand. "Meet me at the best hotel in Tupelo, Mississippi!" The bus driver had found the luggage and was handing it to the elderly passenger. "Good-by, dear," Mercedes kissed Rohan quickly, and slipped from the car. "I'll meet you tomorrow ... or Christmas, in Tupelo."

"Graham," he called, "use the name Graham!" She nodded and ran toward the bus, overtaking the driver just as he was climbing back into the large gray vehicle. For a moment they stood talking and the driver shook his head, but to the woman's insistence he finally gave a reluctant agreement. He stepped aside, and she entered the coach ahead of him. Rohan remained parked at the curb until the bus, gathering speed, roared away into the night. Then slowly he continued on his way.

The Chevrolet was now lonely and deserted, and the night was peopled with strange shadows. No longer was the car a safe, secure refuge from the world. The snow had slackened and had been replaced with increasing cold. The heater in the car threw little warmth against the onrushing cold, and Rohan's feet began to ache. Then, as he turned a sweeping corner of the highway, he saw a figure in the center motioning him to stop with a flashlight. On each side of the concrete road, a Missouri State Highway Patrol car was parked, leaving room for only one car to pass. It was a roadblock, and fear constricted Rohan's throat. Frantically, he reached for his gun. The pocket was empty. And he remembered that Mercedes had the pistol in her purse.

For an instant, he debated the possibility of swinging the car around and attempting to flee back in the direction he had come, but he realized that it was impossible to turn on the highway without stopping and backing, and before he could make the swing he would be overtaken. The patrolman loomed ahead of him only a few feet away. Hopelessly, Rohan pulled the car to a stop. The patrolman flashed his light to the plates of the car, and then cautiously approached the window by Rohan. From the darkness, a second patrolman appeared flashing his light into the back seat of the car from the opposite side.

Rohan rolled down his window and in the sudden rush of freezing air, his breath plumed before him. "From Nebraska, huh?" asked the patrolman, tucking his light beneath the pit of his arm, holding it level to Rohan's face.

"Yes," replied Rohan. He turned slightly in the seat, and pressed his hands hard against the steering wheel to steady them. He added, "Omaha ... I'm from Omaha."

"Let's see your license." The patrolman beat his hands together to warm them.

Panic gripped Rohan. He had no license. With a great effort he fought the instinct to open the door and plunge into the night. Mechanically, he lowered his hands from the wheel and began to fumble blindly within his jacket pocket. "There's no one in the back," the second trooper called, walking around the rear of the car and approaching the patrolman by Rohan's window, "this isn't it!"

"Who're you looking for?" Rohan asked. Suddenly, with desperate assurance, he stopped the futile search through his pockets for the nonexistent license, and removing a package of cigarettes poked one into his mouth.

The first trooper ignored his question, and replied to his partner, "I guess not. Jesus! It's freezing!"

"I'm not going to stand out here," the second replied, heading for his car. "This isn't the description."

"It's a Chevy and the right year." The first trooper was undecided, busily trying to warm his hands.

"Yeah, but we're looking for a gray Chevy ... Michigan, Kansas, or Missouri plates ... with a couple in it."

Rohan nodded. He forced himself to smile. "I'm glad I never got married," he said and began rolling up the window. "May I go on now?"

The trooper stepped back, jamming his hands in his pocket, and the flashlight beneath his arm tilted its beam to the ground. He nodded, and motioned Rohan forward. Rohan took a deep breath, and the car moved ahead.

It took him a long time to regain a semblance of calmness.

Chapter 18

On the way back to my hotel, I passed a large drugstore on the corner. In the windows were displays of all kinds, and 1 stopped to look at some toy guns. The barrels were elaborately engraved, and the butts were made of fake ivory with the name "Kansas City" etched on them. The revolvers were imitations of old frontier six-shooters, Colts, and I decided to buy one to take back for Christmas to a kid who lives on my block. The same guns are sold in New York, of course, but to the boy I was thinking about, the name Kansas City meant the same as Dodge City or Tombstone, the Far West.

I walked into the store and it was jammed with customers. The toy counters, located in the center of the sales room, were near the rear of the store. A large number of other shoppers were looking at the toy guns, too. They surrounded the counter, holding the cap pistols, waving their money in their hands, for the busy sales girls to wait on them.

It was very warm and steamy in the store, and the noise was pretty bad. The shoppers around me were dressed in heavy winter overcoats, damp from the cold and snow. Odors of food from the fountain reached me; and porters carrying large boxes, hordes of sales people, and customers all mingled in the aisles. As I stood near the counter, waiting, I found myself staring at an employee of the drugstore. He was stooping over, his face turned partly away from me, and a coarse twill jacket bunched at his shoulders as he filled a counter with perfume bottles.

There was a familiarity about the man's face which I was unable to place instantly. I stared at his partly visible profile, waiting for him to turn so I could see more distinctly. He seemed to sense that he was under observation, and began glancing around uneasily. I quickly shifted my gaze; after a few moments when I returned to look at him again, he was retreating hastily down the aisle, and approaching a back stairway. It was at that instant I realized it was Rohan!

As quickly as I could, I attempted to force my way through the crowds of people after him. It was obviously impossible to attempt to use my gun, both because of the bystanders and the fact that I had no authority in Missouri. He had disappeared down the stairs by the time I reached them. In the basement, a merchandise ramp led into an alley. I ran up the ramp to a truck that was unloading and asked the driver if anyone had just left the building by way of the truck dock. "Yeah," he told me, "a guy came running out of here bareheaded about a minute ago. He beat it down the alley."

The alley was deserted, and I ran to the corner where the alley intersected a street. But I saw no sign of Rohan.

I flagged down a cab and rushed over to Overton's hotel. He opened the door to his room, undressed except for a pair of shorts. His bed had been pulled down, and his pajamas were on it. In two more minutes he would have been in bed. He looked at me in surprise. "You look like you've seen a ghost," he said.

"I've seen more than a ghost," I told him. "I've seen Rohan. The Turner woman and Rohan are still in Kansas City!" I recounted to him, as rapidly as I could, what had happened.

"You're sure it was Rohan?" he asked.

"Positive! What threw me off at first was his head was lowered and turned to one side. Also his hair has been dyed brown. Of course I wasn't expecting to see him, and it took me a few seconds to realize who I was watching. Rohan sensed it like a fox!"

"Okay," said Overton, "you know what you're talking about."

"I'm not wrong about this. I wasn't too sure they'd still be here, but I am now. I didn't think the woman would stay this long, but something happened to make her change her plans." An idea was nagging at my mind, and suddenly it hit me. I slapped my fist. "Of course! The ad!" Overton was staring at me, and he was standing with his pants in his hand in the middle of the room. "Get dressed!" I urged him.

He nodded and I picked up the phone to call the newspaper office. There was no time to waste, and the switchboard put me through to one of the night editors. I asked him when the Saturday morning edition would be on the street and he told me at ten thirty. It was now nine fifteen. My hands were shaking with excitement. "Look," I said, "you have a makeup form of some kind with the personal ads in it, don't you?" He seemed a little reticent to give me any information. I identified myself, told him the situation, and said, "Look it up, the personal form, right now. I can call our Kansas City man ... his name's Burton, and have him call you back to confirm this. But we'll lose too much time!"

"Okay," he said, "hold the phone."

Overton was dressed. He finished tying his shoes, and straightening, slipped into his coat. "I'll go down to the lobby and get Burton on the phone. We'll hold the line until we hear from you." He hurried from the room.

In two minutes the newspaperman was back on the phone. "Yes," he told me, interest creeping into his voice, "I think we're running the one you're looking for. Tomorrow. ... This one is for jewelry, private owner proposition."

"Read it!" I urged him. He did. It followed the same pattern of the others and gave Room 927 of the Towbridge Hotel. "Thanks!" I slammed down the receiver and rushed into the hall. I had to wait a few moments and fumed at the delay. When I reached the lobby, I looked around for Overton. He was in a telephone booth, with the door open, and he waved an arm at me. "I've got Burton on the phone," he said. "What do I tell him? Or, here, you tell him!"

I took the phone. "They're at the Towbridge," I said. "Room 927." The time was now 9:22. "Where are you?"

"I'm at the station. I'll meet you in front of the Towbridge!"

"Okay." Overton and I hurried out of the hotel. He asked the doorman directions to the Towbridge. It was seven blocks away. "Can you get us a cab?"

"I'll try, but with this weather ..." The doorman hustled out into the street and began blowing his whistle. I kept looking at my watch as precious minutes slipped by. Turning to Overton, I said, "We've got to split. You wait for the cab and if you get there first, you know what to do. I'm going to try to walk it. One of us will get there to meet Burton." Overton agreed, and I took off into the night. Gradually, I felt my stride begin to lengthen until I was running, slipping, and skidding on the wet pavement. People on the sidewalks stared at me with curiosity, and I prayed that a cop wouldn't stop me on suspicion and make me lose time in explanations. Then down the street I saw the Towbridge sign, big, white, electric blazing in the night. I fixed my eyes on it as if it might disappear, and my feet pounded the sidewalk. I sprinted the last block. A squad car was pulled up to the front lobby, but there was no sign of Overton. A plainclothes man was seated at the wheel, while another detective in gray topcoat, with his collar pulled up, left the hotel and walked to the car. He leaned through the window to speak to the driver. As I ran up behind him, he whirled suspiciously and a gun leaped into his hand.

"Burton!" I gasped, my throat throbbing. "Are you Burton?" His eyes studied my face suspiciously. "Yeah." We'd never met before.

"I'm with Overton," I panted, "from New York."

"Oh." He relaxed, although he was still surprised.

"Are they in the hotel?" I asked.

A cab swerved to the curb, and Overton leaped out. He hit the street limping, and stumped over to us. Burton nodded to Overton and gestured toward the lobby of the Towbridge. "They blew," he said.

I could feel the sinking sensation of disappointment in the pit of my stomach. "Don't worry," said Overton, his voice sympathetic, "we'll get them." He turned to Burton. "This guy's been eating and sleeping this case ... it's his baby," he explained.

I looked at my watch again. It read the passage of the minutes of their escape. "Fifteen minutes," I said.

Overton spoke quietly. "Why don't you crawl into the car and have a smoke? You're blowing like a porpoise. Burton and I'll dig out what we can from the desk. We'll fill you in."

"Sure," agreed Burton, noncommittally.

I climbed into the car and sat down by the driver. I offered him a cigarette and we both lit up. Overton and Burton entered the hotel as a stranger hurried up and looked into the car. His eyes passed over me to the driver. "Oh," said the stranger, "Lewis, how are you?"

"Okay," replied the cop.

The stranger jerked his head in my direction. "An arrest?" he asked.

The driver grinned and said, "Hell, no." Then turning to me he explained, rather embarrassedly, "This guy's a reporter."

I didn't say anything. I didn't care. The reporter said, "I was told by the night desk there might be something doing over here at the Towbridge."

"Nothing now," replied the driver. "We missed 'em." Overton and Burton returned to the sidewalk. "Ask Burton about it," the driver added. The reporter withdrew his head from the window and turned to the two men. They stood talking for a few minutes, and I just sat in the car waiting for the disappointment to wear away.

Eventually the two detectives returned to the car and climbed into the back seat. Overton said, "Burton phoned the station and got an alarm out."

"Yeah," said Burton, "maybe we can still pick 'em up before they get too far out of town." He tugged at his coat collar. "It's a hell of a night," he added.

"There's nothing else we can do tonight unless they stop them," Overton said. "Let's knock it off." He yawned. "God, I'm tired."

"We'll drive you to the Moreland," Burton offered. The squad car nosed into the traffic, swung in a half circle around the street, and started back. At the hotel we both got out.

"What's the routine for tomorrow?" asked Burton.

"Unless something breaks in the meantime, I suppose we'll fly back tomorrow afternoon. I'd like to be home for Christmas." Overton turned to me. "Is that okay with you?"

"Sure," I agreed, "but I'd like to talk to that woman who wrote the letter."

"Suppose I meet you here in the morning," Burton suggested. "We'll see her first thing." After he drove away, I walked back in the snow to my hotel. It wasn't far, and the snow felt wet, and cold, and good to my face. I was nearly exhausted, and in my numbed state it seemed as if I were walking in a winding sheet of white, down a long highway. Ahead of me, just out of reach, Rohan was driving and the snow was sweeping against his windshield and blowing back into my face.

The snow had stopped, however, when I reached my room. Just before I fell asleep I wondered: Why had Rohan been working in the drugstore, while Mercedes Turner had plenty of money?

The woman who wrote the letter was a Mrs. William F. Arms, and she lived in a nice prosperous, but not large, house out in the Plaza district. The house was stucco with white wood pillars, and had a large fireplace made of fieldstone. We hadn't called Mrs. Arms before we arrived because if she had anything on her mind, we didn't want to give her a chance to prepare any answers.

She wasn't too anxious to have us come in, but Burton politely insisted and she let us in, with some reservation. We all went into the living room. Mrs. Arms was a pleasant-faced woman, with mixed gray and blonde hair. Well groomed, and entirely self-assured, she answered Burton's questions easily.

"Mrs. Arms," he said, "I believe you wrote a letter to a Mrs. Hartman at the Jefferson Hotel. Are you a friend of hers?"

"No," replied Mrs. Arms. "I only met Mrs. Hartman once, when I went down to her hotel to look at a fur coat she wished to sell."

"Is that the coat she advertised for sale in the paper?"

"Yes. I read the ad and called her. We arranged for me to visit her to see it."

"You didn't buy it?"

"No." Then she smiled. "But I wish I had." Suddenly, the smile left her face and she looked at Burton expectantly, "Or perhaps I was lucky? Was the coat stolen?"

"No, it wasn't stolen. It belonged to Mrs. Hartman all right." For a brief moment Mrs. Arms looked disappointed, then she shrugged politely.

"Would you mind telling us everything that happened? asked Overton.

"Certainly," agreed Mrs. Arms, "although there's not very much to it.

I've wanted another mink coat for … ever so long. My husband bought me one, years ago, before they were so terribly expensive, although they certainly cost enough even then. I've worn mine, and worn it, and finally had the few good pelts that were left in it made into a stole. However I've always wanted another full-length coat, although neither my husband nor myself have wanted to put all that money into another new one."

Overton asked, "So you saw Mrs. Hartman's ad?"

"Yes. I've been keeping my eyes open, hoping I'd find a bargain someplace, and when I saw her ad, I went down to see her coat. Mrs. Hartman said she wouldn't set a price on the coat but would sell it to whoever made the best offer. It was a full-length coat, and it really was beautiful. She said she'd paid eight thousand for it and I can believe it. The coat was in excellent condition and she's only had it for a year. But one thing bothered me; the label had been removed from the coat. Mrs. Hartman assured me that she had bought it new in New York, but wouldn't say where.

"Of course, the first thing I thought was that the coat had been stolen, but I could hardly imagine Mrs. Hartman selling stolen goods … she was such a nice person."

"Did you meet her husband?" I asked.

My question had suddenly switched her chain of thought, and she regarded me curiously for a moment, then replied, "No … I didn't see Mr. Hartman."

"I'm sorry to have interrupted you," I said, "please go on."

"There's not much left to tell. I told Mrs. Hartman I would give her two thousand dollars for the coat." She smiled deprecatingly, "You know how women are … always looking for a bargain. I was too greedy and I realize it now. Mrs. Hartman said she'd already been offered twenty-five hundred for it, and thought she'd get at least three, possibly four, thousand for it. Of course I had no way of knowing if she had really been offered that, so I decided to wait a day and perhaps she'd call me. I left my phone number with her. When I got home, the more I thought about that coat, the more I wanted it. When I didn't hear from her, I decided to drop her a note. I did, and offered her three thousand."

"Why didn't you call her on the phone?" asked Overton.

"Well, I'd thought about it, but I decided that if I did she might think I was anxious. A note would be more … casual. More of a take-it-or-leave-it gesture."

"You've heard nothing more from Mrs. Hartman?" asked

"No. Not a word."

"She didn't say if she were leaving?"

"No," replied Mrs. Arms, "but naturally … living in a hotel…"

Burton looked at Overton and me. "Any more questions?" he asked.

Overton shook his head, but I said, "Yes. Mrs. Arms, will you please try to think back to when you were in the hotel room. Can you recall Mrs. Hartman's face distinctly?"

"Yes. I remember what she looked like."

I handed her the sketch. "Have you seen this woman before?"

"Yes. That's Mrs. Hartman."

"Good. Now in the lobby, or anywhere around the hotel, did you see a man resembling this picture?" I showed her the photograph of Rohan, but she couldn't identify it. I continued, "While you were there did you see any object in the room, other than what would've been there naturally?"

"I don't quite understand," she said.

"Well ... other than the bedroom furniture and the things the hotel would ordinarily furnish ... what else do you remember seeing?"

Mrs. Arms squinted her eyes in thought. She considered my question for several long minutes. "Well ... when I first went in, Mrs. Hartman met me at the door. To the right of the door was a dresser, and I think there was a hand mirror, a comb, and hair brush on it." I nodded. "Then she said something to the effect that she was happy to show me the coat. She took it from a closet; it was on a hanger." Mrs. Arms paused, then went on. "She stood facing me ... holding the coat ... and sort of stroking if with her hand while she told me about it. She suggested I try it on ... and I put my coat on the bed."

"Just like that?" I asked. "Weren't you wearing gloves and carrying a purse?"

"Oh, yes. First, I removed my gloves and placed my purse and gloves on a small table beside the bed. A bedside reading table. Then I put on the coat and examined it ... and made her an offer. She told me about the other one."

"Just a moment. When you placed your purse and gloves on the table, was there anything else on it?"

"No. Yes! An ashtray, and some cigarette ashes. I remember because I was careful not to soil my gloves in the ashes, which had blown out of the tray."

I nodded. "After telling you about the other offer, what did you do?"

"As I remember ... she helped me off with the coat. And then held mine for me to put back on. Then I picked up my purse and gloves and left."

"Mrs. Arms," I said, gently nudging her memory, "you mentioned leaving your phone number with Mrs. Hartman. Did you just tell her your number, or did you write it down?"

"Oh, that. There was a writing desk in the room, and I walked over to it. On top of the desk were some sheets of paper, hotel paper, and a pen.

I stood at the desk and scribbled down my name and telephone number."

"With your gloves on and carrying a purse?"

"My!" she half laughed. "You certainly are a stickler for details. No, I hadn't pulled my gloves back on, yet ... I had them and my purse in my hands when I walked to the desk. I put them on top, while I wrote down the information."

"You left the note on the desk?"

"Yes," she said.

"Then you once again picked up your gloves and purse?"

"Yes."

"Was there anything else on top of the desk ... besides the paper, the pen, the note you had written, and your gloves and purse?"

She thought. "No, nothing important. As I remember there was some kind of folded road map ..." she thought hard, and I held my breath; "the map had a red cover with blue and white letters. It said ... it was ... Louisiana."

I exhaled my breath. I'm sure everyone in the room heard me.

Chapter 19

They met Christmas day in Tupelo. Rohan arrived first, burning with fever, and checked into the hotel registering for Mr. and Mrs. Henry Graham. He was verging on pneumonia, the result of escaping the police in Kansas City without a coat, and the long, cold drive to Tupelo, a country town in the northwest corner of Mississippi, without either an overcoat or an adequate heater in the car. The hotel, at Christmas, was nearly deserted and Rohan sprawled on the bed, his temperature raging, his mind fuzzy and blurred with the fever. Above the bed was a large, wood, ceiling fan which, in the winter, was not operating, but its four blades, and the shadows thrown by them, made it appear like a monstrous spider clinging to the overhead.

In the late afternoon, Mercedes arrived and the man struggled from the bed to meet her. Grasping her, holding her in his arms, he greeted her anxiously and hungrily. She laughed, pleased with his eagerness, not realizing that he was ill. "You seem happy to see me," she said gaily.

"I thought you'd never get here!" he exclaimed, his words slurring. "I've been worried."

"Let's not worry," she said. "Today's a holiday from worry. It's Christmas. Wish me a merry one."

He staggered to the dresser, and his unsteadiness caught the woman's attention. "Darling," she asked, "are you ill?"

"No ... no, it's just awfully warm in here." Opening the drawer of the dresser, he removed a large box. It was wrapped in holiday paper—white, with red and green mistletoe decorations. "Merry Christmas!" he said, smiling awkwardly. "Oh, yes," turning away, he tossed the roll of bills she had given him, carelessly on the dresser, "I bought it with my own money."

Tears started abruptly to her eyes, and she lowered her head. When she faced him again, she had resumed her smile although the sparkle in her eyes was from the dampness of her tears. She sank slowly to the bed, and with fumbling fingers unwrapped the package. Within was a large, partly soiled box lined with pink rayon. In numerous cut-out niches were small, oddly shaped bottles and jars wrapped in red cellophane, bath salts, dusting powder, cloying perfume, toilet water, bars of heavily scented soap, and a skin lotion. It was a tawdry, unimaginative packaged gift such as is sold in chain stores and cheap retail establishments at holiday time. An ill-advised assortment of spurious objects, outstanding only in their numbers and cheapness of items.

She refrained from showing her disappointment and forcing herself to speak with enthusiasm, exclaimed, "How wonderful! Where did you ever find it!"

Half anxiously, half shyly, he explained. "I was going to get something else in Kansas City ... but you know ..." He stumbled ahead. "I bought it on the way here.... I didn't have any time to shop. It wasn't from the money you gave me, either."

"No?" She lifted her eyes, and asked the question she knew he was anxious to have her ask. "Where did the money come from?"

"Oh," he said, "I didn't tell you. I got a part-time job in Kansas City. You thought I was just out walking, but I got a job."

"Just to buy me a Christmas present?" she asked softly.

"Yes."

Slowly, she rewrapped the package in its cheap decorations. "It's the nicest present I ever had," she said gently.

"I don't care too much for the perfume," he told her nonchalantly.

"It's lovely!" Then rising, she picked up her bag and opened it. From it, she withdrew a small box. "Merry Christmas to you, darling," she said, "from ... your wife!" She kissed him when she handed him the present.

Opening the box, he examined the pipe carefully. It was a beautiful object. The bowl was a deep burnished brown, the color of old cordovan leather, and it was inlaid with a delicate silver design. "I hope you like it," she said. "I bought it yesterday in Memphis."

"Like it!" he exclaimed, unable to say more. For a long time he held the pipe gently in his hands. When he finally spoke, he said, "So you remembered?"

"Yes. I hope you still wanted one."

"I've always wanted one." Memories of Royal and Argyle surged through his mind, the golden days when he was studying for Annixter. He had wanted a pipe such as this. It had always been part of his early dreams ... to be a doctor, a famous, respected doctor who smoked a silver-chased pipe. The pipe, then, had been a symbol, the ultimate sign of success. "After all these years," he said, his voice very low, "you haven't forgotten about my silver pipe."

She laughed, her voice ringing with merriment she didn't feel. "After all your descriptions of the pipe, how could I ever forget?"

He polished the bowl of the pipe gently against the sleeve of his jacket. "Why couldn't God have left us alone?" he asked.

"Don't say that. Please ... not today."

"But it's true," he replied slowly. "All I ever wanted was you ... and to be a doctor ... and," he added wryly, "my silver pipe. That wasn't very much to ask, was it?"

"You have me ... and the pipe. That's more than most people receive who ask for things."

"Up in Bordeaux, the chaplain used to talk to the men—at least to those who would listen. He liked to say, 'Go out! Go out and find God ... seek Him until you find Him!' But I don't think you can find God. I think God finds you! You don't know where He is ... but *He* knows where you are. When He's ready ... He'll find you ... and what He does, sometimes, isn't very pretty!"

She began to cry silently. Turning her back, so her lips might not betray her, she said, "We were very young. Many youngsters have troubles in the beginning ... so many troubles."

"And now we're in such trouble that we will never get out," he said heavily, hopelessly.

She dropped to the bed, and he followed her, sitting by her side. She took his head and held it gently against her breast. The heat of it burned through her dress, and in dismay she held her hand against his forehead. The skin was hot and dry. "Someday ..." she assured him gently.

"No," he said thickly, "it isn't someday. There's never going to be a someday." Abruptly he raised his head, pulling away from her, and the room whirled before his eyes. "If I tell you something, you won't laugh?" he asked.

"How can I laugh?"

"Where was it? I've nearly forgotten all the places we have stayed ... one place runs into another, and they all seem to be the same. But it was after we left Richmond. That night we stopped over in a motel somewhere by the side of the road. I told you then that I knew the police were after me, too. Before that they hadn't connected me with being at your apartment. And then in Kansas City ... I knew the cops were there."

"Yes," she agreed, "I know."

His face was flushed, and it was creased in concentration so that white lines appeared against the redness of his skin around the nose and mouth. He swallowed, finding it difficult to talk around the numbness of his tongue. "Well ... this sense ... this feeling of awareness ... each week it grows more and more ..." he struggled in difficulty for his words, "well ... more intense. Sometimes it seems that I can feel another mind, which is ... right there side by side with my own. Often I have the sensation that whoever owns this other mind is listening to my thoughts ..." His voice trailed away.

The woman regarded him anxiously. "Darling," she said, "you're ill ... you had better lie down. Here, let me help you." She began to unbutton his shirt.

He attempted to shrug away her hands. "It's like ... my mind ... left invisible trails in the air behind me ... and then they are picked up," he swallowed heavily, "by this other mind." Stopping for a moment, he breathed heavily, sucking air into his parched mouth. "Each of us is part of the other ... and because we are ... the two parts of us will have to come together."

"Shhhh," she told him quietly, not arguing, attempting to calm his mounting fear and horror. "We'll just have to be more careful. More careful than ever." She attempted to press his head back against the pillow.

"Yes," he agreed with heavy acceptance, "but he'll find me just as I'll find him." Suddenly, he pushed her to one side, and struggled to the dresser where he retrieved the pistol from her purse. "When I do, I'll kill him ... because if I don't, I'll never be free. He'll live with me, side by side, forever!"

"Yes ... yes," she agreed softly, rising and putting her arm around the man. "Now," she said, "you must lie down. Go to sleep." She led him back to the bed, and removed his shoes, loosened his tie.

"He'll always be listening to my thoughts, following us wherever we go...." The man's voice stopped. He was asleep. Gently, the woman pulled the covers over him, and sat down beside the bed. Looking out the window, at the deserted streets of the ugly little town, she began to cry. Now there was no necessity to hide her tears. She cried for a long time.

Around midnight, Rohan awakened for a few minutes. In the darkness of the room, he said, "Mercy, are you there?"

"Yes," she replied and took his hand.

"Do you remember the little apartment we had ... the one on Forty-ninth?" he asked.

"Where you lived before you sailed for Beirut?"

"Yes." She could hear his heavy swallow in the silence of the room. He said, finally, "You'd come there, after we were married, on the weekends from school, and try to act like a married woman?"

She nodded. "I'd shop in the Italian delicatessen ... and try to haggle about prices ... and always lose." She laughed softly.

"And the gas plate with one burner which sat on top of the icebox?" the man whispered. "You'd try to cook my dinner, but you could only cook one thing at a time?"

"I wasn't a very good cook," she said. "I tried for you, darling, but I was awful."

"You were wonderful," he said. He went back to sleep. She placed her hand on his head. It was wet with perspiration. The fever had broken.

Chapter 20

Overton returned to New York. He was anxious to get home to his family for Christmas. I had no family. Besides, I decided that I would go on to New Orleans where I expected the two fugitives to be heading. Before Overton got on his plane, he appeared worried, although he attempted to hide it. "You'll have problems, you know," he said.

I told him I knew it. "But I can't help that. I've got to get there. I'll go strictly on my own, and do my own digging and my own leg work."

Overton seemed a little surprised. "Aren't you going to report to the New Orleans cops?"

"They won't even know I'm there."

"You could lay yourself open to a hell of a jam," he said.

"Not if we handle it right," I told him. "When you get back, tell Skors to maintain all the contacts by wire and phone with the authorities in New Orleans. When the time for an arrest comes, I'll let you know, and you can go through the approved routine."

"Yeah ..." Overton still appeared doubtful, "but what about you?" He looked me straight in the eyes.

I ignored it. "If I need any information or help that I can't get by myself, I'll phone Skors in New York. He can request it from the New Orleans authorities and relay it to me. Later on, you and Skors can come to make the pinch."

"What do you think you can do by yourself?" Overton asked.

"I can try," I told him. "They'll be ready to make their move soon. I want to be there when they make it."

"Well," said Overton, "I'll keep the fire burning, and so will Skors. Good luck." We shook hands, and he boarded his plane.

When I reached New Orleans, I changed into an old pair of trousers and a ragged, unmatching jacket. I took off my tie, left my shirt open at the collar. Carefully repacking my suit, I walked the streets, carrying my suitcase, until I found a boardinghouse.

The halls were damp and dirty ... and paint peeled from the walls. In spots, the plaster had broken away to display the laths like dirty white bones hidden in the walls. It was no better and no worse than places you can find in New York. I know, because when I was a kid I had to live in them. Looking at my room, I remembered a professor I had at Columbia ... where right after the war I had gone to night school on my GI Bill of Rights. He had called such places as this scabs of humanity. At the time I had thought that when people were very poor, a scab is sometimes preferable to an open wound. But I didn't say anything to him about it.

Making a trip to a drugstore, I returned with a big bottle of disinfectant which I poured around the cracks of the room, and sprinkled over the lumpy mattress. After that I could only hope for the best.

New Orleans is almost like an island, lying between the Mississippi River and Lake Pontchartrain. The river front stretches for miles with terminals and wharves along the east bank. There are approximately ten miles of them. At the city, the chocolate brown Mississippi is three quarters of a mile across, wide enough and deep enough to accommodate the largest vessels afloat. From New Orleans, four thousand ships a year go down the river to the Gulf—over a hundred miles away—to voyage to all the ports of the world. Somewhere in this great waterfront jungle, Rohan and Mercedes Turner must come out into the light for a minute, running, to grasp their chance to escape.

I knew that I would pick up their trail again. Rohan was the type of man who insists on running away—even if he runs straight into the arms of his pursuers. The woman, if she had been by herself, would have moved just once—to some town, some city; she would have assumed a new name, a new personality, and might have disappeared forever. But because of her love and pity for Rohan, she was compelled to carry him with her. And by taking him, both would be lost.

That they would attempt to leave the country, I was convinced. But where would they go? Well, one of the problems that most criminals fail to realize is that they can never do anything new. Everything has been done before; the police eventually begin to anticipate the criminals' own problems. Other criminals have often been faced with the same problems confronting Rohan and Mercedes Turner.

Neither of the two fugitives spoke a foreign language—at least not fluently. There is no country, anywhere, today that does not have immigration laws and a police force. To hide from the authorities, and to escape the eyes and ears of the public, a fugitive must remain inconspicuous. Unless he can speak the country's language as fluently

as a native, he can't stay hidden. This means that Rohan and Mercedes
Turner had to go to a place where English is spoken.

As nearly as I could determine, through the sale of her furs and jewelry, Mercedes Turner had somewhere around ten thousand dollars, in
addition to the four grand she checked from her bank. This would take
care of them for a long time if they picked the right place.

England, Scotland, and Wales are too efficiently policed. The rest of the
British Commonwealth can be eliminated for one good reason or another by the average criminal. The two fugitives were not average, I realized, and I believed they would try to head for Australia or New
Zealand. So on these two countries I concentrated my attention. The
usual information went out to the State Department: the police and port
authorities were alerted in all the ports along the eastern seacoast and
Gulf.

I hung around the wharves and docks during the day. The ships
berth parallel to the Mississippi and—in a tangle of forklifts, gantry
cranes, slings, hooks, conveyor lifts, continuous belts, nets, and overhead
cranes—disgorge bananas, sugar, molasses, aluminum ore, and var-
nishes. Later, they take on corn, wheat flour, soybeans, cotton, and sul-
phur, and with their great iron bellies lying low in the water leave again
on their endless rounds of the ocean. From the port bulletins, I could anticipate their arrivals and sailings with their destinations.

Most of the ships were freighters and carried no accommodations for
regular passengers, but it was possible to book passage on them. Each
had to be watched, evaluated and, usually, discarded as the potential escape ship. The ships with destinations to British Guiana, Australia, and
New Zealand were watched with extra precaution by the immigration
and port authorities through the efforts of Skors in New York. I'd call
Skors long distance, relaying my information and he'd teletype re-
quests to the New Orleans authorities.

Lounging around the docks, I'd meet and talk to the longshoremen,
stevedores, porters, and members of the crews. The bits of information
I picked up were negative—but important because they helped elimi-
nate useless investigation.

At night, I'd take up my vigil in the Vieux Carré, the section of the old
original town, the French Quarter. Rohan, I felt sure, would have to contact the underworld in New Orleans to make arrangements to get fake
passports. He had the money, thanks to the Turner woman, to get them.
Who his contact was, or when he'd make it, I didn't know, as we had been
unable to dig up any known criminals with whom he was friendly. The
Canadian authorities couldn't help us in that direction either. But it was
reasonable to assume that during his sentence in Bordeaux he had
made criminal connections of some kind, and he would attempt to use

them now.

The French Quarter is the night life section of New Orleans. It is a warren of narrow winding streets with many of the old French and Spanish houses and buildings still standing—converted into cafés, restaurants, night clubs, and bars. Usually a small wind off the river wanders through the narrow streets, along the alleyways, rustling dry banana leaves in closed patios, making the shutters tap and creak. Walking through the streets, I'd search the faces on the banquettes, and stop to peer into the lighted doors of the cafés, bars, and restaurants ... looking for the two faces that I could now visualize as easily as staring at my own in a mirror. If the two were here, surely, I believed, Rohan would come here either for his contact, or at least once for dinner with the woman.

Often, as I was returning to my boardinghouse near the docks, I'd pass Pirate's Alley, and the bells of St. Louis Cathedral would begin their first calling for early mass, and Jackson Square, with its pink crepe-myrtles under which old men returned each day with their checkerboards, would be growing light.

But days and nights went by, and I found no trace of the two fugitives. I grew anxious. My anxiety resolved into the ultimate realization that I had slipped up. First, I had underestimated Mercedes Turner. The woman was too clever to be seen in the French Quarter. Rohan, by himself, would have appeared. Because of the section's great tourist attraction, it is too well policed, and the woman knew that the appearance of the two fugitives might easily result in an identification.

Rohan had made his contact, away from the French Quarter, too. He had made it, and by now they were gone. But they hadn't escaped on the ships we had been watching. I was convinced of that. Then on what ship had they slipped away?

Disappointed and depressed, I searched for the old feeling, the sensation of awareness invoked by the presence of Rohan. It was gone, too. During my first days in New Orleans, I had known that Rohan would be there; the conviction that he was somewhere in the vicinity was with me constantly. This feeling, however, had left me and the invisible spoor had faded.

In my heart I knew that the red-haired man had finally escaped.

That night, I bought myself a bottle of whisky and returned to my room. I began to drink it. The liquor warmed my stomach, but it could not dissolve the cold, frigid thoughts inside my head.

Chapter 21

"How much do I love you?" He laughed, holding her to him closely and gently.

She smiled, relaxing in his arms, taunting him, "You are misquoting your Browning."

His arms tightened around her, and through their window he could see the garden with its oleanders, wisteria, and camellias. "Yes," he agreed happily, "and although I will say 'let me count the ways,' we will take leave of Elizabeth B. because what I have to count, she never had. I love you more than my freedom, my life!" She kissed him, and he loosened his body, dropping gently down beside her. "I loved you in New England," he continued softly, "when we were young, on the shore of Beirut in the days of disaster, in the gray decade of Bordeaux. I've never stopped loving you!"

She pressed her face against his cheek. "Ah ..." she chided, love in her voice, "my husband is so illiterate that he forgets: 'He who gives a passion-flower, Always asks it back.'"

"For your information," he said, pretending a deep concentration, "that was Grace Hazard Conkling, if I ever read her!"

Her laughter filtered happily through the room. "Hush," she said, running her fingers through his hair, "hush ... hush ... hush. And now you can boast that you have loved me in New Orleans."

In New Orleans they had found a great, lovely room in an old home in Metairie, a suburb in Jefferson Parish composed of beautiful homes and gardens. There was a tropical beauty about it which cheered their hearts and warmed their bodies. In the garden, in season, were flowerbeds of petunias and poppies, phlox, lilies, violets, and roses ... and large oleander trees, some pink, some white. There was clematis, and honeysuckle, and coral vines twined with moonflowers climbing on the walls. Lightning bugs in the night, sometimes the far-off voice of a hound baying at the moon, darktime sounds of gate chains clinking, twigs snapping, a gray squirrel running along a branch ... the moon climbing higher, and a mockingbird coasting from a treetop.

When first they had arrived in New Orleans the man had been weak from his recent illness and they had stayed a single night in a motor court, far out on the edges of the city. The second day, they had driven around, and had noticed the tiny restrained sign on the gatepost, with the single word: GUESTS. They were the only guests in the ancient house, other than the old lady who owned it, and it was nearly as if the house belonged to them.

They were content to remain near the house, walking in the garden which was maintained with only a minimum of attention by a gardener who came to work half a day each week. Carefully the man and woman remained away from the downtown area, ignoring the famous restaurants and cafés, satisfying themselves with meals purchased in outlying neighborhood restaurants.

One night they drove into the parishes. Far out in the country, before an elaborate gambling casino, Rohan parked the car and went inside to make inquiries concerning Bert Crosley. A tall slender man, hard and bald as a steel bearing, met him just within the door. "I'm a stranger here," Rohan told him, "and I'm trying to get in touch with a friend of mine."

The eyes of the bald man hooded over, although when he spoke his voice was softly polite. "If Ah can help ..." he murmured, spreading his hands slightly. "'Course Ah don't know many people."

Behind the closed doors leading from the ornate lobby, Rohan could hear the muffled voices of players, the occasional low whir of the wheels. There was no pretense, no effort at concealment, only well-bred, self-contained quiet. Rohan accepted the man's evasion. "I'm trying to locate a friend of mine ... named Bert Crosley." The bald man gave no indication of recognition. "His name isn't in the phone book." Rohan smiled easily, but there was no returning smile.

The gambler shook his head, "Crosley's a familiar soundin' name, but Ah'm sure Ah don't know a Bert Crosley."

Rohan could not be equally sure. He was careful, however, not to indicate his doubt. "I knew Bert up in Canada ... at a spot called Bordeaux."

The bald man listened indifferently. "A club perhaps?" Rohan appraised a note of cynicism in the gambler's voice. "You can call it that," he replied, following the gambler's lead. "Anyway, Bert claimed he came from these parts ... and he also had a brother ... who worked around here."

"What did the brother of Mr. Crosley do, suh?"

"Sort of in the insurance business, I guess. He figured percentages and odds on calculated risks." Rohan thought he detected amusement in the gambler's eyes. "Anyway, I'd like to get in touch with either Bert ... or his brother. Even by phone would be all right."

"Important business, p'raps?"

"Yes. Good business for either of them."

"If Ah should ever run across either of the Crosleys," replied the gambler, "Ah'll be mighty glad to give him your number."

"I don't have a number ... at present," replied Rohan, not wanting, at this time, to give away the hideout in Metairie. "Suppose I call here, each evening, and if you've seen them ... they can give you a number I can reach."

The gambler's eyes went suddenly hard at Rohan's evasion, but his voice remained smooth. "What is your name, suh?"

"Cargill," replied Rohan. "Just tell Bert that Red Cargill wants to talk to him."

The gambler swept his gaze to Rohan's dun-colored, dyed hair. He shrugged, his glance and voice impassive. "If it should ever happen ..." he murmured. Rohan returned to the car.

The next night, and the following, Rohan called the casino. He received no information, not even the satisfaction of speaking to the bald-headed gambler. On the third night, however, after some delay, the gambler came to the phone. "Cargill," he said, "through a most remarkable co-incidence, Ah happened to meet a Mr. Crosley ... not Bert Crosley, but his brother... Mistuh Whit Crosley. Mistuh Whit Crosley wanted me to tell you that his brother is ... indisposed ... he's away takin' a rest. But Mistuh Whit Crosley says he will be most pleased to talk to you con-cernin' business. He left this number for you to call tomorrow, promptly, suh ... at 'leven o'clock in the mornin'." He gave the number to Rohan, who jotted it down.

Following the instructions, Rohan made the call. The phone was an-swered immediately. In the distance, he could hear voices and the scuf-fling of feet, and he knew that the phone was a public one. Over the line, he repeated to Whit Crosley that he had known Bert in Bordeaux. Whit Crosley said little. "We can't talk now," he told Rohan, "but I'll meet you tonight."

Rohan met Crosley in a bar lying outside the Vieux Carré. It was a quiet inconspicuous place decorated with chrome and leather in a mod-ern manner, and indirect lighting. Crosley led the way to the back of the bar, and walking down a short hallway turned into a small room. He closed the door behind them. Rohan looked around and saw that he was in an office with a desk, business table, and several chairs. The office was neat and plain, businesslike, and gave the impression of being well used. On the desk, a brass goose-necked lamp was lit, and the shade deflected the light to a fresh green blotter. Crosley seated himself in the chair be-hind the desk.

He was a short, pudgy, middle-aged man with stiff gray hair and pale, expressionless eyes. He wore a light blue, flannel suit and dark blue, suede shoes with elaborate perforations in the toes. Crosley sat staring at Rohan for a minute before speaking. When he spoke, his voice car-ried no Southern accent. Chicago, Rohan thought, he must be one of the old Chicago mob.

"Cargill," said Crosley, "I'm getting rid of a couple questions to start with. Are you hot?"

"Yes," replied Rohan, "plenty. I busted out of Bordeaux."

"You've run pretty far. Anything else?"

Rohan debated for a moment, then answered slowly, "There might be something else...."

Crosley examined his fingers; picking up a letter opener, be deliberately began cleaning his nails. "Okay," he said, "I guess I can find out."

"I'm sure you can."

"What you want from me or Bert?"

"I want to get out of the country ... my wife, too."

"You got a broad with you?" Crosley's expression was veiled.

"My wife."

"We don't throw muscle around down here ... unless it's necessary. I don't think you're necessary. If you're hot ... too hot ... I don't want to touch you or your wife!"

"I may be hot," replied Rohan quietly, "but not down here. If I'm wanted ... it's up north ... way up north, and it isn't the Feds. I'm not asking for any favors that I can't pay for!"

Crosley's attention remained on his manicuring. "How much dough you got?"

"Enough to get a couple of passports fixed up, and to pay off somebody to get us through customs."

"That depends on what you mean by 'enough,'" replied Crosley. "Have you got any passports now?"

"My wife has two."

"That helps ... they can be doctored. It's going to cost you a grand each for the new art work; it's going to cost another twenty-five hundred for the time and fixing ... and five C notes to the captain. That makes a flat five grand for the job. Have you got it?"

Rohan nodded.

"Where do you want to go?"

"Australia."

Crosley hunched his shoulders. "We got to see. I don't know what contacts we got coming in. Sometimes they come in ... but they may not be going to where you want to go."

"Australia is where we'd like to go. New Zealand would be all right, too." Rohan watched the face across the table. "As a matter of fact, most any place where they speak English."

"England?"

"No. Not England or Canada."

"Okay." Crosley arose from his desk. "Come in tomorrow and leave the passports ... and the dough! All of it. I'll have some people get to work. Where can I reach you?"

Rohan gave him the telephone number of the old lady's house in Metairie.

"I don't know how long it'll take," Crosley told him, "but when it comes, you may have to move fast. After tomorrow don't try to come here again ... don't try to contact me. You keep your end of the phone covered, and when I get it lined up, I'll call you. Got it?"

"Yes," said Rohan, "I've got it."

Rohan returned to Mercedes jubilant. That night they bought a bottle of champagne and drank it, sitting in their room; the lights out ... the moonlight pouring through the windows.

Then came the days of waiting ... waiting for Crosley's call. They drove separately to take their meals, so one could always be near the phone. They waited in the evenings, tied to the house, tense with the waiting. And then, one day, Rohan said, "We're running out of time."

"No," said Mercedes, "you're just getting edgy ... it's the waiting."

"Yes. I know he's here ... waiting and watching."

"If he is here, he'll never find us. He can't search the whole city and parish house by house. It would take him years! We're safe now for a while. All we have to do is wait until Crosley calls."

Rohan shook his head. "He'll find us." Nervously, he chewed his lips. The woman watched his face gravely, and he turned partly away to hide his agitation. Then he began to speak again, his words rushing quickly ... tumbling one upon another. "Sometimes I feel like a rabbit running across a meadow. And as I run, I see the black shadow of a falcon flowing smoothly by my side. If I stop to look into the sky—I see no hunter, no bird, no falcon. But beside me is the shadow—always beside me!"

The woman made no reply. She couldn't.

But at night she attempted to comfort him, to give him something of her fatalism. They would sleep in each other's arms, and in his sleep he would sometimes grow quiet. In the mornings, they would lie in bed, late, looking into the garden. Finally, he would get up and, taking the car, drive away to return with containers of coffee and breakfast rolls. And then the day would begin, and the endless waiting for Crosley to call.

It was late in the afternoon when the phone rang. Both were near it, but Mercedes stood aside while Rohan answered. It was Crosley's voice. "Get downtown right away. You're leaving in an hour." He added, "Just you!"

"But my wife!" exclaimed Rohan. At the sound of protest in his voice, the woman moved closer and putting her arm around his shoulder, she shared the ear piece of the phone with him.

"Look," said Crosley, "there ain't time to be wasting. I haven't been able to do anything about Australia. But a ship I know pulled in an hour ago to drop off a sailor for an emergency operation. I can fix the captain."

"Where's the ship going?"

"Ireland!" snapped Crosley. "You better take it. The ship ain't berthing here, but I can get you aboard in a launch. She's got a day's call in Miami and your wife can join her there."

Mercedes nodded. "Take it!" she whispered urgently to Rohan. "Take it. It's a good idea!"

"Okay," Rohan told Crosley, "I'll meet you as soon as I can get there. Where do you want me to show up?"

"Come over to the bar," Crosley said. "Bring your wife along, I guess. I'll give her the dope about Miami while they're taking you to the boat."

Swiftly Rohan pitched his packed suitcase into the car, and gathered his coat and hat. "Don't wait for my things," Mercedes urged him. "I can come back for them."

They raced to meet Crosley. He escorted them to his office. "I'll stay here with your wife," he told Rohan, "and give her the details. You get going with Miller. ... He'll see you aboard." Miller, dressed in faded dungarees and shirt, wore a dark, peaked mariner's cap without insignia. He nodded to Rohan. "Come on," he said, "we ain't got much time."

Mercedes slipped her arms around Rohan's neck. "Goodbye, darling," she said softly, "I'll meet you in Miami."

Rohan held her anxiously. "If anything happens ... I mean ... if you shouldn't get there ... I'll get off and wait until you arrive."

"Nothing will happen. I'll be there!" She kissed him again, and patted his arm. "Hurry, darling."

Miller and Rohan disappeared down the hall to the rear of the building. She could hear Miller's tuneless whistling fade down the corridor. In a moment, a car started, and then it drove away.

Crosley regarded her with his head tilted slightly to one side. "This ain't no good for you," he said, "taking it on the run all the time. Why don't you stay here? Let him go on."

"I have to go with him."

"Why? Is he wanted for murder?"

"*I'm* wanted for murder," she replied simply.

Crosley lit a cigarette and regarded her through the smoke. "So it's that way, huh?" He appraised her slowly. "You'll be better off here," he said finally. "I got connections around New Orleans. Long as you behaved yourself, you wouldn't have problems." He added, intimately, "I can promise you that."

She shook her head. "You're very kind, but I must go with him. I promised." She raised her head and gave him a small, brief smile. "I do appreciate your kindness, though. You've been very nice."

"I could be nicer," he said. Then he turned and walked behind his desk. "I never make an offer twice," he said, his voice brisk, businesslike. "If you change your mind, you gotta ask me."

"I'll remember," she replied. "Now ... about my catching the boat in Miami?"

"How're you going to get there?"

"I can drive."

"Well," he said, "here's how it is." Carefully he gave her instructions, and a phone number in Miami. "You only got three days to make it," he explained. "When you get there, call this number and ask for Tommy. He'll be expecting you. Larsen, the captain of the ship, will be in touch with him. They'll get you aboard, okay. When you leave Tommy, give him the keys to your car. He'll get rid of it so nobody can trace you." He leaned over the desk and watched her intently. "This is a good setup," he assured her. "Your husband gets on the boat in New Orleans, you get on her at Miami. The *Dirmuid* ain't scheduled for the stop she made here, so the cops won't never put it together."

"Oh, yes!" she said, forcing herself to show her gratitude. Crosley swelled with pleasure and importance. "I think you've worked out just the right plan!" Gracefully she got to her feet, clutching her bag. "I must hurry," she said, "even though I'd love to stay to talk. But I have to start for Miami."

"Don't forget what I told you," Crosley said. "Next time you ask me."

"I won't forget," she replied, leaving, closing the door softly behind her.

On the way to Miami, she drove carefully, maintaining a lawful, steady speed, but her thoughts were long ones ... long, and very frightened. Once the *Dirmuid* had sailed from the United States, she realized, she and Rohan would be embarked on their last journey. If all went well, they might, with luck, remain concealed for years; if they were discovered, there would be no place else for them to run. To the Continent, possibly, if they had time, but once in Europe they could be picked up easily. Given time, however, in Ireland they might settle down and become part of the country, of the people. She prayed silently, "Time, just time, please give us just a little time."

The two passports she had taken on their flight, her own and the one belonging to Turner, had been skillfully altered. The serial numbers had been changed, together with the names and addresses. Turner's photograph had been exchanged for one of Rohan, and the perforation stamp exactly duplicated on it. Even a visa stamp, with date of entrance, had been duplicated for Ireland. Crosley's forger had done an excellent job.

By-passing customs and immigration officials in both the United States and Ireland would leave no record of either their departure or entrance. Later with the forged date of entry, they could ask for permanent residence.

All they needed, she told herself again, was time! As she drove, her mind concerned with her thoughts and worries, she knew, somehow, that they would not receive it. In New York, or in New Orleans, an unseen man was tearing the days and weeks from the calendar of their lives. Soon he would come to the last day. She shuddered. When that day came, she must then do what she had to do for Rohan.

Chapter 22

In the morning, I had no hangover—felt no illness from the liquor. My despair of the night before had passed, although an emptiness had settled upon me. I knew what I must do.

My concern, my identification with the red-haired man was not of my making, but my duty I had chosen myself. Once again I became a cop. It made no difference. If Rohan had shot and killed Turner, he could not, as an escaping felon, plead self-defense; if Mercedes Turner had killed her husband, she must stand her trial.

That afternoon I talked to Skors on the telephone. "I'm pretty sure they've gone," I told him, "but I'm staying on for a while."

"If they've beat it, what more can you do down there?"

"The trail's here. I'll find it again," I assured him, feeling the certainty, but it carried little satisfaction.

It was no longer necessary to spend my evenings in the Vieux Carré, and I also began to spend less time on the terminals and wharves. More and more hours I devoted to hiring halls and bars where sailors spend their time. In one of them, named The Hull, I met a slender, wiry, very black man from Jamaica. A wiper, he spoke English with a startling British accent. Striking up a conversation with him, I bought him a drink. "Cheers," he told me. He stood at the bar and tossed it down. "Just nipped out of the infirmary. Brought down by a beastly attack of appendicitis ..."

"That's rough," I told him.

"Right you are." He nodded and his grin flashed white against black. "Captain had to shore me in New Orleans ... between Galveston and Miami. A nasty bit of business."

"What ship?" I asked idly.

"*Dirmuid*," he replied, pronouncing it Der-mot. "From Sydney. Captain Larsen, master." He fingered his glass. "Now I must find another berth."

"That won't be too hard," I said.

"No. Sorry I missed her, though. Sailing to Galway and Dublin. Never been there, you know."

"Neither have I," I told him. I placed my glass on the bar and lit a cigarette. Then I suddenly realized what he had said. I turned quickly. "You said the *Dirmuid* was sailing to Ireland?"

"Yes. First port of call, Galway."

I could feel the old familiar excitement working up my arms, tingling my muscles. "When did she sail?" He told me, and I counted off the dates on a mental calendar. The ship had sailed after I had arrived in New Orleans. "What'd be her time to Galway?" I asked, fighting to keep the excitement from my voice.

"Probably around two weeks. An old tub, you know. Not very fast."

Two weeks ... two weeks! It had been four since the *Dirmuid* had left New Orleans. "Any stops between?" I asked.

"One day only ... Miami."

Of course! Now I could see it. Ireland ... it was obvious ... it was ideal. While I had been watching the front and back doors, the escape had been made through the window. During the second week I was in New Orleans, the *Dirmuid* had stopped ... without berthing ... just long enough to discharge the sick seaman. It had not been a scheduled stop and departure, and it was not carried in the port bulletin. I had missed it.

Buying the wiper another drink, I asked, "Who're the owners?"

"Benson and Swift, Sydney."

"Do they have an agent here?"

"Must have, you know."

Impatiently, I waited for him to finish his drink, then I called Skors. When he answered I said, "I think I've got it. See if you can locate a ship's agent for a firm called Benson and Swift, of Sydney, Australia." I gave him the name of the ship and the date she had stopped in New Orleans, together with the tentative date of arrival in Galway. "Also check the immigration officials and see if we can pick up the names they're using on the passports."

"What makes you so sure they've left on the *Dirmuid?*"

"It's the only possible answer."

"Where can I reach you?" he asked.

My room didn't have a phone, and there was no place he could call me. "I'll call you back tonight," I told him. Walking back to the docks, I sat down on a concrete wharf. Near me, an engine from the Public Belt Railway chugged and hustled cars into position for loading. The thick waters of the great river glittered with opalescent colors as patches of oil, diluted into gossamer-thin films, floated past. I pulled my hat down over my eyes, propped my back against a pillar. Restlessly, I lit a cigarette, but it didn't taste good. Settling down, I began my wait. Once again the chase had been renewed.

That night, I received the news from Skors. It was pretty much what I had expected, with the exception of the details. "The agent for Benson and Swift in New Orleans is H. H. Jamison & Son. They know nothing about the stopover. In Miami, the agent is John T. Thorndyke Company. Thorndyke didn't know until the *Dirmuid* had sailed from Miami that the captain had booked a passage for Thomas Hart ... New Orleans to Galway; and Jane Sterns from Miami to Dublin."

"That's it!" I told him. "That must be it. Rohan sailed from New Orleans, and Mercedes Turner picked up the ship in Miami. They split up ... very smart."

"According to Thorndyke," said Skors, "Captain Larsen forwarded the money, by mail, for the passage in Miami. He'd been in the Atlantic two days before his letter reached the office. Of course, it didn't make any difference to either Thorndyke, or Benson and Swift, as long as they received the dough and the books were kept straight."

"What do the immigration authorities say?"

Skors laughed sourly over the phone. "What can they say? Not much. The fugitives didn't clear customs before sailing ... evidently they hopped straight aboard."

"The captain?"

"Sure. He was in on it. Somebody got next to him and paid him plenty. And the hell of it is, Immigration can't nab him the next time around, because all he has to do is plead negligence, a big mistake, he thought everything was in order."

I agreed with Skors. "When did the *Dirmuid* reach Galway?" I asked.

"About two weeks ago."

"Okay," I replied, "I'll probably see you tomorrow. I'm coming home."

"Overton will check the Irish Embassy here in New York, and he's wired the authorities in Dublin. Okay?"

"Sure." I hung up the phone. I felt tired now, and I wasn't happy either. This was it. Hugh Rohan and Mercedes Turner had traded millions of people and a great continent for a tiny island. It was time for the beaters to go to work, and the hunt would close in.

The police in Ireland are called the Civic Guards. The force is a national organization, with headquarters in Dublin. The country is divided into districts, and a district is composed of one or more counties under the charge of a superintendent. Through the superintendent, authority passes into the towns, hamlets, and tiny settlements.

The *Dirmuid* had put into the city of Galway, a port on the extreme west coast of Ireland, before continuing to Dublin. The Irish authorities believed the two fugitives had gone ashore at Galway. Superintendent

O'Hara, in charge of the Galway district, was pressing his search through the county of Galway particularly in the area of Connemara, Murrisk, and the Joyce country.

Back in New York, the waiting wasn't easy. Ten days went by before we received substantial information from Ireland. During those ten days I lost a lot of sleep. My thoughts kept constantly on Rohan. Mercedes Turner was incidental to my thoughts, but not, of course, incidental to the picture. The terrible chain which had linked them together in murder had held them together in their escape. I could not shake free of the sympathy I held for the red-haired man and his love, a deep pity for the two of them, running, running, running. Reflected in the mirror of my thoughts, I could see Rohan's face, the flaming crest of his hair. I knew that now it was dyed brown, but in my thoughts I always saw it as red, and I guessed that Mercedes Turner always saw it that way, too.

What was it, I thought, that in this life turns one man into a hunter, the other into the hunted? Is it that all men are born with the instinct to kill? I with my badge? Rohan with his love? These thoughts worried me; they had never bothered me before.

Not that I doubted the law, nor the respect which must be shown to it; nor did I have any doubts that in a society in which there was no law, the depraved would prey on the moral, the strong on the weak. No, that I had never doubted.

But I found I was doubting ... myself.

My life, my thoughts, had become so entwined with those of the red-haired man that I could no longer think of him simply as a criminal to be hunted. I knew that regardless of his gun and my gun, his red hair, my black, that we were brothers. And I knew that in the end we must face each other and be killed.

When the cable arrived, there was nothing I could do; it was part of the end of the red-haired man. Superintendent O'Hara had located the two fugitives who were living in a place called Letterfrack in Connemara. He sent their descriptions and there was no question regarding their identification. They were unaware of their surveillance by the Irish authorities. We had not yet issued warrants or requested extradition so O'Hara had not arrested them, because the matter of identification first had to be established. Now that the couple had been located, there was little chance that they might escape.

I wired O'Hara to keep them under wraps ... not to tip them off, or arrest them, and that I would cable additional information immediately.

When I told the Chief of Detectives, he smiled with satisfaction. "That's good news," he said. "I'll be glad to get Albany off my back. Are you going for them?"

"If you think I should, sir. Skors or Overton could go if you preferred?"

"No. This has been your case from the start. You finish it up." He found a cigar and carefully bit off the end. "Have you ever been to Ireland?"

"No, sir."

"Your family didn't come from there?" He smiled, and added, "According to the public all cops have families who came from Ireland."

"Mine didn't," I said.

"Okay, then. You deserve to go." He put a flame to his cigar. "Besides the D.A.'s office has to pay for your fare.... I don't." He chuckled. What he meant was that as soon as the District Attorney's office issues a warrant for a fugitive's arrest, all expenses for an officer going to secure the prisoners and returning them, are paid by the D.A.'s office and not by the Police Department.

"I'll get Overton to issue the warrants and arrange for the extradition papers," I said.

"Good luck." He walked around the desk and shook hands with me.

Overton took care of all the paper work. At first, he was going with me, then because of the expenses involved the D.A.'s office decided to have me go alone. I would have the help of the Irish authorities in getting the fugitives to the plane, and once aboard it was nonstop to New York where Skors and Overton would meet me at Idlewild.

I wired O'Hara that I was coming and would meet him in Galway. Standing beside the cable desk, I attempted to decide what further instructions to send. I could request that O'Hara arrest them immediately, and he would do so; then all that remained would be to pick them up in Galway. On the other hand, I had followed them for so long, running with both the hare and the hounds, that I felt I should be there when the red-haired man was taken ... that I owed him that obligation. Somehow, it seemed unfair that he should be taken impersonally, indifferently, simply through the exchange of a paper. I drew the cable pad to me, and added the lines: "Hold up arrests until my arrival. Will accompany your men."

My plane left in the late afternoon. The following morning early, we arrived at Shannon Airport. With my official papers, I was passed quickly through customs into the airport dining room where I had a big breakfast of eggs and Irish bacon. Then I caught an ancient rattling bus from the airfield to the town of Limerick. The bus stopped for passengers along the narrow winding roads, grinding to a lurching halt to pick up and discharge passengers at their pleasure in crossroads, cottages, and fields. The passengers, friends and strangers alike, carried on easy, informal conversations across the length and width of the creaking vehicle. Sitting near the rear of the bus, by the little open platform, I huddled in my coat against the dampness. It was winter, but although there was a rawness in the air, it was not cold, only damp.

The bus straggled its way leisurely to the town. Limerick is an old city ... as all towns in Ireland are old, I suppose, and it is located on the Shannon. There is only one railroad line in Ireland and it is owned by the Irish Transit Authority, and while I waited for the train to carry me to Galway, I walked the cobbled crooked streets of Limerick. Old battles had been fought here, and old heroes buried, and I stopped in a narrow, gabled shop to buy a tie of Irish wool.

Boarding the toylike train, I rode in a compartment upholstered in a faded pattern which reminded me of what carpetbags must look like, although I've never seen a carpetbag. The train seemed to run mostly through the aid of a thin, piping wail of the tiny whistle. Outside the windows, embankments and hedges grew higher than the eyes and it was necessary to look over and above them, and then all you could see was the sky and the purple mountains in the distance.

An Irish priest came into the compartment and sat on the seat facing me. He glanced at me in a friendly fashion, and brandishing a heavy pipe he began to fill it. When he had finished, he offered his pouch to me. I thanked him, and lit a cigarette. The smell of the burning tobacco was rich and fragrant in the compartment. He asked, "Are you going far?"

"To Galway."

"'Tis your first trip?" I told him it was. "Ah ... a fine city. There's a legend, you know, concerning Galway. Of course you will not find the Spanish or the Italians agreeing with the legend, but the story remains. And, if a legend remains for five hundred years, it is not to be dismissed lightly now?"

"No," I told him, "it isn't."

"Well, this is the legend." He drew heavily on his pipe and watched me closely. "Christopher Columbus after sailing from Spain, stopped in Galway port before finally heading into the Atlantic. He stopped and drew fresh water and supplies, and prayed in the Irish churches." He stopped and began drawing op his pipe, making it glow. "Galway is the westernmost port in Europe, and 'twould be a sensible thing for the man to do."

"I know very little about Galway," I told him.

"And neither does anyone else," he assured me. "'Tis said that Galway port has been there since the beginning of time, that the old Phoenicians traded tin there for Gaelic gold and silver. And before the Phoenicians ... I'm sure there were others." He shook his head and looked at me sadly. "Ah, I'm giving a synopsis of Irish history, perhaps unwittingly, but it would seem that Ireland has always been trading her gold and silver to the world and, poor soul, has been receiving in exchange ... tin." He glanced out the window. Rising, he knocked his pipe briskly against the window frame. "I'll be getting off shortly," he said, "and I hope you have a pleasant journey."

I nodded, but I didn't reply. I couldn't tell him that I had come to Ireland to trade lead and death, for the life and freedom of the red-haired man. Lead, the father knew, was worth even less than tin.

It was late when I arrived in Galway City, and an inspector met me at the train. His name was Greene. He said to me, "I've made arrangements for you to stay at the hotel. Give me the papers and I'll have them approved this night."

I handed him the warrants and the extradition papers. "You aren't planning to pick them up tonight?"

"No. It's a bit of a drive to Letterfrack, and when we get there 'twill be late. And then we would have to return here again. In the morning will be time enough to make the arrest." We climbed into the inspector's small Austin, and as we drove to the hotel, he asked, "Are you carrying a gun?"

I was surprised by his question. "Naturally," I said. "Why?"

"Well, you see," he sounded nearly apologetic, "we don't carry them here."

"Oh." I looked at him and he nodded. "I think you'd better tomorrow," I told him.

"It won't be necessary."

"I'm afraid it is. This man is armed, and I believe he will shoot it out." Greene didn't reply. "Is it permitted for me to carry mine?" I asked.

"If you insist, perhaps I can arrange it. But it's most unusual, you know." He turned to look me full in the face. "I'll ask the super in the morning."

That night I lay awake in my bed. I hadn't slept much the night before on the plane, and I was tired and sleepy. But I couldn't sleep because of the red-haired man.

My mind kept asking. What is he doing? How is he spending his last night of freedom ... or life? Does he have his arms around Mercedes Turner? Is he laughing, is he warm in his love, is he happy?

Twisting the pillows into a hard knot brought me no relief. And no answer. I rose and pulled a straight-backed chair before the window, and sat on it ... staring out into the empty street below. Somewhere in the distance, a bell tolled the hours, and the waves rolled into the harbor. I sat in the chair, keeping a vigil, holding a death watch for myself or the red-haired man, until I was exhausted, and my mind was numb.

I sat until the dawn, and I didn't sleep.

Inspector Greene picked me up at the hotel at eight o'clock. It was a chilly morning with a half-mist, half-rain floating damply in the air. Two officers accompanied Greene; both were dressed in dark blue uniforms with high, hard collars. I climbed into the seat beside the inspector and we drove away, leaving Galway, heading north and west.

There is a good highway through Connaught and Connemara, and we drove through hamlets with names which fall from lips like the notes of music, Moycullen, Shindilla, Derryneen, and Ballynahinch. There were the moors and the rolling hills, and the mountains dressed in winter browns and tans and violet blue, with always the greens in little hidden places; the gray rock crags of the inlets were sprayed by the lead-colored waters of the Atlantic ... and over it all, softening, smudging, undefining, the gentle mist-like rain. Small black cattle ranged the land, and tiny burros, straight from out the nursery books of children, dressed in their winter coats of shaggy fur, gazed at us curiously, from the wayside, as we passed in the car. It was a hard land, a frugal land, and one that was lonesome, but it carried itself proudly in the pride of its own fierce beauty.

We stopped in Clifden, by Ardbear Bay, and Inspector Greene climbed from the car. "I'll be checking with the constable here," he said, "and returning shortly." Within a few minutes, he slipped back of the wheel again. "It was a quiet night, and the two suspect nothing," he explained. "A local constable posted at Letterfrack just reported in."

"How far to Letterfrack?"

"Not far ... nine or ten miles."

I nodded and sat silently beside him. From Clifden, the road swings out, then returns in a half circle to Letterfrack in the north. No one spoke; there was nothing to say; Greene covered the distance in a deep concentration.

A crossroads settlement, which intersected the highway, was made up of several small buildings, a tiny post office and grocery, a garage with a gas pump, and several cottages. This was Letterfrack. From the post office, a constable, dressed in his old-fashioned, blue uniform, stepped into the road and signaled us down. He saluted Inspector Greene, smartly. "The man and the woman, sir, are still in the cottage," he reported.

Chapter 23

The cottage contained three rooms. It was whitewashed and had a tile roof; the tiles, washed by the rains and bleached by the sun, were weathered to the color of deep-stained wood. A flagstone path led from the unpaved road to the cottage and in the summer the path blossomed with flowers while the upper half of the cottage door could be swung open. On each side of the doorway was a battered terra cotta figure, a miniature Sphinx crouching by the two shallow steps.

Behind the cottage was a large vegetable garden, lying fallow now that it was winter, and along the back boundary of the garden stretched a hedge as tall as a tall man and a tiny chicken house which stood empty. There were no trees, however, by the house, or even within the sight of it, but this was not unusual because there are very few trees in this part of Ireland. Up the road, toward the west, was the crossroads and the hamlet of Letterfrack; down the road, to the east, descending in a steep grade, the land ended in the harbor of Ballinakill, used only on occasion by small fishing boats. On clear days, Rohan could stand on the cottage steps and see far beyond the harbor the islands of Inishbofin and Inishark, unreal, faintly blue on the horizon. In the winter, though, the days were usually cloudy, cloudy with a heavy grayness and a gently falling rain ... so fine, it was mist and hardly perceptible to the skin.

When they had found the cottage, they had rented it immediately, believing that its isolation would give them the security for which they searched. Each day, Rohan walked up the road to the small store to purchase food, but other than this daily call, they made no friends and no acquaintances, hugging their solitude closely to themselves. The loneliness of the days, however, bore down upon them hard.

In the small living room, a tiny fireplace with a heavy iron plate burned turf. The turf, at night, smoldered somberly giving off little heat, but filling the room with an aromatic smoke, clean and pleasant. Against the wall was a high chiffonier, the top covered with souvenirs gathered by the son of the owner of the cottage ... seashells and conches with delicate pink lips, birds' eggs blown and fading, a chip of stone from a Druid mound near Dowth, a tiny metal souvenir bottle of Guinness from Dublin.

A round, heavy table occupied the center of the room directly beneath an electric light which hung on a cord from the ceiling. A silk shade encircled the bulb, and the combination of light and shade gave off a weak yellow glow which, in the evenings, washed the room with a pale haze of amber. Outside, the westerly winds tugged and pulled at the foundations of the cottage, making it tremble and moan throughout the nights.

The circular table became the center of their social life ... where they ate their meals, or read the thin, strange Irish papers. Here the two often sat, saying nothing, their elbows on the table, each occupied with his thoughts. It might seem that they had found the peace for which they had been searching, except that Rohan again began to grow uneasy.

It began with only a slight uneasiness nagging his mind, picking at his nerves with tiny invisible fingers. He became more and more preoccupied with a sense of foreboding, and his thoughts hovered between reality and superstition. Desperately, he searched for an explanation within himself, never finding it, and then he turned to extravagant fancies. It grew a little each day until one night he could contain the thoughts no longer. They burst forth.

"Mercy," he cried, his voice disturbed, "don't you hear them? There's something walking abroad tonight."

"Your imagination," she replied lightly, but he refused to rise to her lightness.

"No!" He arose from the table and walked to the door, opening the upper half and resting his forearms on the lower section. With the light of the room behind him, he could see nothing but darkness, and the wind whistled around the door, picking at his hair, pushing it away from his face. He shook his head and closed the door, returning to stand beside the woman, staring at her silently, his face twisted by strain. "It's there," he said, his voice dead and hopeless, "the past ... it's out there in the night."

Mercedes rose hurriedly, and rushed to the kitchen. Rohan's fear had grasped her, too, and she ran to conceal it, to hide it from him. Quickly, she dragged forth a light, sheet metal tub ... high to the shoulders, low to the feet. "My water is hot," she called, "and I'm going to take a bath. Do you want me to heat you some, too?"

"No."

She filled the tub from a great pot of water boiling on the iron range, and added cold water from a wooden bucket which she pumped in the kitchen. Moving the tub closer to the range for warmth, she undressed and slipped into the soothing heat of her bath. Her golden honey-colored hair had been piled high on her head, caught in place with a narrow piece of ribbon, and she sat in the water her body trembling, indifferent to the warmth. She was cold, so cold the water couldn't warm her, and she shivered. "Darling," she called, her voice lost, "come to the door ... come talk to me!"

"I'm busy," he replied, hardly hearing her call, missing the loneliness in her voice. Rohan sat at the table, a sheet of paper before him, a pen in his hand. He started to write, beginning slowly to scrawl the date and then writing more rapidly until it seemed his pen barely touched the paper.

To the Police, New York City, N. Y., U.S.A.
This is my true and complete confession. It is made freely and without duress. I shot and killed Albert Turner in his apartment in New York, in a burst of anger and jealousy with a gun which I was carrying. His wife, at that time Mercedes Turner, now Mercedes Turner Rohan, was not responsible in any way. There was nothing at the moment she could

have done to prevent me from shooting, and I accept the full responsibility for the murder.

HUGH ROHAN

He read it over carefully, placing the pen aside, his hand tired and heavy. I should have included everything, he thought, places ... dates ... names ... addresses. There's so much to tell that no one except Mercedes would ever understand. I neither hated nor wanted to hate Albert Turner, but I killed him because there was no time for anything except death. There was no life left for me, except the little that I could steal from Turner. But it's there! I told them I did it! Abruptly he picked up the pen again and added a postscript: I firmly believe that I will be dead in a very short time, and I do not want this murder on my conscience.

He grimaced, a sorry twisting of his lips. That will please them, he thought, they can interpret it any way they like. Rising, Rohan folded the sheet of paper and walked into the bedroom. From beneath the bed, be pulled out one of the suitcases belonging to Mercedes. He opened it, found a small, black, woman's purse, and tucked the paper inside it. Replacing the purse in the suitcase, he closed the bag and shoved it back beneath the bed. Walking wearily to the kitchen, he said, "If anything should ever happen, be sure to look in that black pocketbook of yours ... it's in one of your suitcases."

She looked at him, alarm in her eyes. "What are you saying?" she asked. The water in the tub was suddenly freezing.

"Nothing. But remember ... that purse of yours! Will you?"

She nodded. "Yes," she whispered, "but ..."

He turned and left her in the kitchen. "I'm going out for a walk," he called, putting on his overcoat and stepping out into the night. In the darkness his feet searched unsurely for the path, following it until he reached the road. His eyes growing accustomed to the dark, he turned in the direction of the harbor. The steady, westerly, night wind blew in his face and the cold dampness seeped through his coat. Throwing back his head, he looked into the sky, but he could see nothing, no stars, no moon. He walked uneasily, stumbling occasionally, until he heard the surf against the rocks of Ballinakill. Then his eyes picked out the lighter colors of the spray and the spume riding the crests of the waves, and he hurried forward until he was running ... tripping and falling on the rocky uneven ground, his hands bruised and the knees of his trousers torn. He gained a small promontory, with the water below him throwing itself wildly against the jumbled jetting rocks. Standing above it, he watched the ocean visible only by its spuming edges, but he could feel nothing ... no courage, only a bottomless emptiness. In desperation, he turned his ears to the wind listening for the voice of the night, but the wind had nothing to say and, as if it could try only to assuage his fear, it carried the spray from the rocks against his face, kissing it with a thousand ice-cold lips.

But the moment of his free decision was gone. It would not return. Slowly, he backed away from the cliffs and turned, searching for the road back to the cottage. When he returned, Mercedes was in bed and she called to him. He made no reply, but he undressed and lay down beside her. "Hold me," he pleaded, "I'm cold."

In the morning Rohan arose early, dressing and shaving with care. The woman made breakfast, and they sat at the table drinking their coffee. "What are you planning to do today?" she asked.

"I don't know," he replied indifferently, his voice heavy. "I understand there's a beautiful abbey at Kylemore ... why don't you go to see it?"

"I might...."

"If you like, I'll get dressed and come with you."

"Perhaps," he replied, his voice empty. "Perhaps we might go after lunch." Outside, the day was heavy again; rain was falling and the daylight was diffused to gray. He sat, buried in his thoughts, and he remained at the table throughout the morning until the car drove up.

It was the woman who saw them first, and for a moment she watched without comprehension. Four men climbed from the leading auto, and a single man from the second car. Three of them, she noticed, were wearing the blue uniform of the police; two of the men were not in uniform. At the distance to the road, she could not see their faces as momentarily they grouped solidly together. The leader issued orders, and two of the uniformed police ran briskly around the house, cutting behind it into the garden.

"Hugh!" she cried, "they've come!"

"Yes," he said. His voice held no surprise. "I've been expecting them."

She ran to the table, kneeling beside him, catching his hands in hers. "Darling," she keened, "darling, darling, darling!" He sat woodenly, deafly, his eyes on the table. "Remember how much I love you?" she sobbed. "And remember ... how we always said when this time came ... we'd buy all the time we could?"

He nodded slowly. "Yes," he said, his lips not moving, "but it's useless."

"No!" She replied sharply; her voice now determined and firm. "It isn't useless!"

They heard the sound of a hail from the front yard. "We are officers of the law," an Irish voice shouted, "and we have the warrants for your arrest!"

"Listen, darling!" Mercedes' voice was urgent. "They have two cars out there. Two of the police are out in back. If you can get out the front door ... shoot. We'll get to a car ... and you can disable the other."

"It's useless," he said. His face was drawn and pale.

She grasped his face and kissed him, her lips wet and warm against his, her eyes dry and hot against his cheek. "Darling ... for me ... for me! You must! It's our only hope."

A new voice called from outdoors, an American voice. "Hugh Rohan and Mercedes Turner, I have come from New York with warrants for your arrest. Come out! Come out peacefully, or I will come in!"

"Listen to that, darling!" she cried. "Listen ... they're coming in! Now! Now! Do it for me."

Rohan forced himself up from the table, his eyes dead with a terrible fear. For only an instant, he stood beside her, and then he pulled her to her feet ... hugging her against him. "I'm cold, Mercy," he said, his voice was a whisper, "but it's always been ... for you."

He reached behind him, to his pocket, and withdrew the short automatic. Holding it in his hand, he walked to the door.

The American voice called again, "Rohan! Come out!"

He opened the door, and stepped out between the two crouching Sphinxes. Deliberately he raised his automatic and shot at the face of the man before him.

Chapter 24

We swung away from the post office in Letterfrack and turned to our left at the crossroad. There was a narrow unpaved road which ran at right angles in the direction of the coast. The local constable followed us in the second car. About a quarter of a mile from the store, there was a solitary white cottage with several pottery figures at the sides of the door. Greene said, "This is the place." He stopped the car and we got out.

It was raining now, hard, and somehow I felt that the rain was for me. They were tears for me to run down my face, because I could shed none for myself or for the red-haired man.

Greene ordered the two uniformed men with us to go around to the rear, covering the back door. Behind the house, I could see a high green hedge, but beyond the hedge there was nothing ... only rolling ground and stones half concealed in the hillside. No place to hide, Rohan, I said to myself, no more places to run. Greene and I approached the front of the house, and the local man followed us, although to one side. Greene looked around approvingly. Then he called, "We are officers of the law, and we have warrants for your arrest!"

There was no answering voice from the house, and slowly we drew nearer to the door. "Not too close," I warned Greene, "I'm sure Rohan has a gun!"

"He won't use it," Greene was unruffled.

I shook my head. "When he comes out, he'll come shooting," I said.

The rain continued to fall, and it dripped from the brim of my hat, splashing against my collar, running down my neck. I walked past Greene, centering my steps in the path; the door was directly in front of me and it was so close that I could nearly touch it. The figures flanking the door, I saw, were miniature Sphinxes; their faces stared past me, seeing nothing ... but waiting, just waiting. "Yes," I told them, "we will know soon."

The seconds were filled with an unbearable tension and I could stand it no longer. "Hugh Rohan and Mercedes Turner!" I called. "I have come from New York with warrants for your arrest." The rain splashed over the heads of the little stone beasts and ran from their eyes. Suddenly, the wind stilled, and the house was listening. In the stillness, I could sense movement ... the movement in the house, and I knew my waiting was nearly over.

Once again I called. "Rohan! Come out!"

The door swung open and he stood on the steps.

His automatic was raised, and the deadly black eye of it stared me in the face. It spoke, biting my cheek, burning and searing. Twisting, I threw myself to the ground, and falling, I fired, as Rohan's gun blazed the second time.

Rohan pitched forward from the steps and lay with his head near the paws of a Sphinx. His blood spread slowly through his hair, staining it once again a brilliant red. The Sphinx stared straight ahead. The waiting was over.

"Are you hurt?" It was Greene's voice. Bending over me, he put out his hand to help me to my feet. "Your cheek is bleeding," he said, "but it doesn't look nasty. Lucky bit for you he missed."

I said nothing. Rohan's automatic lay by his outthrust hand. I picked it up and saw it was a Spanish Astra. Pulling out the clip, I held it in my hand ... shielding it from the eyes of Greene.

The clip was loaded with blanks.

"If you don't mind," I said to Greene, dropping the clip into my pocket, "I'll go in alone to arrest the woman." The inspector nodded.

Walking through the door, I saw her standing by a table. Her hair was gold and shining ... even in the darkness of the room. She stood with her head lowered; waiting and weeping.

"Are you Mercedes Turner?" I asked.

"I'm Mercedes Rohan," she replied. She raised her head and looked past me; her face was empty except for her grief.

I withdrew the clip with the blanks from my pocket, and held them out. "Did he know there were only blanks in his gun?" I asked softly.

"No," she replied, "he didn't know. I put them in."

"Why?"

"Because," she said, and suddenly her face was proud and her eyes no longer empty, "it was all I could do for him."

Chapter 25

The concrete runways spread in a web across the flat fields. Dimly, in the distance, the purple hills hunched into the gray skies, and the misting Irish rain glistened on the great Trans-Atlantic Clipper. The plane rested, gathering itself, refueling for its flight, petted and curried by its swarm of attendants. Over the loud-speaker from the low, flat airport building came the announcement: "Clipper Flight ... 417 nonstop to New York ... now loading."

Mercedes Rohan turned slowly, and escorted by a police matron walked toward the silver plane.

Greene shook hands with the American by his side. "Good-by," he said, "and luck to you."

A small boy stood by the gate. Blue eyes in a thin sensitive face, which was dusted with a handful of freckles, watched the two men with awe and fascination. Slowly, he edged past Greene and, screwing up his courage, tugged at the jacket of the man beside him. "Sir," asked the boy, "are you an American detective?"

The detective turned, and smiled down at him. "Yes," he said, "I am."

"Are you an Indian?" asked the little boy, watching the detective's face carefully.

"No, sonny," replied the detective, softly, "I'm a Negro."

Then he turned and walked to the plane.

THE END

Bill S. Ballinger Bibliography
(1912-1980)

Barr Breed series:
The Body in the Bed (Harper, 1948)
The Body Beautiful (Harper, 1949)

Joaquin Hawks series:
The Spy in the Jungle (New American Library, 1965)
The Chinese Mask (New American Library, 1965)
The Spy in Bangok (New American Library, 1965)
The Spy at Angor Wat (New American Library, 1966)
The Spy in the Java Sea (New American Library, 1966)

Non series novels:
Portrait in Smoke (Harper, 1950)
The Darkening Door (Harper, 1952)
Rafferty (Harper, 1953; reprinted in PB as The Beautiful Trap, 1954)
The Tooth and the Nail (Harper, 1955)
The Black Black Hearse (St. Martin's Press, 1955; as by Frederic
   Freyer)
The Longest Second (Harper, 1957)
The Wife of the Red-Haired Man (Harper, 1957)
Beacon in the Night (Harper, 1958)
Formula For Murder (New American Library, 1958)
The Doom Maker (Dutton, 1959; as by B.X. Sanborn)
The Fourth Forever (Harper, 1963)
Not I Said the Vixen (Fawcett, 1965)
The Heir Hunters (Harper, 1966)
The Source of Fear (New American Library, 1968)
The 49 Days of Death (Pyramid, 1969)
Heist Me Higher (New American Library, 1969)
The Lopsided Man (Pyramid, 1969)
The Corsican (Dodd Mead, 1974)
The Law (Warner, 1975; novelization)
The Ultimate Warrior (Warner, 1975; novelization)

Non fiction:

The Lost City of Stone (1978)
The California Story (1979)

Short Stories:

Tooth and Nail (*Cosmopolitan*, March 1955; condensed version of
  novel)
My Husband Is a Redhead (*Cosmopolitan*, Oct 1956; condensed
  version of *The Wife of the Red-Haired Man*)
The Absence, the Darkness, the Death (*Cosmopolitan*, July 1957)
The Private Affair (*Sleuth Mystery Magazine*, Oct 1958)
You Better Be Right (*Sleuth Mystery Magazine*, Dec 1958)
Save Me in San Salvador (*Mike Shayne Mystery Magazine*, Aug
  1959)
The Passionate Spy (from *Spy in the Java Sea* [Joaquin Hawks], *For
  Men Only*, Apr 1967)
The Mice (with Louis R. Morheim; *The Outer Limits: An Illustrated
  Review* v2, 1978)